MY GOVERNMENT MEANS TO KILL ME

MY GOVERNMENT MEANS TO KILL ME

RASHEED NEWSON

FLATIRON
BOOKS
NEW YORK

MY GOVERNMENT MEANS TO KILL ME. Copyright © 2022 by Rasheed Newson. All rights reserved. Printed in the United States of America. For information, address Flatiron Books, 120 Broadway, New York, NY 10271.

www.flatironbooks.com

Designed by Steven Seighman

Library of Congress Cataloging-in-Publication Data

Names: Newson, Rasheed, author.
Title: My government means to kill me / Rasheed Newson.
Description: First edition. | New York : Flatiron Books, 2022.
Identifiers: LCCN 2021055569 | ISBN 9781250833525 (hardcover) | ISBN 9781250833532 (ebook)
Subjects: LCSH: African American gay men—Fiction. | LCGFT: Bildungsromans. | Novels.
Classification: LCC PS3614.E688 M92 2022 | DDC 813/.6—dc23/ eng/ 20220119
LC record available at https://lccn.loc.gov/2021055569

Our books may be purchased in bulk for promotional, educational, or business use. Please contact your local bookseller or the Macmillan Corporate and Premium Sales Department at 1-800-221-7945, extension 5442, or by email at MacmillanSpecialMarkets@macmillan.com.

First Edition: 2022

10 9 8 7 6 5 4 3 2 1

CONTENTS

Lesson #1: The Boss Doesn't Love You   1

Lesson #2: A Sanctuary Can Be a Sordid Place   14

Lesson #3: Don't Wear Straitjackets   34

Lesson #4: Enemies Have Their Value   40

Lesson #5: A Big Lie Can Build Character   53

Lesson #6: Romantic Notions Are Delusions   67

Lesson #7: Devils Have a Weakness   80

Lesson #8: Victory Can Be a Thorny Crown   95

Lesson #9: Touch at Least One Dead Body   108

Lesson #10: To Change the World, Have a Selfish Goal   124

Lesson #11: Allies Don't Always Harmonize   139

Lesson #12: Learn to Take a Punch   164

Lesson #13: The Best Spontaneous Moments Are Planned   181

Lesson #14: No Sense Crying Over Blood Money   196

Lesson #15: Sometimes It's Not About You   210

Lesson #16: There's No Preparing for Every Circle of Hell   221

Lesson #17: Leave the Fallen Behind   234

Lesson #18: Bury Your Old Self   256

Acknowledgments   *275*

MY GOVERNMENT MEANS TO KILL ME

Lesson #1

THE BOSS DOESN'T LOVE YOU

It is true that before moving to New York City in May of 1985, I turned my back on a six-figure trust fund. I was seventeen, and I wanted to be able to lay sole claim to my successes and failures. My parents considered me foolish, stubborn, and, worse yet, ungrateful. "You'll regret it," my mother told me. Yet I didn't miss the money—at first.

Here's what I do wish I'd brought with me when I boarded a Greyhound bus in Indianapolis bound for the city: a working knowledge of how to operate a laundry machine; experience writing checks and balancing a checkbook; familiarity with padlocks and dead bolts; the rudimentary cooking skills to fix a grilled cheese sandwich without setting off a smoke detector; and the ability to sense when I was being hustled.

Savings from summer jobs and a lifetime of birthday money left me with $2,327 to my name. I burned through it quicker than I should have by renting a room by the week at the Chelsea Hotel. I had read about the storied hotel in *Rolling Stone*. Dylan Thomas, Bob Dylan, Patti Smith, and Madonna all called the place home at one time or another. I never saw any of them in the halls.

I did cross paths with heroin addicts who dozed off on the furniture in the lobby. I shared elevator rides with agitated schizophrenics. I met a pimp who got quite hostile when I declined his proposal that

I should become a sex worker and allow him to represent me. Despite my longing to make friends, I kept to myself.

The best thing to come my way at the Chelsea Hotel was Gregory Yester. He was gorgeous. Haitian. Six foot two. Three years older than me. Broad shoulders. Dark skin. Hazel eyes. Dimples so deep that they showed even when he wasn't smiling. Gregory said whatever was on his mind, which is a habit that society punishes, but I found it exhilarating to be around. He helped bash the repression of prep school right out of me.

Gregory approached me while I was checking my mailbox one night, and he was shameless in his appeal. "Can I borrow five bucks? I owe my dealer, and listen, lil man, do me this solid, and I'll not only pay you back, I'm gonna roll you the best fuckin' joint you ever put between your sweet lips."

"Okay, let me see what I've got," I said, pulling my leather wallet from my pocket, opening it in front of him, and fishing through the two hundred dollars in cash I kept on my person. "Here, take a ten."

"Really?"

"I don't have anything smaller."

"You serious? I get the whole ten?"

"Yes," I insisted.

I held out the ten-dollar bill, and Gregory plucked it gently from my fingers.

"What's your name?" he asked.

"Earl, but everyone calls me Trey."

"Trey, I'm Gregory." He put a hand on my shoulder, kissed me on the cheek, and whispered in my ear, "Thank you from the bottom of my heart."

"You're welcome."

I leaned forward to kiss him back but stopped myself. He had already stepped to the side and turned away to put my money in his wallet.

"Which room are you staying in?" I asked. "I'm in 315."

"Oh, I don't live here," he explained. "My dealer does. I'll catch you later, Trey."

Then he took off up the stairs. I wasn't sure I'd ever see him again. But he'd been so charming and sexy that I wasn't angry at him.

Gregory, bless his heart, did track me down in my apartment a couple of days later, and he rolled me a joint. He smoked half of it with me as we sat shoulder to shoulder on my stiff orange futon. I tried to act casual, despite my fervent hope that getting high together would lead to sex. Sylvester's album *All I Need* was under the needle on my record player.[1] I pressed my left knee and thigh against Gregory's right leg.

"Got you a nice place here," he said, eyeing my apartment. "Who's the daddy payin' for all this?"

I misunderstood the question and answered, "My father is Ward Singleton, but my parents aren't supporting me."

"Nah, I'm not talkin' about them." Gregory handed me the joint. "Your *daddy*. The man turnin' you out and payin' your bills. What's his name? I probably know him."

"I don't have a daddy," I said, realizing that once again a man was assuming that I had a calling in the sex trade. "I'm not doing that. Do I look like I do that?"

Gregory smirked. "Yeah. You're gay, and you ain't hidin' it. Hell, you advertisin' with them tight pants and the way you sway your ass

---

1. Sylvester (1947–1988), an African American singer-songwriter who performed an avant-garde blend of R&B, soul, and disco music, was open throughout his career about his homosexuality and was forthright when he was diagnosed with AIDS. In an *LA Times* interview two months before he died, Sylvester drew attention not only to his personal plight but to how the AIDS epidemic was disproportionately ravaging the African American community while mainstream coverage was focused elsewhere. Sylvester said, "It bothers me that AIDS is still thought of as a gay, white male disease."

when you walk. Plus, you got that clean, young look that chicken hawks go crazy over."[2]

"Well, I'm not into that."

"Okay." Gregory pointed to the joint dangling between my fingers. "You just holin' that to look pretty or what?"

I put the joint to my lips and enjoyed it. The weed that Gregory had scored was sublime: a mellow ride that not only banished worries but induced easy laughter. Gregory and I got increasingly comfortable under its influence. He put an arm around my shoulders. I draped a leg across his lap. He quizzed me about my plans in New York City, and I had to admit that I hadn't thought much beyond just arriving and finding a place to live. I didn't have a job lined up. I didn't have a network of contacts to help me find my way. I didn't have a master plan. As we finished that first joint, Gregory and I found my aimless existence hilarious.

I didn't know Gregory well enough yet to tell him that actually I felt quite accomplished having escaped a life in Indiana among the damned: the fallen women, the broken men, and the godless sex perverts. Public sinners. Cautionary tales to the good people I grew up among. Lessons apparently lost on me because by the time I reached high school, I was considered destined to dwell on the outskirts of polite society.

There were no two ways about it. I was gay and notorious. Mind you, I didn't come out as a homosexual while living in Indiana. Given my mannerisms, that step wasn't necessary. I was fooling no one, and before I reached puberty, I stopped denying the playground taunts.

As for my notoriety, it stemmed from a family tragedy. My younger brother, Martin, died when he was nine years old. His death would have been harrowing enough to process had it remained a private matter. When it became a news story, my pain was amplified,

---

2. *Chicken hawk* is a slang term, popularized in the 1970s, for an older homosexual male who prefers (often exclusively) and pursues (often aggressively) younger sexual male partners (who in some cases are underage).

and my grief was distorted. I was eleven years old. I didn't know how to handle the whirlwind. Along with the other surviving members of my immediate family—my mother, my father, and my younger sister, Jackie—I was initially the recipient of unrelenting pity and curiosity from locals who followed the story of Martin's loss. But I managed in short order to dash the sympathy that people held for me, and I seemingly confirmed, to all who suspected, that my homosexuality was indeed a sign of my depraved soul.

Since it was already clear what my fate would be on Judgment Day, the good people of my hometown wouldn't dream of associating with me. I was a social leper. My respectable family—pillars of the bougie Black community—would see to it that I didn't starve, but my days were to be lonely and squalid. I was taught there was no place on Earth that would accept me—a queer marked like Cain. And that message was unrelenting. For years, I ingested so much hate, and in a thousand painful ways, I prepared myself to be the subject of whispered gossip, the target of gay bashings, and the recipient of shameful sex.

Only in my senior year did another path begin to emerge: New York City. No one I knew had anything good to say about the place. It was crime ridden and drug addled. It was the epicenter of moral decay. I set my heart on living there, and for a while, doing so felt like enough.

As we puffed our way through a second joint, Gregory explained, "I'm kinda in a jam, Trey. You see, I can't crash where I've been stayin' 'cause the guy's wife is comin' home from the hospital, and I had a new spot lined up, but the renovations ain't done yet. Can I sleep here for a few nights?"

I blamed the weed for my momentary struggle to process everything Gregory said. Was he really asking me for another favor, despite this being only the second time we'd interacted? Who does that? And who was this man that had let Gregory stay with him until his wife was discharged from the hospital? And why was she in the hospital in the first place?

"What do you say? Three, four days, tops," he pleaded. His voice was deep and hypnotic, and he smelled like baby powder and cocoa butter.

I told him, "You can stay as long as you want."

Gregory kissed me on the lips, finished the joint, and left me with blue balls while he went to take a shower. We didn't have sex that night or any other. I wasn't his type. Gregory was only twenty, but he loved topping white closet cases who were forty-plus. Looks weren't what turned him on. He was attracted to drama and power, and secrets, and hurried sex, and the contrast of Black skin against white flesh. That's why he was willing to be the clandestine, Black fantasy for someone as decidedly ugly as Mayor Ed Koch.[3]

Being a dominant top wasn't Gregory's only skill. He could also type 120 words a minute, and his fast fingers enabled him to work whenever he felt like it for a temp agency that staffed law offices. Otherwise, he made a living as a sex worker, sharing his time and affections with old, rich, married white men. He considered it a fair deal.

Gregory broke it down like this: "If they wanted they wives and they wives wanted them, then there'd be no need for *me*. I'm the answer to *allllll* they prayers."

I was having a harder time earning money. My dream was to work in radio. As what exactly, I didn't know or care. I was just crazy about music. Chaka Khan, Patti LaBelle, and Stephanie Mills were the goddesses I prayed to. During my boring teenage years in Indiana, I read *Rolling Stone* and *Billboard* religiously, and I could recite the number one songs on the Top 40 and R&B charts for the past four years.

There were nearly a dozen Black radio stations throughout the five boroughs. I typed up my résumés, put on one of the tailored

---

3. Claims that Mayor Ed Koch (1924–2013) was homosexual were never substantiated, and Mayor Koch addressed the rumors with an unequivocal denial: "No, I'm not a homosexual. If I were a homosexual, I would hope I would have the courage to say so."

dress shirts that my thirteen-year-old sister, Jackie, made for me, and presented myself for employment. My sales pitch was simple: I'd do the lowliest work for minimum wage.

I got to the interview stage on several occasions. Assistant programmers or deputy station managers would question me about music, and I'd get so excited to show off what I knew that my hands would wave this way and that, and my body would sway and rock, and I'd shout things like, "Tina Turner in *Mad Max* is sure to be the living end!"

My hetty inquisitors would grin at me and nod. One time, a station manager brought in a couple of other employees to sit in on the interview. I quickly realized that they considered me a flamboyant spectacle. My mannerisms were their amusement. I wish I'd had the courage to curse them out, but I did have enough self-respect to stop talking mid-sentence, stand up, and leave. I heard them laughing as I headed for the exit. I'd assumed that people whose work revolved around music would be more liberal minded.

Gregory set me straight. "Trey, you ain't nothin' but wastin' time with those people. They don't want your gay ass around."

I insisted, "I don't see why it should matter. I can do the job."

"Bein' able to do the job is never enough," he said. "You gotta give them somethin' they can't get from no one else."

What unique skills did I have to distinguish myself from every other job seeker in the city? Damned if I knew. I was unemployed through May, June, July, and August. Instead of working, I spent money palling around with Gregory, who slept cuddled up next to me off and on for the summer. During the day, we'd smoke joints together and go share sandwiches at diners, where I'd pick up the tab, or we'd watch shirtless b-ballers hoop at Rucker Park, or we'd kill hours wandering through art museums or listening to albums in my room. He taught me how to get around on the subway lines, bus routes, and surface streets. We cut each other's hair with clippers that Gregory stole from a drugstore on the corner.

At night, Gregory talked bouncers and doormen into allowing me into gay bars and clubs—Private Eyes, Uncle Charlie's, Rawhide's, and Alex in Wonderland—despite my being a minor without so much as a fake ID. We danced with our shirts off until men bought us drinks. If we didn't land a benefactor, we'd steal unfinished drinks from patrons too sloppy drunk to catch us in the act.

———

I moved out of the Chelsea Hotel in September and split a studio apartment with Gregory in SoHo. We made SoHo our home a decade before reasonable people deemed it a desirable neighborhood. Paying my half of the October rent was going to wipe out the last of my savings. I'd applied for jobs in retail and in restaurants. No takers. It was Gregory who hit upon a solution that had been whizzing by me since I'd stepped foot in Manhattan.

"Can you ride a bike?" he asked.

"Of course," I said.

Gregory punched me in the shoulder. "Okay, then, lil man, you can earn."

Bike messengers were ubiquitous in the days before emails and Amazon drones. They weaved through traffic and onto sidewalks with a single-minded savagery. Few used helmets. All of them wore scars, burns, and tattoos like badges that separated them from regular people. This was to be my new tribe.

Except the first four bike messenger companies that I applied to rejected me. Gregory thought it was because I appeared too short, too young, and too preppy. He dressed me for my fifth interview. Laced in thick-soled high-top sneakers to elevate my five-foot-seven frame, and sporting ripped, gray jeans and a black T-shirt, I looked like a baby-faced punk rocker, especially once Gregory applied the eyeliner. We hotboxed a joint together so that I smelled of weed. Then I walked over to Swift Pedal Delivery on Mott Street in Chinatown.

It was a small, gutted garage. Bike messengers not out on assignment were sprawled around like junkies in the park. They played cards, drank beers, arm-wrestled, bragged about who they fucked last night, and reminisced about their best acid trips. White, Asian, and Latinx—not one of them was Black, and not one of them looked at me twice.

Swift Pedal was owned and operated by Zhilan Mah, an abrasive Chinese woman in her sixties. Everyone called her Zee. She spoke English with a British accent and chewed gum every minute of the day. She rarely, if ever, made eye contact. There was always a pile of paperwork that she found more riveting than whoever she was speaking with. Zee was perched on a stool behind a podium against the back wall of the garage. Her posture was ramrod.

My interview was short. Zee sized me up in a glance as she filled out some form. "You've biked in traffic?"

"Yes," I lied.

"How long would it take you to get from here to Harlem?"

"Forty minutes," I guessed.

"Thirty is ideal."

"I'll get faster with experience."

"Or you will get terminated with failure." Zee handed me a start-work packet that consisted mainly of various liability waivers. "Sign every document. Find a bike, and you can start today. I can pay you on or off the books. In cash if you like, but there are fees, understand?"

"Which way do I get paid the most?" I asked.

"Off the books pays more, but if you want to file taxes, stay on the books."

"Pay me off the books."

"Smart move." Zee gave one last look at my résumé before sticking it into a stack of papers. "So, Mr. Earl Singleton III, what do you like to be called?"

"Trey."

Zee spit out a worn wad of gum into a wastepaper basket. "Word to the wise, Trey." She put several sticks of Wrigley's Doublemint into her mouth and chewed them into one cohesive mass while I stood at attention. "I'm the only friend you must have in this dump."

Zee needn't have worried about me getting too chummy with my coworkers. The other messengers paid no attention to me for weeks until I learned to make myself useful. I carried tire patches, a lighter, and Newport cigarettes, and I shared them upon request. Despite my generosity, a loving kinship never developed between me and the seventy-five bikers in Zee's revolving fleet. That was a bit disheartening. Even this group of renegade misfits didn't know what to make of me.

———

Zee was shrewder than I'd realized at the time. She sent me for pickups and deliveries in Harlem, but never to Skadden or Cravath or other leading law firms in Midtown, or to Goldman Sachs or Lehman Brothers or their ilk on Wall Street. She handed me assignments that took me to Bedford-Stuyvesant. She drew me a map that led to Jamaica, Queens. Zee grinned when I returned from a ride. I thought she was happy to see that I was safe. Chances are she was just pleased that I'd completed my assignments.

Within a month of hiring me, Zee brought on five more young Black men to join the fleet. I was the test case that proved to her that Black messengers could go into Black neighborhoods without getting jumped and robbed. This opened a new frontier for Zee. For years, she'd occasionally dared to send white or Latinx riders into the Black hoods, and she lost not only employees and packages but also dozens of perfectly fine bicycles. Now she had a way in.

I became one of Zee's favorites. She smiled at me when others got nothing except grunts or dismissive flicks of her hand. She padded my pay with bonuses. Twenty-five dollars here and there. When I turned eighteen on January 11, 1986, Zee presented me with a lemon cake that she'd baked herself, and she made every messenger in the garage gather around and sing "Happy Birthday." I thought she appreciated that I was reliable, uncomplaining, cute, and, above all, quick on a bike. The truth was much more superficial.

It was Monday, March 3, and I felt settled into the job. I'd biked through the worst of the winter, which had earned me frostnip on three fingers and two toes. Spring was arriving. Riding was getting easier as my mile count climbed into the thousands and the bike shaped my body to meet its needs. My pencil legs grew thick and defined, and my torso, once baby-skin smooth, was scaffolded with hard ribbons of muscle. I felt confident, perhaps too much so.

I was zipping down West Broadway on a one-way, just past Canal Street, when an asshole getting out of a cab swung the passenger door open into the street. Why this dipshit didn't get out curbside, I'll never know. I had a split second to avoid ramming into the open door.

I didn't panic. This sort of thing was routine. I had dodged hundreds of doors by then. I swerved around into the center lane—just as a town car started to fill the lane from the left. A bystander on the corner saw the whole thing, and she shouted, "Oh, fuck!" in anticipation of a collision that could easily kill me. I glanced down, and my bike pedal came within a rat's whisker of scraping against the side of the honking town car.

I held steady. The town car came no closer. Within five feet, the town car sped past me, and I exhaled just as my front tire hit a pothole as wide and deep as a kitchen sink. My bike flipped, and I went flying. Before I smashed into the pavement, a simple wish came to mind: *Don't let the street knock my teeth out.*

My left collarbone was broken clean through, and my left radius sustained a hairline fracture. I probably suffered a concussion, but no one checked me for that. Unconscious, I was admitted into St. Vincent's Hospital. Since I was separated from my wallet during the accident—whether by the force of my fall or by a pickpocket—I had no ID on me, and the medical staff warehoused me on a floor with disturbed vagrants who didn't know their own names. I didn't wake until the following morning.

No one knew what had happened to me or where I was. Gregory got worried about me when I didn't return to our apartment in the evening, but he silenced his concerns by chain-smoking several joints. Zee, of course, noticed that I failed to complete my delivery. She called the police—and reported the bike I was riding stolen.

An hour after I awoke in St. V's, I was discharged under the name John Doe 1347 so that I wouldn't receive a bill. That was the only kindness I can recall the hospital showing me. No one talked to me about how to care for the cast on my left forearm, or about follow-up appointments, or about pain management.

I self-medicated in my apartment with tequila and weed, and slept as much as possible. Three days after the accident, I took the subway to Chinatown and strolled into Swift Pedal to collect my paycheck. I was higher than the skyscrapers.

Zee greeted me by demanding to know, "Where's my bicycle?"

I explained the situation as best I could. She was not sympathetic.

"You should have slammed into the cab door," she said, adding another stick of gum to the wad in her mouth. "I could have sued the taxi company for damages. Maybe even gotten you some money, too."

"Sue the city," I said. "I hit their pothole."

"The city never accepts blame."

"Then I don't know what else to tell you. The bike is gone, and I'm hurt."

"This is all on you," she said. "You're in no condition to work, so you're fired, and I'm docking your last paycheck for the cost of my bicycle."

I was too hazy to muster much of a coherent defense, but I did yell, "That's bullshit!"

Zee looked down at her paperwork as she spoke her final words to me. "Go see Jason about your final check. Otherwise, I will call the police."

On my way home, I considered what Zee had said to me, and I concluded that she was right. This was all on me. Not just the accident but my life. I needed to assert myself more in times of crisis. Because the average person was never going to bestow pity or mercy on me. The average person—depending on his or her social status, age, sexuality, or race—dismissed me as an expendable worker, or a social delinquent, or a faggot, or a nigger, and if I was bleeding to death in the middle of the street, the assumption was that I must have done something to deserve it.[4] Other people suffered misfortune and received sympathy; not me. Other people made mistakes and were granted second chances; not me.

I finally accepted, once and for all, the harsh truth of my standing in our society when Zee fired me, but I'd already been shown in the spring of 1979 how very cruel the world could be to me, even when I was vulnerable and distraught. I was eleven years old when infamy attached itself to my name. My mistake in '79 and with Zee had been expecting anyone else to look out for me ahead of their own interests.

Zee had only grinned at me when I was valuable to her. I'd go on to tangle with other bosses and authority figures, and that dynamic never changed. Affection never outlasted need. This was the first lesson the city taught me the hard way. The vast majority of us are merely pawns in someone else's game. Don't get defensive over this point. Embrace it. Once you do, you can begin to manipulate the board. Positioned correctly, pawns can checkmate kings.

---

4. Trey's and his contemporaries' use of derogatory language like *faggot* and *nigger* (or even less heated, but still objectionable words like *sissy* or *twink*) are presented to provide an accurate view of Trey's and his contemporaries' mindsets and worldviews—outdated and offensive as they are to many people.

Lesson #2

A SANCTUARY CAN BE A SORDID PLACE

In late April of 1986, Gregory and I sawed the cast off my arm because the itching became too much for me to live with and the stench became too much for him to tolerate. We used Gregory's pocketknife to cut through the filthy plaster. I'm lucky we didn't slice open a vein. Only after the cast was removed did I notice that my left arm was a fraction shorter than my right arm.

Around this time was when I began to suspect that my parents were having me followed by a private investigator. Because of their jobs, my parents, Ward and Fiona Singleton, would employ a PI the way other families hired a babysitter. Ward ran the Department of Governmental and Regulatory Relations (read: lobbyists) for the pharmaceutical giant Eli Lilly and Company. He kept private investigation agencies on retainer in Indianapolis, D.C., and New York City, and their discoveries were his leverage against bullheaded regulators and senators.

In my mother's line of work, gathering incriminating information about a target was called "opposition research." Fiona was a speechwriter and domestic policy advisor to a slew of midwestern Democratic politicians, most notably the Reverend Jesse Jackson during his 1984 presidential campaign. While she didn't give the orders to invade the private lives of political rivals, she gladly peppered her candidate's remarks with veiled allusions that warned opponents, "We've got the goods on you."

My parents weren't above using their business methods on our family. I know for a fact that they had my cousin Percy Singleton followed. Percy was a drug addict with a history of relapsing, and my parents would foot the bill for his studio apartment so long as their investigators assured them that my cousin was staying clean.

The telltale sign that my parents had me under surveillance is that my sister, Jackie, started calling me frequently. Now I loved my sis. She was a smart, bighearted fourteen-year-old with an uplifting laugh. We shared a love for camp, although neither of us used that word then. Jackie adored the Weather Girls.[5] She watched *Dynasty* for the catfights and the clothes. Her interest in fashion turned into a passion. Jackie designed and sewed dresses for herself, and created tailored dress shirts and tuxedo pants for me. We spoke once every month or so.

Yet I held my breath and braced myself every time I picked up the phone and she said, "Hello." In the following fraction of a second, I would scrutinize the tone and inflection of her two-syllable greeting because the day would come when it would not be sunny and full of love. The day would come when someone—a classmate, a neighbor, our parents—would tell her the truth about me and our brother, Martin, and what really happened down on the banks of Fall Creek in the spring of '79. That knowledge would sever the delicate bond between Jackie and me. I imagined a final call that would begin with a distressed "hello," move on to recriminations, and end with my sister telling me that she never wanted to speak to me again. The last of my relatives to love me unabashedly would vanish before I hung up the phone.

So I loved my sister, but held that love loosely in my arms, anticipating its death and mourning it as it lived.

---

5. The Weather Girls, an African American female duo act formerly known as Two Tons O' Fun, released its most successful song in 1982, the camp classic "It's Raining Men."

When suddenly in April, Jackie started calling me several times a week, asking more probing questions than usual about how I was doing, my guard went up. I suspected that she was building up the nerve to confront me about Martin. That she had dialed my number intent on interrogating me, only to default to questioning me about what I had eaten for lunch that afternoon.

I became totally convinced our parents were using her as part of the spy operation during a call late one Sunday night.

"How's your arm?" Jackie asked innocently.

"Fine for the most part, although sometimes it aches for no reason," I said, before realizing that I had never mentioned my bike accident or broken arm to her.

The private investigator must have reported my condition to my parents, who must have mentioned my broken arm in front of my sister. I didn't let Jackie know that she had slipped up in her attempt as our parents' mole. I didn't blame her either. My mother and father had a shared talent for manipulation. I did, nonetheless, protect myself by taking Jackie's calls far less often.

———

The private dick following me certainly started to get an eyeful in May. Because to get my mind off my uneven arms and my renewed unemployment, Gregory took me to Harlem for my first visit to Mt. Morris Baths, one of the few gentlemen-only spas allowed to stay open after the New York City Department of Health closed almost all the other sex clubs and bathhouses in a futile attempt to stem the spread of HIV among homosexuals engaged in unprotected sex.

Closing the bathhouses passed for prudent public policy to average straight people and to assimilation queers, but it was a moralistic act of oppression. The battle against AIDS was never going to be won by getting humans to quit fucking bareback. Sex is a desire as natural and strong as hunger. The government should have been pouring resources into efforts to develop drugs that helped those infected survive and that prevented the spread of HIV to those who were not infected. But all that came later—much too late for many.

Mt. Morris Baths remained open because its owner promised that the staff would discourage sex among the patrons. Or so we were told. I always suspected that city officials didn't bar the doors to Mt. Morris because the patrons were Black, and city officials didn't care a lick if Blacks caught AIDS.[6]

Whatever safe-sex promises were made, the reality inside Mt. Morris was stark and graphic: men were having sex with men, often in the open, frequently in groups, and almost never with a condom. To me, it was invigorating. The crowd consisted predominately of closeted or low-key, butch, working-class Black guys. My type at the time.

When Gregory told me that we were headed out to Mt. Morris, I imagined the bathhouse would announce itself from the street with a streak of faux grandeur or dingy seediness.

"There she is," said Gregory, pointing at a drab, five-story, brick building with faded white paint on the arched, stone inlays.

Nothing special would have been my first-blush architectural review. The bathhouse itself was in the basement of the building. On the way down, there was a corroded black railing that I was loath to touch but found necessary to grab because the stairs were steep, chipped, and worn smooth. Countless daydreamers and drunks must have busted their asses in the red glow of the neon sign by the front door that read: MT. MORRIS BATHS.

The sign wasn't visible from the street, and it buzzed like an electric mosquito zapper, and it was my first clue that I was about to step into a hidden society of Black sodomites. Much later, I would learn

---

6. It is an enduring political mystery why the Mt. Morris Baths was allowed to continue operating after the city shuttered nearly every other gay sex club and bathhouse in 1985. Its location outside of a gay enclave, as well as its discreet and predominately African American clientele, may have allowed the bathhouse to fly under the radar. However, even Mt. Morris met its end. Established in 1893, the bathhouse closed in 2003 when New York City building inspectors deemed the facility structurally unsound.

that generations of Black men who had sex with other men had been frequenting Mt. Morris since the Harlem Renaissance. Rumor had it that Countee Cullen[7] ditched his wife after he and Harold Jackman[8] made Mt. Morris their regular rendezvous in the late 1920s. In the time since, thousands upon thousands of Black men used their bodies to create this delicate, invisible web connecting the queers of old to newcomers like me.

As Gregory and I checked in at the front desk, I peeked through a glass partition into the lounge and saw a passing parade of Black men in every shade. Looked like heaven. Gregory, of course, had no interest in the Mt. Morris clientele. He soaked in the hot tub and sweated in the sauna, ignoring the acts of sodomy occurring less than an arm's length away from him. I only witnessed one person take offense to Gregory's aloofness. A muscular and hairy Black man with crooked teeth.

He yelled at Gregory, "What the hell is you here for if you ain't gonna suck or fuck?"

My friend pointed at me and said, "I'm just here lookin' after that

---

7. Countee Cullen (1903–1946) was an African American poet and novelist who flourished during the Harlem Renaissance, and he is a prime example of how sexual inhibitions and mores make it tricky to pinpoint the sexuality of a queer person during his era. Cullen's first marriage to a woman ended in divorce, allegedly due to an affair with the best man at that wedding, Harold Jackman, but the poet's second marriage to a woman endured until his death. Cullen is believed to have had relationships with several men between the marriages, and during his lifetime, he wrote a trove of letters that allude to his homosexuality without confirming it. Was the poet a homosexual who conformed to heterosexual norms, or a bisexual who was afraid to affirm his attraction to men? Was he sexually fluid or sexually ambivalent? The world may never know, and Cullen may not have known either.

8. Harold Jackman (1901–1961) was an art collector and archivist who also served as a muse to a circle of gay African American artists. Never married, Jackman's social connections gave him access to art and insights on the artists that have contributed to historians' understanding of the Harlem Renaissance. In an allusion to the biblical story, Jackman and Cullen were known as the "Jonathan and David of the Harlem Renaissance," and the Cullen-Jackman Memorial Collection at Atlanta University is named in honor of the two men.

Bambi. Make sure you ex-cons don't gang-rape him up against the lockers."

I feared a fight was going to break out, but the muscular, hairy Black man roared with laughter. He admitted that he was on parole after serving five years in Rahway State Prison over in Jersey, and he did like the look of me. "A tasty redbone punk," he called me. Then he flexed his chest for me and walked off into the corridors of the bathhouse.

True to his word, Gregory was prepared to shadow me around Mt. Morris. I had to beg him not to. "I'll scream if I need you," I said. He didn't find that amusing but agreed to let me go off alone into the wild.

Naked except for a thin towel that covered me from waist to mid-thigh, I roamed the bathhouse's dimly lit hallways in a state of frightened arousal. I was young, skinny, fay, and fair game. The aggressive clientele didn't just eye me as I walked by. They pawed me, slapped my ass, squeezed their hard cocks, and catcalled their lewd intentions. Their lust gave rise to my euphoria.

I wasn't accustomed to being wanted. Growing up in Indianapolis, my slight build and timid manner got me branded early as a "sissy." That slur came with a social death sentence. It wasn't uncommon for me to attend school for days without another student speaking to me. Hell, only a few of my classmates would even bother to make eye contact with me. It will come as no surprise that I got beat up whenever hateful straight boys needed a punching bag, but I found the isolation to be more painful than the physical abuse. No love letter; no slow dances; no kisses—I grew up starved for affection.

Now, being stalked into a dark corner of a bathhouse maze and submitting to the carnal demands of an aggressive man that you've never spoken to might seem like a strange substitute for the teenage mating rituals I missed out on, but it had raw drama every inch as thrilling as schoolyard puppy love. This was my scene. The guys that I fooled around with were physically stronger than I was, but, in this realm, I had the power. I chose the men I wanted with a coy smile and a nod. They initiated the ferocity of our sex, and I retained the right to do as much or as little as I pleased.

That first visit hooked me. Within a few weeks, I was a regular in room 27 most Monday and Tuesday nights, as well as every Friday and Saturday night. Because I was young, the workers at the check-in desk stopped charging me the admission fee. I thought they were just being kind. Now I know that I was chum in the water.

———

Mt. Morris wasn't only about sex. Over time, I made friends with bathhouse employees and some of the other regulars. One of the patrons I became pals with was the underappreciated social justice advocate Bayard Rustin.[9] Rustin—we all called him by his last name—had been a key organizer of the March on Washington. He'd sat alongside Martin Luther King Jr. at countless strategy meetings for the Civil Rights Movement, and Rustin would be a household name but for his open homosexuality, which included an arrest record for "engaging in public sex," and his ties to communist and socialist ideologies. He was scrubbed from mainstream African American history and consigned to be a minor notable of the Gay Rights Movement. It was nearly two decades after Rustin's death before his legacy was given more of the credit it was due.[10]

"You shouldn't smoke, kid," were his first words to me.

He and I were alone in the break room: a small back office crammed with cold metal chairs, a slanted table, and an unreliable vending machine. I turned to look at him. Rustin wore thick-framed glasses, his hair was full and bright white, and his body was wrinkled, sagging, and slightly stooped. He was seventy-four years old

---

9. There is no evidence that Bayard Rustin (1912–1987) was a customer at the Mt. Morris Baths or any other gay bathhouse or sex club.

10. Bayard Rustin was posthumously awarded the Presidential Medal of Freedom in November of 2013. The Presidential Medal of Freedom is the highest honor the United States government bestows upon citizens.

and clad in a much longer waist towel than the rest of us bathhouse patrons got. He looked vaguely familiar to me. For a split second, I thought he might be some character actor that I'd seen play bit parts in the Blaxploitation films that my father enjoyed screening in our home theater.

"I rarely smoke," I explained. "I never buy my own. I only take them when they're offered, and I don't want to be rude."

Rustin laughed. "You might become the first person to end up with cancer by way of good manners. How about next time someone offers you a smoke, you say, 'No, thank you,' with a smile?"

"Yeah, okay," I said, turning away from him sharply, signaling my sexual disinterest.

"You've got me wrong, kid. Telling you to quit smoking isn't my pickup line," Rustin insisted. "I wouldn't bed you, even if you were offering. You remind me of too many brothers I used to run with ages ago. Brothers long dead. Nah, if I'm going to bed a fella, he's got to remind me of no one. I need a clean slate to turn me on."

His voice was so melodic and laid-back that it lowered my guard. I put down my cigarette, letting it continue to burn in the ashtray between us.

"How often do you score?" I asked.

"Once every now and again. I'm currently on a five-week dry spell."

"And what kind of guys want it from you?"

My questions came out ruder than I'd meant them, but Rustin didn't seem offended. He enjoyed talking to anyone and was especially flattered, I think, that someone as young as I was would even be curious about someone as old as he was. In those days, the age gap in gay culture was akin to racial segregation in the North, an unspoken divide that kept one group from mixing with or understanding the other. Young gays frequented clubs like Limelight, older gays haunted bars like Julius', and rarely did the two intersect. The old men who hunted youth were considered pervs, and the youth who lusted for the old were assumed to have daddy issues. It was a conservative, narrow-minded era in almost every corner of society.

"As of late," said Rustin, "I've had my best luck with the Asian men that come here occasionally. Often there's a language barrier, but we make up our own sign language to express our desires." He laughed as he showed me the rudimentary hand gestures for blow jobs, jerking off, and fucking. Lust is a universal language.

His crass humor sealed the deal. I wanted to know this guy. I extended my hand and said, "I'm Trey."

He shook my hand and said, "Nice to meet you, Trey. I'm Bayard Rustin."

He kept talking, but whatever words came out of his mouth were drowned out by the soundtrack in my head, where the name *Bayard Rustin* was repeated in an overlapping loop voiced by my father, my mother, their political friends, and a teacher or two. His achievements—his very life—had flickered at the edge of my awareness since I was a boy. Now he stood front and center before me. He was a man who had shaped history, and if I had been introduced to Rustin at a dinner party, I wouldn't have presumed that I could become friends with the likes of him. Chalk it up to one of the great powers of gay bathhouses: they strip men of their clothes and their worldly social status. Inside Mt. Morris, Rustin was an old cruiser in a big towel, and we could be buddies.

We talked for more than an hour that first night. Rustin was unlike any other adult I'd ever met before. He was intelligent without being condescending. He was open in his sexuality and opinions without a hint of shame. He could be quite serious when giving advice, but he never bullied anyone into agreeing to do as he had instructed. Rustin was the exact opposite of my father.

I started arriving at the bathhouse earlier in the evening, during the hours when it was nearly empty, just to have uninterrupted time to speak with Rustin. Why he tolerated me, I'll never know. This is how young and crass I was: in the middle of my conversations with Rustin, men would proposition me, and I'd ask Rustin to "hold that thought." I'd scurry off to fornicate in shadows, then return to find

Rustin waiting for me. He'd pick up the thread of our conversations as if these interruptions were natural and proper.

Rustin schooled me with such a light touch that I didn't realize that I was getting smarter about gay culture and politics. He opened my eyes to movies like *The Children's Hour, The Boys in the Band,* and *Portrait of Jason* and to books like *Dancer from the Dance, Just Above My Head, City of Night, Loving Her,* and *Faggots.* He taught me the history of the Daughters of Bilitis[11] and the Mattachine Society.[12] He spoke of the exclusion of gay rights from the Civil Rights Movement, the Women's Rights Movement, and the Democratic Party agenda.

He awakened me to the AIDS crisis, which again underscores the myopic worldview of my younger days. I lived in Manhattan, and AIDS was ravaging the gay community of New York City more quickly than fire had destroyed ancient Troy. Why was I so slow to smell the smoke? Well, for a long while, Gregory was my only friend, and everyone else was a passing acquaintance. If the bald gay cashier who never charged me for gum stopped coming to work at the corner store, I didn't wonder why. If I no longer crossed paths with the cute queer dogwalker on my way to the Strand Book Store, I figured he changed his route. I was blind to the magnitude of

---

11. The Daughters of Bilitis (1955–1995), originally founded by lovers Phyllis Lyon (1924–2020) and Dorothy Louise Taliaferro "Del" Martin (1921–2008) as a social club for lesbians in San Francisco, grew from eight members into a national organization dedicated to educating lesbians about gay history and gay rights. The Daughters were the first lesbian rights group in the United States. The national office closed in 1970; several local chapters survived until 1995.

12. The Mattachine Society (1950–1969), a gay men's rights organization that took a clandestine approach similar to a secret fraternal order when it came to its membership and affiliate cells, was founded in Los Angeles by Harry Hay Jr. (1912–2002). For nearly two decades, the society exerted the most influence in shaping the struggle for gay rights in the United States. While local cells of the Mattachine Society endured into the 1970s, as a national force, the group rapidly lost its power to set the agenda and tone of the Gay Rights Movement in the months after the Stonewall Riots in 1969. A new generation of bold gay activists emerged, and the Mattachine Society was suddenly passé.

death and the politics responsible for so many lost lives until Rustin educated me.

The very course of my life was changed by Rustin, and here I must give Gregory due credit. For if Gregory hadn't taken me to a dilapidated bathhouse in Harlem, I wouldn't have gotten the chance to learn from Rustin. One of the best suggestions Rustin ever made to me was simple: "You ought to go to a meeting of the Gay Men's Health Crisis." It took me several months to get my ass in gear and join the GMHC, but even that didn't frustrate Rustin. "You'll do the right things in your own time," he reassured me.

When Rustin wasn't around, Marcel Kincaid helped me pass the time at Mt. Morris between sexual encounters. Marcel assumed the role of general manager, loosely speaking, and worked the night shifts because "that's where the action's at." I'm not sure he'd been granted special authority by the bathhouse's owner, but Marcel had worked there the longest, and by force of personality, he held sway over the patrons.

A fifty-one-year-old ex-Marine with a compact bod, Marcel served two tours of active duty in Vietnam before he was dishonorably discharged in 1967 for being a Class II homosexual.[13] He made no bones about the gruesome carnage he witnessed and created fighting in the humid jungles. Civilian casualties, hand-to-hand combat, mutilation, and slaughter, Marcel shared the details of his warfare with the detachment of someone reading the phone book. His years as a soldier gave him an unshakable confidence. He could face down anyone, anywhere.

Marcel hailed from the backwoods of Alabama, and he was for-

---

13. Class II homosexuals were dishonorably discharged from the United States military on the grounds that they had solicited a homosexual act. The regulation was one of several discriminatory pretenses that facilitated the dishonorable or less-than-honorable discharge of more than one hundred thousand soldiers, on account of their sexual orientation, from the United States military. A dishonorable discharge resulted in a loss of military benefits and severely limited employment opportunities.

ever embarrassed about his thick Southern accent, his lack of rigorous education, and his loose command of grammar. He took a liking to me because he said I had "proper schoolin'." This made me uncomfortable at first. I'd caught hell from other Black kids in my neighborhood because I attended Catholic school in starched uniforms and "spoke white." But Marcel's interest in me was sincere. He'd listen to me talk and ask me to define several of the words I'd used. If he was working a crossword puzzle—a hobby he took up to expand his mind—he'd come to me for help with the more difficult clues.

I never teased Marcel about his accent, spelling, or vocabulary. He was so clearly sensitive about all that, and it quickly became apparent to me that he was at heart a sweet, earnest man. Marcel sent money every month to his family down South and hid his homosexuality during his holiday visits, so as not to upset his parents, whom he adored. He had a green thumb and tended to a couple of dozen plants he stationed throughout the bathhouse. When he believed no one was within earshot, he whispered loving encouragement to his devil's ivy, rubber figs, succulents, and jade plants.

Marcel also had a sense about people that I lacked in those days. He credited his ability to read the hearts of men to his combat experience during the Vietnam War. Marcel told me once, "I seen enough evil in men to smell it on the ones tryin' to hide it inside." He made good on that boast.

———

It was Fourth of July weekend—Friday or Saturday, I can't recall— and Mt. Morris was packed with out-of-town closet cases. Black married men, visiting the Big City, were paying five dollars at the door to rent a locker, find a willing mouth, unzip for a blow job, and rush back to their wives and kids after only fifteen minutes inside the bathhouse. Marcel was grinning at everyone that night. The quick turnaround times gave him a chance to skim off the top. He confided in me that since he could tell which of the tourists weren't even going to get naked and towel up, he'd rented out more lockers and rooms than the bathhouse contained.

I was enjoying the holiday crowd, too. Closet cases loved me. Those self-hating sodomites looked at me with such desperate yearning. They would whisper in my ear, "You're fucking prettier than my wife," or "You got a face like a girl." I wasn't enlightened enough yet to find their compliments and attention demeaning. No, in fact, I got off on their hurried lust. One after another, they were so pent-up and afraid and anxious for relief, it made for quick, hot action. Less than five minutes from initial contact to completion. I would see how many I could get off in an hour, then spend the next hour trying to break my own record.

There was something gratifying about seeing these professed hetty paragons—Reagan Democrats, churchgoers, Little League coaches—hiding their faces in the labyrinth where I walked without shame. These men were petrified but longed for a release they couldn't get in the regular lives they claimed to hold dear. They had lied to their wives to sneak away, and they had come to this run-down bathhouse in Harlem, risking ruin if caught. And they were searching for me. They needed me. I set them free with an orgasm. Call it what you will, but I played my role with glee. It seemed like harmless fun.

Shortly before midnight, in walked a tall, strapping brother. I'd guess he was in his early thirties. He had a shaved head, light eyes, and a brooding air—a combination I adored. He looked like he could have played for the Knicks, so I dubbed him All-Star and cruised him from the moment he checked in.

I figured he'd rent a locker like the other suburbanites. Instead, All-Star's key opened the door to a private room. Those rooms, equipped with a plastic mattress, flimsy sheets, an ashtray, and a trash can, cost eight dollars on the weekend. Renting one also meant that All-Star could stay in the bathhouse for up to five hours. Locker-renters could only stick around for two. I'd long ago been granted house privileges; I could arrive in the afternoon and stay until dawn.

All-Star ignored me even though I grazed by him and let my towel slip to reveal the top half of my ass as he unlocked his room. I waited patiently at the end of the hallway, and when he emerged, I felt rewarded. I was the first one to see him in seminude glory. He wore sandals, a crotchless, red leather Speedo, and a metal cock ring. His towel was flung over his shoulder.

I stepped forward and said, "What are you into?"

His square-jawed face remained expressionless and his voice had an African accent as he said, "Slaves."

I had heard him clearly, but I couldn't help repeating, "*Slaves?*"

All-Star reached out and pinched both of my nipples between his thumbs and index fingers. "Obey, and you'll cum on my command." He pinched harder, and I winced and tried to pull away from his grip, but he didn't let go for another couple of seconds. "You're not ready," he said and walked into the dark maze that led to the sauna.

Naturally, the rejection pissed me off, and I tried to erase All-Star from my mind. Who needed him? The bathhouse was packed with men. To hell with All-Star. I gave head to a half dozen more guys, but those encounters all of a sudden felt bland. I would literally be going down on a man and wondering what it would be like if it were All-Star's dick in my mouth. I even focused on the pain throbbing from my sore nipples to put me over the edge when an unremarkable married father of three failed to arouse me sufficiently.

I went to the check-in booth, described All-Star to Marcel, and asked him, "What do you know about him? Have you seen him around before?"

Marcel recoiled and looked at me like I'd smacked the joy off his face. "Fuck," he groaned, "you don't needa be sniffin' 'round him—noway, nohow."

"He's sexy," I teased, "with a smoldering intensity."

"Nah, stay far clear. He come up questionin' me before he done paid." Marcel folded his arms across his chest. "Askin' if we got a sling or a piss room. I said, 'No, sir. We ain't open to that kinda action. Just plain suckin' and fuckin' is what we allows.'"

"What did he say to that?" I asked.

"Fucker gave me some lip, talkin' 'bout, 'What if faggots scream while I fuck 'em, is that alright?' I told him if his dick is that strong, more power to him. Then I double charged him for a room."

Nothing I heard dissuaded me. "So, he's power top."

Marcel shook his head. "I'm tellin' you, you's too sweet for his kind."

"You're probably right," I said.

About an hour later, I decided to go into the dark room. Situated in the back-left corner of the bathhouse, the dark room—as its foreboding name suggests—was a ten-by-ten-foot space with no lights. The sole entrance was draped in black silk curtains. It took at least a few minutes for your eyes to adjust to the darkness, giving you then a slight chance of making out the faces of the men near you.

The dark room existed to provide anonymous sex in its purest form. Some patrons were devoted to the space. After checking in, they stripped down and headed straight to that back-left corner, parted the silk curtain, assumed the position against a wall, let their towels fall to their feet, and welcomed whoever touched them, without saying a word.

That wasn't my approach. I wouldn't have dreamed of engaging in anal sex in the dark room; I insisted on a clear view of whatever man was fucking me. Call me old-fashioned. Usually, I stepped into the dark room to close out a humdrum night when I didn't like my options in the dimly lit hallways but still wanted to get off before checking out. It never took long to attract attention in there. Hands and mouths would be upon me. The men would attempt to push and pull me to serve their purposes. It could get aggressive, but a firm refusal was respected. I liked to keep my visits to the dark room brief. Get in, get sucked off, and get out.

All-Star's eyes must have been adjusted to the darkness. I slipped through the curtain, and he moved toward me with purpose. He grabbed the knot in my towel and pulled me close. It happened with such swiftness that I didn't have a chance to react. All-Star pressed against me, towering over me. It was frightening, and that aroused me, too.

"Last chance," All-Star whispered into my ear. His accent gave the words edge.

"Let's go to your room," I suggested.

He yanked my towel off my body and tossed it aside. "We do it here or nowhere."

I considered the options.

"Say *yes*," All-Star commanded.

My hormones got the better of me. I said, "Yes."

There might have been between eight or a dozen guys in the dark room. My eyes could only make out silhouettes, and as was custom, the curtain parted with regularity for men going in and out. I heard the moans and dirty talk of several other patrons. A speaker was playing Chaka Khan's "I Feel for You." It was past two in the morning. I was eighteen. Maybe my mindset can only be understood by people who've been in similar scenes at a tender age at the wrong hour: I felt like rules didn't apply. Everything I knew about danger and consequences abandoned me. I just wanted a hot experience. Nothing else mattered.

I got down on my knees. All-Star bent forward and kissed me. I relaxed. I began to suspect that his ultramasculine posturing was a front. He french-kissed me passionately, his hands cupping my face.

Then he bit my tongue—intentionally. He held it hostage between his teeth, pulling straight up. I was like a fish on a hook. Too scared to pull away, I tried to stand up, but his hands pressed down on my shoulders. Panic surged through my body, but I suppressed it. If I continued to protest, he would continue to punish me. So I stayed calm. I held still. I gave him control. After a few seconds, his teeth released my tongue.

He patted me hard on the side of my neck. "We're gonna have fun," said All-Star.

I stood up. "Get the hell away from me."

He grabbed me by the waist and rammed me into the wall. "You wanted to play," he growled.

"Not like this."

"Don't be scared now. Go with it."

"Let go of me!"

Other voices in the dark cried out:

"What's goin' on over there?"

"Trey, is that you?"

"We got a problem in here?"

"We can turn these damn lights on and whip an ass."

"Trey, you alright?"

All-Star realized I had defenders at the ready. He let go of me and hurried out of the dark room.

"I'm alright," I said. "He got the message."

I spent a few minutes collecting myself and talking to some of the regulars who wanted to know what All-Star did to me. They all winced when I told them about the tongue biting. Once my heart rate slowed to normal pace, I ventured out into the maze.

A regular named Aaron or Ernie followed me, sort of acting as my bodyguard. He was a firefighter in his late thirties, and I think he had always had a crush on me although we'd never fooled around. Once we got to my room, I made out with Aaron/Ernie while giving him a hand job. Then I got dressed and went to check out.

Marcel shook his head at me. "Didn't I say, 'Steer clear'? Didn't I?"

"You were right," I admitted. "Totally right."

"I wish someone had told me what he done before I let him go. I could've busted his head in."

"I'm glad it didn't come to that. No serious harm was done."

"If you say so. Irregardless, that muthafucker is banned for life."

"I appreciate that. Good night, Marcel."

"Go straight home and get some rest," he said, hitting the buzzer to unlock the exit for me.

Outside and below street level, the red neon sign hummed an

unbroken song, and I noticed that the *i* in *Morris* was fading. Not quite out but dying. Walking up the stairs, I tripped and banged my knee. That should have been all the proof I needed that I wasn't as steady on my feet as I had thought.

When I got to the top of the stairs, I turned left and checked for traffic before crossing the street. An oncoming delivery truck kept me rooted to the sidewalk. I felt a little hungry, and I considered stopping by Claudia's Diner for a chocolate malt. The delivery truck passed, and the street was clear. I remember how quiet and abandoned the block looked. It was as if the whole city was sleeping, and I was the one unruly child who had dared to get out of bed. It was peaceful.

The blow to the back of my head was a complete surprise. I hadn't heard or seen All-Star approaching. I fell to my hands and knees, and I crawled several feet away. When I turned to look at him, he stood silently, holding a switchblade in his hand.

"Don't!" I begged.

"You started this," he said.

He came toward me, and I couldn't decide whether I should run or fight. He was definitely faster and stronger than me. I wanted to sprint to Mt. Morris and bang on the door, but All-Star was between me and the stairway to the bathhouse. I felt paralyzed. Then from behind All-Star, I heard the bang of the bathhouse door swinging open, and out came Marcel brandishing an old silver revolver.

"I shoot to kill!" he hollered as he ran up the stairs two at a time.

All-Star fled into the night. When he reached me, Marcel took me by the arm and hustled me back into Mt. Morris. He let me sit with him in the checkout booth, and he gave me a shot of whiskey for my nerves. I was rattled, and my head was throbbing.

"How did you know?" I asked. "Did you hear us?"

"You think I wasn't gonna keep an eye on you?" said Marcel. "I thought that son of a bitch might come lookin' for seconds."

"Are you going to call the police?"

"No goddamn cops."

I immediately understood why. A gay man attacked in or coming out of a bathhouse couldn't expect sympathy. Besides, the police hated us two times over. The white cops were driven by racism and homophobia; the Black ones were motivated by shame and rage at brothers who "debased themselves." Instead of investigating the assault, the cops would search every room and locker for an excuse to arrest, abuse, and humiliate as many of us as possible. Cops were latter-day Gestapo.

Marcel said, "I take you to the hospital if you hurt."

I shook my head. "I'm not that hurt. Just embarrassed."

"You sleep here, then. I'll give you a room. When I clock out in the mornin', you and I catch a cab to your apartment. I'm makin' damn sure you get home safely this time."

I tried to say, "Thank you," but the words caught in my throat. The fear, the adrenaline, the evil, and the trauma of what I had just gone through landed on me. I burst into tears. Marcel sat next to me and put an arm around my shoulders. He didn't tell me to toughen up or quit my crying. He stayed beside me and told me to let it all out. I don't remember how long it took, but eventually I wiped my eyes and stood up. Marcel gave me a room for the night, and I slept more soundly than I had expected. I felt safe.

———

I was determined not to let the attack spoil my affection for Mt. Morris. I returned the next evening as an act of defiance, and I visited the evening after that, and so on for years to come. The way I figured it, if I'd been mugged and beaten in Central Park, joggers would have ignored me without breaking stride. If I'd been stabbed and left for dead in the stairwell of my apartment building, any tenant other than Gregory that noticed me would have turned around and taken the elevator. Only in that run-down bathhouse was there a group of people who I could count on to care enough about me to get involved, to come to my defense. It felt liberating to know that I could warrant that kind of protection.

So I kept cruising and teasing; and making small talk; and giving head; and reading books in the break room; and letting my towel slip for attention; and gossiping with the regulars; and having sex in the rented rooms, the sauna, and the hallways with newbies; and seeking wisdom from Rustin; and solving crossword puzzles with Marcel. I'd found the haven for my mind, body, and soul. Everyone needs such a place. Don't reject the space you gravitate toward just because the windows aren't stained glass and the congregation isn't saved.

Lesson #3

DON'T WEAR STRAITJACKETS

Gregory didn't share my feelings about Mt. Morris. He swore that he would never again step foot in that joint after I was assaulted, and he urged me to do the same. Once, we got into an argument about it as I was getting ready to head over to the baths. My attire consisted of a tank top, short shorts, and a jockstrap. Gregory was smoking a joint in our cramped studio apartment that only had one window that opened a quarter of the way up. Subsequently, I was high off the contact smoke.

"I'll never go again," I said, "if you can explain why it's more dangerous now than it was the night you first took me there."

Gregory loved concocting unlikely hypotheticals. "Alright, hear this. You got someone out to get you now."

"Who?"

"All-Star, asshole."

I laughed in his face.

"You think I'm jokin'? Okay, tell me this. Whatcha gonna do, lil man, if All-Star turn up to finish the job and Marcel don't come to save your ass?"

"Don't be absurd," I said. "He was a sex freak hopped up on, like, angel dust—not a serial killer."

"You don't know that. You don't know shit about him except he tried to kill you."

I let Gregory yell that last line at the back of my head as I left the apartment.

A decade later, I imagined how Gregory would have rubbed it in my face when I read an article about a serial killer who seduced and murdered as many as sixteen gay men in San Francisco in the 1970s. The serial killer was never caught, never brought to justice. His build, ethnicity, and age lined up with All-Star, and when I saw the composite sketch based on the recollections of three victims who survived . . . I recognized him as the man who tried to stab me outside of Mt. Morris. I owed Gregory an apology. All-Star was a homicidal psychopath known as the Black Doodler.[14]

———

In August of '86, Gregory and I got completely fed up with the ratty, uninsulated studio apartment we shared on Mercer Street in SoHo. The ten-by-twenty-foot room had been a sweatbox during the summer and was promising to become an icebox during the winter. Gregory and I had complained repeatedly to the building manager about the faulty front door lock, the army of ants who marched through the kitchen cabinets, and the perpetually broken elevator, as well as about the frequent surprise power outages and the scalding brown water that arrived unannounced during showers. The building manager did nothing to help us, so on a matter of principle, Gregory and I decided to stop paying the rent. Our ethical stance also suited our financial desires: we felt damn near rich once we quit writing those rent checks.

After recovering from the injuries of my aborted bike messengering career, I worked off and on cutting grass at Calvary Cemetery in Queens. The pay was $3.50 an hour (which was fifteen cents above

———

14. The Black Doodler was known for sketching his victims before stabbing them to death. He "went dormant" in September 1975. His identity and the full extent of his criminal activities remain a mystery.

the minimum wage), all cash, all under the table—if you could manage to get one of the thirty open mowers. Securing a position meant being in line outside the cemetery when the gates opened at 7:00 a.m. I had to leave my apartment at 5:30 a.m., catch the E train, and transfer to the 7 before walking the last half mile to Calvary. Some days the trains ran late, and all the mowers would be spoken for by the time I reached the cemetery. Some days it rained, and no one cut grass or got paid. Some mornings I overslept.

When I did reach Queens on time and was among the fortunate laborers with a mower to push for a nine-and-a-half-hour shift, the job itself was beatific, hypnotic, and grueling. Not that I ever shared such observations with my grizzled, hefty coworkers, but I loved how the morning dew would turn into steam under the summer sun, making the crowded metropolis of jagged tombstones appear as if they were smoldering. I never got bored of looking at all those graves.

During my shifts, I learned to read the headstones with passing glances. I'd do quick math to figure out how long the deceased had lived. I would consider the words carved into the stone, words meant to sum up lives: FATHER, BROTHER, SON . . . MOTHER, WIFE, SISTER . . . DEVOTED, BELOVED, BLESSED. Family plots intrigued me. Was everyone present and accounted for, united in the same soil for all of eternity? Or had some wayward niece or rebellious cousin snubbed this final reunion in Queens and had the audacity to get buried in Brooklyn?

My family on my father's side owned a large mausoleum in Crown Hill Cemetery, where members of three generations of Singletons were already entombed in the marble walls. Earl Sr. and Gertrude, my grandparents, had to be dug up from their shabby plots when the mausoleum was built in 1977. With macabre foresight, there were enough slots for the coffins of my parents, my father's siblings, several cousins, Jackie, and me.

I, of course, had zero desire to spend my eternal rest in Indianapolis, but when I thought honestly about my death, it seemed quite likely to me that my mother and father would outlive me. After all, I was living in a wild and dangerous city, and random violence had a knack for striking you if you were poor, gay, or Black. I belonged to all three targets and had already survived a madman's attempt to kill me. How long could I expect to outrun death? And if I died before my parents, I figured the decisions about my burial would be theirs. Crown Hill it would be. Indiana forever.

While my mind wandered as I worked, my body hardened. Calluses formed on my fingers and palms from gripping and pushing the lawn mowers for hours on end. Overexposure to the sun naturally darkened my complexion but, also quite surprisingly, dyed some of my black hair reddish gold. My physique, which had always been unremarkably skinny, took on muscle tone and bulk. I didn't notice until several weeks after I started cutting grass at the cemetery. I was walking around shirtless in the apartment, and Gregory awed over the definition in my back, pecs, and arms.

He wasn't the only guy to admire the changes in my appearance. Being more muscular flipped the script when it came to who was pursuing me. Riding the subway home from Queens, I found myself appealing to a new audience: overt *bottoms* were daring to lick their lips and eye-fuck me. This reversal in the gay natural order, as I knew it, amused me.

Before my transfiguration, these very same young men would cut their eyes at me as we crossed paths at gay bars and clubs. Like types must be fast friends or rivals, and rivalry tends to be the default. But as I clung to the subway rail in the evenings, my body tanned, sweaty, and ripped, I appeared butch. Up was down; black was white.

This realignment presented an erotic challenge. Given what I have revealed of myself so far, it probably comes as no surprise that throughout my sex life, I had served exclusively as a bottom. I had no complaints about my role. Getting penetrated made me hard. The idea of having to top gave me performance anxiety. Yet curiosity, easy targets, and the summer heat led me to wonder what it would be like to take on a new position.

I asked Gregory for tips about how to top, and I'll never forget his sage advice: "Just fuck like you own the ass in front of you, and you can't go wrong."

I pretended as if I understood what he meant. The first few young guys that I picked up riding on the subway were subjected to my clueless fumbling and embarrassing failures. More than once, my cock refused to get hard enough to do the deed. Another time, I hit the mark with no finesse and promptly came before I reached full insertion. The bottoms that I disappointed weren't sensitive to my plight. They complained bitterly, insulting me, my manhood, and my mama. One beautiful Mexican bottom slapped me across the face.

My luck changed when I followed a white, curly-haired, punk rock fan back to his apartment. His name was either Frank or Hank, his curls hid a forehead dotted with zits, he wore too much cologne, his body was skin and bones, and he wasn't much of a talker. But he had a silent confidence, and he had a wide mouth with full lips, and he liked kissing, and he led me by the hand into his bedroom, where he cleared the dirty clothes off his mattress and pushed me onto my back. Frank/Hank moved with a quick efficiency that left me no time to think, no time to worry. We were making out. He took his clothes off. He undressed me. He blew me. He fitted me with a condom, and he was riding my cock. I was in heaven. Frank/Hank mumbled instructions, and I learned the fundamentals of topping.

We parted ways without exchanging phone numbers. The very next day, I searched for him on the subway. Days passed, and I didn't see him. I went back to the neighborhood he lived in, and I wandered the streets hoping to recognize his apartment building or bump into him. I wanted to fuck again, and to thank him.

With a sense of purpose, I went on to top dozens of guys over the next few months. My newfound sexual prowess wasn't extraordinary. Legends weren't born about my cock skills. But the impact on me was lifelong. I learned that I wasn't locked into how I'd been perceived by others and how I had perceived myself.

My whole life, I'd been viewed as a sissy. Some people found my effeminate mannerisms disgusting; others found them alluring. I came to believe that I had been stamped a certain way, and that the stamp was immutable. This is not to say that I was rebuking my effeminate side; this wasn't about subtraction but addition. On the train to and from Queens, I discovered I was capable of expansion.

We are not so narrowly defined as society would have us believe. Yet the limits placed on our appetites, talents, and potential are implanted in us when we are children—too young to recognize the prisons built with words. We could blame it all on our families, but then we'd never find the keys to unlock our cells. The awful genius of our confinement is that we are both the prisoner and the warden. We tell ourselves daily that we aren't free to do *this* or *that* because we are *that* or *this*. To escape such limited thinking, we don't have to look far. The keys are in our pocket.

ENEMIES HAVE THEIR VALUE

Winter arrived early and hard in October, and there was no need for men to cut the grass at Calvary Cemetery in Queens. I applied for jobs, but no one hired me. I sold some of my collection of gold cuff links (gifts from my father) and several first-edition books (gifts from my mother) and lived off my meager earnings.

Money was lasting longer since Gregory and I hadn't paid rent since August. Eviction notices were posted on our apartment door. We tore them down and threw them away. We didn't take them too seriously because our fellow tenants didn't either. More than half the eighty units in the building were under threat of eviction. No one came home to find they were locked out of their apartments and their belongings were tossed on the curb. I wasn't sure how long we'd be allowed to rip up eviction notices, but I didn't care. My plan was to somehow get enough cash to put down a deposit on a new place with Gregory and to leave our current landlord high and dry.

To that end, I toyed with the idea of swallowing my pride and phoning my parents to beg them to wire me money. Several times I even picked up a pay phone and called them collect at their gray stone mansion in Indianapolis. Jackie usually answered, and I'd shout over the operator to tell her that I loved her and then hang up. I gave up on the notion of pleading for money because I simply couldn't imagine how I was going to get either of my parents to send me a dime. My mother didn't believe in second chances, and my father hated making what he deemed to be bad investments.

———

I made the mistake of leaning too hard on Gregory for emotional support. He was, after all, my best friend in the city, and from my blinkered point of view, he had his shit together. At least better than I did, or so I believed.

Gregory temped three or four days a week, earning decent pay. His problem was that he increasingly wanted to live like he did when he was riding the tab of his old, rich sugar daddies. He'd come home with bottles of Dom Pérignon, or a gold Pulsar calculator watch, or a pair of front-row tickets to see Prince perform at Madison Square Garden. I assumed these were gifts from old men, and I had no qualms about enjoying whatever Gregory was willing to share with me.

For instance, witnessing Prince in concert was nothing short of a revelation. Gregory and I danced together like possessed lovers for every song, and no one looked at us funny once. I felt safe and free in a world where the voice of God belonged to Prince.[15] I was certain that Gregory and I would return to our hellhole apartment and finally have sex.

That didn't happen. After the concert let out, Gregory saw someone else he wanted to say hello to and left me waiting for him in the corridors of the Garden. He said he would be back in a sec. I didn't see him again for two days.

---

15. A virtuoso singer-songwriter and musician, Prince (1958–2016) cultivated an androgynous, pansexual persona during the height of his groundbreaking, award-winning career. His liberated sexual views, however, seemed to narrow once he became a practicing Jehovah's Witness in the 2000s. In a 2008 interview with *The New Yorker*, Prince was asked about gay marriage, and he said: "God came to earth and saw people sticking it wherever and doing it with whatever, and he just cleared it all out. He was, like, 'Enough.'" Thereafter, Prince's position on gay rights remained murky and offered less than the full-throated support one might suspect given his earlier work.

My devotion to Gregory, however, didn't waver. I didn't call him on his thoughtlessness, his habit of drawing me near and casting me off at whim. As I saw it, I was fortunate Gregory had chosen me as a friend and roommate. On more nights than I dare to count, I lay awake on my narrow cot in our studio apartment, and I prayed that Gregory would get out of his cot, cross the room, and fuck me. I loved him madly. He seemed sexy, street-smart, and glamorous. Everything I wanted to be one day.

But, in truth, Gregory's reality was as far from glamorous as my own. During a windy, cold night when we got too high at a party that we crashed in Lenox Hill, he confessed to me that he'd blown through his money and that he'd racked up $10,000 in credit card debt. Gregory and I discussed his financial ruin while we helped ourselves to a bottle of whiskey and food in the party hostess's pantry. She walked in on us eating Lucky Charms with our hands straight out of the box and chugging Maker's Mark, and she threatened to kick our asses if we didn't leave at once.

Outside, Gregory groaned, "I don't have cab fare. I ain't even got subway fare."

"I'm broke, too," I said with a smile. "We'll walk home. No big deal."

It was a long, drunken, stumbling trek along unfamiliar streets, and our feet were aching, and our hands were going numb, and the freezing air smelled of piss and garbage—and there was nothing remotely cool about being poor in the city.

Gregory insisted we rest on stairs leading up to a brownstone, and as soon as we sat down, he leaned over and cried on my shoulder. "They're gettin' tired of me."

"Who?"

"The men, my daddies. They want younger, they want new."

"You sound like one of their wives," I joked.

Gregory wasn't laughing. "The judge used to cover whatever I bought at Lord & Taylor. I went there last week, and that fucker cut me off. Everyone gets tired of me."

"That's only one guy. Plenty of—"

"It's happenin' with all my daddies. They're talkin' to each other, I know it. Everyone wants to cut me off, and my dealer chooses now to fuckin' jack up the price of coke. Like I need that headache."

"How much coke are you doing?" I asked.

"That ain't the point. Are you even listenin'? They're tryin' to put me out, run me out of the city. They had their fun. Now they want new dick, and there ain't shit I can do to stop it."

"Calm down. No one is putting you out. You make your own money, and you could temp full-time. You don't need these old guys."

Gregory blew his nose into the sleeve of his jacket. "My mother threw me out of the house when I was fifteen. One of my uncles told her that I was chargin' men to suck my dick in our church's bathroom. Like I was the only rough trade in Flatbush." He sobbed. "She ain't spoken to me since. I went to try and stay with my dad, but he'd heard already. I knocked on his door, he pulled me inside, and he beat the shit out of me."

I held Gregory as his words gave way to tears. I didn't know what to say. We didn't make it back to our place that night. Following Gregory's lead, we got hopelessly lost, headed to the wrong side of Manhattan, and wound up sleeping until dawn in Carl Schurz Park.

———

Yet Gregory deserves credit for getting me out of my head when I spiraled over my directionless life. He'd only let me brood for a day or two before forcing me out into the world. I was content to cuddle up next to our illegal kerosene space heater and read Kurt Vonnegut's latest novel, *Galápagos*, until he badgered me to put on slacks, a dress shirt, and tie, and accompany him to the Dakota.

It was to be a ritzy dinner party thrown by one of Gregory's open-secret sugar daddies and a permissive wife. This time, the host was Nathaniel "Tex" Udel, a wealthy construction company owner.

"C'mon, and I'll show you the spot where Lennon got shot," my roommate promised as an enticement.

That was of no appeal to me. I cared little for the Beatles, and even less for John Lennon and Yoko Ono. His death was tragic, but I wouldn't be leaving roses at the site. My dream was that the party would be blessed with a visit from another Dakota resident, Ms. Lauren Bacall. I worshipped her. In my estimation, she'd given one of the three top femme fatale performances on-screen, in *The Big Sleep*. (The other two wicked turns belong to Barbara Stanwyck in *Double Indemnity* and Dorothy Dandridge in *Carmen Jones*.) I could just see her cutting through the old-money crowd and helping herself to a stiff drink at the bar.

It never happened. The likes of Ms. Bacall wouldn't have been welcome in this decidedly right-wing soirée. The likes of Gregory and me barely made the cut.

A Black butler dressed in formal Uncle Tom attire blocked our path when we stepped foot inside the lavish apartment.[16] "Whatever you selling, we don't want it. Now get."

"We were invited," said Gregory.

"I seen the guest list, and a pair of colored hoodlums wasn't on it."

I was prepared to retreat.

Gregory was having none of it. "Take our coats before you lose your job, bitch."

The butler raised his voice and started poking his finger in Gregory's chest. "I'll have the cops get rid of you Negroes faster than I throw out the trash."

"You about to have a broken finger."

"Sir, he's for real," I warned.

---

16. *Uncle Tom* is old slang for an African American male with self-hating and subservient devotion to white authority figures, as well as to institutions and power structures that favor white people. The character of Uncle Tom comes from the novel *Uncle Tom's Cabin; or, Life Among the Lowly* (published in 1852) by Harriet Beecher Stowe (1811–1896). Ironically, when it debuted, the novel was considered a progressive work of art and advocacy that advanced the cause of antislavery.

The growing commotion caught the host's attention, and he hurried over to us and sent his butler away with our coats.

"Call me Tex," he said as he shook my hand, "and remember my son's name is Dustin."

"What college do we attend?" Gregory asked.

"Regent. It's in Virginia outside Norfolk."

I was confused until Gregory explained, "We go to college with his son, Dustin," and winked.

Tex was legitimately handsome. Square jaw, button nose. Gregory had really scored this time. In his late fifties, Tex was still built like a linebacker, and his tan looked as if he'd earned it working under the sun. His hands were calloused and roamed liberally along our shoulders and spines as he led Gregory and me into the living room, where most of the seventy-five guests were mingling. The crowd was predominately white, male, and pushing sixty. A chorus of polite chatter and clouds of cigarette smoke filled the air.

Gregory lightly patted Tex on the ass. "You've got a guy for Trey, too?"

"Damn straight. There are a couple of gents interested in meeting a new friend. Follow me to the fireplace."

This was news to me. I wasn't terribly eager to be matched up, and my enthusiasm flatlined when I saw my would-be suitors. One was a sixty-three-year-old white man hampered by a hound-dog face and a neck wattle. He wore an ill-fitting blue suit, and his teeth were stained with red wine. The other was sixty-one and a bit more dapper-looking, but his aura was unsettling. His eyes had the glint of a sociopath, and his face twitched as if it were a mask he was wearing.

Tex introduced me to the hound dog first. "This here is Marvin Liebman."[17]

---

17. Marvin Liebman (1923–1997) was a prominent advocate and writer in the conservative political movement; he contributed regularly to *National Review*; and he revealed he was homosexual in 1990. However, Trey's recollection of Mr. Liebman making sexual advances at him in 1986 while surrounded by a conservative crowd that included William F. Buckley Jr. runs contrary to Mr. Liebman's claim that he was discreet and closeted in his sexuality prior to coming out.

The name meant nothing to me, and it showed on my face.

Tex quickly added, "He's one of this country's leading minds. A champion of conservatism and a foe to godless commies. You can read his brilliance in *National Review*."

"Yes, but only when I deign to transmute and publish his Byzantine manifestos," said the dapper sociopath, grinning with self-satisfaction.

The hound dog affirmed the hierarchy. "He's correct. My copy looks more brilliant in your magazine than it does when I turn it in."

"I'm Bill Buckley, *the* leading mind our country has on political science and yachting. I'm also founder and editor in chief of *National Review*."[18]

The name was vaguely familiar; I'd heard of *National Review* and was aware that it was the opposite of *Mother Jones*. I pretended to be impressed.

"I'll leave you gents to your devices," said Tex. He squeezed my ass before walking off with Gregory.

Bill and Marvin stepped closer to me. Marvin offered to get me a glass of wine. Bill held his glass to my mouth and told me to go ahead and drink some of his. I declined. Desperate to get sex off their minds, I turned the subject toward their other shared passion: politics.

"My father has met with President Reagan several times in the Oval Office," I said. "He says the president isn't as out of it as you might think."

Bill pounced on the opportunity to be bitchy. "The cerebral light

18. William F. Buckley Jr. (1925–2008) was a conservative public intellectual, author, journalist, and founder of *National Review*. He was a strict Roman Catholic and opposed gay rights such as same-sex marriage; he was in a heterosexual marriage with his wife, Patricia, for more than fifty years; and he tolerated but refused to condone the homosexuality of his close friend Marvin Liebman when Liebman came out as gay. Trey is the first person to publicly claim Mr. Buckley was homosexual. There is no evidence to corroborate Trey's assertion.

emanating from our current commander in chief was never, even at its zenith, a shining beacon."

"What line of work is your father in that he gets the honor of meeting with the president?" asked Marvin.

"He's a lobbyist for Eli Lilly, specializing in public health."

Bill cupped the side of my face in his hand. "Young lad, do you know the greatest public health care crisis plaguing this noble republic of ours?"

I'd learned enough by then to give the obvious answer. "AIDS."

"Wrong," he boomed. "AIDS can be snuffed out in its tracks if we have the courage of our convictions. All that's necessary is that we round up everyone infected with this dreaded disease, and we tattoo a warning on the forearms of the drug addicts and on the buttocks of the queers.[19] Do that, and there won't be a new case of infection among anyone worth keeping alive."

I pulled away from his hand.

Marvin turned to gaze into the fireplace as he lodged his objection. "Tattooing a segment of the population, I suspect, could be more destructive than the disease."

"You say that because you're Jewish." Bill sighed. "Think it through empirically and remove your traumatized heritage from the equation."

I tried to return the conversation to smoother ground. "What is our greatest public health crisis?"

Bill leaned in and stage-whispered, "It's the dismantlement of the traditional family in accordance with Judeo-Christian morality."

"Oh, I've heard this one before," said Marvin. He arched an eyebrow at me. "Buckle up, son. The ride is long."

Bill ignored his friend and tried to hypnotize me with his searing analysis. "Look at your community. The best Blacks are God-fearing. They believe in hard work, law and order, and incremental economic

---

19. On March 18, 1986, *The New York Times* did publish an op-ed written by William F. Buckley Jr. in which he proposed tattooing "AIDS carriers." In the same op-ed, Mr. Buckley also suggested that if a woman was willing to marry a man living with AIDS, she should be sterilized before being issued a marriage license.

gains across generations. They don't demand fortune for themselves. No, no, they simply want a middle-class life for their progeny. Upward mobility is a steady climb, not a holy ascension made manifest by the machinations of Big Government.

"And the worst of your people," he continued, "have traded in their moral fiber for libertine delights. The high of drugs, the riches of crime, the carnal thrill of siring children out of wedlock. These vices, celebrated as mere personal preferences by the left, have torn apart the traditional family, leaving Black babies and often Black women caught in its undertow. Ill-housed, ill-fed, ill-cared for. This is the legacy of liberalism, and the health of your people has suffered. Life expectancy is lower than for whites. Death by violence is higher. Even this AIDS epidemic will ravage your community as it has the homosexuals. Both communities are victims of their lack of willpower to resist baser temptations. The queers can't quit sodomy. Too many Blacks can't quit pushing junk in their arms with needles. It's easy to blame AIDS, but look closer—we are living in the hangover of the 1960s."

He said all of that without pausing, and I'm not sure how he took in a breath because the outpouring of words was unbroken. It was impressive for a parlor trick. He was so proud of himself, and I just had to wipe that smirk off his face. Fortunately, Old Rustin's tutelage at the Mt. Morris Baths had prepared me for this moment.

"At the risk of being rude, I have to disagree," I said.

Marvin beamed. "How about it? The boy's got gumption."

"You endeavor to debate the matter with me," Bill said before laughing at the notion. "Do your best. *Dominus tecum.*"

"Okay," I said, flashing a devilish smile. "You think the Black family was destroyed by vice, and that's a good play for an elderly white man because it's safer than looking in a mirror. What wrecked the Black family was white oppression, white political choices, white violence, white men. The likes of you did more damage to us than crack rocks. I think the Black community actually deserves credit for not being driven into total madness. We have survived your attempted genocide."

When I finished, Marvin clapped—not out of political solidarity but in the doomed hope of earning my sexual favor. Bill put his hands on his hips and reassessed me.

"I hope I haven't been insolent," I joked, invoking an adjective used by nuns to describe me in grade school.

Bill slicked his silver hair off his forehead and to the left. "*Insolent* misses the mark by a degree or two, you militant scamp. You're redoubtable, bewitching, and cocksure. Wrong, of course, but winsome in your form." He pinched my right earlobe between his thumb and the knuckle on his index finger. "You should be dragged by the ear to the headmaster's office. A few rounds of corporal punishment ought to be sufficient to realign your muddled thinking."

Marvin looked away as his ideological compatriot moved in for the kill. Anyone watching us could be forgiven for believing that Bill had drawn me to him so that he could whisper the most sensitive of covert foreign intelligence to me.

In reality, he groped my cock with his right hand and told me, "Sodomy isn't a sin if we stop before we ejaculate."

My dick had never been limper, my sex drive never less stimulated. He wasn't my type, and he hadn't stood a chance from the start. Our encounter could have ended quietly, rejection being a message I usually sent with dispassionate efficiency.

However, a flash of anger ran the length of my body, although it wasn't Mr. William F. Buckley Jr.'s forwardness that upset me. I'd grown accustomed to men touching me without asking me first. It was his hypocrisy that pissed me the fuck off. This old man could lecture and condescend to me with his right-wing, homophobic, racist screed, or he could cruise me at a dinner party with the mothballed tactics that must have been effective enough during the Eisenhower administration. But he couldn't do both.

I shoved him back and shouted, "Get your hands off me!"

Every white man's head turned in my direction.

Bill pleaded with me as if I were a volatile thug. "Calm down, young sir. I only meant to straighten your tie." He turned away and headed to the bar, where I supposed he would tell a distinctly different version of our brief time together.

Marvin didn't miss a beat. "Are you alright?" he asked. "Bill tends to go too far after a few glasses of wine."

"Oh, is that what's wrong with him?" My tone was hostile, and my voice was louder than I had intended.

"Please, accept my apology. He shouldn't have treated you like a—"

"A two-dollar whore."

"Please, you don't understand. An attractive young man like yourself . . ." Marvin's hands shook while he explained his (and Bill's) vantage point. "We don't get many opportunities. There aren't a lot of men in our circle who are accommodating like Tex. Only two, three times a year, we'll be introduced to a young man like yourself. We can get . . . too excitable. I'm sorry. Is there anything I can do?"

I took the wineglass from his hand and drank from the rim that hadn't been smudged by his lips. We drifted away from the fireplace and into two chairs by a window overlooking West Seventy-second Street. Marvin kept offering to be of service to me, and the more I refused, the more insistent he became.

Whereas Bill was contemptable, Marvin was just pathetic. A closet case too bound and gagged by fear to do much of anything. He didn't have the guts to make a move, but he was desperate for some kind of connection with me. He wanted me to like him. Doing me a favor might make me grateful. Why not play along and get a benefit for my troubles?

I told Marvin that I was looking for a job in the music industry after abrupt endings to my careers as a bike messenger and a graveyard grass mower. He had no contacts in music. I mentioned that I was months behind on the rent for my dilapidated apartment, and Marvin asked me to describe the condition of my unit and the building. I spared no grimy detail.

Marvin thought aloud. "The state of the building sounds horrible, but nothing newsworthy like that World War I vet who got killed in that faulty elevator. But listen—you're a very appealing kid—if you go to your landlord, tell him your personal hard-luck story . . . poor Black youth, injured on the job—he might forgive the outstanding back rent."

Then an idea struck him, and he reached for my knee but lost his nerve. His hand hung impotently in the air.

"There's a better way," he continued. "All these building owners know each other. I've got a friend who could advocate on your behalf. Maybe even horse trade to your benefit. Find out who owns your building, and I'll set you up with an appointment to meet with Clive."

Marvin scribbled a name and number on the back of his business card, and I took the card. Marvin's generosity, such as it was, would lead to the searing campaign that introduced me to the unruly arenas of political organizing and advocacy work in New York City. Naturally, Marvin never intended for me to head in the direction I did, but that's not the point.

The fact remains that I should raise a glass and toast to the vile Bill Buckley, the cowardly Marvin Liebman, and the lascivious Tex Udel—men who dedicated their energy and fortunes to politically disenfranchising people like me—for serving as accidental angels in my life. If we never meet our despicable adversaries, we'd never be forced to find out how brave, resilient, and cunning we can be.

Of course, I don't ever literally raise a glass in memory of my enemies. To the contrary, I take immense joy in having outlived them all. Bill Buckley was rotten to the grave; the laurels he believed that history would bestow onto his reputation didn't come. In 1992, five years before he died, Marvin Liebman wrote a memoir titled

Coming Out Conservative, about his sad-sack existence as a homosexual dedicated to the Republican Party. It was a textbook example of too damn little, too damn late. And Tex Udel burned to death in a house fire; a stroke had left him bedridden. Before you think of feeling sorry for him, remember he was a self-loathing homosexual who donated millions to denying the civil rights of the LGBTQ+ community. He also gave Gregory chlamydia. To hell with all three of them.

A BIG LIE CAN BUILD CHARACTER

It was a week before Halloween when I finally learned the name of my landlord. He'd done a good job of hiding. Gregory and I, back when we were paying our rent, made out checks (from me) and money orders (from him) to Plutus Property Management LLC. To trace back who owned Plutus—in the age before public records were digitized—meant a trip to 280 Broadway, the headquarters of the New York City Department of Buildings.

"If you can't find what you need, don't come crying to me," said the middle-aged woman working the Building Department's help desk. She exhaled her cigarette smoke through her nose and gave me directions to the catalog of records. "And the city's not responsible if any bodily harm should come to you down there," she warned.

The building records were in floor-to-ceiling file cabinets in the cavernous basement of 280. Long fluorescent lights, many of them flickering, hung precariously overhead. The smell in the room was a mixture of festering mildew and a rotting, dead rabbit. No windows, no vents, no air circulation. It was at least warm in the basement, which I imagine was why it attracted a half dozen homeless people who searched for nothing more than quiet spots to rest.

I assumed the task would be straightforward and easy. In high school, I'd memorized and mastered the old Dewey decimal system.

So an hour, I figured, would be sufficient in the bowels of 280. I looked up the property records for my building, and Plutus Property Management's owner was listed as Sawyer Real Estate Investment Group. This required me to find a "master list" of all the buildings owned directly by the Sawyer Group. I then had to look up the deed for the oldest property on record to see who was listed as the owner of the Sawyer Group because information on ownership isn't included on the master list.

It was a ridiculous way to store the information and a brilliant way to dissemble the information. The tortuous scheme reminded me of a topic my mother, a political speechwriter, often lectured me and my siblings on: the insidious ways of municipal, state, or federal governments. Fiona had a special turn of phrase for what I was experiencing through this small branch of local government: "the intentional secondary consequence."

The theory goes that governmental agencies don't accidently make accessing information or resources difficult. They do this shit on purpose. The forms are confusing, and the record keeping is ass-backward because it reflects a policy choice. A decision has been made to repel the average citizen from gaining certain knowledge or opportunities.

When most people encounter the seemingly arbitrary and capricious workings of, for instance, the IRS or the DMV, they accept it because they've been trained to assume that the government is run by half-wits. They yell at the lowly staffer in front of them, then sulk away and comply with the absurd rules or give up. Yet what the vast majority of citizens see as mistakes are the result of calculated design. Some high-level political functionary stipulated that the form must be completed in triplicate. A few billionaire donors drafted the fine print that disqualifies the neediest from touching the bounty. These are very smart motherfuckers. To think otherwise plays into their hands.

Case in point, my search for my landlord's name. Why should that have been such a difficult fact to uncover? Why hadn't I known his name from the day I became one of his tenants? Hell, during the wanton age of the antebellum South, even slaves knew the names of their masters.

My landlord's identity was a secret because he belonged to a powerful constituency of wealthy building owners and real estate developers. None of them wanted tenants hounding them to provide safe living conditions. So they shielded their names by using shell companies like Russian nesting dolls. Plutus Property Management was a subsidiary of Sawyer Real Estate Investment Group; Sawyer Real Estate Investment Group was owned by Middlebrook Unlimited; Middlebrook Unlimited belonged to Firemort Holdings; Firemort Holdings was but a spawn of Williamdale Inc.; Williamdale Inc. was held by Bellriver Enterprises; Bellriver Enterprises lived in the shadows of the Greater Horizon Project; the Greater Horizon Project answered to Marigold Operations; and, finally, Marigold Operations was owned by Frederick Christ Trump.[20]

His reputation did not precede him. The name *Fred Trump* rang no bells for me. Even his son Donald Trump would have only stirred vague impressions back then. My working assumption was that my landlord was your standard rich prick who didn't give a flying fuck about the poor. He was far worse than that.

Fred's activities as a racist slumlord are a matter of public record: In 1973, the U.S. Department of Justice's Civil Rights Division filed a civil suit against the Trump Organization—Fred was chairman; Donald was president; and Roy Cohn was their lawyer—for violating the Fair Housing Act of 1968. The main evidence in the suit rested on the fact that several Black test applicants had inquired about vacancies in a Trump-owned apartment building and were turned down, despite being as financially stable as whites who were accepted. The rental applications denoted the race of the prospective tenants, and one rental agent claimed that Fred Trump had instructed him

---

20. Fred C. Trump (1905–1999) was a wealthy real estate developer and apartment building owner. He was also the father of the forty-fifth president of the United States of America. The Trump family categorically objects to the characterization of Fred Trump in this book, which they dismiss as "the fake memoir of a nobody."

"not to rent to Blacks." The Department of Justice and the Trump Organization settled the matter with a consent decree in 1975 that included a directive that the Trumps "thoroughly acquaint themselves personally" with the Fair Housing Act of 1968.

With that legal scrape behind him, Fred went on to get himself more directly embroiled in another housing complaint against him in 1976. This time, he was ordered by a county judge to fix serious code violations (e.g., broken windows, missing fire extinguishers) in a five-hundred-plus unit complex he owned in Seat Pleasant, Maryland. Despite the court order, Fred dodged and stalled efforts to make the repairs. He eventually agreed to meet with county officials at the complex in question to discuss the matter. When he showed up for the meeting, Fred was handcuffed and arrested on the spot. He was released on $1,000 bail and begrudgingly brought the building up to code.

This was the man that I was hoping to persuade to forgive my unpaid back rent.

———

True to his word, Marvin Liebman got me an appointment with Clive Oswyn, a commercial real estate owner who specialized in leasing to hundreds of bodega owners throughout the five boroughs and parts of New Jersey. I dressed like the cleanest-cut Catholic schoolboy ever to walk out of the pages of *Blueboy* magazine.[21] I figured if Clive was a conservative like Marvin, he'd look favorably upon my groomed appearance, and if he was a closet case like Marvin, his gaze would fall even more appreciatively on my fitted white dress shirt and tight navy-blue pants.

———

21. *Blueboy* (1974–2007) was a pioneering gay men's lifestyle magazine that featured softcore photos of sexy young males. The magazine was referenced in the Cyndi Lauper song "She Bop."

I needn't have bothered. Clive, a hunched senior citizen with a head of uncombed thinning hair, was hopelessly hetty. His suit was baggy, wrinkled, and plaid. His shabby office was a shrine to the New York Mets with signed baseballs, helmets, posters, and hats everywhere I turned. It was a bold decorating choice considering that his office was located in the Bronx just a short stroll away from Yankee Stadium. Clive ate a chili dog at his desk while I sat on a lumpy stained sofa.

"Marvin told me you quit paying your rent," barked Clive.

"Yes, sir, I lost my—"

"That's a violation of your rental contract."

"I know, sir, but Marvin said—"

"Your landlord is within his rights to initiate eviction proceedings against you."

Flustered by his scolding tone, I shouted back, "I know that! I'm here because—"

"Who's your landlord?"

"Fred Trump," I said.

Clive fixed me with a hard stare, put down his chili dog, and wiped his fingers with a napkin. "Oh ho," he said, "I see your game."

"I'm not playing any games."

"Don't get loud with me, boy."

I stood up. "I'm not your boy."

"I see, this is the warning shot," said Clive. "Let me guess. You couldn't get a meeting with Fred, so you used Marvin to get to me, since I'm in tight with Fred. Pretty slick. I'll give you that."

I realized, of course, that he misunderstood my intentions, but I didn't correct him because I could also feel I had become more substantial to him. That gave me a surge. I stepped forward, approaching his desk, and enjoyed seeing Clive squirm in his chair. This man was afraid of me, and not because he thought I was a street thug. He believed I had some sort of legitimate white-collar power.

I played along. "Are you going to help me or not?"

"Fred doesn't like to be muscled. He's faced down the Justice Department before."

I smiled, confident it would unnerve him. "I'm not with them."

"Then who's backing your play?" I shut up and let Clive do the guessing. "Urban League? NAACP? HUD? The ACLU?"

I tilted my head at the mention of the American Civil Liberties Union. Old Rustin had taught me a thing or two about the scope and might of the ACLU. "The corrupt tremble when they hear those four letters in that particular order," Rustin had assured me. And here I was seeing it in action. Clive wasn't admonishing me anymore.

"Jesus fuck me with a wrench Christ," he groaned. "Is this courtesy call just to let Fred know you're gonna slap him with the RS49s on the cover of the goddamn *Times*?"

RS49s, RS49s, RS49s, RS49s—I needed to find out what those were as soon as I got out of this office. And what he said about *The New York Times* guided me. Clearly, he (and Fred) feared bad publicity in a respectable newspaper.

"This doesn't have to be on the front page. I'd—we'd—prefer to handle it quietly. And next time, Mr. Trump had better meet with me."

"Alright, alright, young man. I'll pass on the word. But you uphold your end and keep this out of the goddamn papers."

———

Outside of Clive's office building, I realized that I'd clenched my fists so tightly during our tête-à-tête that my fingernails had made impressions on my palms. I raced to the nearest library, went straight to the research section, and asked a librarian where I could find information on an RS49.

The librarian was family. He grinned and said, "You want to start a rent strike. Good for you. Follow me, and I'll make sure you have everything you need."

A rent strike. Alright, so that's what I was up to. Good to know.

The shift in tactics didn't bother me because my objective remained the same. Whether I wasn't paying the rent because I'd personally been granted mercy from the landlord or I wasn't paying the rent as part of a collective action, the bottom line remained I wasn't paying the rent. Besides, the rent strike approach seemed more viable than convincing Fred Trump to take pity on me. I figured he would be relieved to bestow a six-month rent holiday on me and the other tenants in exchange for us not going to the press with the details of our ACLU-backed rent strike. The snag in my plan, of course, was that I needed to organize a rent strike that was backed by the ACLU.

"I straighten up this section once a month, but when citizens help themselves to it, alphabetizing nose-dives out the window," said the librarian as he and I huddled over a large file cabinet filled with mimeographs of New York City government forms.

He kept sneaking glances at me as he thumbed his way through the thicket of file folders. He was in his mid- to late thirties and by no means conventionally handsome: pockmarks along his left cheek and jawline; a prominent nose that was angled to the right, possibly from a break that didn't heal correctly; and eyes that were set a smidge too far apart.

All the same, I could imagine him outside of this staid branch and his buttoned-up librarian's uniform. Strip him of that tweed sports coat, the collared shirt and argyle tie. Put him in a tank top and short shorts and discover that his arms and legs are quite muscular. I could see him dancing with abandon under flashing lights at a big club like the Saint. Free of the library's hush, I bet he scored guys with ease.

Teasing out the scope of that duality between the professional/public life and the untamed/private life—a double consciousness that I first experienced as a Black boy growing up in Indiana—was something of a game I had recently started playing in my head. I would see someone I suspected of being queer and wonder how deep undercover they were. Did they hide it from everyone in the office, or were there a few coworkers in on the secret and equally dedicated to keeping the boss in the dark? When they went out to party, did they style their hair, apply makeup to their face, and wear clothes so foreign to their nine-to-five appearance that they could pass a colleague without being recognized? The bifurcation of one's identity, I would learn, is damaging and can even be lethal. At eighteen, I found it titillating—like I had a special ability to see through Clark Kent and recognize him as Superman.

The librarian pulled out dozens of blank RS49 forms. "You need at least seventy-five percent of your building's occupants to sign their names to this and follow through," he explained. "I can't tell you how many rent strikes I've seen fall apart because everyone acts all brave when signing the form, but then they turn chickenshit and send their rent in anyway."

"Thank you," I said as I took the RS49s from him. "How many of these have you seen work?"

He looked up at the ceiling and whisper-counted. "Fourteen," he said. "Fourteen successful settlements and nearly a hundred losses. Solidarity is the key."

"Why do you know so much about rent strikes?"

He put his hands on the back of his waist and smirked at me. "Where you from, cutie-pie?"

"Indianapolis."

"And you're, what, twenty? In college at NYU?"

"Eighteen, out of school."

"Ahh," he cooed. "You missed all the fun we had here in the 1970s. Inflation, heat waves, crime waves, serial killers, and the city went broke. And when the city went broke, paying the rent was more than a lot of us could manage." The librarian sighed. "We thought *those* were the worst of times."

———

I got to Mt. Morris before sunset, and Louise greeted me with a broad smile. "What a delightful surprise," she said as if I were a beloved nephew dropping by unannounced to visit her. Louise worked the check-in booth during the day shift, Tuesdays through Saturdays, before handing over her duties to Marcel, who ruled the night. Like all the other regulars, I adored Louise.

When I met her, Louise was pushing sixty, her voice warbled in a singsongy tone, and her gray hair was cut pageboy-style. When she wasn't busy processing customers, she sat perched on a stool reading romance novels. Forever cheerful, Louise seemed completely at ease in her soul with being a white woman working at a gay bathhouse that catered mostly to Black men. She greeted us as if she were a bank teller and we were millionaires.

"Room 27 as always," she said, offering me the lockbox and waiving the entrance fee.

"Yes, thanks," I said.

"Nothing to it, darling. It's slow today."

"Is Rustin around?"

"Yes," Louise whispered, "and he brought a guest."

"Who?"

"Never seen him before, but he's a dreamboat. Asian, looks young, almost too young. I carded him, and turns out he's twenty-eight. I apologized, but I think he took it as a compliment."

The very idea of Rustin bringing a date to the bathhouse blew my mind. "Did he and Rustin look like they were going to get it on?"

Louise beamed at me innocently. "I'm told that's what men come here to do." She buzzed me in, then gave me my room key and towel.

"What room is Rustin in?" I asked.

"Room 25," she said.

When I reached the room, the door was closed, and I didn't dare knock. Let it be known there was decorum at Mt. Morris. Instead, I put my ear to the door. What I heard were not the carnal moans, oohs, and aahs that porn has programmed the public to expect from sex. The sounds coming from inside room 25 were strained and halting. Skin slapping against skin, yes. But uncomfortable grunts and quick apologies, too.

Patiently, I waited against the wall across from Rustin's door. Even though traffic was light in the hallways, temptation appeared: a man only a few years older than I was made a point of cruising past me a few times. He was exquisite. His head was shaved bald, his cheekbones were high and chiseled, and the muscles in his thick legs were defined and flexed with every step he took. I later learned he was a ballet dancer in the Dance Theatre of Harlem. He beckoned me to follow him, and I would have under normal circumstances. I just couldn't risk missing Rustin because I was off flip fucking.

As I waited, I listened to the Big Band music that Louise liked to pipe through the sound system during her shifts. She tuned in to a local radio station, so we got the songs, the commercials, and the weather reports. Some patrons complained, but it was her call. I simply marveled at how almost everyone holds tight to the music they loved when they were young. I wondered if I'd still be listening to Patti LaBelle belt out "If Only You Knew" when I got old. (Turns out the answer is yes.)

After half an hour, Rustin's door opened, and a Taiwanese man exited. He was fully dressed and nodded at me as he left. I was impressed, quite frankly. Old Rustin had bedded a hot number.

With the door ajar, I felt free to poke my head inside Rustin's room. He was naked and sitting on the edge of the rubber mattress. He looked up at me, and that craggy face of his was beatific.

"He must have really laid it on you," I said.

Rustin chuckled and covered his lap with the thin bedsheet. "And how," he said.

I couldn't resist prying. "Where did you pick him up?"

"Over in the back of Holloway Books."

"By the porn mags?"

"So you've been there," Rustin teased.

"I'm just trying to picture you thumbing through *Honcho*."[22]

"Truth be told, I'm rather partial to *Drummer*."[23]

I leaned dramatically against the doorframe and pretended to be a Southern belle. "If you tell me you're a leather daddy, I'm going to faint dead away."

"No, I don't dress the part, but I like seeing other men that way."

"But your new friend didn't fit that mold."

"So you got a good look at him?"

"Yeah."

"Then I shouldn't have to explain why I was willing. He started in on me. I thought I had to be imagining it. What's someone like him gonna want with me? But he asked if we could go back to my place, which is impossible at this hour. Walter is there."[24]

"He wouldn't want to join in?"

"That's not the nature of our relationship." He punctuated his words with a tight smile that told me to change subjects.

I didn't have the guts to dive directly into my confession. "My mama liked to warn me, 'Don't start nothing, won't be nothing.'"

"That saying is much older than your mama," said Rustin. Then he noticed the worry in my eyes. "Trey, what's wrong?"

"I started something."

"Is it criminal?"

---

22. *Honcho* (1978–2009) was a pornographic magazine for gay men who had a sexual interest in male models striking traditionally masculine poses in traditionally masculine roles.

23. *Drummer* (1975–1999, and relaunched 2019) is a pornographic magazine for gay men who have a sexual interest in leather and rubber gear, bondage, S and M, and other related kinks.

24. Walter Naegle was Rustin's partner from 1977 until Rustin's death in 1987. Because gay marriage was outlawed during Rustin's lifetime, he legally adopted Naegle in 1982 to create a legal bond between them that would afford Naegle rights ranging from hospital visitation to inheritance. The practice of one person in a gay couple adopting his or her partner was a "legal work-around" in the days before marriage equality.

"I'm not sure. I lied. Could be fraud, I guess."

Rustin scooted over to the far end of the mattress. "Close the door, sit down, and tell me everything."

I did just that. We sat side by side on the rubber mattress. There was no confessional screen between us, but our roles were set. I was the sinner; he was the priest. There wasn't a detail I omitted, from why Gregory and I stopped paying rent to how I insinuated that I was leading a rent strike with the ACLU's support. I floated the idea that Rustin might graciously open up his Rolodex of liberal icons and pull strings to get the ACLU to do what I'd claimed they were already doing.

Rustin looked down at the ground in deep concentration throughout my monologue. When I was done, he rubbed his face with his hands and said, "You've fucked this up seven ways 'til Sunday."

I'd never heard him curse before, and his assessment hit me like a gut punch. "Please, Rustin, there must be somebody you can call. I get it's a huge favor to ask—"

"It doesn't work that way."

"But you've—"

"I'm not who I used to be," he said. "I'm out of step with the times. Hell, I always have been."

I slumped back on the mattress. Here I was, in New York for more than a year, and I had failed to secure the most basic of adult milestones—a paying job and a decent place to live. I felt like a loser.

"Don't lose heart," Rustin said. "Success can take root and bloom out of manure. Or, at least, that's what Martin told me once."

It took me a moment to register that the *Martin* he was referring to was Dr. Martin Luther King Jr., but when it did, my sense of awe overrode my self-pity.

"When did he say that to you?" I asked.

"Late one night when we hit yet another snag trying to pull together the March on Washington."

I screamed like Little Richard and laughed.[25] "How am I supposed to live up to that? I mean truly, Rustin. You and all the other civil rights giants must find everyone younger just puny and irritating."

"Not at all," he insisted. "Your challenges are different, but no less legitimate."

"You planned the March on Washington, and I'm fronting a nonexistent rent strike. We're not on the same level."

Rustin waved his hand as if shooing away my argument. "You're eighteen. I was fifty-six when I helped organize the march. See why it doesn't line up?"

I nodded, although still convinced that I was a laughable lightweight compared to Rustin.

He must have been able to read my thoughts. "You underestimate yourself," he said. "You've backed yourself into a corner—no two ways about it. But see this as an opportunity. You presented yourself as a brave community organizer willing to confront a powerful man for a noble cause."

I shrugged. "But it's a lie."

"Not if you live up to it," he said. "Not if you make it true."

Rustin spent the next two hours giving me a crash course in how to build support for a rent strike among my fellow tenants. He thought through scenarios on how to ensnare the ACLU into the campaign. He proposed remedies that Fred Trump might accept if presented in the right light with the appropriate amount of pressure. However, the most valuable thing he gave me was his personal assurance—built on a lifetime as a political radical—that all great activists start off as

---

25. Billed as "the Innovator, the Originator, and the Architect of Rock and Roll," Little Richard (1932–2020) was a flamboyant performer and a practicing bisexual when he began touring in the late 1940s. Throughout his life, his commitment to his sexuality and to rock and roll music wavered. In the 1960s, Little Richard quit playing rock and roll for five years in favor of performing gospel music. In the 1980s, he embraced Christianity and renounced homosexuality and bisexuality, referring to them as "unnatural affections" that needed to be resisted.

young people who don't really know what the hell they're doing. Our mouths give voice to goals, dreams, and even lies. Ultimately, we will be judged on our follow-through, on our ability to turn our stirring words into reality. My cause was born of a lie, but a lie can be the spark that leads to virtue.

ROMANTIC NOTIONS ARE DELUSIONS

He had a girlfriend. Her name was Brianna Sothers, and she disliked me on sight. I figured she was nothing more than a basic Black-church homophobe, but in short time, I gave her valid reasons to hate me. In the aftermath, I realized that she had seen it all coming. From the moment I appeared asking her and her man to sign the rent strike petition, she knew that I was wanton and that he was susceptible. Brianna knew, and she couldn't stop it.

The guy in question was Harrison Coleman, and I would classify our first encounter as purely asexual. I was on the fourth floor of our apartment building, sweet-talking residents into signing the RS49 forms for the rent strike. The pitch that I developed with Rustin had two different appeals: 1) For those who were already behind on the rent, joining the strike could help legitimize their delinquency. Sure, Fred Trump might prevail and evict them, but the tenants could use the rent strike as an excuse when they sought a new apartment. Their story would be that they hadn't withheld rent because they were poor. They did it because they were trying to bring a slumlord to heel. 2) For the tenants who could afford to pay the rent, I whipped them into a lather over the deplorable and dangerous conditions of the building. Then I assured them that the rent strike was a safe gamble for them, so long as they set aside their rent money in a savings account. If we were successful, the building would get fixed.

If we lost, they could just use the saved money to pay the back rent, stopping eviction proceedings against them.

Turned out, I had some talent for the task at hand. Apparently, I'd learned more than I'd thought from my mother and father, who earned their salaries by finding the right arguments and angles to persuade voters and politicians into supporting their candidates and causes. I remembered how Fiona liked to tee up the end of stump speeches that she wrote by posing a question that was sure to spark righteous indignation in the listeners. So near the conclusion of my hallway pitches, I'd ask, "Are we going to keep letting Trump screw us?" My mother would then have her candidate reiterate what he wanted from the listeners. "Then you've gotta join our rent strike," I'd say, and that's where my father's influence came into play. Once I went silent, I kept my mouth shut. The person might waver and talk through their concerns aloud, but I didn't interfere. I let them talk their way to *yes,* just as I had seen my father do during cocktail parties at our house.

I wasn't sure if my parents would have approved of how I was using what they'd taught me, but no one could argue with my effectiveness. People were signing once I was able to speak with them. The tough part was getting folks to come to their doors or to keep it cracked open long enough for me to explain what I was proposing. Some tenants seemed never to be in their apartments.

Harrison and Brianna fell into that latter category. I'd stopped by their place, apartment 409, several times at different hours. It was always dead quiet inside, and I'd already learned the difference between a truly empty unit and the soft rustle of someone pretending to be gone when there was a knock at the door.

It was a Monday evening when I spotted Harrison and Brianna in the hallway waiting for the elevator. She wore a chunky yellow knit sweater that went past her knees and dark gray leggings that tucked into brown boots. He sported a pin-striped dress shirt and khakis that could have used more ironing. Both were bundled in scarves, hats, and winter coats. In their midtwenties and with a casual elegance, Harrison and Brianna could have been one of those trendy Black couples that were featured in magazine ads for Newport cigarettes.

"Hey, got a sec?" I shouted.

She clutched her purse tightly against her body, and he pressed the elevator button a few more times as I approached. I'd grown so use to such defensive reactions that they didn't offend me or slow me down.

I ran up to them. "I live in the building, and a lot of us tenants are organizing a rent strike."

"We have dinner reservations," Brianna said as if that should bring an end to the matter.

"It won't take but a minute for me to explain and a second for you to fill out the form."

"What are you after?" she asked. "Five dollars? Ten?"

"No, ma'am, this isn't a solicitation. We're trying to get the landlord to repair the building."

Brianna looked at me and curled her upper lip in disgust. The elevator dinged, and its doors slowly parted.

"We'll think about it," she said as she got onto the elevator with Harrison.

I hurried in behind them. "There is some urgency involved. We want to start the strike on November 1." The elevator hiccuped, jerking up then down before beginning a steady descent. "See, this is one of the things we want fixed," I added.

"Now is not a good time for us to get into this."

Harrison furrowed his brow and took a shallow breath. I would discover that this was what he did as he gathered the courage to say something he feared would be upsetting. "Bri, you are always saying that this place needs a renovation."

She looked at him as if he'd committed treason. "Well, I'm just not comfortable being rushed into a rent strike. Is that even legal?"

"It's perfectly legal, ma'am, if it's done by the book."

"Please stop calling me 'ma'am.' I can't be that much older than you."

"Well, if you told me your name, I'd be happy to call you by it."

Harrison stifled a smile. The elevator reached the lobby, and Brianna fled it as if she hadn't heard me.

I spoke to the back of her head. "I'm Trey, by the way. I'm in apartment 704."

Harrison turned toward me and extended his hand. "Trey, I'm Harrison."

I shook his hand. "Nice to meet you."

"Now please forgive us," he said. "We are running late. Some other time, though, brother. Okay?"

"Sure," I said.

Harrison left me in the elevator, and I watched him and Brianna hurry out to the street to hail a cab before the elevator's metal doors sealed shut. Her perfume and his cologne mixed in the air as I rode up to my floor. I tried to think of how I could have played it differently and been more persuasive. Then I looked up at the mirrored ceiling and realized why I was never going to get anywhere with those two bougie strivers. I was wearing tight red jeans and a white T-shirt bearing the slogan: SODOM TODAY, GOMORRAH THE WORLD.[26]

———

The campaign to get 75 percent of the building's tenants to join the rent strike was going very well. Gregory was helping me follow up with people, and I have to credit him with recruiting several of the more cynical and rougher-edged residents into the fold. Gregory used a tactic I didn't dare try: he questioned the Black pride of Black tenants.

———

26. The SODOM TODAY . . . T-shirt was most notably worn by British gay rights activist and historian Alan Bray (1948–2001) at a gay pride event in 1979. Bray is said to have coined the slogan and designed the T-shirt. Trey's T-shirt would have been a knockoff of the original.

"The landlord ain't gonna give you shit for tap-dancin' like a Tom," he told a scrappy Black guy with neck tattoos.

The scrappy brother puffed up. "I ain't no Tom."

"Good. Then get on our side and help us stick it to this fuckin' honky."[27]

The scrappy Black guy signed to prove he was willing to fight the Man.

Gregory loved telling that story, and it was beautiful to see him strutting around proud of himself. Organizing the rent strike grounded him. Gregory stopped disappearing for days at a time. He snorted less coke. His mood swings were less pronounced. We hung out even more, smoking weed, listening to music, swapping sex stories, and talking about whatever crossed our restless minds late into the night.

Not that Gregory totally refrained from being an erratic pain in the ass who enjoyed flustering me in front of other people. So I was on guard when Harrison showed up at our studio apartment on Tuesday night, a surprise visit that I should have kept brief.

Bare-chested and in checkered Gucci pants, Gregory answered the door and barked, "What you want?"

"I'm looking for Trey," said Harrison.

I was lying on my cot, eating peanut butter out of a jar with a steak knife and reading that month's *Rolling Stone*. Tina Turner was on the cover, and the interview with her was juicy. But when I heard Harrison's voice, I abandoned Tina and the jar and hurried to the door to stop Gregory from toying with Harrison. Unfortunately, I wasn't quick enough.

"Yeah, he's here. C'mon in," said Gregory. "You come to talk about the rent strike, right?"

Harrison entered. "Yes, I'm interested in learning more about it."

Our apartment was small, so after two steps inside, Harrison spotted me scrambling to my feet. I stood before him in tuxedo pants

---

27. *Honky* is an old derogatory term meant to demean white people.

that were a gift from my sister, Jackie, and a black mesh shirt that I bought at the Goodwill store in Chelsea.

"Thanks for dropping in," I said, and only when I went to shake his hand did I realize I was holding the steak knife stained with peanut butter.

Harrison recoiled. "Whoa, there's no need for violence."

His delivery was dry, and it took half a second for it to register that he was joking. I decided to play along.

"Oh, don't worry about this," I said. "If I wanted to cut you, you'd never see the knife. You'd just feel it."

Harrison rocked back on his heels, and I could see that he wasn't altogether sure if I was joking. Gregory savored the awkwardness between me and Harrison, and he stoked it.

"Have a seat," said Gregory. "You must be the yuppie. Your girl-friend or wife blew Trey off, right?"

"I didn't say she blew me off."

"That's true, that's true," Gregory conceded before stage-whispering to Harrison, who sat in a wobbly chair next to our tiny kitchen table, "What he said was, if he'd been on fire, the bitch wouldn't have pissed on him to put it out."

I pointed the steak knife at my roommate. "You can shut up any-time now. And go put a shirt on."

Gregory did neither.

To my surprise, Harrison laughed, and the broad smile that broke out across his face transformed him from blasé to startlingly hand-some. His eyes, which seemed slow to move and spiritless when he was in repose, flashed with mischievous charm. His nose and mouth went from cold and statuesque to delicate and inviting. You could see the unbridled boy inside the uptight man when he laughed.

That was the first hint of attraction I felt toward Harrison, but it lasted only a moment. To my eyes, he lacked edge, and I thrived off men who could be wild cards. What would be the fun in fooling around with a guy who woke up every morning three minutes before the alarm clock rang, who remembered to floss after every meal, who never failed to walk the dog and pay the electric bill, who drank enough water and ate enough fiber to stay regular, who said *please* and *thank you,* who behaved like the voice in his head was calm and rational?

"Brianna mistrusts strangers," Harrison said. "She's from Jersey. If you get to know her, she's very nice."

"So she your wife?" asked Gregory.

Harrison held up his ringless left hand. "No, but we've been together for six years."

"Six years? Damn, what you waitin' on? You still ain't sure if you like her?"

I said, "Ignore him. He lives to be outrageous."

Harrison's grin didn't fade. "It's okay. Neighbors are naturally curious about each other. You can ask me anything."

I attempted to put the conversation on conventional terms. "How long have you and Brianna lived in the building?"

"Two years. We knew the place wasn't the best when we moved in, but we're saving for a house."

Gregory spoke with a genuine sense of awe. "You pay rent and have money left over to burn?"

Harrison started to answer, but I cut him off.

"What do you and Brianna do for a living?"

"I'm in grad school for architecture, and I bartend nights part-time at Schaffer's. Brianna works the swing shift as an operator for the phone company."

"No shit!" yelled Gregory. "If I dial zero, I could get her!"

"Totally. It's happened to friends of ours."

"Schaffer's is pricey," I said.

"That makes the tips bigger. I only have to work there a few nights a week to make it worth my while." Harrison raised an eyebrow. "Have you dined at Schaffer's?"

"No," I said, "but my father has been coming to the city on business my whole life, and he raves about the lobster at Schaffer's."

"I been there a few times," Gregory boasted. "This old Broadway producer—he put a lot of money into that one called, uh, *The Tap Dance Kid*—he used to take me to Schaffer's. I'd have the crab cakes. Then we'd go check into a suite at the Warwick Hotel, on one of them high floors way up where you can see all the big lights of the shows, and I'd fuck him against the window."

Harrison cleared his throat and asked simply, "At the Warwick?"

"Oh yeah, it's one of my favorite spots. The staff don't care, the daddy pays, and if I can send him home after we nut, I get the room to myself, and checkout ain't 'til noon."

Harrison was speechless.

"I warned you he gets like this."

Gregory shrugged. "What? We all adults here. We can't talk about sex?"

"You didn't have to go there," I argued. "He came to talk about the damn rent strike."

"I'm not upset or offended or anything," said Harrison. He furrowed his brow and took a shallow breath. "I've seen the two of you around, and . . . I've been curious as to how you boys . . . operate. You're both so young and . . . very homosexual."

"Trey and me ain't fuckin'," said Gregory. "Let me assure you."

I groaned my disapproval, but Harrison laughed again and admitted, "I had wondered about that."

Since we were being real, I volunteered, "Gregory likes his men white and geriatric."

"What do you like?" Harrison asked me.

Before I could answer, Gregory replied, "He used to like his trade rough, but now he'll screw with any dick that makes for a good story."

"A good story?" I echoed.

"Oh yeah, Miss Thang here likes there to be something to gab about later." Gregory imitated my voice, exaggerating how formal my enunciation and how high my pitch can get when excited. "Nothing satisfies him more than to tell me, 'You should have seen the piercing in this gentleman's scrotum. A *hafada*, it's called.'"

Harrison looked at me to see how I took the teasing, and when I laughed, he allowed himself to do so, too.

With a rapt audience at his feet, Gregory kept at it: "'I was in an alleyway behind the UN building blowing a Cuban in green fatigues. I can't be certain, but I'm fairly sure I deep throated *Fidel Castro*.'"

As my roommate kept riffing, I found myself checking out Harrison. His dress shirt and khaki pants were a couple of sizes too large to hug and showcase his body. It was only when he turned to face Gregory or doubled over in laughter that the fabric caught against his skin that I got a glimpse at the tightness of the muscles in his back and came to realize that he had a tapered waist. My interest in him baffled me even as I ogled him. Harrison stayed for another hour. Only the last fifteen minutes were spent discussing the rent strike. He filled out and signed an RS49 and bid us good night.

Gregory was kind enough to wait until he heard Harrison walk down the hall and the elevator ding before giving me the business. "He got you sprung!"

"He's cute, but he's not for me."

"Why? Because there's no chance he's gonna treat you like a trick in the bathhouse?"

"No one pays me for sex," I said. "You're the rent boy."

Gregory cocked his head back and waved his finger in the air less than an inch from my face. "No, no, no, lil man. I'm no rent boy. Rent boys get tossed five-dollar bills and dime bags. I'm gettin' Ralph Lauren and other shit worth bank. And if they leave me cash, it's a fresh stack of hundreds."

I scoffed. "So you're more of a call girl?"

"I'm getting the better end of the deal. I fuck a man, and he buys me a Rolex. You get fucked in Mt. Morris by three muscle-heads on parole, and you leave there with nothin' but cum up your guts."

"Oh, I'm stupid for not selling my ass?"

"Yeah, because you're a whore, same as me. You just get used for free."

I grabbed my winter coat and headed for the door, ending my fight with Gregory by making one final point: "You could have your pick of men, but you choose to top old white guys. I take what I can get."

————

I walked the streets wiping tears from my eyes. Crying while I made my way past fellow pedestrians was not an uncommon way for me to travel. In fact, plenty of people sobbed and wailed on the sidewalks in those days. Emotions ran free and raw.

It wasn't what Gregory had said about me that set me off. It was what I'd said about myself. *I take what I can get.* It sounded desperate and weak as it came out of my mouth, and I wished it were different. There were moments when I imagined what it would be like to have a man approach me in a record store and strike up conversation and invite me to go have coffee with him. Or a less common scenario, but applicable to me: after fucking each other's brains out in a bathhouse, the man at my side asks for my phone number and suggests we grab dinner and catch a movie sometime. Nothing of the kind ever happened to me. And while I did suspect that a square, decent man would bore me, it also ate at me that none ever approached me.

The men with a sexual interest in me saw what, exactly? A young male that they could dominate. A baby-faced preppy they could defile. A young Black stud who could dick them down. A sexual deviant who was seducing them into breaking their moral codes. I was forbidden fruit. I was a living sex doll. I was a dirty secret. Alas, I wasn't first-date material.

My self-pity and defeatist thinking did eventually lead me to a useful realization as I waited on the corner for a red light to change. I saw the Empire State Building beaming in the skyline, and my mind replayed my favorite parts of *An Affair to Remember*. The old film was an obsession of my great-aunt Vera's, who had served as our family's summer-break babysitter. She made me, my brother, and my sister play quietly at her feet whenever *An Affair to Remember* aired as a midday movie on Channel 8. It was of no interest to my siblings, but even as a seven-year-old, the fraught romance, as well as the polished appeal of Cary Grant, hooked me. What I found remarkable was the fortitude driving Cary Grant's love. He had every reason to write off Deborah Kerr, but his affection made him persistent. That's what I craved—a guy willing to pursue me despite my hang-ups, my past, my mistakes, and my own misgivings about him.

Of course, when my Hollywood desires became clear to me, I saw how ridiculous they were. What flesh-and-blood man was ever going to immediately recognize the inner beauty and value in me, then make the effort to machete his way through the thorny thickets of insecurities and defense mechanisms surrounding my heart? And if such a man somehow existed, how long was I supposed to wait until our paths crossed? The odds against it coming to fruition had to be astronomical, which made sense because the very notion I had concocted was a fairy tale.

Turns out Prince Charming and white knights and unwavering love don't exclusively plague the expectations of basic hetties. Here I was, nothing if not sexually liberated. I didn't pine for marriage, children, or a house in suburbia. In fact, I'd become devoted to the steadfast fraternity and open polygamy of homosexuality: *every gay man can be a brother to me; every gay man can be a lover to me.* Yet I harbored these unspoken and awfully wholesome expectations about the love stories that were destined to animate my life. I wanted a boyfriend. Even Gregory, who was tiring of sex work and sugar daddies, wanted a boyfriend. Our boyfriend fantasies were part of a larger collection of common, saccharine notions. Once I detected the useless gnawing desires embedded in me, I was hell-bent on cutting myself open and removing them immediately.

I quit my crying and sprinted back to the apartment building. I must have looked wild—sweaty, out of breath, and with red-rimmed eyes—when Harrison opened his apartment door. The only relationship rule I could trust was: *if you have strong feelings, let them be known.*

"I want to be your first," I said.

Harrison leaned against one side of the doorframe and extended his arm to grip the other side. "My first what?"

"Guy you fuck, guy you kiss. How far have you gotten?"

He furrowed his brow and took a shallow breath. "I messed with a few guys back in high school and college. Not sex, really. Nothing serious."

"But you want to do more," I suggested. "You're in luck. So do I."

"Honestly, I'm not sure what I want." He sighed. "You should go."

I ducked under his arm and entered his apartment. "Try me once. If you don't like it, I'll leave, and no one will ever know I was here."

Harrison's face gave nothing away. We squared off silently for several seconds. Then he closed the door.

"Tonight, we're only gonna jerk each other off," he insisted.

I stripped out of my clothes fast. Harrison was still unbuttoning his dress shirt by the time I reached him and unbuckled his belt and lowered the zipper on his pants. He wore baggy Hanes briefs, and I barely managed to keep from making a wisecrack about his uninspired, lackluster choice of underwear. He wasn't the type I was used to, and that was the point. I needed to keep my inner smart-ass in check if this was going to happen.

Once we were both naked, he grinned at me and grabbed my cock.

"Bigger than you expected?" I asked.

"Thicker," he said.

"I'm surprised you're uncut."

"My dad was against circumcision," he explained.

We went to work stroking each other. He closed his eyes, and I licked his hairy nipples. He used his free hand to pull my head tighter to his chest. His cock stiffened to rock hard and was leaking precum, and I knew he was going to shoot quick at this pace. So I let go and stepped back.

Harrison panted, "What? Why'd you stop?"

"I need more than a jerk-off buddy."

"Hey, I told you I'm not comfortable doing more. I don't want to catch nothing, no offense."

"Bullshit," I said. "Only thing you're scared of is if you put a dick in your mouth, you'll like it too much and have to stop pretending with your girlfriend."

"This was a mistake."

I stood my ground. "I don't want to be your girlfriend, and I don't care if you stay with her or not, or if you call yourself straight or whatever. But I won't pretend I'm at a middle-school sleepover and jerking off is going to be hot enough for me."

"My goodness, middle school?"

"Imagine what I've learned since then." I picked my boxers up off the floor. "It's up to you. We do this for real, or you can spend your time wondering how good you could feel if you weren't so afraid."

I had pulled my boxers up to my thighs when Harrison fell to his knees in front of me and began giving me head. His effort was fervent, although far from commendable. He had all the hallmarks of a novice: he didn't go as deep as he should, his teeth scraped my skin, and his tongue didn't know what to do. I came in his mouth anyway because he'd crossed the line for me. He'd met me on my own terms. This was adult romance.

DEVILS HAVE A WEAKNESS

My meeting with Michael Ossani, a young, tight-ass ACLU lawyer, was a disaster. He brushed aside the stack of RS49 forms I brought as my credentials, and he repeated several of the points Rustin had leveled at me back in Mt. Morris. I tried to present my behavior as an innocent, panicked response, but Michael would have none of it.

His assessment was brutal: "You and your roommate quit paying rent, and you wanted to see if a friend of a friend could pull strings so you could weasel out of paying what you owed. Failing that, you lied about your intentions, who you represented, and who your allies are. You are not the leader of a cause, Mr. Singleton. You are running a shakedown. The law is not on your side, and neither is the ACLU."

Michael showed me the door, but not before I swiped one of his business cards. My backup plan had begun to form shortly after the ACLU lawyer had started to denounce me. It struck me that my hustling, my lying, and my frantic efforts to cover my ass had produced some legitimate results. I had, in fact, organized eighty-nine percent of the current tenants in my apartment building to unite in a rent strike, and I did have a meeting on the books with Fred Trump for the following day, Tuesday, November 4 (Election Day). My tactics were unconventional and improvisational, but not without promise. While Michael scolded me, I decided to follow my wayward instincts.

Out on the streets, I twirled Michael's business card, holding its two sharp corners between my thumb and index finger. An exhilarating burst of confidence warmed me against the windchill. For once, I didn't feel lost. I knew my next moves.

If anyone had asked me then how I'd come up with my new plan, the eighteen-year-old me would have credited his quick thinking. Yet more than half a century removed from the days of my youth, I can see the influence of my father, Ward. To say that Ward and I had a strained relationship suggests that there was more between us than there was. Before I was five years old, he reached the conclusion that I wasn't the type of son he could father. I was too tenderheaded when the clippers touched my neck in the barbershop; at family cookouts, I spent too much time sitting on my aunts' laps; in church, I was reprimanded for staring at the choir director instead of the reverend; and in the backyard of our family's gray stone mansion, I walked away from the basketball court to go daydream in the garden.

Ward didn't try to mold me or toughen me up. No, he fucking passed over me and instilled lessons in my brother, Martin, who was born eighteen months after me. On weekends, I was taken to museums or swap meets by my aunts or my mother, if her political work allowed her to spend time with us. Ward took Martin to playoff games or daylong rap sessions with Indianapolis's other prominent Black men and their favored sons. Our family divided so quietly and peacefully, in fact, the existence of the fissure was never discussed.

Ward could go days without saying a single word to me. The silent void between us grew even more pronounced when my younger sister, Jackie, came into her own as a child. Overnight, she quit being a shy, doe-eyed kid and bloomed into a sharp-witted, irrepressible mini-diva. She was four or five. My father loved trotting Jackie out during adult dinner parties and eliciting her opinions on headline news. Whereas previously I'd been ignored, now I was altogether invisible.

My father was blind to me, but I continued to study him. Some part of me hung on to the childish notion that I could learn how to make him love me. Futile, I know. The most reliable occasions for me to even be in Ward's presence for an extended period of time came during large family holiday parties and formal dinners designed to further his business dealings. As the lead lobbyist for the pharmaceutical company Eli Lilly, my father played host and dealmaker to countless politicians and drug regulators in our grand dining hall.

One of Ward's most effective tactics was to tell stories on himself. It was his way of assuring powerful white men that he was a team player, willing to sacrifice his pride for the sake of an advantageous alliance. The tale that made the greatest impression on me involved Ward's first meeting inside the Oval Office. It was March of 1969, and President Nixon's administration was less than one hundred days old. Ward was the most junior member of Eli Lilly's lobbying department, and he shouldn't have been invited into such a high-level meeting.

With a whiskey in hand, Ward recalled, "My boss, Dennis Knight, God rest his soul, was honest with me. He said, 'Nixon is still courting Black leaders. We need your skin for the picture.'" Ward threw his head back and guffawed, letting his white guests know it was safe to laugh. "I appreciated knowing the score," my father continued. "So I walk into the White House expecting to sit in the back and take notes. I figure Nixon won't notice me none. We enter the Oval, and President Nixon is standing there, grinning next to the only person in the room more clueless than I am, Commissioner Ley.[28] All of us

28. Herbert L. Ley Jr. (1923–2001) was commissioner and head of the U.S. Food and Drug Administration (FDA) from July 1968 to December 1969. After he was ousted from the FDA, Ley claimed in a *New York Times* article that he faced "constant, tremendous, sometimes unmerciful pressure" from drug company lobbyists to quickly approve their companies' products. Ley added, "The thing that bugs me is that the people think

shake hands. About a dozen of us at the meeting, and I look for a chair against the wall, but the president called me over, 'I want you next to me, Ward.'"

My mother, Fiona, who made her living writing biting lines against conservatives, interjected, "Nixon just loved havin' a Sammy around."[29]

"Oh, he treated me better than Sammy," insisted Ward. "He asked for my opinion on everything discussed. If a decision was reached, he turned to me, 'That sound alright to you, Ward?'" My father's Nixon impersonation was spot-on. "My team went to lunch after the meeting. I'm the only Black face at the table, and Mr. Knight puts his arm around me and sings my praises. You see, Mr. Knight had told Nixon's people that I was in deep with the NAACP *and* the Black Power movement. The bastard had practically made me out to be a minor Black messiah. I took it all in stride, and by dessert, I'd convinced Mr. Knight to give me a promotion and a raise befitting a minor Black messiah."

My parents and their guests laughed uproariously. As a boy at the far end of the dining table, I didn't get what was so funny. I suppose the adults considered the story an amusing show of realpolitik: my father was willing to be used so long as he was compensated on the back end. But I came to see it quite differently: my father was a pawn—likely not for the first and definitely not for the final time—and he was alright with it because he received a payoff that he deemed worth playing his part. The person to emulate was not Ward but his boss.

The key to my new strategy was persuading a man I'd only met

---

the FDA is protecting them—it's not." Ley's detractors dismissed him as a political novice lacking the talent to run a large administration.

29. Sammy Davis Jr. (1925–1990) was an African American entertainer known primarily for his singing, tap-dancing, and comedy routines. Davis hugged President Richard Nixon onstage at a youth rally during the 1972 presidential campaign. Davis received considerable backlash from many in the African American community for endorsing a Republican candidate, especially one as divisive as Nixon.

once to lie about who he was—and to make him feel that he would come out ahead if he did so.

———

I returned to the Melrose Library in the Bronx just before noon. My plan was to see if I could find the gay librarian who'd taught me how to organize a rent strike and talk to him during his lunch break. I searched his section, but there was no sign of him. I described him to a sour-faced, female librarian and asked if she knew where he was.

"He clocked out early for lunch," she said with a wisp of disapproval.

"You wouldn't happen to know where he goes to eat, do you?"

She blushed and whispered, "Brummell Café."

"Where's that?"

"I've never been," she said.

I couldn't resist getting bitchy. "And I'm not inviting you now. Give me directions, and I'll let you get back to dusting books."

She complied and was relieved to be rid of me. Brummell Café was four blocks away, and its narrow storefront was at odds with the street, the Bronx, the whole of New York, and the United States of America. A Union Jack waved high above the café's doorway. The two large front windows were blocked by tall shelves that displayed sterling silver tea sets, busts of Queen Victoria, a framed portrait of Florence Nightingale, clay sugar bowls and plates with the Royal Arms painted on them, and porcelain salt and pepper shakers shaped like a lion (salt) and a lamb (pepper).

I opened the front door, and a bell announced my arrival. Walking into the café was like crossing into a time warp. The style paid homage to the Victorian age with antique armchairs, ornate lamps, circular wooden tables draped in lace, and threadbare rugs. I approached the counter lined with fresh scones, biscuits, and cookies, and I could feel the eyes of the customers and staff upon me. No surprise there,

I figured. This was a café for British ex-patriots and Anglophiles. I didn't appear to belong to either camp.

However, there was more to the furtive glances I was attracting. I looked around for the gay librarian and didn't spot him, but noticed that everyone in the café was male and white. Okay, not *that* unusual. Then I realized that many of the customers were dressed as dandies. So many colorful silk suits, double-breasted vests, puffy pocket squares, and finely polished shoes that I felt suddenly as if I were wearing rags. For the record, I was sporting a blue oxford dress shirt and yellow slacks because I'd wanted to seem professional but not too corporate for my meeting with the ACLU lawyer.

"Are you lost?" asked the squat man behind the counter. His British accent wasn't nearly as posh as I expected, and his mouth twitched as his bravado wavered. Of course, I'd seen this paper-tiger posture in shop owners, clerks, and bartenders before. He was afraid a robbery would soon be in progress, and if he had a gun tucked under the counter, he wasn't sure he had the nerve to use it.

I did my best to put him at ease by raising my hands and promising for all to hear, "I'm not here to rob you. I'm looking for a friend."

The squat man relaxed, then remembered his manners. "Right, very good—not that I was implying that you were going—"

In no mood to hear him excuse his casual racism, I cut him off. "My friend works at the library—white, crooked nose."

"That would be Simon." The squat man nodded toward the back of the café. "You'll find him in the tearoom."

I was confused, and it showed.

"The bogs," he said. "No need to be shy. You'll be more than welcome company."

I walked to the back of the café, where the men's and women's restrooms were located. Little tables lined the wall as I made my way, and several of the men sitting in their finery cruised me, but much more subtly than I was used to at Mt. Morris. The signals would be nothing more than a slight arch in an eyebrow or a quiver in an upper lip. Positively quaint.

As I passed, I'm afraid I chuckled, and probably hurt the feelings of a guy or two. My reaction must have come off as dismissive, but what I found comical was my own slow thinking. I hadn't immediately recognized that this café was a gay cruising spot because bathhouse culture had deadened my antenna to softer frequencies. Apparently, if men weren't walking around with towels over their shoulders and their hard cocks in their hands, it took me a minute or two to pick up on the gay vibe. I was the ridiculous one in the Brummell Café.[30]

The men's room had a swinging door, and when I pushed past it, I discovered the main attraction of the café. The owners had transformed the kitchen space into a men's restroom / powder room / theater space. Delicate screens embroidered with flowery patterns divided the room into sections and gave additional privacy to the toilet stalls and urinals along the walls. There were large vanity mirrors and fainting couches throughout the space. Classical music played over a phonograph. Without question, it was the best-smelling men's restroom I have ever taken a breath inside of. The air smelled of lavender.

I had never dreamed of being a British dandy in the age of Oscar Wilde, but I stood in awe of these gentlemen's commitment to their fantasy. They'd elevated and brought historical context to the scene of British tearooms, which from the scant amount of erotic fiction that I'd read in gay porn magazines were depicted as working-class, alarming, rough, and dingy. Almost as a rebuke to those notions, Brummell Café was about more than circle jerks and blow jobs through glory holes, although that was happening, too.

This was cruising by way of performance art. A few men sat about reading old periodicals like *The Idler* or *The Lady*. Another man combed his long, wavy hair methodically with an ivory-handled hair-

---

30. Brummell Café was named after Beau Brummell (1778–1840), a British socialite credited with being a trendsetter in men's fashion and the first famous dandy. Because Brummell never married or sired children, his dandy style gave rise to the perception that he was a homosexual.

brush. Four men played bridge, and only one of them fondled himself openly while he held his cards.

I went to the row of toilet stalls to look around for Simon. Half of the doors were cracked open, and I was flattered to be invited into a few of them, but I stayed on mission. As I reached the last stalls, a middle-aged dandy cloaked in a purple cape rushed out of one. He kept his head down as he exited. I peeked into the stall he'd vacated, and there was Simon zipping up his fly. He was in a green tweed suit and a full-length, navy-blue overcoat with a brown fur collar.

"Simon," I asked softly, "do you remember me?"

He snapped his fingers and pointed at me. "Rent strike."

"Exactly. I need your help bad."

"How did you track me down here?"

"The librarian who looks like she's sucking on a lemon."

"Natalie," he spat. "That nosy bitch. I knew she followed me last month."

Whatever drama was brewing between them could wait. "Is there somewhere we can talk?" I asked.

Simon bought half a dozen small cookies; three ginger snaps for me and three snickerdoodles for himself. He drank tea. I had a hot chocolate. We hunched over a table located beneath a photo of Prince Albert, a joke not lost on me. I asked Simon how many Prince Alberts he guessed were in the café, but he didn't see the humor in it.

"You should read *Albert, Prince Consort: A Biography*," he suggested. "His royal highness turned a kinder eye to our persuasion than the current leader of the free world."

"I thought Victorians were . . . puritanical."

"No, the Puritans despised sensuality wherever it lurked—in brothels, in private homes, in the mind. Victorians believed in privacy and discretion. Men like us could enjoy ourselves as long as we adhered to a sense of decorum."

"That's what this place is about—decorum? That's why you come here?"

"Sure, that's the highfalutin reason."

"What's the real one?" I asked.

"I like to forget that it's 1986."

Before I realize it, I seized the opening to begin my pitch. "It's a shitty time to be alive and a shitty time to die. Everything is stacked against us. Hey, I took your advice and got damn near ninety percent of my building to sign the RS49s."

He perked up. "That's fabulous."

"It's not going to matter. We're going to lose anyway. I met with an ACLU lawyer, and he spelled it out for me."

"What did he say?"

"My landlord is too rich, too plugged-in to take on."

"Who's your landlord?"

"Fred Trump."

Simon pounded the table with his fist, rattling our cups and drawing the attention of everyone around us. He muttered, "All the wrong people are dead."

"Amen." I let him stew in his anger for a minute before I continued, "If I play by the rules, most of the families in my building are going to end up on the streets, and I'll be to blame."

"No, it's Trump's fault."

"I convinced my neighbors to roll the dice with me. I should have met with the lawyer first."

"No, no, listen, I don't care what the lawyer said. You can't give up. There has to be a way to stick it to this miscreant."

"Not unless . . ." I trailed off for effect.

"Unless what?"

"The lawyer suggested this crazy idea. I wanted to run it past you. We'd be scamming Trump into doing the right thing."

Simon smirked, and that's when I knew he'd be my accomplice.

———

My first chance to vote in a general election had arrived, and I squandered it. I didn't vote. Neither did Gregory. I wasn't even registered to vote. Neither was Gregory. No one gave me a hard time about neglecting my civic duty besides Rustin when I let it slip to him weeks after the fact. My mother, for sure, would have been apoplectic about my failure to take advantage of a right that earlier Black generations fought and died to secure for me. I did have a nagging fear that if my parents still had a private eye keeping tabs on me, the fact that I didn't cast a vote was included in the weekly report.

I wish I could give an account of the reasons why I felt voting wasn't worth the time and effort. Truth is, I had no overarching principles on the value of voting. In the day-to-day demands of life, voting just wasn't a subject I gave much thought to. There's surprisingly little that I regret in my life, but I regret not voting in every fucking primary, special, and general election possible. The country could have improved so much sooner if I and those that shared my indifference had cast ballots religiously.

Instead of heading to my polling station, I met Simon at 9:30 a.m. outside of Trump Tower. He was dressed in a gray tweed suit, and I wore a black sweater and brown corduroy pants.

After we traded good-mornings, Simon put on glasses and asked me, "On or off? What's more believable?"

"What makes you feel more comfortable?"

"Off." He put the glasses away. "I'm just scared they'll get one whiff of me and know I've got nothing more than a two-year degree from Central Milwaukee Tech."

"No one in that room is going to have read more about the eviction code than you," I assured him, despite doubting my words as I said them.

Simon stared up at the skyscraper. "If they get wise, can they throw us from the roof?"

"Trust me, they are going to thank us. We are offering them a way out of a big mess. We are their salvation. Let me hear you say that. We are their salvation."

Simon closed his eyes. "We are their salvation?"

"It's not a question."

"We are their salvation." He snickered.

"It's not a fucking joke either."

"We are their salvation."

"Again."

He opened his eyes and stood taller. "We are their salvation."

"Believe it, and they'll believe it."

We entered the tower's gaudy lobby and checked in with security. Two guards escorted us to a private elevator that went to the highest office floor beneath the penthouse. We were left in a large conference room that had a bleak autumn view of the East River. There were drinking glasses on the conference table, but no pitcher of water. We waited for twenty minutes before the doors opened again.

Clive Oswyn entered first. He appeared to have aged a decade since I'd seen him a couple of weeks before. Walking with a cane, he was stooped so far forward that his chest was parallel to the floor. His thin, wind-tossed hair crisscrossed into the shape of an abandoned bird's nest. He had a respiratory infection that forced him to rasp for air. This man needed to be in a hospital bed.

Following on Clive's heels was a jittery, thin man with a boyish face. He repeatedly clicked the button on his retractable pen, and he, too, glanced around the room hoping to spot a water pitcher. When he took his seat, I noticed that he'd misbuttoned the middle of his white dress shirt.

Finally, Fred Trump graced us with his presence. He stood in the doorway, waiting to be announced by one of his cronies. First impressions: he was more vital and alert than I expected an eighty-one-year-old man to be, and he did possess a minor-star magnetism. If I hadn't known his name and profession, I'd have pegged him as the host of a successful daytime game show.

The boyish crony did the honors and proclaimed, "You're fortunate he's able to join us today. Here is *the* Mr. Fred Trump."

Simon and I stood as Fred walked to the head of the table. I was in the seat to his right, so I greeted him and reached out for a hand-shake. Fred bristled and rubbed his bushy mustache with his crooked index finger.

"Just the two of you?" asked Fred. His voice was deep and soothing.

"If we'd brought a pack of lawyers, it would be a hell of a lot harder to keep this quiet," I said.

Fred turned to me. "You're the rabble-rouser who spooked Clive?"

At the mention of his name, Clive coughed himself upright into his chair.

"Indeed. I'm Trey Singleton. This is Michael Ossani of the ACLU."

Simon slid Michael Ossani's business card across the table. "Plea-sure to finally meet you, sir."

Fred didn't touch the card. He leaned forward and inspected it for a long while. My heart was racing. What was this son of a bitch studying the card for? Had he met Michael Ossani? Was he going to call our bluff here and now? I didn't dare look at Simon, and I hoped with all my might that he was keeping his cool.

"David," Fred said to his jittery younger crony, "take this."

David scooped up the card.

Fred took a seat at the head of the table. "Mr. Ossani, how long have you been with the ACLU?"

"Long enough to have seen you weasel your way out of violations in Queens and Long Island."

"David, make a note that Mr. Ossani has a vendetta against me because I bested the ACLU in previous actions."

"Yes, Mr. Trump."

"David is attempting to fill big shoes," Fred explained. "Roy Cohn, bless his soul, used to handle these nuisance cases for me."

Simon scowled at the mention of Roy Cohn's name.

Fred continued, "I wouldn't have had to supervise him. No, I could count on my Roy."

"Fuck Roy Cohn," said Simon.[31]

"David, make a note that Mr. Ossani cursed a dead man, who was one of this city's finest lawyers and one of this country's most devoted patriots."

Simon locked eyes with Fred. "I doubt you'd admire Roy so much if you'd seen him like I did—threatening a young man who refused to have sex with him, no matter how much Roy offered to pay."

I put a hand on Simon's forearm and squeezed. "Can we get to the matter at hand?"

"I'd like that," pleaded David. "Our dispute is over back rent at 22 Mercer."

"We're withholding rent," I said, "as part of a rent strike."

David flipped through a stack of paperwork he'd brought to the meeting. "Yes, I reviewed your RS49 forms, and by my calculations, you don't have enough participation to have standing for a—"

"Forget standing," Fred growled. "The rent strike is bogus. They're only doing it because they're already behind on the rent."

"That's not accurate," I lied. "Many of us withheld rent individually because our complaints about building code violations weren't being addressed."

Fred sneered at me. "What complaints? Do you have a single one of those in writing?"

My mouth went dry. The old man was going to annihilate me and my scheme in less than five minutes flat. I was about to admit that I didn't have one formal complaint about building conditions when Simon hit upon a different line of attack.

Simon zeroed in on David. "Show me your calculations. We have eighty-nine percent of the tenants on board with us."

"Not if you count all the units in the building."

---

31. Roy M. Cohn (1927–1986) was infamous for his unscrupulous tactics as a lawyer, and he was disbarred shortly before his death. A closeted homosexual, Cohn claimed until his final breath that he was dying of liver cancer. In truth, he died of complications from AIDS. For a full portrait of his hypocrisy, read or watch Tony Kushner's play *Angels in America: A Gay Fantasia on National Themes*.

"Drop it," Fred ordered. "Standing isn't the issue."

"But, sir, it is the simplest way to dismiss their action."

"Did you get eighty-nine percent to sign up or not?" Simon asked me.

"I did. I mean, does he get to count the seventeen vacant units?"

Simon's jaw dropped, and he covered his open mouth with his left hand.

"This is immaterial!" Fred yelled as he stood up and walked away from the table, turning his back on us as if he were ending the meeting.

But Simon wasn't done. "Seventeen vacant units. Seventeen . . ." He slapped the table. "We've got you."

David's voice broke as he inquired, "What? How do you figure?"

"Your boss isn't paying to keep the building up to code, he isn't filling vacant units, and he's let a lot of renters in other units fall behind on rent. I see it. I see what you were up to." Simon was giddy off his revelation. "You were waiting until after Christmas to start a mass eviction. I mean, you're an evil bastard, but you're not stupid. You can't evict a couple of hundred poor people during the holidays. But once they were gone, you could tear down or renovate the building."

"Mr. Trump wouldn't need to go through such a hassle. He can renovate or demolish the property without—"

"He didn't want to pay the tenants to relocate," said Simon. "He'd have had to cough up at least three months' rent per unit if he planned to reno the building and jack up the rent for new tenants."

"True," David conceded, "but Mr. Trump is a wealthy man. He could afford to—"

Fred walked over to a window. "Not another word out of you," he said to his lawyer. Then he turned to face us and wagged his finger at Simon. "You'll never prove this garbage in court."

"Maybe, maybe not. But the papers will run with it," I said. "They'll crucify you."

Fred began to tremble from head to toe. He steadied himself against the window. His face flushed beet red, and I thought he was about to drop dead in front of us. Instead, he let out a piercing scream like a wounded animal. I was terrified by the sound and captivated all the same.

"Thirty years back, twenty years back, ten years back," Fred seethed, "I would have sorted the likes of you two with a snap of my fingers. There used to be order. There used to be an understanding of how business must be conducted. The politicians didn't interfere, and the papers wouldn't have wasted ink on anything either of you had to say. Once upon a time, this city knew how to function."

I swear, the old man was on the verge of tears. The rest of us remained silent as he regathered his composure. I expected him to rejoin us at the table, but he headed for the door.

David, who kept his head down like an embarrassed toddler, asked, "Sir, what do I do now?"

"Settle, then resign," were Fred Trump's final words on our action.

The door closed behind him, and I can't say I felt sorry for the old man, but I did see a vulnerability in him that I would have assumed couldn't exist. Robber barons, political overlords, and other powerful devils can reign with impunity for decades, and the terror they inflict on those of us beneath them can feel eternal. Yet there is one stone that will slay them all: time. Devils grow old, and the world around them eventually exceeds their understanding and control. Never forget that. Never let them forget it.

VICTORY CAN BE A THORNY CROWN

Winning is like cocaine. There are those who snort a line, feel the rush, and remain amiable. Plenty of others, however, become assholes the second the fine white powder hits their bloodstream. Winning runs the same litmus test on people: you handle it well, or you don't.

Winning didn't bring out the best in me. Not by a fucking long shot. A pernicious strain of righteous arrogance took hold of me after my victory in Trump Tower. I believed my fellow tenants should shower me with eternal gratitude and that the world should give me a reward. I was prepared to take bows. Instead, I began to lose my hold on people that I should have cherished.

Take Simon, for instance. Before he went underground to catch a train out to the Bronx, he and I hugged and exchanged phone numbers and promised to meet up soon. My affection and admiration for him were enormous. Simon had taken a huge risk impersonating an ACLU lawyer, and his keen mind was instrumental in carrying the day. We were brothers in arms.

Yet before nightfall, I was omitting Simon out of the story as I told it to tenant after tenant. It took too long and was too complicated to explain why he was pretending to be Michael Ossani; it also revealed that I'd lied about the ACLU supporting our rent strike. So, in my version of events, Simon the librarian was a real lawyer. He's the one who realized Fred Trump planned to allow enough units to fall behind on rent to justify a mass eviction, opening the door to a renovation and a massive rent hike that only new, wealthy—and let's face it—white tenants could afford. When I finished that part of the story, people praised Simon's ability to see the hidden motives at play. They praised it so much that I began taking credit for having been the one to put the pieces together. I inserted myself into the starring role without pause, malice, or forethought. A taste of winning turned me into a glutton for glory.

I never saw Simon again. We traded missed calls for a while. He left a message with Gregory inviting me to a poetry reading at the Brummel Café. I don't remember why I didn't go, but I'm sure the reason was flimsy. Three years later, I found myself up the street from the Melrose Library. I went in and asked for him. The librarian at the front desk grimaced. All that he'd tell me was, "Simon no longer works here."

I'm sorry to say that I hadn't thought of Simon in years when I came across his obituary online in 2020. He had made a life for himself in San Francisco, where he became a beloved longtime staff member at City Lights Bookstore.[32] Simon died of complications from COVID-19. He survived one needless plague only to die in another. I wish I'd kept in touch with him.

———

When I returned to my apartment building, I raced past a couple of tenants in the lobby and took the stairs up to my floor. I was determined to dodge questions about the rent strike because I wanted to share the good news with Gregory first.

"We did it!" I cheered as I enter our apartment.

32. City Lights Bookstore and Publishers was founded in 1953 in San Francisco, where it has served as a beacon and champion of progressive literature, politics, and art. In 1956, City Lights published *Howl and Other Poems* by Allen Ginsberg (1926–1997), which sparked a landmark obscenity trial. City Lights and Ginsberg prevailed.

Our stereo was blaring Rick James's "Give It to Me Baby," and in the middle of the floor, Gregory was on his back thrusting his cock, to the beat of the music, into the fat ass of a freckled white man squatting above him. The only thing mildly shocking to me about what I was witnessing was that my roommate was actually wearing a condom. The rest seemed, at first, unremarkable. Walking in on Gregory fucking one of his sugar daddies happened, on average, once every other month. He would never cop to it, but I accused Gregory of deliberately arranging some of his assignations so that I would interrupt them in the act. I suspect he got off on it. The thrill of getting caught and the fright in his surprised partners added a jolt of arousal that Gregory relished.

On similar occasions, Gregory held his sugar daddies in place and urged them to let him keep fucking. "Don't sweat my boy. He ain't gonna tell nobody nothin'. And you got me close, daddy."

Gregory's eloquent plea and the pleasure he delivered to their bodies actually kept most of his partners engaged. I would apologize and exit. Gregory would climax with a roar before I got halfway down the hall.

This time was different. The freckled white man stood up before Gregory could grab him. He hollered, "Make it go away!" and fled naked into our bathroom, locking the door behind him.

Gregory scrambled to his feet, rushed over to me, pressed a hand against my chest, and said, "You didn't see his face." He wasn't asking me; he was telling me.

He was both grave and dead calm. I wanted to agree that I hadn't seen the sugar daddy's face, but such an assertion felt too ludicrous. The freckled, middle-aged man cowering in our bathroom was six feet tall, his hair was strawberry blond, he weighed approximately two hundred pounds, his face was puffy but handsome enough, his cock was uncircumcised, and he and I had made brief eye contact.

"You didn't see his face," Gregory repeated.

"Who is he?"

Gregory smacked me on the side of the head. "Don't ask again."

I shoved him, and we squared off. Gregory balled up his fists. He was more than willing to beat sense into me. I backed down and shouted, "I didn't see his face!"

"Thank you," Gregory mouthed to me.

"Fuck you," I mouthed back.

———

As annoyed as I was to be caught up in Gregory's bullshit, what pissed me off more was that his drama kept me from celebrating my triumph with him. I'd imagined us leaping and dancing around the room before splitting a joint and laughing about how we got one over on the Man. Denied that joy, I searched for a substitute and went knocking on Harrison's apartment door.

Harrison and I had managed to meet up merely four or five times since commencing our affair. His schedule of architecture classes, bartending shifts, and social obligations with his girlfriend, Brianna, made it tricky to find opportunities for us to be alone. We'd cross paths in the laundry room or outside by the trash bins. He probably thought it happenstance, but I spent hours reading books and waiting in those spots with the hope that he'd turn up. When we were together, we'd indulge in small talk for a minute or two. I'd learn adorable tidbits about him: he was allergic to cats; he loved DC Comics and wished he were one of their illustrators; he kept a motorcycle in the building's garage, and Brianna was pressuring him to sell the "death trap."

During these chats, we'd check to make sure no one was around and slip off into the janitor's closet, a utility room, a dark corner behind a dumpster. We'd trade kisses and blow jobs, and I'd urge him to try anal (top or bottom, his call), and he'd say he wanted to, but not now, not here. I considered the challenge of getting this guy to go all the way to be a refreshing change of pace.

Going to Harrison's apartment in the middle of the morning was outside our norm, but I had the perfect excuse: we'd won the rent strike. And if I caught Harrison all by his lonesome, maybe one of us could penetrate the other to mark the glorious day.

Luck appeared to be on my side when Harrison opened the door. His face was unreadable, but I detected the smallest hint of glee in his voice. "What's up?" he asked.

"We beat Trump."

He smiled. "Really? That's great. He's going to fix the building up and everything?"

"First of all, I appreciate the happiness, but you can lose the surprise. I told you we'd win."

"Yeah, but you're like . . ." He stopped himself and laughed nervously. "Congratulations is what I mean."

"I'm like a what?"

"Huh?"

"Finish saying what you were going to say. I'm like a what?"

"Trey, don't make a mountain out of a molehill."

I put my hands on my hips and cocked my head to the side. "Don't punk out now. Tell me about myself. What am I like?"

He took a shallow breath and furrowed his brow. "You're not a lawyer. You're not even in college. You show up with these big ideas. I signed, but I didn't bank on you pulling this off. Which is to your credit. You proved me wrong."

Still not satisfied, I tried to put words in his mouth. "You didn't think I'd succeed because I'm so obviously a faggot no one would take me seriously."

"No," he said. "I didn't think anyone would take you seriously because you're a kid."

"A kid? That must make you a child molester."

"Stop it." For once, his emotions reached the surface of his skin. My insult scared and wounded him. "I just meant that you look young is all. I know you're not a kid."

"I'm sorry," I said. "I can be a bratty bitch some—"

"Who's that you're talking to?" asked Brianna.

The apartment door blocked her from seeing me.

Harrison leaned back and looked toward their bedroom. "It's Trey. Did we wake you?"

"It was time for me to get up anyway," she said.

"Trey, come in. Brianna will want to hear this, too."

I entered, and Brianna looked as pleased to see me as you would be to spot a cockroach in your bathtub. Wearing a robe, a head wrap, and slippers, she padded over to the kitchen to pour herself a cup of coffee.

"Hello, Trey. How's the rent crusade going?"

"Good morning. We came out on top."

Harrison put a hand on my shoulder and squeezed it affectionately. "Isn't that the best, honey? The landlord is going to bring the building up to code."

"Not exactly," I interjected. "The settlement is more about money than repairs."

Brianna didn't even blow on her steaming cup of coffee before taking the first sip. If that coffee was scalding, it didn't bother her a bit. "We're getting money?"

"In a way."

"It's a yes-or-no question," she said.

"We'll all save money, but no one will be cutting us a check."

Harrison stepped forward before Brianna could continue her cross-examination. "Why don't you lay it out for us start to finish?"

"Okay, here's the big picture," I said, gesticulating even more than usual because I knew it irritated Brianna. "Mr. Trump is going to tear this building down and put up a new one that he can rent to rich white people. He's been letting units go empty in this building, and he let a lot of us tenants fall behind on rent because then he could put everyone out on the streets at once."

"But we weren't behind on our rent," Brianna griped.

Harrison said, "Please let him talk."

I was smug as I repeated what Simon had told me only a couple of hours ago. "Even tenants who pay the rent on time can be evicted if the building has less than twenty-five percent occupancy. The building is deemed terminable, and the owner can kick out everyone, renovate the building, and start again, charging way more money."

"Forgive me," said Brianna, cutting her eyes at Harrison and daring him to stop her, "but can you fast-forward to the point. What do we get out of this?"

"All back rent is forgiven, and none of us has to pay rent for the next three months."

Ever practical, Harrison pointed out, "Socking away three months' rent will go a long way toward our down payment for a house."

"Yes, that's nice. What happens after three months? Does he have that long to fix up the building? If he doesn't, does our rent stay free?"

"No, it's not like that," I explained. "In three months, we all have to move out."

"You little shit!" Brianna lifted her coffee cup as if she meant to throw it at me, but then decided that she didn't want to break the mug or waste the coffee on me. "You got us evicted all the same! Trump gets to do what he planned to do from the get-go!"

I yelled right back at her. "But we aren't going to get screwed over! Back rent is forgiven!"

"We didn't owe back rent! We pay our bills!"

"Good for you! Maybe you'll be crowned Bougie of the Year! And just so you know, even us poor unwashed masses *want* to pay our motherfucking bills! We just don't have the money you take for granted!"

She turned to Harrison. "Did he just curse at me in my own home?"

"You cursed me first."

Harrison raised his hands. "You should go, Trey. Please."

The bile in my mouth tasted so rancid I almost spit it in their faces. It wasn't lost on me that I could tear asunder their *Cosby Show* imitation of professional, aspirational Black life. Brianna thought they were above the likes of me, and Harrison figured he could cloak himself in the privilege of the strong, silent, hetty type. How laughable and fragile their personas were. I could decimate them both with four words: *Harrison sucked me off.*

I held my fire. I wasn't ready to start a war in their living room. Besides, I'd come to be hailed as a conquering hero. Between my apartment and this one, my victory lap was off to a dismal start. So I left Brianna and Harrison in their delusion: they were upstanding, normal people, and I was the broke, uncouth sissy boy.

———

The reception I received in a lot of apartment units lifted my spirits. An old woman kissed my cheeks. Several families pulled me into group hugs. One old man insisted I drink a shot of vodka to toast to our good fortune. The forgiveness of back rent wasn't trivial to these people. The burden of debt kept them up at night, and it limited everyday decisions they made for themselves and their loved ones. From what to wear to what to eat, they were humiliated by the shoddy compromises imposed on them by their poverty.

Yet about an equal number of tenants were as displeased as Brianna had been about having to move in three months. I could do nothing more than apologize and listen to them as they explained their plights. Quite a few units had more occupants than were permitted by their leases; these extended families would have to separate or find a place they could get away with packing into without a new landlord or building manager catching wise. A single mother feared she wouldn't find another apartment that was walking distance from her job, and she couldn't afford to be taking the bus to work and back five days a week. A half dozen older folks told me they'd have to abandon most of their belongings and leave New York City once and for all. They'd have no choice but to impose themselves on younger relatives down south or out west. To these people, moving was a new crisis, sure to be doomed.

Fortunately, even the residents who dreaded the move didn't direct their anger at me. They rightly blamed Trump. With me, they commiserated, and while it was far from being greeted like a herald angel, it was warmer treatment than I was used to from many of these tenants. Mind you, Gregory and I had lived in 22 Mercer for a little more than a year, and during our residency, I could count on one hand the number of times my fellow tenants behaved toward me in a way that could be described as *neighborly*. Crime was a real threat, and as Black men, Gregory and I were viewed as walking suspects. Before people got accustomed to seeing me around, I'd had to show my fellow tenants the keys to my apartment and tell them what unit I lived in to keep them from hounding me.

Once they'd accepted that I had a right to be in the building, many of them noticed I was gay, and not just gay but a flaming faggot. They overheard me talk with my theatrical intonations and florid vocabulary. They saw me going out at night in tight pants, mesh T-shirts, booty shorts, or crop tops. My more modest attire—tailored dress shirts and top designer slacks—also failed to conform to the frumpy dress code of straight guys. I confirmed any lingering suspicions whenever I staggered in drunk, belting songs from my favorite glass-closet queen, Luther Vandross.[33] My fellow tenants gave me a wide berth. I remember some of them wouldn't even share an elevator with me.

Suffice it to say, I was suffering from a deprivation of civility. So whether they wanted to celebrate the news or fret about the future, I found it intoxicating to be treated like a person worthy of courtesy. People invited me into their apartments. I sat on their couches or at their dining tables. They handed me glasses of water and offered me snacks. They showed me the books they'd have to sell or weathered photos of celebrations on the rooftop of the building. They made me tell them the story of my meeting with Mr. Trump. They launched

33. Four-time Grammy Award winner Luther Vandross (1951–2005) was a phenomenal R&B singer and songwriter. He never stated publicly that he was homosexual, but in 2017, his close friend, legendary soul singer Patti LaBelle, confirmed in an interview that Vandross was gay. She claimed that he didn't come out of the closet because he didn't want to disappoint his mother or his female fans.

into stories of their own about other horrible landlords and wretched buildings. Maybe I should have resented them for their previous slights and simmering bigotry, but I reveled in suddenly being a welcome guest.

It was well into the evening when I reached the last unit in my sweep of the building. The apartment belonged to an old man who was hard of hearing. I had to bang the hell out of his door to get him to answer. I knew he was home because I could hear him yelling at his television, which was cranked to its highest volume. Once he let me inside, he put the TV on mute. Communicating with him was slow going. I had to speak loudly and distinctly, repeating myself to confirm that he'd understood what I'd said the first time. In the middle of our talk, he excused himself to go to the bathroom.

While I waited on a sagging love seat, I watched the silenced TV. Election results were coming in, and the networks were projecting winners. Nationally, the Democrats gained seats to strengthen their majority in the House and recaptured control of the Senate. I wasn't terribly interested until the photos of New York's political delegation started appearing on the screen, and the winner of the state's First Congressional District was a Republican candidate who had been a successful homicide prosecutor in Suffolk County. His name was Leslie Galbreath. It took a couple of seconds for me to recall where I'd seen the Honorable Leslie Galbreath before because in the photo, his strawberry-blond hair was neatly combed and parted, and he was wearing clothes.

The scope of the situation unfolded in my mind in quick succession. Gregory was fucking a congressman. Gregory was fucking a Republican congressman in our apartment on Election Day. The Republican congressman that Gregory was fucking in our apartment on Election Day knew I had seen him get sodomized.

Oddly enough, I had a sudden urge to call my mother. Fiona would have feasted on the details of a lurid political scandal. I could just imagine her giving my news her highest review. "It's a powder keg," she would have raved.

Yet I forced myself to take the revelation in stride and put it into perspective. Gregory juggled a gross of sugar daddies, and the old white men in his rotation were exceedingly wealthy and prominent. A freshman congressman didn't rate, compared to them. I neglected to account for the political possibilities.

What did manage to kill my rent strike victory buzz was realizing that Gregory would now hassle me to keep quiet about his affair. I'd undoubtedly scared the shit out of Congressman Galbreath, and Congressman Galbreath would surely put the fear of God in Gregory. Hours of my life were sure to be lost to my best friend harassing and inevitably threatening me to keep my mouth shut. How was I ever going to get him to focus on what I'd accomplished at Trump Tower? His messy sexcapade would have to dominate every conversation we had for the foreseeable future.

The old man finished up in the bathroom and took a seat across from me in his living room. I walked him through the terms of our settlement, and he was delighted and appreciative. I took my last bow, but the spark was extinguished.

Robbed of my gratification, I decided to head to Mt. Morris. Marcel would be starting his shift soon, and he'd get a kick out of what I'd done. Old Rustin might be at the bathhouse, too, and I deserved to have him beam at me with pride. High praise followed by anonymous sex was the one-two combination to salvage my flagging mood.

I took the stairs down to the lobby. The elevator opened, but I didn't look back to see who was stepping out of it. I kept my head down and braced myself for the cold winds that would greet me outside. In short, I was minding my own fucking business.

"Trey, can I talk to you?"

I recognized the voice, and I wondered if I could get away with pretending that I hadn't heard her. *Yes*, I thought, *just keep walking*. But she wasn't going to let me escape. She rushed across the wet floor to catch up with me.

"Trey!"

I turned around. "Good evening, Brianna."

"Can I give you some advice?" she asked.

Never in my life had the previous question ever led to a productive conversation. Guided by etiquette and a faint hope that I could let whatever Brianna was going to say go in one ear and right out the other, I answered, "Yes, by all means."

"You're making a fool of yourself," she said.

I clenched my teeth, trapping my tongue inside my mouth.

"The way you preen and swish," she continued. "The puppy-dog looks you give Harrison. Gay boys like you—the pretty ones—can't help but come sniffing around him."

My tongue shoved against the back of my teeth, crying out for freedom.

"He's too bighearted to tell you to stop or to punch your lights out." Brianna spoke these vile words with the assured tone of a Sunday school teacher warning her students against mortal sin. "He says, 'So what if this fairy has got a crush on me?'"

Let it be known that I walked away. Through the front entrance and down the chipped stairs and onto the sidewalk, I did my level best to keep from going off on Brianna. She pursued me. She wouldn't let it go.

"I told him it's not right to let you go on embarrassing yourself! Put the sissy out of his misery!"

Pedestrians had stopped to watch Brianna hector me. Her voice was echoing off the buildings. My mind latched onto her last insult and flipped. *Put the sissy out of his misery. No, put this bitch out of her misery.*

I spun around and charged toward Brianna. "He sucked my cock first! In your apartment! While you were at work one night!" I got nose to nose with her. "I came in his mouth! And he spit it out on your dish towel."

"You lie! He's a real man!"

"Keep saying that! Maybe one day, you'll believe it!"

She and I were shouting over top of one another.

"You stay away from us!"

"You want to scare me off! Because you know your man can be had!"

"Never, never! Not in your wildest dreams!"

"But you're too late. I've had him! And I've had better!"

"You're sick and twisted!"

"He likes his balls tugged while I blow him! He said you do it that way, too!"

That shut her down. Mouth agape, eyes wide open—she froze. No sound from her, not even breathing. The people who had gawked at our screaming match clapped, whistled, and laughed. They shouted their thoughts on who had won, and according to the voice vote, it was I. Then, after several seconds, Brianna rolled her shoulders back and stood perfectly straight. I expected her to haul off and slap me, but she retreated to 22 Mercer with her head held high. She walked as if nothing unseemly had occurred.

I wasn't so composed. There was a lurching ache in my stomach, and I wanted to vomit but couldn't. Strangers were smiling at me and complimenting me on how I'd torn Brianna to shreds. Their wicked approval only compounded my sense of despair. Acting like a snide, shrieking, gay minstrel was not how I wanted to be seen or applauded. Hurting people—even clueless, hateful homophobes— also did nothing for my self-esteem. Instead of going to Mt. Morris, I walked into a bar on Christopher Street and got drunk alone while I did some tall thinking.

No epiphanies joined me at the bar that night, and it would take years for me to understand why I'd been unable to enjoy the spoils of victory. Winning rarely changes how people perceive us and almost never soothes our insecurities. Winning, as most of us conceive it, is external and public. I didn't yet know that the most rewarding activities of my life would be those done in secret.

TOUCH AT LEAST ONE DEAD BODY

For a couple of weeks after Election Day, I was at loose ends. My rent was free into the new year, so I felt no pressure to go find a job. I also figured that Gregory and I would find another rat-hole apartment in a snap. Quite quickly, I fell into a relaxing routine. Gregory and I spent a lot of time getting high and wandering the city just popping into stores and browsing the merchandise to kill time, but, by virtue of an unspoken decree, we did not discuss his sexual liaison with Representative Leslie Galbreath. I was reluctant to call him out on it given that I had never told him about my affair with Harrison, who I avoided after my fight with Brianna.

Lord only knows how they carried on as a couple. Maybe she confronted him, and he pled temporary insanity, blaming me for bewitching him. Or maybe when she shared my accusations, he convinced her that I was a deranged, queer fabulist. Or maybe she kept our quarrel to herself, and Harrison was none the wiser. From my apartment window, I would see them on weekends strolling arm in arm to meet friends for brunch.

Most days, I divided my time between reading Audre Lorde's poetry and essays in the palatial New York Public Library and exploring the Morris Louis retrospective and Francesco Clemente's exhibit, *The Departure of the Argonaut,* at the Museum of Modern

Art.[34] I wasted hours with Gregory roaming the aisles and fingering the vinyl records at Headfunk Music. At night, I'd swing by
Mt. Morris, even when I wasn't horny. The other regulars and I
would gossip in the break room and scope out the fresh trade that
checked in.

Every time I entered the bathhouse, I hoped to see Rustin, but
Marcel told me that he hadn't been in since he scored with the sexy
Taiwanese guy. It dawned on me that I could look up Rustin's address or phone number, if he was listed. However, at the time, that
felt like an invasion of privacy. I believed our friendship belonged
inside Mt. Morris.

Despite not running into Rustin, my thoughts turned to him often, and I considered the advice he'd given me months ago. He felt
I needed to participate in the Gay Rights Movement. I believed that
I didn't have much to offer, and it seemed unlikely that I could do
anything to match my parents' experiences as young activists. Ward
joined in civil rights marches and protests in Chicago and Detroit—
since Indianapolis was not a frontline city in the fight for racial equality. Once, a police dog bit him in the thigh. Another time, he walked
behind John Lewis.[35] Fiona, who was born in Oakland, California,

---

34. Audre G. Lorde (1934–1992) was a lesbian African American poet, nonfiction writer,
and holistic civil rights advocate. She recognized the interconnectedness of every struggle
against injustice and thus, in her work, she railed against sexism, racism, homophobia,
and classism.

35. John R. Lewis (1940–2020), a civil rights leader who spoke at the March on Washington and went on to become an esteemed congressman representing his Georgia district for thirty-three years, distinguished himself in addition to his lifelong efforts to
ensure racial equality. Lewis championed LGBTQ+ rights, too. In 1996, he vehemently
opposed the passage of DOMA (the Defense of Marriage Act), which stipulated that the
federal government defined marriage as a union between a man and a woman, and which
gave states the power to refuse to recognize a same-sex marriage permitted in another
state. On the floor of the U.S. House of Representatives, Lewis called DOMA "a slap in
the face of the Declaration of Independence. It denies gay men and women the right to
liberty and the pursuit of happiness."

grew up as a neighbor and friend of Black Panther Party cofounder Bobby Seale.[36] She was an early member and organizer for the Black Panther Party until she resigned in protest over political tactics and sexist treatment.

My parents' activism transformed with time as they grew older and started a family. They drifted from being militant radicals to behind-the-scenes centrists. A natural change, I guess. Yet I tended to romanticize the younger versions of my mother and father. The bold ones who wore dashikis, dreamed of liberation from capitalism, and openly hated the police state. I think I would have preferred them as my parents. A pointless wish, seeing how my mother and father had snuffed out those cool radicals when I was an infant.

Anyway, I couldn't dream of touching history on such a grand scale like my parents had. So I kept my expectations low, and on November 24, I walked into the central office of the Gay Men's Health Crisis (GMHC) at 254 West Eighteenth Street and presented myself as a volunteer. My assumption was that I would stuff envelopes and lick stamps—small, mindless tasks that an eighteen-year-old couldn't screw up.

The front desk secretary had the phone to her ear as she asked me to state my business. I began to explain the entire backstory of where I met Rustin and his suggestion that I engage in the political struggles of the time. She twirled her hand, urging me to hurry my story along. The second the word *volunteer* came out of my mouth, she said, "Peter will handle you," and she pointed the way.

I walked over to Peter Chatsworth, the GMHC's unpaid, indefatigable outreach coordinator, and said, "Hello."

He looked at me expectantly and said, "Good, you're here. Grab

---

36. The Black Panther Party (1966–1982), founded in Oakland, California, was a political organization based on socialist principles and dedicated to revolution. Targeted by the FBI as a domestic terrorist group, the Black Panther Party launched community service programs—such as providing free breakfast for children and health clinics for the poor—but their involvement in good public works has been obscured by a more radical characterization.

those grocery bags off the counter. Careful, there's a carton of eggs in the left one. You're already late, and Angie will crack your skull if there's one broken egg."

I picked up the grocery bags and tried to explain that I was new, that I didn't know Angie, that I didn't know why he was talking to me as if we'd met before. But Peter, as I would come to love, could be quite daffy in a screwball manner.

"You should hoof it before it starts to snow again," said Peter. "But hold on, I promised to send her the money from Sidney. Where did I put that envelope? Can you imagine the hailstorm if I lost three grand?"

Peter went silent for a moment as he searched his cluttered desk, and I looked him over. He had the build of a bantamweight and appeared to be in his midforties, with thinning black hair and an elastic face that defaulted into a content grin. Under his faded blue eyes, there were dark circles, and his clothes were rumpled and worn.

I would never have guessed that he was thirty-seven years old and worked the night shift as a copy editor for the *New York Post*, a job that afforded him the little sleep he did get. He catnapped between wire reports of local shootings and fires. Peter had earned his claim to fame at the *Post*, which was infamous for its irreverent, attention-grabbing headlines, when a trio of hunters were mauled to death by grizzly bears, and he coined the front-page "screamer": BEARS 3, HUNTERS 0.

Just as Peter found the envelope stuffed with $3,000, I managed to say, "This is my first day as a volunteer. I'm Trey. Trey Singleton."

Peter blinked several times before saying, "Oh shit. Sorry about that. You look familiar, awfully familiar. Anyone ever tell you that? It's a good thing, trust me."

Unsure of what he meant, I ventured a hesitant, "Thank you."

"So you have no clue where you're going with those groceries."

"No, sir."

Peter laughed. "*No, sir.* You learn to talk like that in Mineshaft?"[37]
"It closed before I got the nerve to go."

"Our loss, I'm sure. Alright, I'll come with you to Angie's this time. It's not that far. Eighth Ave. between Thirty-fifth and Thirty-sixth." Peter paused and sighed. "Trey, I hope you've got thick skin."

Angela McBroom—or Angie, as she insisted her few friends call her—was an outcast in the community of New York City gay rights activists. It was a distinction she believed spoke highly of her: she was the prophet ignored by the crowd. Indeed, Angie had political and cultural insights that were ahead of her time. She also had a quick temper that was triggered by the smallest of mistakes, and she never failed to voice her disdain for violators of her unwavering moral code. She proved to be a nightmare when invited to serve on any organization's working group or subcommittee because she wouldn't compromise principles to spare feelings. Peter said, "Angie burns bridges like hens lay eggs."

I was drawn to Angie immediately. And I came to disagree with the common rap against her. Sure, Angie could be a gigantic pain in the ass, but there were plenty of men in the Gay Rights Movement who pounded tables, screamed in faces, and crushed the souls of their allies at planning meetings. Angie paid a harsher penalty because she was a woman, and not just a woman but a forty-eight-year-old butch lesbian who didn't wear makeup and rarely styled her frizzy, graying brown hair. Not the ideal spokesperson for a movement controlled far too much by white male assimilation queers

---

37. Mineshaft (1976–1985) was a cavernous members-only sex club and leather bar catering to the community of gay men who engage in BDSM (bondage, discipline, dominance, and submission, and sadism and masochism) role-playing. Famed photographer Robert Mapplethorpe (1946–1989) was a Mineshaft member, and hundreds of his photos document the sexual breadth achieved inside the club. Mineshaft was closed in November of 1985 by the New York City Department of Health.

who wished to convince the public that homosexuals were a meek telegenic people desperate to live discreet little lives.

Two years before I met her, Angie caused an uproar with a quote she gave *The New York Times* shortly after President Reagan was re-elected: "President Reagan and his Christian followers wouldn't care if gays were wiped off the face of the earth. Explain to me how that attitude isn't evil? Where's the humanity in wishing for the extermination of millions of other people?"[38]

To those pushing the assimilation agenda, Angie's remarks were unforgivable. The assimilators were dedicated to coalition building across the political spectrum, and she'd essentially accused the conservative heterosexual population of engaging in a government-sponsored genocide against queers. I'd argue Angie turned out to be correct on that point.

Enough of how her haters saw her. Let me tell you about this astounding woman when she was in her glory. Angie was first-generation Irish American and came from a line of renegade midwives who spared the mothers over their distressed and lethal offspring. Angie explained it plainly, "My foremothers didn't call it *abortion*. There was no such word. They thought it common sense to put the woman's life first."

By dint of her family line, I believe Angie had a comfort with death that most people will never understand. She didn't fear it. She didn't curse it. She knew death could be a mercy, and Angie believed her calling was to comfort people before they reached their eternal

---

38. President Ronald W. Reagan (1911–2004) entered office in 1981, and later in the year, a rare deadly cancer would be linked to 41 homosexuals. In 1982, that cancer would be called GRID (gay-related immune deficiency), before adopting its permanent name, AIDS (acquired immunodeficiency syndrome). Unequivocally, the Reagan administration turned a blind eye to the growing health crisis. Reagan's acting White House press secretary, Larry Speakes (1939–2014), made jokes when questioned about the AIDS epidemic in 1984 and repeatedly asserted that the president hadn't expressed any thoughts on the disease or its victims. President Reagan delivered his first major speech on AIDS on April 1, 1987. By the end of 1987, the cumulative total of reported AIDS cases in the United States was 50,378; and of those cases, 40,849 people were dead.

rest. She'd gotten a year and a half of training in nursing school before having to drop out to take care of her ailing parents. When her parents eventually died, she inherited their apartment and enough money to live comfortably for the rest of her life. Kick up her heels, she did not.

The morning I met Angie, I walked behind Peter into her place. It was the front half of the fifth floor of a prewar, crumbling-brick apartment building. The pipes groaned when required to operate, and the furnace still ran on coal. Yet the grand apartment had a romantic air to it. The furniture was aging art deco meets Goodwill rummage sale.

Peter covered his nose and mouth with his hand as we entered. I couldn't because I was holding grocery bags. The smell was staggering. Stale piss poorly coated by antiseptic cleaner mixed with sour body odor and a hint of vomit. It was the kind of stench that burrows into the walls. Opening a window or mopping with bleach would be exercises in futility. This was the odor of the sick and the dying.

Angie had turned the apartment into a hospice for AIDS patients who had nowhere else to go. Men on the outs with their families; men who were the last survivors in their decimated circles of friends; men with loved ones too poor to support them; men who were days—a few weeks if their bodies refused to quit fighting—from death.

Peter explained that there was an informal network of dozens of home hospices operating in the five boroughs. Almost all of them run by lesbians, and every single one of them an illegal operation, given that they were unlicensed and that regulations, such as occupancy restrictions, were ignored.

The sight of twenty dying men stretched out on cots or propped up in couches and chairs as they wheezed, moaned, spoke to no one, or stared silently into the void so overwhelmed me that I didn't react to the horror. I didn't think at all. I just went into action. I put the groceries away. I helped a man struggling to reach the toilet. I put more blankets on another man complaining about the cold.

There, of course, was more at play than I initially realized. Angie's home hospice was different from many of the others, and that difference created an affinity between me and the men in her care: the vast majority of Angie's patients were Black. Sixteen of the twenty, when I arrived. These men could have strolled into any family reunion in my parents' backyard and introduced themselves to me as distant cousins or long-lost uncles, and I would have taken their word that we were kin. The connection was that natural and recognizable on my end, and I believe they instinctually trusted and appreciated me.

It would be weeks before I discovered that Angie had cornered the market on Black patients because other home hospices found it problematic to shelter Black men in their respective buildings. Nosy neighbors noticed and complained. See, even during a pandemic, racism never fails to insert itself into the equation.

Angie's neighbors didn't dare give her any trouble, and word spread quietly in some circles that her place was the one for Black gay men in the last stages of their battles with HIV/AIDS. Peter, no doubt, assumed that I'd fit right in as a volunteer under Angie. He was correct in more ways than he could have ever imagined. My devotion to Angie and the men in her apartment was instant.

On the first day, Peter stood back and watched me, offering no guidance or judgment. One old man—it was hard to place ages because the disease did such a number on the faces and bodies back then—told me where the vodka was stashed in the kitchen and asked for a glass. Peter didn't say a word as I retrieved the liquor, poured a glass, and held it to the old man's lips as he drank it down in a few big gulps.

Angie exited the primary bedroom, which was reserved for the sick who were thought to have less than a day or two of life left in them. Her face was flushed and her hair a mess. As casual as one would say, "Hello," Angie told Peter, "Walton just passed."

"This morning?"

"This minute."

Almost to himself, Peter said, "I should call the news desk."

Angie huffed. "For fuck's sake, that's your first thought?"

"Sorry, but this is news. His family is worth billions."

"And they disowned him for sucking cock. They won't do a thing for him now."

"So let me call it in. Put it on the record. Make them explain why their youngest son died here."

Angie shook her head. "I don't give a shit about sticking it to them. I want to see that Walton gets a proper burial. The Keller Funeral Home said they can't help me anymore. The few that will take our bodies only do so if I agree to cremation."

"Okay, then, call one of them."

"Walton didn't want to burn. He pleaded with me."

Peter cocked his head. "You suddenly get superstitious. Scared he's going to haunt you."

"He made me promise he wouldn't burn, and if you go blabbing it to your paper, they'll turn that pretty boy into ashes. Now are you gonna make a liar out of me?"

Peter put his hands up in surrender. He and Angie thought quietly for half a minute. Then Peter turned to me. "You're going to have to get knee deep in this if we're going to pull it off. Are you in?"

"Sure thing."

Angie side-eyed me as if I'd just materialized. "Who the hell is he?"

"This is Terry."

"It's Trey," I corrected.

"Right, Trey. This is Angie. Now that we're all friends, let's have a look at what we're dealing with."

Peter led the way into the primary bedroom, where Walton lay curled up in the fetal position. He was one of two white men staying with Angie, and she had been right: he was pretty. Honey-blond hair, alabaster skin, pink lips, and a model's jawline. He couldn't have weighed more than 130 pounds, been taller than five-foot-seven, or older than twenty. There were no signs of lesions or facial wasting on his exposed skin.

I had never been so close to a dead body before, and it scared me a little. I couldn't take my eyes off him. He looked so lifelike. I wondered if Angie had made some sort of mistake. This pretty boy wasn't really dead. He was too young and gorgeous to die. I felt light-headed as my mind frantically searched for a way to change what was final.

Peter had no such turmoil, and he sized up the situation with a cold logic. "He was a drug addict, a hustler, right?"

"Yeah, what's that got to—"

"He overdosed. Passed out in the snow and died of exposure."

Angie put her hands on her hips. "And I found him outside and dragged him up here?"

"No, he can't die here. Too many people will know what that really means."

"So what, then?"

Peter pointed at me. "Trey and I will carry him out the back and put him in an alley. Give it an hour, let him get cold. Trey will go to a pay phone, call the police, tell them he was getting high with his buddy last night, and the two of them passed out in the alley. Trey woke up, Walton didn't."

"You want to fucking dump his body?" shouted Angie.

Peter paid her no mind and continued giving instruction to me. "The cops will ask you for your name. Don't give them one, not even a fake one. You just establish that you were both doing drugs and give them the location of his body. Then you hang up and walk away. Can you do that?"

Before I could answer, Angie shoved Peter on the shoulder. "Do you hear yourself? You want to toss a dead boy in an alley like garbage?"

"He OD'd. His family will accept that. They'll hold a funeral for him." Peter rubbed Angie's arm. "I hate it, too. But it's this, or he burns."

The risks and wildness of the plan didn't alarm me, but then again, I wasn't thinking straight. While Peter had laid it all out, I'd been staring at Walton, trying to place him in my memory. Had we crossed paths at Limelight or Ninth Circle? Maybe we sat near each other while eating at Florent? Did he cruise me once—lick those pink lips of his and beckon me into the shadows of Morningside Park? Did I cruise him—flashing my crooked smile and giving him a sly wink when he looked my way on a street corner as we waited for the red hand to change into a white man? We were young gay men sharing the city. Our lives had to have touched before his ended.

Angie snapped her fingers an inch from my nose. "Hey, buddy, this sit right with you? You're gonna carry a dead body and then lie to the police?"

"I'll do it," I said, then added as a challenge, "unless you've got a better idea."

My back talk earned the faintest smiles from Angie. "Look at the balls on this one. You want to join our mad circus, kid? Have at it."

"Okay, that settles that," said Peter. "Let's get moving."

———

By the time Peter, Walton, and I exited the back door of Angie's apartment building, it was snowing, and the wind was whipping the onslaught of falling flakes into mini-cyclones. Walton's arms were draped over my shoulders, and his head rested against my neck as I carried him piggyback-style with my arms tucked under his thighs. His body was light and still warm, which was a small comfort. I could just about pretend that we were horsing around—that he was alive.

Walton hadn't arrived at Angie's wearing a coat, so she draped a yellow knit shawl around his shoulders and torso. His head was uncovered, and snowflakes clung to his honey-blond hair. The only signs of his earthly wealth were on his feet: he wore black, suede Dolce & Gabbana loafers.

For all my nonchalant courage when Angie had asked me if I

could handle my end of the plan, I was petrified once we hit the streets. If a bystander pointed at Walton and screamed, "He's dead!" I was sure that I'd turn and run. What I couldn't quite decide was if I would carry the dead body with me. On one hand, I didn't want to land in jail for this pretty white boy I didn't know. On the other hand, I felt a responsibility to place him on the ground respectfully. I owed him nothing, and I owed him as much dignity as possible under the circumstances.

Peter walked ahead of us, leading the way. The snowfall and the wind were our friends. The New Yorkers we passed were rushing along with their heads down. Their only concerns were to get out of the cold and to avoid slipping on ice. I received a few sideways glances, but no eyes opened in alarm. Walton must have looked like a friend of mine who'd passed out from too much drink or drugs, and I was carrying him to sleep it off or to continue the party in some other location. That's, of course, assuming that anyone who laid eyes on us thought about us for more than a fraction of a second.

Our plan was to leave Walton alongside the abandoned railway tracks of the High Line. Dead bodies were a common sight on those elevated grounds in the seedy decades before the High Line's renovation into a family-friendly park.

We were approaching Tenth Avenue when Peter stopped suddenly. A block ahead of us stood a white man with a shaved head in blue jeans and a puffy winter coat. The man waved at Peter, and after a moment of hesitation, Peter waved back. I could tell from Peter's stiff posture that we were in trouble. Whoever the man greeting Peter was, he certainly wasn't going to drop his morning errands to help us dispose of a dead body.

Peter bent to the side and forced a couple of fake coughs then barked at me, "He's a cop. Go. I'll deal with him."

Go where? I wondered. But Peter hurried off to meet his pal the cop, and I didn't dare yell after him. My concern over the cop sparked another fear in my mind: What if the private investigator I suspected my parents had hired was observing me now? Holy fuck, how would I explain this to my mother and father? I shook that worry because I had no time to indulge it. If I was being followed, then I was being followed. I had to stay on mission.

I turned around to walk away from Peter and the approaching cop, but I moved too quickly, and Walton's weight shifted on my back. His left arm fell to the side, and the rest of his body started to slide in the same direction. I tightened my grip on his thighs and lunged to the right to get him back in alignment with me. It worked, except for the fact that I overcompensated, and Walton swung back toward me hard and fast. His skull clipped me in the back of my head.

My knees buckled, and the pain blinded me for a second. Failure felt imminent, and that very thought turned my fear into rage. I hated the idea that I was going to let down Peter, Angie, and Walton because I was too weak, too clumsy, too much of a panicking sissy under pressure, too much of all the slurs I'd grown up hearing. Fuck that noise. I caught myself and held on to Walton. Upright and alert, I looked around, and across the street was an entrance to Moore Park. I kept my cool as I walked to the crosswalk and waited for the lights to change.

An elderly woman joined me as I waited. She wore a red wool hat and a thick green scarf that snaked around her neck and up over her mouth and nose. All I could make out of her face were her pale eyes surrounded by hundreds of wrinkles. She sized up Walton and me. She shook her head like the nuns did at my high school. I braced for a reprimand.

Instead, the old woman said, "I had a friend like that. A hopeless lush. You can't help them, you know? They come to no good end."

The light changed, and she crossed the street ahead of us. Walton's body began to slump away from me, so I hunched forward to keep us together. I reached the other side and entered the drab park named in honor of Clement Clarke Moore, the alleged author of the poem "The Night Before Christmas." There were a couple of junkies wandering around with no connection to reality. Otherwise, Walton and I were alone. This would have to be the spot. I found a bench and laid Walton on his side. I took the yellow shawl off his shoulders, folded it up into a square, and tucked it under his head like a pillow. I'm no necrophiliac, but damn, did Walton look handsome. I pressed my lips to his and kissed him before I walked away.

———

Angie was outside on her apartment stoop smoking a cigarette when I returned. She didn't have on a coat or a hat. Yet the freezing winds didn't seem to bother her in the slightest.

"Buddy, you're back," she said. "It must've gone peachy keen."

I gave her a sedate rundown of events. "I left him in Moore Park, went to a diner up the street, ate a bit, killed some time, then called it in to the police. I waited for the sirens to come. They got him."

Angie nodded and tapped the ash off the end of her cigarette.

"Is he some sort of Kennedy or Rockefeller?" I asked.

"Walton's family is a hundred times richer than the Kennedys, and they ain't giving a penny away like the Rockefellers." Angie tossed her cigarette into a pile of shoveled snow. "You heard of Hadamovsky?"

The name sounded familiar, and after a second or two, I placed it. "They make race cars."

"Yeah, that's all they want you to know about them." Angie opened the door to her apartment building, and I followed her inside and up the stairs as she schooled me. "The Hadamovsky family got filthy rich building engines for tanks and fighter jets. They profit off the war machine. Never mind that their engines made the Nazi blitzkrieg possible. When the Hadamovsky clan realized Hitler was going to lose, they ran to the Allied Forces and spilled all their secrets. In exchange, they were allowed to keep going after the war. They downplay their past and their connection to every war on the globe, and instead make cute formula racing cars."

"Walton's one of them."

"The youngest of four boys. His grandfather started the company. His father runs it. His brothers fight over who will be next. And Walton never stood a chance." Angie paused as we reached the third floor. I thought she was winded, but she was choked up, fighting back tears. "His brothers could tell he was gay before he was old enough to realize it himself. They beat him, tortured him. Then his parents wondered why he kept running away, acted out in school, and got hooked on drugs."

"Maybe Peter was right," I suggested. "People should know how his family treated him."

"No," Angie insisted. "It wouldn't work. The Hadamovskys would drown out the story. I mean, the sons of bitches were Nazi collaborators, and they scrubbed that away. Being cruel to their faggot son isn't going to bring them down."

In that moment, Angie appeared so wounded that I couldn't stop my reaction. I hugged her. I half expected her to throw me down a flight of stairs. To my relief, she hugged me back.

———

The death of Walton Elliot Hadamovsky was international news published in all the leading papers of North America and Europe. According to what ran in print, Walton was a drug addict who had broken ties with his wealthy, loving family despite their repeated efforts to get him help. He died of a drug overdose, exposure in subzero weather, or a combination of the two. Walton was nineteen years old. Following his small and private memorial service and funeral at St. Paul's German Lutheran Church, his body was whisked away to the Hadamovsky compound outside of Cologne, Germany, and buried in the family cemetery. There was no mention that he was homosexual, that he was a sex worker, or that he died of AIDS-related complications.

Until he was eclipsed by subsequent cautionary tales, Walton was branded as a spoiled, rich fuckup. He got little sympathy from any quarter of society. The haves resented him, and the have-nots mocked him. I consider carrying Walton's dead body to ensure that he got the burial that he wanted to be the first worthwhile accomplishment of my life.

Lesson #10

TO CHANGE THE WORLD, HAVE A SELFISH GOAL

Peter got back to Angie's apartment an hour after I did. I was in the bathroom, standing by as a man named Terrence showered. I don't recall Terrence's last name, but if memory serves, he'd been a taxi driver. He got fired when a passenger noticed a lesion on the back of his neck and reported him. AIDS had rendered Terrence frail and blind. He didn't need me to wash his body or anything that intimate. I just guided Terence to the shower and waited for him to finish as the room filled with steam. Terrence was thirty-one.

Peter opened the bathroom door, poked his head in, and said, "Way to come through with flying colors."

I answered his compliment with a sharp, "Fuck you."

"Whoa! What the hell?"

"You ditched me."

"You're sore I had to go keep a cop away from us?"

"You could have given me more direction. This was your plan, and you left me holding the bag."

"And you figured it out." Peter threw up his hands. "What are we even arguing over?"

"It scared the shit out of me."

Peter grinned. "I'll bet."

Terrence turned off the shower and asked, "What's all the commotion about?"

"Nothing major," I said. "Peter was just apologizing to me."

"Yeah, about that. Let me buy you a drink when you finish up," Peter offered.

———

We went to the Depot, an old Chelsea dive bar that had a front room with a long, narrow bar and a back room with two pool tables. Along the long bar, most of the stools were occupied by alcoholic bears: coarse men with guts, scruff, aggression, and no shame about drinking before lunchtime. Legend had it that the Depot, despite being older than Stonewall, was never raided or fairy dusted by the cops, and the reason given was naturistic: "Bears eat pigs."

The back room was for rough-trade rent boys: striking, wild-eyed young men that radiated a feral allure. Their johns enjoyed the ordeal of getting these hustlers to shower and eat before fucking, and the challenge of ending the encounter without getting mugged, robbed, and left for dead. The ideal outcome was for a john to rehabilitate a rent boy in *My Fair Lady* fashion, domesticating him and finding him a suitable career like as an attendant in an art gallery or as a hotel concierge. Coming as no surprise, such endings were rare. More often, rough-trade rent boys smacked their johns around, bloodying noses and lips before snatching wallets. The cops were almost never called because they wouldn't give a shit about the abusive kink between two faggots. To each their own, I suppose. It wasn't my scene.

It struck me as odd that Peter took me to the Depot. I figured it would offend his dedication to stamping out the plague since the back room of the Depot should have been ground zero for HIV/AIDS prevention efforts, but early attempts were rebuffed with swinging pool sticks.

"You like this place?" I asked when we perched on two wobbly stools near the drafty front door.

"I had a master who made me meet him here," Peter explained, "and I grew to like the feel of the place."

"You . . . had a master?"

"No need to be shy. I'm an all-star BDSM submissive, open to tit torture and wax play." He raked his fingers through his thinning hair and took pleasure in seeing the shock on my face. "Let me guess. You had me pegged as vanilla, and now you can't shake the image of me in leather, rocking in a sling." Peter laughed so hard it made me laugh.

"Hell," I confessed, "I couldn't picture you having sex, period."

Far from insulted, Peter doubled over laughing. "Good, then my cover isn't blown." He leaned in close, and his voice became a seductive growl. "Because I like to surprise new lovers with the tricks in my bag."

Just like that, I was turned on, curious, and scared. To break the tension, I asked, "When did your master die? Did he stay with Angie? Is that how you know her?"

"Goodness, Trey, do you go around writing sad stories for everyone?" Peter signaled the bartender to bring us two beers. "My master isn't dead. He moved to Miami. Not every homo is dying of AIDS."

"I know, I know. But you said he was gone, all sad like."

"I am sad. I'm angry. Master Yuri and our whole crowd scattered to the wind once they closed Mineshaft. That was our playground, our Garden of Eden—except all we ate was forbidden fruit. I was there on the first night and the last. Now I can't even walk past the damn building. It tears me up inside."

Too young and ignorant to see his point, I asked, "The sex was that good?"

Peter didn't dignify my question with an answer. "You got moxie, no doubt about that. The way you handled yourself in a pinch was first-rate."

"Thanks."

"Why'd you go through with it?"

The bartender put two beers in front of us. Peter grabbed his, clinked it against mine, and took a sip. I could tell I was being tested. I played it cautiously.

"Seemed only right? If we didn't, Walton—"

"Was gonna burn. Yeah, yeah, yeah. What's it to you? You didn't know Walton, or Angie, or me? Why risk it? Why trust us?"

Not sure what he wanted me to say, I sputtered, "I-I-I-I came to volunteer. I want to help."

"Let's back up, Trey. You woke up this morning and marched over to the GMHC. What do you get out of doing that?"

"I get to be a part of the fight against AIDS?"

Peter sighed. "Have you lost people you loved to this thing?"

"No."

"Have you got it?"

"No."

"Then why do you care?"

"I'm friends with Bayard Rustin, and he told me to get involved."

"Bayard Rustin?" Peter whistled. "That's a big name to drop. Tell me, do you do whatever Mr. Rustin orders you to do? Is he your master?"

"Why are you coming at me like this? I did good today, right?"

"Yeah, Trey, today was exceptional, and you did rise to the occasion. It's tomorrow I'm worried about. Six months from now. A year from now. What keeps driving you? What keeps you from burning out? 'I want to fight AIDS' is a bullshit goal. It's too big, too abstract. Besides, the metaphor is horrible. If we were in a fight against AIDS, our eyes would be swollen shut and all our teeth would be littered across the ring."

I took a sip from my beer. "Okay, this is the talk you give new volunteers. You want to see if you can scare me off."

"No, I burn through volunteers all the time. Means nothing to me. Fresh homos arrive by bus and train every day. I'll always have a new kid ready to fight AIDS," he explained. "I'm talking to you because you've got balls on you. You are willing to walk through fire, and that doesn't come around very often. Trouble is, I don't know what makes you tick. What's your selfish goal?"

I think silently for a few seconds. "Help me out here. I don't get it. What's your selfish goal?"

Peter smirked. "This stays between us."

I nodded in agreement.

"We're not going to wipe AIDS off the face of the planet. We're not even going to save the lives of everyone infected with this plague," he said. "What keeps me going is what I think we can achieve. We educate people so they don't fear the disease, we increase condom use among gays, and lower the number of annual infections. We contain this disease, stop it from being a public health emergency, and policy makers can quit policing our private lives. We can open Mineshaft again. That's my selfish goal. I want my playground back."

I considered what Peter said. Did I have an endgame as concrete as his? It took me a minute to locate what was driving me. Why did I leave Indianapolis and turn my back on my trust fund? What was I seeking? What was I trying to prove? The answer struck my heart with a piercing pain, and once I identified it, I had to gather my nerve to name it.

"I'm the reason my younger brother is dead," I said. "If I can, I'd like to do enough good in the world to balance the scales somehow. I just want to wake up one morning and feel like a good person."

Peter clinked his beer glass against mine again. "May we both get what we desire."

———

I moved to New York City to put distance between myself and my role in a tragedy that I could never live down in Indiana. More than a scandal (because scandals fade from memory) and worse than a sin (because sins can be forgiven), my transgressions were immutable. People with knowledge of what I had done could never see past my failings, and on hundreds of occasions, I stood before men, women, and children as their views of me darkened once they realized my connection to the death of Martin Singleton.

Any Black person raised in Indiana during my generation could easily recite the painful details of my brother's murder. Hoosiers my age but of other races would probably need only a little prompting: *1979; missing boy; Douglass Park; Fall Creek; Ashmount.* Some of you from the era may even be vaguely familiar with the case. It was a national news story for several weeks.

By the time I arrived in the city, I wasn't afraid of being recognized when I shopped for groceries. But I did decide to go by "Trey," a nickname my oldest cousin gave me when I was an infant on account of my being the third Earl Singleton in our family tree. I figured that Trey was less distinctive than Earl—should there somehow be someone for whom my birth name rang a bell.

I also told no one in my new world about the defining events in my old world. Gregory was aware that my younger brother had passed away. I didn't give him the specifics as to how Martin died, and Gregory respectfully didn't pry. With Rustin and Marcel, I managed to slide into an alternate reality. At one point, I had shared with them that I grew up with a brother and sister named Martin and Jackie, and down the line, when Rustin or Marcel asked me how my siblings were doing, I would say, "Fine." I left it at that because I didn't want to have to introduce the heavy, sad truth. I didn't want them to see me differently. So what I created, inadvertently, was this realm inside Mt. Morris where my brother was believed to be alive. It seemed like a harmless lie, and I liked pretending it was true.

Perhaps that was the strongest constant between me at eleven and me at eighteen: I was too drawn to wishful thinking. Or, presented with less tenderness, my mind walled off the disgraceful realities I would rather have forgotten. I was afraid to examine my naked soul.

Let's see if I can now provide an unflinching eye.

April 1, 1979, was the last day I shared with my brother. In the aftermath, the news media would attach a lot of meaning to the date being April Fool's Day, suggesting that our awful misfortune was the result of a calculated prank or hoax. For the record, April Fool's Day meant nothing to anyone in my family, and it had no effect on our actions.

What did matter to the children living in my parents' mansion—me, age eleven; Martin, age nine; Jackie, age seven; and our cousin Kareem Singleton, age eleven—was that April 1, 1979, was a Sunday. We had to be up, dressed, fed, and out the door to make it to New Covenant Church for Sunday school by 9:30 a.m. We were trusted and expected to accomplish these weekly tasks without adult assistance. Jackie picked out our outfits. Martin polished the dress shoes. I ironed the clothes. Kareem cooked a pancake breakfast.

There wasn't a single adult in Ashmount (the name of my parents' mansion) to help us that morning even if we'd wanted it. Both my parents were out of town on business trips. My father was lobbying congressmen in D.C., and my mother was in Chicago as part of a small think tank helping Rev. Jesse Jackson decide if he should challenge President Jimmy Carter for the Democratic Party's 1980 presidential nomination. My aunt Roberta Singleton lived in Ashmount, along with her son, Kareem, but since she worked until closing on Saturdays as a waitress in a nightclub, we had standing orders not to wake her on Sunday mornings.

Martin, Jackie, Kareem, and I arrived at church without a hitch. We listened to our Sunday school teacher, then sat through the full 10:00 a.m. service and placed our family's offering envelope in the collection plate.

On the way home from church, the next stop for us was White Castle for lunch. Along the way, we saw two old fishing poles leaning against the tree outside of an apartment complex. Next to the fishing poles was a scrap of cardboard that had the word FREE written on it in black marker. I was so excited to have our boring routine disrupted in even this slight way that I made my siblings and cousin stop.

"We need those fishing poles," I said. "Then we could catch our own lunch at Fall Creek."

"We're not allowed to go down by Fall Creek, and you don't know how to fish," Kareem pointed out.

"I can learn. How hard can it be?"

Jackie pulled at my sleeve. "I'm hungry."

I tried to sound as if I were in charge. "Okay. We'll take them with us and fish after we eat."

"No," argued Kareem, "we're playing basketball after we eat."

"We always do that."

"And we're gonna do it again today."

I hated playing basketball at Douglass Park. The whole pecking order of who got to play on what court and for how long bored and intimidated me. Kareem, Martin, and I were already at a disadvantage for being preteens. We were relegated to the half court with the most cracks in the cement. We then had to stand on the sidelines, waiting to be picked as the ringer on someone else's team or until we found two players who would unite with us to form a squad. We could spend an hour or more kicking over anthills before we even stepped onto the court.

Jackie was the lucky one. She got to climb and swing on the jungle gym. She got to play freeze tag with the younger boys and girls.

Once Kareem, Martin, and I were in a game, unrelenting anxiety seized me by the chest. When the ball came to me, I looked to pass it immediately. Occasionally, I'd be wide open, and an older boy on my ragtag team would scream at me to shoot it. I'd buckle under the pressure and lob the ball toward the basket. I never expected the ball to go through the hoop. I just wanted it to make contact with the rim. If my shot only brushed the nets, everyone gathered around the court chanted, "Aaaaaiiiiirrrrr! Baaaaaall!"

So I was determined not to go back to Douglass Park. The fishing poles offered an alternative, and I pressed the case hard. Unfortunately, Kareem, who was a pretty good baller, held his ground.

Martin proved to be the decisive vote. "Fishing sounds fun," he said.

Kareem groaned, and my brother and I each carried a fishing pole. Jackie was relieved that we could continue our walk to lunch. None of us said another word until we reached White Castle. I didn't even bother to thank Martin even though I appreciated that he'd sided with me.

I doubt Martin had any genuine interest in fishing. What's more likely is that he had picked up on my distress at the prospect of returning to Douglass Park, and he decided to spare me. Well before he was nine, my brother displayed a talent for being startlingly astute. He didn't always say why he was doing kind things for me or Jackie. He simply saw a need and found ways to make the situation better.

At White Castle, we ate our fill of tiny square hamburgers, then headed home to Ashmount to change out of our church clothes. Martin and I hid the fishing poles in the bushes that lined the driveway. Once home, I was worried that Aunt Roberta would sense that Kareem, Martin, and I were up to something. Instead of being suspicious, my aunt was in one of her lonely moods. I could tell because she was still wearing her silk head wrap and red bathrobe. A lit cigarette dangled between her fingers. She stopped us at the staircase.

"Whoa, quit your running," she said. "You all race in and out of this house like a pack of wild dogs." She smiled through her hangover. "Why don'tcha take it easy and stay with me. I'll pop corn on the stove, and we'll find a show or a game to watch on the TV."

"We're gonna play basketball," I lied.

Aunt Roberta narrowed her eyes at me. "Aren't you the eager little beaver?"

Kareem spoke up. "Mama, we're meeting up with friends."

She took a drag off her cigarette and zeroed in on Jackie. "How about you, sugar pie? You want to keep cool with me? I'll even let you rummage through my jewelry box."

My sister beamed. "Can I wear the necklaces?"

"But of course."

Jackie agreed to stay behind.

Martin nudged me. "Let's get going."

———

Dressed in gym shorts, graphic T-shirts, and old sneakers, Martin, Kareem, and I rode our bikes along Sutherland Avenue. The two fishing poles rested on my handlebars. We cut off the street, glided down a grassy hill, and pedaled into a wooded area until mud prompted us to hop off our bikes and lean them against trees. The creek was about twenty yards wide, and its current rushed faster and sounded louder than I'd expected. As we tiptoed onto the soggy bank of Fall Creek, Kareem snatched one of the fishing poles out of my hand.

"I'm fishing first," he said.

"Why's that?" I asked. "You said this was stupid."

"I lied to my mama to get us here. You owe me."

"You can use the other one," offered Martin. "I'll wait."

I said, "Thanks."

Our newly found fishing poles were simple cast rods, so there wasn't much to figure out. We dug in the dirt for worms to use as bait. The woods shaded us from the sun and concealed us from the streets. The three of us were laughing as we competed to find the fattest, longest worm. Fall Creek felt like our own private oasis.

None of us heard the gang of seven teenage boys. We were facing the water with our backs toward the woods. The teenage boys formed a loose semicircle around us, trapping us between them and the creek.

"Youse boys lost?" asked the ringleader.

Martin, Kareem, and I exchanged nervous glances with each other before turning around and seeing the odds against us. Seven teens. Four Black. Three white. Each of them rawboned and gimlet-eyed. The ringleader's left ear was jagged at the top like someone had bitten part of it off.

He couldn't have been older than fourteen, but he had the voice of an angry man. "Youse boys deaf or stupid? I asked if youse lost. Answer me."

"We're fine," said Kareem. "We've gotta be getting home."

"Them bikes of yours shining like they's new." The ringleader casually pulled a can of dip out of his pocket, swung the can rapidly for a few seconds, and put a pinch of dip between his front teeth and lower lip. "Thems bikes liable to get took."

I ran first. I reached my bike before any of the seven teenage boys moved, and I was pedaling alongside the creek before three of the teens gave chase. I looked back over my shoulder and saw that Kareem and Martin had dashed to their bikes, too.

The ringleader yelled, "Get 'em all!"

I didn't look back again. Mud from the banks was caking to my tires, and I was pedaling hard to keep up my speed. I could hear the grunts and huffing of the teens racing to catch me. They were gaining on me.

"We gonna fuck you up!" one of my pursuers hollered.

And he was right. I couldn't bike fast enough to escape them. I had to change course. The creek was to my left, and its current gave no indication as to its depths, but I had to take a chance. I steered into Fall Creek.

My front tire splashed into the water and got twisted in a bed of slick pebbles. I skidded down a steep embankment. For a moment, it felt like I was either going to be pitched off the bike or dragged by it underneath the water. I screamed. The bike bottomed out, and I was on a narrow path where the water reached halfway up my tire. My feet were submerged on the downstrokes of my pedaling, but I didn't care. There was a way forward for me.

The boys running after me didn't hesitate to follow me into the creek. One of them wiped out on the embankment, landing face-first in the water. The second one got several yards into the creek when he suddenly dropped, having in a single step gone from ankle-deep water to shoulder-deep water. And the third one just quit at the water's edge; maybe he couldn't swim.

Once on the other side of Fall Creek, I biked toward Thirty-eighth Street, where I met Kareem up on the overpass. Perched on his bike, my cousin was panting hard.

"Where's Martin?" I asked.

"I thought he'd be with you. He went the same direction as you."

"What way did you go?"

"I biked through them and went back the way we came. A couple of them chased me but stopped once I reached the street."

The thoughts in my head were clear as a bell: *They got him. They got my brother for sure. The teenagers chasing Martin would have stayed after him until he ran into the boys who failed to catch me. Seven on one. They'd beat him bad.*

Just considering that scenario caused such a searing pain in my head that I shut it out. I refused to voice it. I tried to unthink it.

Instead, I said, "He must've gotten away like we did. He's probably on his way home."

"Then we'd better get back. We don't want him telling my mama what happened."

"He won't do that."

"But what . . ." Kareem hesitated before raising the slightest possibility of harm. "But what if he's got a busted lip or a black eye? How's he going to explain that? How's he going to explain why we're not with him?"

We sped off on our bikes. The two of us pushed each other to greater speeds. As Ashmount came into view, I searched for any sign of my brother—his bike parked next to the garage, his wet shoes left outside by the front door. No such luck, of course. My legs felt as if they were about to give out from under me.

"Maybe he's still by the creek," I said with no conviction. "We should go back."

"Let's just tell my mama."

"No, she'll be mad, she'll tell my parents, and they'll never let us do anything fun again."

The panic in my gut contracted into a tight ball that knocked me to my hands and knees. I opened my mouth and retched violently again and again and again. Nothing more than spit and bile came out of me. Kareem helped me to my feet. I was unsteady as he led me into the mansion. I was terrified by what had happened and by what might have happened, and the only certainty was that all the anger and the punishments were going to land squarely on me, and I would become even less than the afterthought I already was.

"Mama! Mama!"

Aunt Roberta hurried into the grand foyer with Jackie on her heels. "Boy, what you—"

She saw me. My panic, my fear, my body coated in sweat. She saw Kareem. His saucer eyes. His trembling bottom lip. She looked for the one who was missing.

"Where's Martin?" she asked.

Without any premeditation, I spoke. "I think that white man at the park took him."

———

A manhunt began within hours of my lie. Cops released a composite sketch, based on my description, of a bearded white man in his late thirties to early forties, weighing approximately 160 pounds and standing anywhere between five-foot-eleven and six-foot-two. A perimeter was sealed around Douglass Park, where I claimed that Martin, Kareem, and I had been waiting to play basketball on the afternoon of April 1.

In my telling, there was a bearded white man lurking around. I didn't think much of this white man until Martin went off to use the bathroom on his own and didn't return. That's when I noticed the bearded white man was gone, too. Kareem and I raced home to alert my aunt Roberta.

Aunt Roberta phoned the police, who sent two officers to Ashmount to question me and Kareem. Kareem said little beyond one-word answers. He didn't contradict me, but he was adamant that he didn't see or notice the bearded white man.

Roberta tracked down my mother in Chicago and my father in D.C. and broke the news that Martin was missing. Fiona and Ward flew home immediately. They worked the phones, harnessing the combined power of their political connections. Indianapolis mayor William Hudnut, Indiana senators Birch Bayh and Richard Lugar, FBI director William Webster, Rev. Jackson, and Vice President Walter Mondale were all pressed to cut through red tape, to garner media coverage, and to deliver resources for the search for my brother.

On the Black radio station Power 105, community activist Amos Brown dedicated dozens of hours to reporting the latest on the Martin Singleton case. Pioneering journalist Barbara Boyd did the same on WRTV. The Black weekly newspaper the *Indianapolis Recorder* printed the missing boy's photo on their front page for a month. Father Boniface Hardin led a candlelight vigil at Martin University. There was talk of putting my brother's face on the little milk cartons that were served at grade schools, but nothing came of it.

Two weeks after Martin went missing, my mother questioned me relentlessly about the day of his disappearance. I stuck to the lies I had told, but I tripped up on some of the details. My mother zeroed in on my inconsistencies. She told me the cops had been unable to find credible witnesses who remembered seeing the white man that I'd described at Douglass Park on April 1. No one even remembered seeing me, Kareem, or Martin in the park that day. I began to sob.

"Goddamn it, boy, tell me the truth," my mother demanded.

I did. I confessed. I recanted. I apologized.

The police refocused their investigation and dragged Fall Creek for Martin's body. The fact that I had given a false statement and doomed the search for my brother from the start was kept out of the press.

It was all supposed to remain a family secret, but within a year, it felt like the whole city—except for Jackie—knew, and for a time, I believe I was the most despised person in Indianapolis. How I wished I was dead. Already living under the damnation of being a suspected faggot, I ruined what was left of my soul and reputation through my cowardice and deceit. In a way, I killed my brother.

Martin's body was never found. No one was arrested or brought to justice for his disappearance. In 1983, he was declared legally dead in absentia. My mother and father never spoke to me about my costly lies, never threw it in my face or lashed out in a rage. But it changed forever how they saw me—when they chose to look at me.

Rather quickly, I managed to think of my brother as dead without calling to mind the details surrounding his death. Never underestimate a Midwesterner's ability to live in a perpetual state of denial. For more than seven years, I had fought off the resurgent guilt that threatened to overrun me while never admitting that I was at war with myself. It took Peter Chatsworth's interrogation to force me to acknowledge the harm I had caused my brother, my family, myself. Grievous harm for which I was now ready to atone.

ALLIES DON'T ALWAYS HARMONIZE

Gregory watched with increasing annoyance as I began volunteering with Angie a few days a week. After my shifts, I would come back to our apartment too tired and emotionally drained to go out clubbing with him. But I would want to talk, so I would tell stories from the lives of the men that I had met—like Jeremiah, who worked the rodeo circuit as a champion saddle bronc rider, or Reggie, who cut diamonds for Tiffany's. None of the tales I shared sparked any interest in Gregory.

I invited him to come volunteer with me, if only for an hour. He kept blowing me off, until one night when I decided to call him out on it. Admittedly, I picked a poor moment to raise the issue. Gregory had recently been let go by a few more of his sugar daddies, and he was getting dressed in a pin-striped Perry Ellis suit (a gift from a former elderly lover) for a first date with a wealthy antiques dealer who was pushing seventy.[39]

---

39. Perry E. Ellis (1940–1986), a prominent fashion designer in the early 1980s, is a case study of the stigmatism surrounding AIDS, even among wealthy, prominent gay men of the era. Ellis repeatedly denied rumors that he had contracted AIDS—despite an obvious loss of weight and facial wasting, despite collapsing in the receiving line at a Costume Institute party, despite needing the help of two assistants to walk the runway during his last public appearance, and despite his long-term lover dying of lung cancer that had metastasized from Kaposi's sarcoma. Ellis's obituaries made no mention of AIDS. His cause of death was given as viral encephalitis.

"Do I look fresh?" Gregory asked me as I thumbed through an edition of *Paper* magazine.

I figured Gregory was just fishing for compliments. Without a doubt, he looked fresh—and sexy with his unblemished dark skin and his cocky demeanor. He didn't need me to tell him that. The mirror he had gotten dressed in front of should have confirmed that Gregory had achieved his goal: he was a walking young-Black-stud fantasy; the kind old, white, gay men paid to fuck them, while they imagined they were teenagers again and Gregory was the son of their family's maid or cook. What these white men wanted and dared not approach at sixteen was theirs to buy at the age of sixty-one. Fresh.

"He's going to love you," I said.

"You didn't even look me over," he complained.

"Are you going to nag me into telling you how hot you are?"

"Fuckin' forget it. I just wanted your honest opinion."

I sat up in my cot. "That so? Okay, okay—my honest opinion. These old men aren't leaving you because you've stopped looking sexy. They're dropping you because your heart isn't in this anymore. You're tired of it, and it's about time."

Gregory wagged his finger at me. "The last thing you is, lil man, is a mind reader. I'm not tired of how I score, and I sure as hell don't want to trade it in for what you got goin' on. No real job. But breaking your back for nothin' to clean up after a bunch of sorry mother-fuckers who are better off dead."

I jumped to my feet. "How do you know that about them? You haven't had the balls to face them. You should see how scared you get when I ask you to join me."

"I'm not scared. I just don't need to be seein' that shit."

"Because one day it could be you?"

The anger that had been animating Gregory's face vanished. He appeared at a loss for words. Then he found a few: "Or you," he said, "Miss Bathhouse Bottom."

I admitted, "You're right, but I've been using rubbers more. I'm even gonna get tested next week. You should do it, too."

"Fuck that. If I'm meant to get it, I'll get it. That'll be how it goes."

"You act like it's completely out of your hands."

"You been workin' with this Angie, but you still don't know the real story about AIDS." Gregory turned his back on me, faced the mirror, and loosened his tie to appear more rakish. "AIDS ain't nothin' but another word for *death*, and when death decides to come for you, it's out of your hands."

"Your life is what you make it," I insisted.

Gregory gave me the finger. "Maybe where you come from."

I fell silent, suddenly ashamed to have been born into money and embarrassed to have turned my back on it. Gregory left for his date, and I imagined how I must have appeared to him. Gregory was a true runaway with no choice in the matter. He had hustled for the clothes on his back and the cash in his wallet. He had survived being poor, Black, and gay in the city much longer than I had. Who the hell was I to lecture him about anything?

So I stopped asking him to volunteer with me at Angie's, and I tried to accept him on his terms. Fatalistic and wrongheaded as his conclusions seemed to me, I figured he had weathered enough trauma and adversity to be entitled to his convictions. Plus, I still loved Gregory. I still desired him and wanted to borrow the best qualities I saw in him.

What I had to accept, however, was that there was a divide between us. Money, with all its advantages and burdens, colored our worldviews and our assessment of each other. On a base level, he could see me as nothing more than an elective runaway, a trust-fund baby from the Midwest. To him, I would never be sufficiently streetwise. I would always be the naive kid brother. I would always be the bougie boy who could hightail it out of New York City and repent on the steps of my parents' mansion if I wanted to shake off the poverty and pressures that shackled Gregory. We were great friends, but not simpatico.

———

Lesbians had no place in my life, or so I thought until Angie schooled me. She and I were in her apartment preparing lunch for the dying men who had the strength to eat. I'd been volunteering with Angie a few days a week for the past two months. At her insistence, I had gotten my first HIV/AIDS test; my status was negative. Without being asked, I made sure to show up for shifts on Thanksgiving, Christmas, New Year's Day, and even on my nineteenth birthday.

Angie and I would bicker with growing affection for one another as we bathed infirm men, removed soiled bedsheets, or pressed cool, damp washcloths to burning foreheads. In the early days, it struck me as odd, almost callous, to carry on chitchatting while performing our melancholy chores. I'd grow quiet with reverence, and Angie would have none of it.

"Talk or go home," she barked.

"Okay, I'll try," I said. "But frankly, this place can make you lose your train of thought."

"Oh, for fuck's sake, just hop on another train. The talking isn't for my benefit. It's for theirs. It helps me gauge who's still working with a full deck and who's misplaced their aces and kings."

There was a method to her madness, as always. A lot of the men found our banter amusing. A few even joined in to snap a wisecrack, usually at my expense; Angie was intimidating. Then there were the guys who couldn't follow our conversations and were becoming oblivious to their surroundings. We tracked their mental capacity with our squabbling.

Most of what I talked about covered the new music I loved and the recent art exhibits I saw at museums. For her part, Angie would dismiss all new music as inferior to her favorite band, the Doors.

Then she'd assail the elitist nature of museums and ridicule modern art as "adult finger painting." Nothing earth-shattering.

Except when I really stepped in it. That occurred about once a week because Angie had primed me to say whatever came to mind, and I would quit filtering my thoughts around her. That's how we delved into the topic of lesbians in my life. I thought I was paying her a compliment, and Angie was astounded by my ignorance.

"You know, you're the first lesbian I've gotten close to," I said with a smile.

Angie harrumphed.

"What?"

"Tell me you're kidding. Tell me you don't honest-to-God believe that I'm the first dyke you've had a meaningful relationship with."

I mixed a cup of mayonnaise into the large batch of tuna salad that I was preparing, and I thought hard as I stirred. "Yeah, you are."

"Think back to when you were even younger than you are now. Think of any unmarried woman you knew over the age of thirty. Teachers, family friends—hell, maybe even an aunt or second cousin. Women who you heard described as 'liberated,' 'strong,' 'a tough cookie,' or 'handsome.' You got some women in mind?"

There was my second-grade teacher, Miss Atkins; my grade school principal, Miss Bridges; the owner of Lavern's Bar-B-Q, Miss Ramsey; the head of my church's fellowship committee, Sister Carson, who, come to think of it, was long-term roommates with my Sunday school teacher, Sister Strickland; my mother's hairdresser, Miss Blair; and my high school counselor, Miss Hammond.

"Can you picture them? See their faces?" asked Angie.

"Yeah."

"Now count backward from five for me. Do it aloud."

I cocked my head at her.

"Do it. This is gonna be like a magic trick."

"Five, four, three, two, one—"

"They're dykes! Every woman you're picturing is a card-carrying muff diver."

I laughed and shook my head. "Look, okay, I can see it with most of them. But Miss Blair was—"

"Beautiful? Ladylike?"

"That's not what I was going to say."

Although it was what I was thinking. Little dumb shit that I was. Sadly, I was in the vast majority for once. The typical gay man in 1987 was hardly more enlightened than the average hetty man when it came to lesbians, and I was no better than the typical gay man. It was as if butch lesbians were the only kind of lesbians that existed on the spectrum of visible light for men. Lesbians who presented themselves outside of the bull-dyke mold might as well have been gamma rays or infrared light. Men were blind to them.

"Call me crazy, but I'd bet all the money in my pockets and yours that Miss Blair is pretty enough to turn guys' heads when she glides all ladylike into a room."

I didn't dare confirm or deny.

"You don't have to admit I'm right. I already know I'm right." Angie mashed steamed carrots into a mush that was easier for the men to swallow. Her temper flared as she continued, "You been looking right through women—all women!—your entire life! You don't stop to consider what's going on inside of us. No, not at all! Why do that, shit for brains? What would be in it for you? That's why you didn't bother to notice lesbians have been helping make your world go round since before you discovered you had a cock and what it was for!"

I had learned not to hang my head or show any sign of fear in the wake of Angie's anger. I looked her dead in the eyes and with a sincere, even tone said, "Angie, I'm sorry."

"You should be!" Then she took a deep breath and said calmly, "You boys needs us more now than ever."

Angie and I remained quiet for a minute as we finished fixing lunch. Then I launched into a glowing critique of Janet Jackson's hit single "Control," and made a case for why the song should be the rallying cry for my generation. Angie argued that "Control" couldn't compare in vision and musicality to the Doors' "Break on Through (to the Other Side)." We were laughing as we fed the men their meals.

That's how I dealt with Angie's infamous temper. I let her rants and insults wash over me, secure in the knowledge that once she finished breathing fire, the dragon smoke would clear, and we would be friends again. Peter told me that damn near every volunteer he sent to help Angie couldn't handle her outbursts.

No two ways about it, Angie could be mean. It hurt when she once called me "the dumbest fairy north of the Mason-Dixon Line." Why, you ask? Because I accidently left the refrigerator freezer ajar and a carton of strawberry ice cream got soggy.

Although her put-downs did sting, I couldn't take them too personally. Her actions belied her words. I couldn't be *that* dumb if Angie relied on me—trusted me—to administer pills to the men in our care. She must have held me in some regard since she bothered to get me a card and gift for Christmas. (The card was blank, and she wrote in it, "Your silly God knocked up a virgin! Let's celebrate the bastard's birth!" And the gift was the Doors' album *Strange Days* on vinyl.) She might have even loved me—at least that's how I interpreted it when she began the ritual of saying goodbye to me after my volunteer shift by yanking me into a bear hug and kissing me on the forehead.

Besides, it was impossible to feel singled out because Angie gave so many people a tongue lashing. She went apeshit on deliverymen, repairmen, mailmen, the paper boy, the woman who lived in the unit above her, the old couple across the hall who let their cat roam through the building, and, without a second thought, the men dying of AIDS in her very own apartment. No one was safe, and that made it fair.

Other than her anger and her compassion, it was difficult to get a read on what made Angie tick. I tried one evening to go beyond our usual safe topics of discussion. It was January 25, 1987, and we let the Super Bowl air on the television in the living room. The New York Giants were playing the Denver Broncos, and quite a few of the guys with us were Giants fans. Others joined the viewing party just to kill time. Angie and I didn't give a damn about football, so we sat at the dining room table playing an epic game of war using two decks of cards.

"You're amazing," I began. "You've opened your home to these guys, and you're dedicating almost every waking hour to keeping them alive. How do you keep going? Why haven't you burned out?"

Angie slammed a jack of diamonds on top of my six of hearts, then scooped up both cards, adding them to her large pile. "Did Peter put you up to this?" she asked. "That pain in the ass has been on me to tell him my *selfish goal* since we were kids and Brenda snookered us into helping organize the first pride marches."[40]

"You've kept him in the dark all these years?"

"And in the dark is where he's gonna stay." She slid a three of clubs across the table. "That one's as good as yours."

I beat it with a ten of hearts. "If you really want to drive him crazy, tell me and not him."

"How much is he paying you to torture me with this nonsense?"

"You don't believe in the selfish goal theory?" I slid a queen of spades in her direction.

"Oh, I bet it holds true for men. You jack-offs can't be bothered to do anything unless you get something in return. Women—well, not all women—work differently." She flicked a five of clubs at me.

I tucked it into my meager pile of cards. "Then you call this altruism?"

The men watching the Super Bowl cheered and clapped as best they could. The Giants had scored another touchdown. With only a few minutes left in the final quarter, "our team" was sure to prevail.

"No," she shouted over the noisy men, "I'm not breaking my back

---

40. Brenda Howard (1946–2005), a polyamorous, bisexual, LGBTQ+ community organizer and activist, has been deemed the "Mother of Pride" for her central role in planning the first LGBT Pride March in New York City on June 28, 1970. She, at the age of twenty-four, recruited scores of people into the cause of turning Pride marches, parades, and parties into a national (and eventually global) monthlong initiative that raises visibility and advances the rights of the LGBTQ+ community.

to be nice! I'm doing this because it needs to be done, and I'd be more pissed off than I am if it weren't being done!"

I played an ace of diamonds and grinned. "Forgive me, for I'm only a man, but it sounds to me like you like being useful. That's what—"

"Wrong! I don't enjoy being useful. I don't enjoy a second of this. See, this is the problem. This is one of the widest gaps between men and women. The concept is foreign to you, but I'll say it plain as possible. Women fill a need because they see a need. We don't necessarily get pleasure from it. We don't expect a reward. We don't expect shit." Angie flipped an ace of hearts.

We spoke in unison, "I. De. Clare. War."

Angie's last card was a king of spades. Mine was an eight of hearts. She pumped her fist in the air and picked up her winnings.

"I used to go out to dinner parties," she said. "I'd be standing with eight or ten queers in a campy parlor, and over cocktails, a guest would tell a sob story about a friend of a friend who was very sick. The bullshit euphemisms. Even in that crowd, hardly anyone had the guts to say *AIDS*. Anyway, in this sob story, the friend of a friend got very sick, and his job fired him, or he just couldn't work, and his lover left him, or he didn't have a lover to begin with, and he fell behind on his rent, or his neighbors harassed him out of his apartment. Whatever the details, this very sick friend of a friend wound up homeless. Dying on the street like a goddamn animal. Everyone at the dinner party agreed it was horrible. Then a bell would ring, and we'd all go to the dining room and stuff our faces with filet mignon."

I reached across the table and took her hand in mine. She didn't pull away.

"I wish I'd rolled up my sleeves after the first time I heard one of those sob stories." She squeezed my hand tightly. "It took at least a year. A year of hearing about one friend of a friend after another. A year of debating who should step in and save these poor, blighted men. The city? The federal government? Homeless shelters? Charity groups? We never decided because our hosts announced dinner. And who would want to talk about something so morbid over a sumptuous meal?"

We fell silent for the next dozen rounds of war. Angie took most of the hands. The Super Bowl ended, and I went to help several of the guys move back to their beds, cots, and couches. One of the men that I had to practically carry was Barney Valentine. He was an elfin man—five-foot-five in heeled shoes—with a baritone voice and perfect pitch. Every word he spoke was imbued with musicality.

Barney stole my heart easy and fast. Radiating joy and mischief, he was a captivating raconteur. I'd listen to him and forget that AIDS was ravaging his body. It was like the sarcoma, the raspy cough, and the facial wasting vanished when Barney was spinning a tale. He had a million stories in him. For nearly two decades, Barney had been a dresser for Broadway shows.

He cherished his place in the theater. His specialty was dressing Black divas. Bigotry handed him that ripe plum. Or as Barney explained it, "Being an inconspicuous Negro, they'd only let me work with the Negro stars. I never let on that I preferred it that way." Then he winked and added, "I pushed for equality, but stopped before they gave it to me."

Barney, who was forty-eight when I met him, loved to dish the dirt on every star he'd zipped into a gown. He'd gotten his big break dressing Pearl Bailey, when she led an all-Black version of *Hello, Dolly!*[41] (Barney on Bailey: "She didn't read the whole play—just her lines, her songs. The director asked her what she thought Dolly's motivation was in her final scene of the first act, and Pearl said, 'I don't

---

41. Pearl Bailey (1918–1990) was a Tony Award–winning actress and singer. Bailey, a Republican who campaigned for President Gerald Ford and received the Presidential Medal of Freedom from President Reagan, costarred with Redd Foxx (1922–1991) in a progressive-for-the-era film comedy in 1976 that promoted acceptance toward homosexuals. In the film, *Norman . . . Is That You?*, Bailey and Foxx play parents who discover their son is gay and living with an effeminate white man. Many of the jokes rely on crude racial stereotypes, gay clichés, and gender norms, but Bailey's character accepts her son's homosexuality with relative ease and helps convince Foxx's character to do the same.

know, I don't care, and I don't see how it's any of my business.'") His favorite gig had been dressing Eartha Kitt in *Timbuktu!*[42] (Barney on Kitt: "She made every moment with her electrifying. It was compulsive. Other actors complained that she upstaged them, and they were correct. She couldn't help but steal focus.") His last show had been *Lena Horne: The Lady and Her Music.*[43] (Barney on Horne: "A workhorse. She could have whispered the lyrics to her songs and gotten standing ovations. But she pushed herself. She wanted to sing like Ella. She couldn't. But she gave her best every show.")

The night of the Super Bowl, I brought Barney to his cot. He sat gingerly on the edge of the steel frame. There were other men in need of my assistance, but it was clear Barney wanted to talk.

"I hate to impose," he said, "but I'd like you to deliver a letter after I die."

Surprised by his request, I flinched.

"I'd ask Angie, but she's not sentimental. You're a sweetheart, I can tell. I used to be the same. It would mean—"

"I'll do it," I said. "Who's the letter for?"

"My ex—Neil." Barney reached over to the side table and yanked a sealed envelope from between the pages of a thick book. "We broke up five years ago. I haven't seen him in two."

"You've got his address?"

"Yes." Barney rubbed the envelope tenderly in his hands. "We

---

42. Eartha Kitt (1927–2008) was an entertainer known for her cosmopolitan sex appeal, the sensual purr in her intonation, and her sultry rendition of the song "Santa Baby." Beyond her image as a perpetual sex kitten, Kitt was a dedicated activist, and her career suffered in the United States after she criticized the Vietnam War during a White House luncheon. Her remarks made First Lady "Lady Bird" Johnson (1912–2007) cry. Kitt also championed LGBTQ+ rights, voicing support for same-sex marriage before it became legal.

43. Lena Horne (1917–2010), who broke color barriers as an African American singer and actress in the movies when she became a contract player for Metro-Goldwyn-Mayer in 1942, leveraged her fame to bring notoriety to the Civil Rights Movement. Horne was also close friends with songwriter and arranger Billy Strayhorn (1915–1967). Strayhorn was openly homosexual, and Horne referred to him as "the only man I ever loved." She added, "He was just everything I wanted in a man . . . except he wasn't interested in me sexually."

split because I quit drinking, and I insisted he do the same. He told me I was being too controlling . . ."

"Hell, Barney, why don't you call him? You need to get this off your chest."

He thrust the letter into my hands. "I couldn't. It's been too long. And his boyfriend might answer the phone."

I nodded.

"Wait until I'm good and dead. Then go and put it in his hand."

Thirty-three men had died since I'd started volunteering at Angie's place. Everyone in our care spoke about their imminent deaths. Most were resigned to it. Some were afraid. More than a few were bitter and enraged. For my part, I'd learned not to annoy them with encouragement. *You can beat this* and *Keep fighting* were the verbal equivalents of salt on an open wound.

I put the envelope in my pocket and promised Barney, "I'll wait until you're dead."

"Thank you, Trey."

I started to leave him, and Barney grabbed my arm.

"You should find you a nice young fellow," he said. "A homebody."

He'd given me this advice before, and I appreciated his concern. He wanted me to survive this plague. A boyfriend who didn't fuck around on the side was the ticket to longevity. I wasn't against the idea on principle, but it was more complicated than Barney wanted to acknowledge. I wasn't exactly tripping over monogamous gay men on my way through the city.

I tried to brush him off gently and said, "If you know a sexy homebody, give me his number."

"I'm not in circulation like I once was," he said, "but there have to be other young men like yourself. Dedicated, politically minded. Are you going to be part of Larry's army?"

The Larry in question was Larry Kramer.[44] I hadn't met him ex-

---

44. Larry Kramer (1935–2020) was an indefatigable activist, strategist, organizer, playwright, author, and firebrand in service to the LGBTQ+ community for more than half a

actly. No one had introduced us, that is. I had, however, once listened to him address a small crowd on a street corner outside the Gay Men's Health Crisis (GMHC) headquarters. Larry had cofounded the GMHC but had subsequently broken ties with the organization. In a hectoring voice, Larry railed against the group's members and political approach so vehemently, I wondered if he regretted getting the ball rolling.

"Larry's got an army?"

Barney shrugged. "He's building one. It's sort of a secret but not. Who knows? Larry's crazy. My pal Charlie told me about it the other day when he popped by to visit me. Word is it's attracting a lot of young blood. You should look into it. Might land you a man."

I laughed and bid Barney good night. Over the next hour, I tucked in another half dozen men. Then I went to get my parting hug and kiss from Angie.

"You gonna shove off and head home?" she asked.

"Yeah, after a pit stop."

"How in the Sam hell can you spend hours with these bastards and still go frolic at a bathhouse?"

"I got condoms on me."

Angie erupted, "They're not a hundred percent safe!"

I ignored her outburst and asked, "Larry Kramer is starting an army?"

She muttered, "More like a cult."

"How's it going to work? What's the purpose?"

"That blowhard's read one too many books about the Student Revolution in Paris, and he's dreaming of leading an army of young queers who will take to the streets and throw bricks at cops."

"Where do I sign up?"

"Don't fucking joke," she said. "This ain't 1968. This ain't Paris. We throw bricks, and they will crack our skulls in."

Angie's opinion flat-out astonished me. I didn't want to get combative. I was just curious as to how she arrived at her conclusions. In retrospect, I could have been more tactful.

"Since when do you back down from a fight?" I asked. "Weren't you rioting at Stonewall?"

"Stonewall was different."

"How?"

"Back then, a disease wasn't slaughtering our men!" Angie covered her mouth with her hand.

"Isn't that all the more reason for us to take to the streets?"

"Lord, you're young."

"Don't give me that shit."

"No, I don't mean it like that. It's not a put-down. It's a fact," she said. "When I was nineteen, I thought marches could end wars. They don't."

"So we're wasting our time every June?"

"No, those marches matter. They raise visibility, they unite us, they give us a chance to regroup and reenergize. But marches can't solve what's happening in this apartment. We need to pool our own resources. You know how many rich fags and dykes there are in this country? We don't need to shed blood trying to force the government to do right by us. Because they won't. How is that not obvious by now? Burning down city hall won't solve shit."

I didn't know how to counter her argument. So I offered a qualified concession. "I see what you're saying. I can't say I agree. I need to think on it."

Then I stepped forward to claim my hug, and Angie wrapped her arms around me extra tight and held me close for longer than usual.

She kissed me on the forehead before whispering in my ear, "Don't get roped into Larry's ego trip. If he goes unchecked, he's gonna get a lot of innocent kids like you killed."

Walking through Mt. Morris's battered front door normally took away my worries. Tension would drain from my shoulders. My mind would pause its incessant chant of errands undone and problems unsolved. The only other place that managed to hush my anxieties as reliably as the bathhouse was the Museum of Modern Art.

Marcel spotted the strain on me as soon as I stepped up to the check-in booth. "What's got you down, brother man?"

I placed my wallet on the ledge. "A friend just begged me to stay away from this guy, and now I want to meet the guy more than ever, and I can't tell if that's just because I was told to stay away from him."

"Temptation be a muthafucker." Marcel put my wallet in a lockbox. "Adam only ate the apple 'cause God told him not to."

"Right."

"No good came from it, though. Adam probably didn't even like the taste of the apple."

"Or he could have loved it more than anything."

Marcel shook his head as he passed me a towel and room key. "You gonna do what you wanna do. Now go get some tail. Gotta good crowd tonight. Mostly room buyers."

He buzzed me in; I stripped naked in room 27 and headed to the sauna with my key around my wrist and a towel around my waist. The halls had a kinetic pulse. Men were going in and out of rooms. Doors were slamming shut. Beds were squeaking. Moans came through the walls. I felt charged. There was action everywhere.

I could have dived in and gotten my rocks off before I turned the first corner. Every guy I passed reached out to caress or grope my ass, cock, or nipples. A bull of a man beckoned me into his room. A threesome fucked with the door open and invited me to join them in putting on a show. This was going to be a fun night. Multiple scores. For whatever reason, I just didn't want to blow my first load yet.

My restraint was rewarded. I entered the sauna, and as to be expected, the light bulb had been unscrewed. The only light was coming through the square window in the wooden door. There were seven or eight men interlaced by their limbs, mouths, and cocks. Even in this free-for-all of hand jobs, blow jobs, grinding, and kissing, there was a focal point: one man that all the others were maneuvering to get their hands on. They were auditioning their sex talents on each other for his approval. He sat in the corner on the upper bench, and he decided who would be called forward to blow and rim him.

He was positioned so that the light from outside shone on his face and torso. He'd done this before. I respected his poise and artistry. He was gorgeous. Made perfect sense that he would be the shot-caller. I stood back and calculated how best to enter the scrum.

Then it hit me: I had seen him before. Tonight's shot-caller had cruised me when I'd been waiting to speak with Rustin, but Rustin had been scoring with a hot Taiwanese guy. What reminded me of our brief history wasn't his shaved head, his high cheekbones, his plump-lipped bow of a mouth, or his sinewy torso. It was his legs—thick thighs, bulging calves. His legs were shaped as if every muscle and curvature was in its ideal state.

I had to have him. This was the only score that mattered. He looked at me, remembered me, too, and smiled. I smirked, nodded at the door, and left the sauna. I didn't look back as I walked into the showers. It was a bold play, but I was banking on his earlier interest in me and the allure of unconsummated desire.

I wondered if I should have chosen a different spot for a rendezvous: six showerheads in an open room that was floored and walled in yellowish, pentagon-shaped tile. I got under a spray and washed up using the gritty, pink, industrial liquid soap in the wall pump. There were a few other men stroking themselves, and I gave them no signs of interest.

Despite my intention to act nonchalant, I stared at the entrance, trying to will the shot-caller into the room. A minute passed. Nothing. Another minute passed. Shit. Had I been too cocky to expect him to chase after me? Would he know to look for me in the showers? I should have waited in the hall outside the sauna. While I cursed myself out in my head, the shot-caller strolled into the showers and got under the spray next to me.

"I about started a riot because of you," he said with the coolness of a casual aside. "The men in the sauna complained, and a couple got pushy when I got up to leave."

"I hope I'm worth all the fuss."

"Me, too."

"My name's Trey. I've got a room."

"Nice to meet you, Trey. I'm Erik." He turned off his shower. "Lead the way."

We toweled off and hurried to room 27, and I locked the door behind us. I wanted no lookie-loos jerking off in the doorway and no assertive patrons helping themselves to our bodies. Erik hung his towel up on a hook. He stood naked with such ease and confidence.

"What are you into? Top, bottom, kissing, fucking?" I asked.

"I'm vers," he said. "There's nothing I can't do."

By God, he proved it. Erik set a relaxed tempo for our carnal pas de deux. His hands guided me, never tugging or forcing me into position. He dipped me onto the mattress, and once I was on my back, he mounted me without the usual bumps and lurching. Erik's ability to multitask was sensational. He kissed me while fingering me. He blew me while massaging my inner thighs. He was sucking my nipples as he tore open a condom wrapper and then rolled the latex sheath onto my erection. His body control and grace should have given it away that he was a ballet dancer.

I was scared I was going to cum too quick when he took my cock inside him and rode me to a four-count beat. His ass was milking my dick, and his tongue was licking inside my ears, and I almost cried out for him to stop. This was too much of a good thing. I didn't want to be a trick he conquered and discarded in less than fifteen minutes.

Erik decoded the tightening of my shoulders and the hesitation of my thrusts. "Don't hold back," he said.

I obeyed. My orgasm was volcanic. Erik marked my neck with

hickeys, and I let myself float on waves of warm bliss. Sex redefined. And we weren't done yet.

Erik asked, "What's your deal?" He removed the spent condom, tied it off, and threw it on the floor in the corner of the room. "You got a boyfriend waiting for you in the dorms? Or you got a papa bear who realizes that he's gotta let you have your freedom if he hopes to keep you?"

"Neither. I'm single. How about you?"

"Same. I prefer it this way." He slid down to my stomach, planting kisses, and heading lower. "I'm old and jaded—shacking up isn't for me."

"How old are you?"

"Twenty-four."

"That's not old."

"You'd be right if I was just twenty-four, but I'm a New York twenty-four." Erik lifted my cock and balls up and tongue-bathed my taint. "I've been making my own way in the city since I was sixteen."

"I moved here at seventeen," I managed to say before he hoisted my leg up onto his shoulders and started to eat me out. I moaned.

Erik worked me over for a couple of minutes, then picked up our conversation. "Wait and see, you'll be an old twenty-four one day. You'll find out that single is where it's at."

I couldn't see his hands, but I heard the crinkle of a condom wrapper being ripped open. "Did you have a bad breakup?" I asked.

"No, not especially. I've gotten bigger headaches from the men I refused to fuck than the ones I have." Erik sat back on his haunches and fitted himself with a condom.

"How so?"

"I'm a ballet dancer, and the men that pull the strings, the men that write the checks, treat us like whores. I can't count how many times I've been told to *entertain* a donor."

Erik's cock penetrated me in a soothing, steady push. He let me adjust to the feel of him inside me. Then he fucked me in every position I knew and several others I had never imagined were possible.

The keys to his stellar performance were his powerful legs. They never tired, they never failed him. I almost applauded him at several points.

Not that I just lay there. Erik's sexual prowess spurred me to heighten my game. I sensed that he enjoyed edging, and I repeatedly brought him to the precipice of climax, then walked him backward until he was pleading (in delicious anticipation) for me to get him off. When I finally did, Erik was breathless. He collapsed on top of me, and I could feel his heartbeat racing.

He sat up and stretched his arms out to the side. "What time is it?"

I reached over for my watch, which was buried in my pile of clothes, and my pants shifted, and Barney's letter slid out of my pocket and onto the floor. "Eleven fifty-two," I answered.

Erik picked up Barney's letter. "What's this?"

"Long story."

"Goodie! I love long stories. Tell it to me."

I prepared myself to hate him. This could have been the turn where I realized Erik was little more than an amazing lay. Because if he made one wisecrack about Barney or the letter, I was going to tell him to fuck off and get out of my room.

But he didn't. Erik curled up naked on the rubber mattress and listened. At the end of my explanation, he climbed onto my lap and made out with me. I wasn't prepared to like him so damn much.

"I've got rehearsal in the morning," he said.

I resorted to my standard closing lines. "I really enjoyed this . . ."

He fished through my clothes and found a pen and a crumpled receipt. "Here's my phone number," he said as he scribbled. "If you call, I'll answer."

"Thank you. I'll call."

"Don't promise anything. I like surprises."

We kissed, and he left wrapped in his towel. I lay back on the mattress and stared at the ceiling for a while. I don't think I'd ever checked out of Mt. Morris after only one score. It felt against the rules. Could I call it a night? Or should I do a lap through the maze and see what turned up?

Sick of my own dithering, I found a quarter in my coat pocket and flipped it. Heads, I stay. Tails, I go. The quarter landed in my palm. I was dressed and headed for the exit. Erik would be my one and only that night.

On my way to the front, I caught a glimpse of Rustin in his jumbo towel a second before he walked into the break room. We had celebrated my victory over Fred Trump weeks ago. I had no pressing issues to discuss with him—except I was curious what he would make of what Angie had said about Larry Kramer.

I entered the break room, and there was Old Rustin attempting to rock the vending machine side to side. I could see why: he'd paid for a Snickers, but the spinning coil in row C5 had failed to release the candy bar. Rocking the machine was the cheapest solution. The other fix was to put another quarter in and repeat the selection. The first candy bar would surely fall, and a second one, too, if you were lucky.

"Rustin, let me help you," I offered.

"I'd kindly appreciate it."

I retrieved the quarter from my coat pocket and moved to deposit it into the vending machine.

"Stop," said Rustin. "Don't put any more money in that contraption."

"I don't mind."

"I do. I paid already. It should give me what it owes me."

"Okay. Why don't we rock it together?"

I pushed on one side, and Rustin shoved the other side. We had the vending machine swaying and striking the floor with a rhythmic bang until the candy bar dropped. Rustin hooted and slapped me on the back.

"Thank heavens you came along," he said. "I tell you things were better before they installed that big vending machine. They had a fellow who sold sandwiches, apples, and Pepsi-Cola. You didn't have to shake him to get what you paid for. Nice fellow. He lost his job to the machine."

"When was this?" I asked.

"Nineteen sixty-seven or sixty-eight."

Astonished, I asked, "How long have you been coming to this sex pit?"

Rustin sighed as he thought. "Let's see . . . Jimmy's the one who first brought me. I'd heard of Mt. Morris, but I wouldn't have had the nerve to walk through the door in those days, if Jimmy hadn't pressed me to join him one night. I think it was after he returned from Paris. So probably '58. Although it could have been a year or two later because Jimmy used to read to me whatever he was working on, and I distinctly recall hearing the first half of *Another Country* in the sauna."

Rustin leaned against the vending machine and started to eat his Snickers.

My mind went into overload. Jimmy. *Another Country*. My mouth fell open, and Rustin noticed.

"What's the matter?" he asked.

"James Baldwin!" I shouted.[45] "James Baldwin dragged you into these baths and turned you out!"

"Turned me out," Rustin repeated, unsure what the expression meant. "Jimmy and I didn't have sex with each other, if that's what you are implying."

Well, Rustin had indeed answered one of the dozen questions about Baldwin that raced to the tip of my tongue. None of the questions were about the acclaimed author's writing because that wasn't a topic of much interest to me. I was a fan of Baldwin more out of obligation than passion. I liked his essays, but never finished his novels. I respected his activism during the Civil Rights Movement, but it gnawed at me that arguably the most famous gay Black man in America didn't use his status to advance the gay agenda. Not that

---

45. A writer, civil rights activist, and public intellectual, James A. Baldwin (1924–1987) is a lionized and influential figure in literary sets and liberal political circles. While Baldwin made no efforts to hide his homosexuality, he took no significant role in the Gay Rights Movement.

I thought about Baldwin often or deeply, but when I did, he was forever a dry, cold subject.

Now, the revelation that Baldwin had been dicking down tricks in Mt. Morris during the Eisenhower administration got my blood going. I couldn't help but strip the author out of his dark suits and picture him clad in a little white towel.

In an unabashed torrent, I asked, "When's the last time he came down here? And what's he like on the prowl? Does he hunt, or is he more of a watcher? Does he go to the dark room? Do you think he would cruise me?"

Rustin laughed, which caused him to choke a little on his candy bar. He coughed and cleared his throat as he took a seat in the break room. I fetched him a cup of water from the lukewarm watercooler.

Rustin drained the cup before answering, "In his prime, Jimmy would have seduced you in a heartbeat. He had a way about him. Regrettably, he's been ailing of late."

"Baldwin was a player," I mused. "I wouldn't have guessed it. He always looks so serious and buttoned-up, and even though he's gay on sight, I pictured him talking about sex more than having it. Like an academic homo, not a fucking one."

"No, no," Rustin said, "Jimmy's an open, proud, red-blooded gay man. I can testify to it."

"Proud? Has he ever waved the rainbow flag?"

I spoke without considering the decades of friendship between Rustin and Baldwin. It was impolite of me, but also honest. To me, Baldwin was neither a sacred icon nor a lifelong intimate. He was a man; he could be called into question.

Rustin sat up straight. "Since the day he was born, Jimmy's presented himself as he is, and he's written openly in his novels about the gay life."

Rustin's defense was too easy, too pat, and it pissed me off that he'd try to shut me down with the kind of line fit to silence a child.

I sniped, "But—and correct me if I'm wrong—Baldwin doesn't

lead pride parades. He's not out there on gay rights the way he was on civil rights. He hasn't said or written a thing about AIDS."

Anger flashed in Rustin's eyes, but it didn't register in his voice. "Trey, you're being too harsh on Jimmy. Have mercy. You don't understand the choices he and I and other gay Black men were forced to make. Neither movement welcomed us to lead the parades. You had to sort of choose one, knowing that the side you cast your lot with would still question your loyalty."

Rustin was correct: I didn't understand. Not then. Not for many years. Neither of us said a word for a minute or two as other men breezed in and out of the break room.

Finally, I broke the silence. "Rustin, can I run something by you?"

"Most certainly."

I recited Angie McBroom's remarks on Larry Kramer and the rumors of him forming an army of confrontational activists. About a minute into my spiel, I notice that Rustin had knitted his brow and pursed his lips. He grew increasingly dour as I continued, but I didn't know why. I felt like a kid unwittingly tattling on himself to a teacher. Yet I couldn't shut up.

When I was done, Rustin's first question was, "How did you get mixed up with the likes of Angela McBroom?"

My guard was up. "A friend of mine in GMHC introduced me to her."

"I thought she'd washed her hands of organized political work. She had a breakdown in '80 or '81 at one of the last big Gay Activist Alliance meetings.[46] Stood up on a table in front of everyone, screaming and carrying on."

"Was she screaming crazy, or did she have a point?"

---

46. The Gay Activists Alliance (1969–1981) pursued a moderate approach to advancing the rights of gays and lesbians by working through the political system. The alliance was created by dissatisfied members of the more radical Gay Liberation Front (1969–1973), which itself was formed as a reaction to frustration with the centrist philosophy of the North American Conference of Homophile Organizations (1966–1970).

Rustin ran his fingers through his shock of white hair. "If I recall, it was the same lament every haggard activist gives before stomping off into the wilderness. 'You're not making my priorities your priorities, you're not following my strategy, and you can all kiss my ass.'"

"Yeah, but what did she want everyone to do?"

He huffed. "Angela is provincial, small-time. She's got no interest in a national or global movement. She believed we could create a world where we looked after our own. Zero government support. Insanity. We'd just pass the hat among ourselves, and we'd open soup kitchens and homeless shelters. Anything grander than that is beyond her. She can't see the big picture."

I'd heard quite enough against Angie. "Does Larry see the big picture?"

"Yes and no. He does get that we need government involvement to combat AIDS *and* to end the discriminatory laws that target homosexuals."

"But?"

"He's got no patience for the political process. He rejects compromises and incremental gains. I've seen him in action. He's a bully and a zealot. Now, it can be useful to have an agitator like Larry in the movement. His threats can convince politicians to work with more moderate factions. But Larry's a liability because he doesn't know where the line is."

"How do you feel about this army he's starting?"

"Makes me uneasy. If he instigates violence or destruction, it could set the movement back years."

I flashed a wry grin. "Then you and Angie do agree on something. She doesn't want me to get involved in it either."

"Actually, Mayor Koch asked me personally to help monitor the Gay Rights Movement in the city," Rustin confessed in a hushed tone. He put a hand on my shoulder. "If you were willing, there could be tremendous benefits to you joining Larry's ranks."

———

What Rustin proposed gave me so much to think about that I walked from Harlem to SoHo after midnight in winter. He wanted me to be his man inside Larry's army. Track the group's progress and report back to Rustin on its intentions. A spy? I'd asked. No, Rustin assured me. Spies want to destroy the people they monitored. I'd be protecting this young band of activists from becoming Larry's sacrificial lambs. I hesitated to accept the assignment. Think it over, Rustin suggested. Think it over—I agreed to do so.

The arrangement felt like one my father would propose, although I realized that alone wasn't a reason to reject it. Only when I was lying awake in my apartment did I conclude that I was grappling with more than *Should I* or *Shouldn't I.* The thornier question was *Where the fuck am I?* The landscape as I recognized it had become jumbled. Bayard Rustin, Angela McBroom, and Larry Kramer were lifelong, far-left-of-center gay rights activists, and I'd taken it for granted that they'd be more or less comrades in arms. To my nineteen-year-old brain, it was disturbing enough to be exposed to the ideological fissures and deep-seated animosity between the three of them. To also find myself at the intersection of their political agendas was disorienting.

Super Bowl Sunday of 1987 was my introduction to the thankless work of recalibrating the shifting alliances of the individuals in my orbit. Charting out the crosscurrents between peers and friends can be maddening and painful, but the benefits are akin to self-preservation. You can't protect your interests if you don't have an accurate understanding of everyone else's.

Still, it is a task I loathe because it requires you to take a hard look at the history, the shortcomings, and the motives of people you respect, maybe even revere, and perhaps even love. Among a host of unflattering conclusions that will be laid bare, the most common one will be that a good person has become warped by defeat, success, or jealousy, and can no longer adapt to the current political moment or the ascendant leaders shaping the scene. It's just one of those things. People lose their touch; people lose their way.

LEARN TO TAKE A PUNCH

Gregory promised to take the lead in finding our next apartment because Fred Trump had had me blacklisted throughout the five boroughs. We had already wasted a month before I figured out that putting my name on the rental application was the kiss of death. So we decided to have Gregory apply for apartments alone, and I would just move in with him and pay half the rent. This plan also hit a snag: Gregory's credit history was shit. Unbeknownst to me (yet coming as no surprise), Gregory had bounced checks and over-drawn accounts at a few of the country's largest banks. He also was delinquent with payments on his outstanding balance for more than $25,000 in credit card debt.

The first of February came and went, and Gregory and I had less than a week to vacate our apartment. Panic set in. I contemplated a move to Brooklyn. I floated the idea to Gregory while he was using clippers to cut and line my hair.

"Nah, we not movin' out there," he said.

"Why not? There are places in Bed-Stuy that don't care about bad credit."

"Hold still, or I'mma mess up."

I moved my mouth as little as possible as I said, "We don't have much time left."

"The temp agency won't be able to call me in last minute if I'm out in Bed-Stuy, and we'd be in trouble with you. Too many Black closet cases for you to be turnin' out."

He'd gotten me good. I was stunned speechless.

Gregory cackled. "That's your thing now, right?"

"When did you find out about me and Harrison?"

"Lil man, I seen you two were gonna fuck from the jump."

"I could have sworn when we met him that he was a hundred percent hetty."

"Hold still. I'm almost done." Gregory blew on the clippers to clean some of my hair out of the blades. "He kept licking his lips when he listened to you talk. I knew what he was hungry for, and I knew you wouldn't say, 'No.'" He finished lining up my hair and turned the clippers off. "Plus, I seen you two sneak off into the parking garage."

"Damn, I thought we were careful."

"No one ever fucks around without tippin' off somebody who ain't supposed to know."

I checked out my hair in a hand mirror. "Looks sharp. Thanks."

"C'mon, now that I done told you about yourself. You don't wanna do the same to me?"

"You threatened me, you hit me upside the head. You told me I didn't see what I saw. So forgive me for not being gung-ho to talk it over with you."

"I'm sorry. I freaked out. I shouldn't've. But that guy—"

"The congressman," I clarified. "Congressman Galbreath."

"Oh, alright, so you're wise to him." He wiped the clippers clean and put them away in our bathroom medicine cabinet. "I was gonna have to tell you about him, because he's how we're going to get our new apartment."

I brushed the loose hairs on my head and shoulders directly onto the kitchen floor. Fuck Papa Trump. We weren't leaving the unit clean.

"Let me guess," I teased. "We're going to live in his district."

Gregory rolled his eyes. "They got this lottery for public housing in Harlem, and all we gotta do is fill out these forms, claiming we're brothers."

"I'll sign whatever, but if we don't win a lottery space—"

"They done had the lottery already. But Leslie—the congressman—fixed it so we can have one of the apartments. See, they hold some units out of the lottery to give to whoever they want to. We just gotta turn in the forms. I thought of just signing your name, but it's important we act like brothers."

"Okay."

"Okay? What about, 'That's awesome. You're the man, Gregory.'"

I forced a smile. "I'm happy. It's just that this congressman makes me nervous. Have you read up on him?"

"He's a Republican, but you know I don't give a shit about politics. Most the daddies I fuck are Republican."

"He still refers to AIDS as gay cancer! He's said that anyone who gets AIDS through sex or drug use should have to pay for all their sins and their healthcare without government assistance! He—"

"Don't yell at me. I didn't vote for him."

"He's evil, and you're sleeping with him, and we'll both owe him a favor if we do this."

"Whatta you mean *if*? I can't pull another rabbit out of the hat. We do this, or we're on the streets."

———

Gregory and I moved into the Harlem River Houses three days later. The redbrick apartment buildings looked vibrant in contrast to the winter gray skies, and our two-bedroom unit on the third floor had fresh paint on the walls and a working heater. The rent was fifty dollars less a month than we'd paid to live in Trump's hellhole. We were welcomed as warmly as I expected. Our new neighbors eyed us warily while offering faint smiles. To establish how we hoped to be seen, Gregory laid it on thick, referring to me as his brother whenever another tenant was within earshot.

Erik declined to help us carry any of our bags, but he bought us meatball subs for lunch, and he gave me a pink orchid. I had called Erik the evening after we had sex in the bathhouse. Gregory had warned me against appearing too eager, but Erik had sounded excited to hear from me. He invited me to meet him in a Greek restaurant that was up the street from his apartment in Chelsea.

I hadn't spent much time in the city's fabled gayborhood. On the occasions I was there, I bumped up against an insider bravado that repelled me. I quickly realized that Chelsea gays not only shared every New Yorker's disdain for tourists but expanded their circle of contempt to include anyone who didn't live in Chelsea.

But now I had Erik by my side, and I felt comfortable and accepted. It was in Chelsea that I finally got to experience the minor freedoms that should imbue every life. At dinner, Erik and I held hands and stole kisses from one another. Our waiter told us we were a cute couple and didn't charge us for a round of drinks. On the way back to his place, Erik and I walked the streets arm in arm.

The sex between us remained athletic and invigorating. Our conversations were delightful, too. Although Gregory immediately started referring to Erik as my "boyfriend," we didn't put a label on our relationship. We were too progressive for such antiquated notions that one person had ownership claims over another person because the two were fucking. Or, at least, that was how Erik explained it to me when I jokingly (not jokingly) asked if we were "going steady."

Usually, Erik and I met up about every other day when he wasn't out of town. I still went to Mt. Morris regularly, and I know Erik did, too, because we ran into each other at the bathhouse unplanned more than once. Jealousy didn't rear its head. I felt I was getting the best of both worlds: intimacy with one special man on some nights, and anonymous sex on others. In a way, I was living the dream of most homosexual men.

Besides, even a dating novice like me could see that the smart move was to be low maintenance if I wanted to keep Erik's attention and affection. His career alone stressed him out plenty and sapped his energy. He was a principal for the Dance Theatre of Harlem; a guest artist for the Joffrey Ballet in Chicago; and a principal guest artist with the Dayton Ballet. In addition to those commitments, Erik would rearrange his packed schedule at a moment's notice if Arnie Zane asked him to perform with the Bill T. Jones / Arnie Zane Dance Company.[47] Erik worshipped Arnie and therefore envied Bill.

The rehearsals, performances, plane flights, and jet lag meant that Erik often dozed off if we went to the movies or watched television in his dark bedroom. Sometimes I would grab takeout and bring it to his place because he was too sore to move or he had to elevate and ice his legs. Then there were the days he was gone or too busy to see me at all. Sounds frustrating? Well, in truth, I liked that I couldn't take him for granted. I felt so adult managing and rolling with the demands of his creative life. I got a charge out of *not* being able to count on seeing him when I wanted to. It made me appreciate the minutes we were together.

———

My stomach was in knots the evening I disobeyed Angie. I'd tried to behave like nothing was out of the ordinary, but during the last hour of my volunteer shift, I kept catching her eyeing me. We were rotating Kenny Purdue—a twenty-six-year-old short-order cook, who deteriorated from coherent to catatonic in less than two weeks—to prevent him from getting bedsores. As I wrapped a blanket around Kenny, Angie asked me where I planned to go after I left her apartment.

"I'll go over to Erik's for dinner. I'm in the mood for tomato soup, and there's this deli that serves the—"

47. The Bill T. Jones / Arnie Zane Dance Company was founded in 1983 by its two namesakes, who choreographed together, danced together, and were lovers. In 2011, a merger between Jones/Zane and the Dance Theater Workshop created what is known as New York Live Arts.

"Erik's in Chicago." She sized me up. "That's what you said when we were feeding Mateo."

"Damn, you're right." I rubbed my eyes with my hands. "I've gone and gotten my days mixed up. He's in Chicago, so I'll swing by Mt. Morris."

Angie grunted. "Or here's an idea—give your prick a rest, go home to your own bed, and get some sleep. You've been cloudy-headed all day, and you know if you so much as suspect that you might be coming down with something, you have to stay away. The common cold would be a serial killer in here."

"No, no, of course. I would never come here sick."

She sent me out the door with a hug and a kiss. Fifteen minutes later, I was standing outside of 2 Fifth Avenue in Greenwich Village waiting on Peter. He was plugged into the clandestine assembly of Larry's army, and with Peter vouching for me, I was invited to attend this hush-hush planning meeting. At least twenty militant queers marched by me and up to the call box before getting buzzed into the apartment building. I didn't have the nerve to go in without Peter.

"About time," I said when he arrived.

With that unabashed goofy smile of his, Peter danced a jig. "Loosen up. These meeting always start late."

"You're the one who told me to be here at seven o'clock sharp."

"And I congratulate you on your punctuality. How's Angie doing?"

"She's good. She doesn't know I'm here, and we've got to keep it that way."

"Hey, I don't want her all over my ass for leading you to the dark side."

"Shall we?" I asked.

I took a step toward the call box, and Peter held me back.

"I don't mean to scare you, but whatever it is we do upstairs is gonna be page one of your fed file, and tonight isn't exactly a boiler-plate informational meeting."

"What is it?"

Peter ballooned his cheeks, then blew the air out in an exaggerated exhale. "I've been meaning to call you and give you a heads-up. I wrote it on Post-it note after Post-it note. Call Trey. Talk to Trey. But the Post-it notes don't stay put and—"

"What am I walking into?"

"A proving ground."

On the way up to Larry Kramer's apartment, Peter explained that I had missed the gentle recruitment meetings where they'd served pastries and coffee. The current stage was focused on testing the mettle of would-be participants and weeding out the weak ones. It was going to be intense, but he was sure I would make the cut.

"Larry was impressed with how you came through for Walton, and Larry is impossible to impress."

"You told him about that?"

"I had to. He wasn't going to let you just walk into this. I had to show him that you've got chutzpah."

I was flabbergasted, and Peter threw his arm around my shoulders, ushering me into Larry's apartment. We were greeted by the commotion of three dozen side conversations underway simultaneously. Not all the discussions were friendly. More than a few people were shouting their points at the tops of their lungs. I only picked up snippets of the various debates as Peter led me into the living room, and that was all the evidence I needed to believe that everyone in Larry's apartment was smarter than me.

The crowd skewed young, but these weren't wide-eyed freshmen who trusted priests, cops, and elected officials. These kids—my peers—were dissecting the nuances of structural racism, unconscious misogyny, the prison industrial complex, the moral decay of capitalism, and the cycles of violence condoned by religion. Now, I was still working my way through my Rustin reading list, but I have to admit that I grasped the biographies (Myrlie Evers's *For Us, the Living*) and struggled to digest books on political theory (Frantz Fanon's *The Wretched of the Earth*). The gaps in my knowledge were vast. In Larry's apartment, I overheard the word *intersex* for the first time in my life, and I didn't have a clue what it meant. I suddenly worried that I didn't have anything to contribute to a group this intellectual.

Peter brought me to where most of the older—and by that, I mean midthirties to midsixties—activists were gathered. They were balding, going gray, or completely silver haired; they were plump around the middle or gaunt; they were stooped by age or remained upright in defiance of it. If I had passed any of these seasoned rabble-rousers as individuals on the street, I wouldn't have considered a single one of them a threat to anything. Together they looked like a staff of undistinguished high school teachers. Peter introduced me to them en masse with a casual, "Boys and girls, this is Trey."

Six or seven of them shook my hand and introduced themselves in such rapid succession that I had no hope of remembering their names. I noticed a few smirked at me, and I realized they assumed that I was Peter's boy toy. Not the first impression I aspired to make, but I wasn't sure their assessments of me would improve if I blurted out, "I'm not a rent boy, I'm not rough trade, and I'm not fucking Peter."

Conversations ceased when Larry emerged from his bedroom. An elegant Black woman with her head wrapped in a blue turban walked beside him. She was in her fifties and had the sanctified aura of a church mother.

Larry climbed up onto a coffee table to address the sixty people crammed into his living room, hallway, and kitchen. Peter and I stood to Larry's right with our backs to a window. I was struck by how Larry fidgeted while cleaning his glasses on his untucked, white dress shirt. He opened his mouth to speak a couple of times only to close it with a sigh. He was not naturally ferocious or eager to roar. He was a lamb who had to rev himself up to become a lion.

"Thank you for coming," said Larry. "I have an urge to play host and offer each of you food and wine, but I'd go broke trying to feed this many people."

There was polite laughter, and the boisterous ones among us clapped and whistled. Larry flashed a quick grin. His shoulders relaxed.

"Actually," Larry continued, "it's good I can't play host because this is *not* a party. We are here to find out who can take a punch. *Take* being the operative word. The group we're forming will require discipline. When we confront our enemies, it won't be like that fist-fight you got into with a drunk closet case at Rawhide's. You won't get to trade punches. And it's not going to be like the night you got whipped and fisted at the Anvil.[48] There won't be a safe word to make it stop. We're charging into a war where we don't get to fire back, and yet we can win it, if we train ourselves properly."

Larry offered his hand to the Black woman in the blue turban. She kicked off her heels and joined him on the coffee table.

"We are lucky to have with us tonight Ms. Dorothy Cotton.[49] She graciously drove down from Ithaca to lead us in a workshop on how to engage in effective nonviolent resistance without getting our teeth knocked out."

"I hate to be contrary," Dorothy said with a trace of a Southern accent, "but there is no guarantee that teeth won't be knocked out. I have difficulty hearing out of my left ear on account of an attack I suffered during a wade-in." She put her right hand to her chin and regarded her audience, predominately young and white. "Who under the age of thirty knows what a wade-in is?"

Dead silence for a second or two.

"It's what you did to integrate a whites-only beach or public pool," I found myself saying before having decided to speak. "You sit in at a lunch counter. You wade in at the shore."

---

48. At first blush, the Anvil (1974–1986) had the hallmarks of a regular gay club: a dance floor, pop music, and a bar. Downstairs is where it earned its notoriety. That's where patrons could watch gay male porn on a big screen and enter a large, dark room that catered to the BDSM crowd. In 1986, Anvil was closed by order of the New York City Department of Health.

49. Dorothy Cotton (1930–2018) was the educational director of the Southern Christian Leadership Conference (SCLC). In that role, she served as an influential leader of the Civil Rights Movement, as a dynamic teacher of nonviolent resistance, and as an organizer of voter registration drives in African American communities in the South.

Dorothy pointed at me and jabbed the air. "Exactly. I marched twelve children into the water with me that day. Down in St. Augustine, Florida. The sky was clear and bright. We weren't in the water but ankle deep before them white people were on us. Vicious." She closed her eyes and took a cleansing breath. "Not one of the twelve children let me down." She opened her eyes and scanned the room slowly. "Not one of those children abandoned the lessons I taught them. The same lessons I will attempt to instill in you."

After a nod from Dorothy, Larry gave us instructions. "We're doing this five at a time. We'll select you at random. The chosen five will go into my bedroom for their crash course with Dorothy. It should take thirty to forty minutes a round. We've got a lot of people, so prepare to stay late. If you've got a problem with that, there's the door. It's going to be intense. I anticipate crying and cursing and people storming out. So be it. We can't have weak links when the cops are out for faggot blood. If this is too much for you, we need to know it now."

Dorothy raised her hand. "There is no shame in not being able to complete the training. I believe God gives us different missions to perform. It is not everyone's calling to face evil as I have. If you learn tonight that this is not your calling, the true shame would be if you fail to go forward and find out how else you can serve the cause."

"Alright, let's get to it!" Larry shouted.

An older man offered to help Dorothy step down from the coffee table, but she waved him off and hopped onto the floor. She reminded me of my aunt Maxine: militant and cheerful. Larry did indeed just select five people willy-nilly. They followed him and Dorothy into the bedroom, shutting the door behind them.

Peter poked me in the ribs. "You ready for this?"

"I think so. I'm nervous, but somehow this feels right. Probably sounds crazy, but I feel like I've been waiting to do this. How about you?"

"I didn't care for that joke Larry made about S and M at the Anvil, and I'm going to let him know it when I get the chance."

"Out of everything those two said to us, that's at the top of your mind?"

"He belittled relevant experience. All the years I've devoted to torture play are going to be tremendously helpful." Peter pulled me in close to whisper in my ear. "When the cops beat my ass, I'm liable to cum."

He doubled over laughing, and I pushed him away. Secretly, I appreciated Peter's puckish irreverence. His humor was my canary in the coal mine. If Peter stopped kidding around, then we were in serious trouble.

Those of us not in the bedroom reverted to small group conversations. Peter and I were speculating about what exactly our training would entail. Only Peter kept looking past me while I was talking. Eventually, I followed his gaze and discovered that he was checking out a spiky-haired, twenty-five-year-old Puerto Rican man with a nose ring.

"You're cruising him—right now, right here?" I asked.

"For starters, we're cruising each other," said Peter. "Secondly, any place is fair game to cruise. I've picked up guys waiting for STD results at the free clinic. Finally—"

Muffled yelling came out of Larry's bedroom. It startled and quieted everyone in the rest of the apartment. Then we all pretended that it was nothing that we should continue to acknowledge, and we resumed our conversations.

"Finally," Peter concluded, "couples with common interests, such as political activism, last longer."

"Your master teach you that?"

"No, but before Master Yuri, I dated Liam for four and a half years."

"Liam?" I teased. "You've never mentioned Liam."

A white man in his thirties stormed out of Larry's bedroom screaming, "Fuck these mind games!" He pushed through the crowd with his head down. His hair was dripping wet, and the top of his sweater was soaked. He left slamming the door behind him.

Seeing the first person flee was unsettling, but I kept my cool. Larry had told us this would happen. So an irate man shoving his way out of the apartment made sense in context. I reminded myself that we, in fact, needed people to run out of here. This was natural selection.

I prodded Peter. "Liam?"

"He left me to join the priesthood. One day, I'll tell you the whole saga. Promise. Right now, my next great love is coming toward us."

I turned, and the spiky-haired man with the nose ring was already less than a foot from us. He leaned past me to greet Peter with a hug and kiss on the cheek. I received a handshake.

He introduced himself as Eduardo Ramirez.

"Great name," said Peter. "I can already imagine myself moaning it."

Peter and Eduardo flirted relentlessly while I played the third wheel. A woman left Larry's bedroom trembling and in tears. She fled the apartment with her face in her hands. My heart went out to her. I wanted to give her a hug or offer her a Kleenex.

Against the wall near me, there was a frail man talking to a bald woman, and I heard him whisper, "I bet she was a plant."

"Without a doubt," the bald woman agreed. "No one I know had ever seen that bitch around before."

Shortly thereafter, two young men exited the bedroom holding each other as they departed together. The first group was whittled down to one: Nuwa, a young, lesbian, Chinese Ph.D. student who weighed less than a hundred pounds and stood four-foot-eleven.

The next five were chosen. Two made the cut. Another five disappeared behind the bedroom door. On and on, group after group. The majority of the chosen were soaking wet when they returned to the living room, eliminated or triumphant. The shouts coming out of Larry's bedroom got harder to ignore as our numbers thinned out into the night. Some groups lost all five members. I remember only one group that produced three survivors. I wondered if either of my parents had gone through anything like this when they were young activists.

Those that graduated from the training kept to themselves in the kitchen. They'd been forbidden from discussing their experiences with the uninitiated. Many of us who were still waiting to be tested grew pensive and quiet. The notable exceptions were Peter and Eduardo, who were cracking each other up discussing their hysterical mothers.

I read the titles of the hundreds of books on the shelf-lined walls in Larry's living room, and my mind drifted to Erik. I wondered what he would make of me auditioning to join Larry's army. I hadn't mentioned it to him because he and I didn't contemplate heavy issues. Easy, breezy, uncomplicated—that was our code. Would Erik deem this righteous or ridiculous?

There was no question as to Gregory's opinion. I'd had to teach him who Larry Kramer was and explain the underground desire for an army of activists who would take dangerous steps beyond marching peacefully. He had listened respectfully until I mentioned joining the radical band of activists. Then he shouted, "Why? You tryin' to be the muthafuckin' queen of drama queens!" We argued off and on about it for the next three days.

At 11:30, Larry picked four people, then said, "Peter, join me in my boudoir."

It was a setup Peter couldn't resist. He started to sashay across the living room and delivered a perfect vocal impersonation of Mae West. "Oh, Larry, I thought you'd never ask."

The room erupted into laughter and catcalls. The tension mercifully subsided. Even Larry chuckled, and he slapped Peter on the ass before following him into the bedroom.

Since I was too intimidated to talk to anyone new, I was left with Eduardo for company, and neither of us made an effort. He thought I was sore at him for cruising Peter, and I wasn't interested in getting to know Eduardo because I didn't think he'd last the night. He struck me as the kind of party boy who snorted coke at Limelight and made important decisions based on his horoscope.

Peter and a stocky white man who worked as a paralegal were the survivors in their group. I studied Peter when he walked through the living room. No impish grin, no arched eyebrow. His head and dress shirt were drenched. He didn't do anything cheeky until he reached the kitchen, where, unlike everyone else, who sipped tap water out of plastic cups, Peter opened Larry's refrigerator and helped himself to a beer.

Another hour passed before Larry pointed at me and Eduardo. "Boys, you're up."

————

The floor in Larry's bedroom was covered in several layers of plastic, which prevented the sloshing puddles of water from soaking into the carpet. The curtains were drawn, and light came from one dim lamp in a corner. Dorothy sat on the edge of the bed, and Larry leaned against the bathroom door. To my surprise, there were two white men, both built like nightclub bouncers, standing with military posture in front of the far wall. The stocky duo must have been stationed in the bedroom before any of us prospective advocates arrived.

In the middle of the room, five tall stools were lined in a row. I perched myself on the one farthest to the left. Eduardo sat next to me; an older white woman took a seat next to him; next to her was a young woman who had dyed her hair pink; and on the end was a young, gawky white guy wearing too much cologne.

Dorothy got up and circled me and my four battle buddies as she talked. "My daddy, bless his broken soul, had a hair-trigger temper. He would beat me and my three sisters for stepping on a squeaky floorboard. Many were the days that he whipped me with a switch until his arm got tired."

She stopped in front of the pink-haired woman and locked eyes with her. "You need to have hurt like that in your past. You need to have long ago been hit by the devil."

She moved on to get in Eduardo's face. "The reason so many Black folks of my era could march against fire hoses and biting dogs, the reason we could sit-in while white men and women spat on us, pulled at our hair, and clawed at our skin is because we'd dealt with worse in our daily lives."

I sat up straight when Dorothy walked to my left and spoke directly into my ear. "Who among us didn't know of a colored woman who had been raped by white men? Who among us didn't know of a colored man who was lynched to entertain white families? Who among us hadn't already lived through pain greater than what old Bull Connor could throw at us?"[50]

She paced in front of us. "Good intentions will not sustain you and prayers will not save you when cops kick you with steel-toed boots. You will need wounds you can draw on. You will need the confidence that comes from having endured loss and suffering more excruciating than a police-sanctioned ass whoopin'."

Dorothy waved over the two stocky white men. "You will also have to keep your emotions from leading you to fight back. This is the hardest part. It will feel counterintuitive. It will upset your pride. But it is necessary. If you fight, it will legitimize the unchecked savagery of your enemies. You must remember that your victory comes from unmasking the senseless brutality that the government chooses to sanction against you, a collection of nonviolent demonstrators. The point is to let your bruised and bloodied bodies serve as evidence that the government means to kill you, if you so much as protest its bigoted policies."

A childhood spent attending church services, and the first time I ever felt the Word touch me was during a sermon from Dorothy Cotton delivered in Larry Kramer's bedroom. It was like I'd finally reached a long-sought destination and tasted the purest water. The answer to a gnawing, central question was made manifest. Why had I always felt persecuted by authority figures? Why did the promises of America the beautiful, America the land of liberty, and America

---

50. Theophilus "Bull" Connor (1897–1973), a Democrat, was the elected commissioner of public safety for Birmingham, Alabama, from 1936 to 1954 and from 1957 to 1963. As the public safety commissioner, Connor had authority over the local fire department and police department. A racist opposed to the Civil Rights Movement, Connor gave the orders for fire hoses and police attack dogs to be used against peaceful protesters, some of whom were children.

the shining city upon a hill ring false to me? Why didn't I trust cops?
Why did I have no faith in the justice system? It was obvious now.
Until Dorothy removed the scales from my eyes, I'd had one hundred
ways of asking one thing: Why did I feel hunted in my homeland?
Because my government means to kill me. Amen! Amen and glory hal-
lelujah! At last, I could explain the force shaping my existence.

"I've said just about enough." Dorothy stepped back, and the two
stocky men approached us. "We're going to see how each of you per-
forms under pressure. During this training, I will give you instructions that I expect you to follow immediately. Remember, you can
quit any time you want, and if you lash out against these two gentlemen, you will be expelled. We start now."

The tallest gentleman struck the older white woman upside the
head with an open palm. She shrieked, spun off her stool, and fell to
the floor. The shorter gentleman kicked the front of Eduardo's stool,
sending him flying backward.

The over-cologned white man jumped out of his seat, yelling,
"No, stop! Stop!"

"Sit back down, sir, and quit your screaming," Dorothy ordered.

The shorter gentleman used the web of his hand between his
thumb and index finger to jab me in the throat. On contact, I couldn't
breathe, but I held on to the edge of my stool and stayed upright.

"Larry, how can you just stand there?" asked the over-cologned
white man.

"Leave if you don't approve," said Larry, and the white man exited before anyone had laid a hand on him.

The pink-haired woman had been forced onto her feet, and the
tall gentleman was handcuffing her.

Dorothy told her, "Go limp, honey."

She did, and the tall gentleman slammed her to the floor. Her
face splashed into a shallow puddle, and she began sputtering and
coughing.

I saw the open palm of the shorter gentleman coming at me, and
I preemptively dove to the floor.

Having missed me, my attacker announced, "This faggot's a trickster. Let's see him dodge this." He kicked me in the stomach.

The taller gentleman poured a pitcher of hot water on the older woman's head and threw another pitcher of hot water into Eduardo's face. The older woman fled the room. Eduardo started to sing softly in Spanish.

"If you're going to sing," Dorothy said, "sing loud."

Eduardo complied. His voice was beautiful. I rolled over onto my back, able to breathe once more. A pitcher of hot water was dumped into my open, gasping mouth. The verbal and physical abuse continued for another half hour. I was cuffed, I was dragged around the room, I was tossed like a rag doll, I was hit in the balls. More hot water, more personal taunts.

Close to the end, the pink-haired woman begged to be uncuffed and let go, and her request was quickly granted. Eduardo didn't quit singing the whole time, and I owe him for that, although I'd never be able to tell him exactly why without insulting him. In essence, I thought if Eduardo can take the heat and sing, then there's no way I can't take the heat in silence.

Dorothy said, "Time. It's over. Well done, fellas."

The shorter gentlemen released me from the handcuffs and helped me to my feet. My throat felt swollen, and it hurt to swallow. I'd banged up my knees and sprained my right ankle somewhere along the line. I was proud of myself. Eduardo winked at me. Dorothy handed me a dry towel.

"Congratulations," said Larry. "You two are founding members of the AIDS Coalition to Unleash Power. ACT UP, for short."

THE BEST SPONTANEOUS MOMENTS ARE PLANNED

Political movements aren't born of happenstance. However, there's a narcissistic appeal to the saga of the accidental history-maker. People want to believe that as they go about their own humdrum lives, the day could come when out of the blue, they'll spark a revolution. It's bullshit, but the myth of the unplanned uprising has persisted, in no small part, because the movements themselves often package their origin stories to fit the fanciful narrative.

Look at the common (mis)understanding of Rosa Parks. School-children usually get a thumbnail sketch of her one afternoon during Black History Month that goes like this: on December 1, 1955, Rosa Parks, a mild-mannered, God-fearing seamstress in Montgomery, Alabama, got arrested because she refused to relinquish her seat on the bus to a white man.

For the local Black community, the arrest of Rosa Parks was an indignity they couldn't abide, and her individual rebellion inspired them to start the Montgomery bus boycott. The successful boycott was an early triumph in the Civil Rights Movement and brought Dr. Martin Luther King Jr. onto the national stage. And we owe all of this to Rosa Parks's tired feet. They always stress that in schools—she wouldn't give up her seat because her feet were sore.

Admittedly, even I thought the third-grade version of Rosa

Parks, "Mother of the Civil Rights Movement," was the whole truth until Old Rustin set me straight a few months after he and I first met in the break room at Mt. Morris.

"Mrs. Parks was plugged into the movement and had been for many years before the bus incident," he explained. "She was secretary of the state and city chapters of the NAACP. She ran the NAACP's youth leadership organization, and she was an active member of the Montgomery Improvement Association (MIA), which put her in Martin's circle before me."[51]

"Ah, they told her to do it," I assumed. "Her getting arrested was part of the plan."

"No, it wasn't like that. No one gave Mrs. Parks orders." Rustin tapped his fingertips against his temple. "Mrs. Parks is shrewd, and she knew that MIA wanted a test case to challenge segregation on the buses, and they'd thought they had one with that fifteen-year-old girl . . . Claudette . . . Claudette Colvin."

"Who's she?" I asked.

"An angelic troublemaker. She refused to give up her seat on a bus in Montgomery in March of 1955, and she was arrested. Mind you, this was nine months before Mrs. Parks. Miss Colvin, at first, was considered very sympathetic because she was a child, cuffed and jailed and the like." Rustin shook his head. "Then the ministers in the MIA got wind of Miss Colvin being pregnant. The father of her baby was a married man. Details on the nature of their affair were . . . unclear at best."

"So they dropped her?"

"Like a hot potato. Subsequently, spring, summer, and fall passed by, and the MIA was without a test case. Mrs. Parks was aware of these events and more. She understood the fear that time was slip-

<hr>

51. The Montgomery Improvement Association (1955–1969) was an African American grassroots organization dedicated to challenging segregation on the local level. Co-founded by E. D. Nixon (1899–1987) and Jo Ann Robinson (1912–1992), the Montgomery Improvement Association was led during the bus boycott by Dr. Martin Luther King Jr. (1929–1968).

ping away, the demand for action was going untapped. The leaders were ready, the lawyers were ready, and the people were ready. All that was missing was someone to take the hit. Someone who could withstand scrutiny from the Negro churches and the white legal system." Rustin bit his bottom lip and tilted his head at me, silently challenging me to finish putting the pieces together.

"Then this was a wink-wink situation. No one told her what to do, but she knew exactly what she was doing."

"Yes," he said, "although if you went out to Detroit and asked Mrs. Parks, she'd tell you there was no premeditation in her refusal to give up her seat on the bus that evening."

"Why would she deny it?"

"Because if her actions were premeditated, then she could have been branded a political radical who willfully broke the law to instigate the boycott. That would have turned off a lot of white people we needed to be sympathetic to our cause. That's why Mrs. Parks has been cast as a meek seamstress with aching bunions. It's the version of events that garnered the most goodwill with white folks."

———

ACT UP also had to tailor the details of its inception to placate the sensibilities of a key demographic: assimilation gays. With their seven-figure salaries or inherited wealth, assimilation gays kept their homosexual lifestyles discreet and their politics mild for the comfort of their tolerant straight neighbors. They prided themselves on attending dinner parties in the Hamptons, where the topic of their homosexuality was never broached by the Wall Street hosts or their respectable guests. Assimilation gays took this to mean that their keen intellect and upstanding character had tucked away their queerness into a footnote that no one would bother to read. As a gauge of how fucking warped assimilation gays could be in 1987, many of them wanted to frame the AIDS pandemic solely as a public health crisis, de-emphasizing how the disease was killing gay men at a genocidal pace.

Despite being dangerously myopic, the assimilation gays were a sizable constituency that couldn't be ignored. First of all, as a class, they had tremendous wealth at their disposal. We're talking about the kind of obscene family fortunes that even the heedless expenses from a generation of drunk dilettantes and their litter of ex-wives and ex-husbands and mistresses and secret love children can't manage to dent. These jack-offs owned beachfront mansions in Newport that they let crumble to the ground.

However, somewhere between throwing lavish birthday parties for their dogs and paying six figures to own kitschy furniture from the estate of Brenda Frazier, the assimilation gays would occasionally make a large donation to a nonprofit organization.[52] They did have a sense of noblesse oblige. The key was to stroke them just right. They needed to believe that they were the saviors.

The other reason most gay rights groups kept a dedicated fluffer on staff to attend to the assimilation gays was because they were political tastemakers. Elected officials consulted them for their advice on how to deal with "the gays," and publications like *The New York Times* printed think pieces from them about "gay issues and trends." Invariably, the message from these milquetoast motherfuckers was one of caution. Pragmatism was their religion. They yearned to reassure the hetty population that they shared its concerns about radicalism and the unruly side of the gay agenda. If the assimilation gays

---

52. Brenda D. Frazier (1921–1982) was a wealthy socialite who was marginally famous for being a wealthy socialite. She was a figure of glamour and envy in 1938 when she appeared on the cover of *Life* magazine as part of the press coverage of her debutante ball, and she was the subject of ridicule and pity in 1966 when a photo of her in *Esquire* magazine revealed that she still dolled herself up in her signature white face powder and red lipstick—an aging debutante stuck in a bygone era. Frazier entered the canon of gay camp in 1971 when her name appeared as a lyric in Stephen Sondheim's song "I'm Still Here" for the musical *Follies*.

declared that a group or campaign was out of bounds, mainstream opinion followed suit.

Given the urgency of its mission, ACT UP couldn't afford to have assimilation gays out to smother it in its crib. So to keep the would-be assassins at bay, a quixotic tale was concocted, and all these decades later, that fabrication is accepted as official history. The lie, I must concede, has a romantic sweep to it, if one finds beauty in the magic of accidents and perfect timing.

According to the lore, the Lesbian and Gay Community Services Center was in the middle of presenting its rotating speaker series.[53] Nora Ephron held the March 10 slot but had to bow out at the last minute due to an ear infection and a cold.[54] The spur-of-the-moment replacement for Nora was our one and only Larry Kramer. Met by an unexpectedly large crowd for the center's speaker series, Larry delivered a fiery broadside about the Gay Men's Health Crisis's ineffectual nature and lack of political courage. The audience was enthusiastic and receptive to the speech, which differed sharply from the boos and heckles Larry usually received when lambasting the gay response to AIDS. The positive reception led him to end his remarks with an impromptu question: "Do we want to start a new organization devoted to political action?" Two days later, several hundred gay activists held a meeting and formed ACT UP. Voilà.

Naturally, the training I attended in Larry's apartment three weeks before his speech at the center debunks the fable of ACT UP's

---

53. The Lesbian and Gay Community Services Center, founded in 1983, changed its name to be more inclusive of the entire LGBTQ+ community. It is currently called the Lesbian, Gay, Bisexual & Transgender Community Center.

54. Nora Ephron (1941–2012) was a famous and successful journalist, essayist, playwright, director, and screenplay writer. She was nominated three times for the Academy Award for Best Original Screenplay. Romantic comedies were considered her specialty. Yet her first Oscar nomination was for cowriting the 1983 drama *Silkwood*, which included a sympathetic supporting character who was a lesbian—a groundbreaking portrayal at the time.

immaculate conception. But what I learned drying myself off later that night in Larry's living room was that there were already several initiatives in motion that would culminate to give ACT UP its potency.

"Eat as much as you want," said Larry. "Dominic is family. He didn't charge us for any of these pies."

It was 1:30 a.m., and the two white men who'd roughed us up in the bedroom had run out and brought back five large cheese pizzas from Dom's Authentic Italy. The other sixteen newly baptized members of ACT UP and I chowed down while Dorothy hugged Larry, then bid us all good night. I sat on the end of a cramped couch with Peter wedged next to me and Eduardo sitting on Peter's lap.

I tried not to roll my eyes at them. Queers can get lovey-dovey at the drop of an orange hanky.[55] And I knew I had no right to judge them for hooking up at a political event; Erik and I met in a bathhouse. What I think bothered me was that Eduardo wasn't who I would have chosen for Peter. I'd imagined someone erudite, to match wits with Peter, and a bit curmudgeonly, to balance out Peter's playfulness.

"Strange bedfellows," Peter whispered to me.

"Who?" I asked.

"The three musketeers who just arrived. Edie, Dylan, and Felicia. They barely get along with each other, and none of them can stand Larry."

"You know, I find him a lot nicer than people give him credit for."

"He arranged to have the shit kicked out of you tonight, and you adore him."

"I'm saying he's not the screaming killjoy I'd imagined."

Peter disagreed with an assertive, "Eh, you barely know him."

Eduardo kissed Peter on the neck and chimed in, "I saw Larry

---

55. In the hanky code, which originated in the 1970s and was a subversive, silent way for gay men to signal their sexual interests and roles to each other, the color orange meant "anything goes" when worn in the back left pocket.

chew out a doctor at St. V's. The doctor treated a friend of mine, Diego, and it was a day or two before Diego died. There was nothing anyone could have done to save him, but Larry had this poor doctor up against the wall crying. Larry kept calling him *Mengele*."[56]

"Case in point," said Peter, who rewarded Eduardo with a peck on the forehead. "That doctor broke the cardinal rule with Larry. You can't ever disappoint him. He goes unhinged. He hits below the belt with brass knuckles. I guarantee the doctor he bawled out lost family members in the camps."

"If he's such a monster," I asked, "why are you here? Why are you friends with him?"

"Because we traveled in the same circles before anyone had heard of AIDS. He was a pain in the ass then, too, but he was a good friend," explained Peter. "The kind you called after your boyfriend threw you out or you got shitcanned from a job you hated anyway. I can forgive his anger since I know where it comes from. We've buried a lot of friends together. But I don't kid myself about what this struggle has done to him. He's not the guy I met on Fire Island in '76. He can hurt the people around him, and someday, he'll drive me away, too."

Naivete hadn't completely lost its hold on me, and I couldn't fathom why Peter would resign himself to a doomed relationship. If heartbreak and recriminations were inevitable, cut ties and bolt before the pain comes to pass. I remember how obvious that seemed to me.

Larry clapped his hands softly, gathering everyone's attention. "If we all focus, we can be out of here in thirty minutes."

"Promises, promises," said a redheaded woman in her late twenties.

"Interruptions only slow us down, Helena." Larry gestured to Edie, Dylan, and Felicia. "For those that don't know the distinguished people to my right, allow me to introduce the brain trust for ACT UP."

---

56. Dr. Josef Mengele (1911–1979) was a high-ranking Nazi officer who was nicknamed the "Angel of Death" because of the cruel and fatal experiments he performed on captives at the Auschwitz concentration camp.

"Not the brain trust," insisted Dylan. "This group is to have no hierarchy. No executive committee, no leader. The four of us are not in charge."

Larry bristled. "What the talented Mr. Dylan Stalder, who is representing the Silence=Death Project, means to stress is that *I* am not in charge.[57] Otherwise, ACT UP will be saddled with my baggage. Next to Dylan is the steadfast Edie Galecki, representing the PWA Coalition—"[58]

"Damn it, Larry, we just discussed this, and you weren't listening," said Edie. "I'm not representing PWA in an official capacity. I'm offering my contacts and know-how, but I'm not disavowing PWA the way you did GMHC. I'm here because I'm interested in doing work that falls beyond the current scope of PWA."

"Did everyone get that?" asked Larry. "Great. On to the illustrious Felicia Hall. Felicia, dare I say you're joining us as a representative from GLAAD?"[59]

"I am here as a GLAAD representative," she said, "but whether I formally join ACT UP remains to be seen. I've come on a fact-finding mission, if you will."

Helena Costas, a defense lawyer who specialized in representing battered women on trial for attacking or killing their abusive boyfriends or husbands, raised her hand, but didn't wait to be called on to speak. "Does this mean Vito isn't with ACT UP? Because his support will go a long way with people Larry has, no offense, alienated."

---

57. Silence=Death Project (founded in 1987) was a six-person art collective dedicated to raising public consciousness about the AIDS epidemic.

58. People with AIDS, a.k.a. the PWA Coalition, and later known as the National Association of People with AIDS (1982–2013), was at one time the largest and oldest patient advocacy group for persons living with HIV or AIDS.

59. Founded in 1985, GLAAD, formerly an acronym for Gay & Lesbian Alliance Against Defamation, is a media watchdog group that monitors the portrayal of LGBTQ+ people in the media. The group's original focus was to combat biased news coverage against the homosexual community. More recently, it is known for presenting GLAAD awards that recognize distinguished portrayals of the LGBTQ+ issues and people in the media.

Larry snapped, "I'd say, 'No offense taken, Helena,' but I really mean, 'Fuck you.'"

There was an uproar of objections from a dozen people in the room. The ensuing bickering lasted ten minutes. The displays of white-hot passion were breathtaking. I'd never witnessed the inner workings of a grassroots organization before. I was taken aback by the open hostility. Peter, on the other hand, nestled into the couch; Larry and company were players in a soap opera he had been following for years. These kindhearted people upbraided each other without hesitation or restraint. No point went unchallenged; no nuance went unparsed. Clearly, we were going to be meeting for longer than half an hour.

Larry apologized and addressed the question about Vito Russo.[60] "I spoke with Vito yesterday, and he agrees that this group will serve a vital need."

"Then why isn't he here?" demanded Helena.

"Because I asked him to stay away until this group has held its first demonstration, and before anyone impugns my motives, let me make them clear. ACT UP can't afford to be sucked into these cults of personality that are hampering our community. We've got to free ourselves of these high school popularity contests. This isn't Larry's army. This isn't Vito's clique. ACT UP has to be organic—of the people, by the people."

"Yes, yes," droned Dylan. "Can we finally discuss how we're going to orchestrate this organic happening?"

"The floor is yours," said Larry with a contemptuous smile.

Dylan, who with his bushy beard and broad shoulders looked more like a tanned, young lumberjack than a graphic designer, opened up his artist's portfolio and pulled out a poster. The images were sparse

---

60. Vito Russo (1946–1990), a gay rights activist and a film historian, was a cofounder of GLAAD. He also traveled the country delivering a lecture about the portrayal of homosexuality and homosexual characters in movies. The lecture was titled "The Celluloid Closet," and after Russo died, a documentary film with the same title was produced using Russo's lecture and research notes.

but evocative: a pink triangle sat in the center of a black background, and below the triangle it read SILENCE=DEATH.

"You might have seen these already posted around Chelsea. The next step is to plaster Manhattan with these bad boys. I've got boxes with thousands of flyers. Let's canvas the subways, Wall Street, the churches, the hospitals, the streets around Gracie Mansion. And if you're caught posting bills, don't explain shit. You don't know where you got it. You just believe it and had to mark the city with this message."

"A pink triangle?" complained a middle-aged man with salt-and-pepper hair.[61] "Is that in good taste?"

"We inverted the triangle," Dylan explained.

Helena said, "My objection is that it doesn't say a word about AIDS. Silence equals death, but the poster itself doesn't dare say the word."

"It could be confusing!" shouted a guy I couldn't see on the other side of the living room.

Dylan threw his arms up in the air. "The design is not up for debate! Jesus Christ, it's already on the streets. I'm asking this group to help make it ubiquitous."

Felicia, a thirtysomething Black woman with a crown of braids, proposed a compromise. "Perhaps those who have objections don't have to participate in posting the leaflets."

"Yes, yes," Dylan conceded. "I want helpers, not hostages."

"Thanks," said Larry, obviously pleased that Dylan's plan had met with friction. "Alrighty, I've written a call to arms, and everyone in this room should be in attendance and bring some friends to pack the room when I deliver it. My question for Edie is, when and where will this battle cry take place?"

Edie stepped forward. With short hair slicked back and parted

---

61. In concentration camps, Nazis used pink triangle badges on prisoner uniforms to identify homosexual men, bisexual men, and transgender women.

on the left, and dressed in a bespoke double-breasted men's suit, I would have, at the time, pegged Edie's age as forty, and I would have classified Edie as a severe butch lesbian. I was wrong on both counts: Edie was forty-eight, and he was a trans man. Oh, and his named sounded like *Edie,* but it was actually *E.D.*

"You'll be speaking at the Lesbian and Gay Community Services Center on March 10."

"Impossible!" yelled Larry. "The faggots and dykes running that joint despise me."

Dylan quipped, "I can't imagine why, when you speak so highly of them."

Larry ignored the dig. "Seriously, E.D., there will be a revolt if I'm announced as part of the speaker's series."

"It's being handled," he said. "I don't want to get into the mechanics in front of everyone."

Peter shouted, "Why not? I thought there was no hierarchy."

I scoffed because I knew Peter hadn't protested on principle. He wanted gossip. Despite his impure intentions, Larry backed him and urged E.D. to let us all in on the plan.

"Fine," he said, "but if this leaks, we're screwed hard and forever. Nora Ephron is slated to speak on the tenth, and she's going to withdraw on the ninth. She'll say she's got a cold or a migraine—doesn't matter. Point is, she's gonna bail, and I've got a couple of contacts on the inside, Alex and Ted, who will push Larry as Nora's replacement. They'll argue that on such short notice, how much trouble can you cause?"

Half the room broke out laughing and applauding.

Larry raised his hand to quiet the crowd and asked, "Nora Ephron agreed to take a dive so we could do this?"

"Yes," said E.D. "She's a straight ally. There are some out there, you know."

———

On March 10, Gregory, Erik, and I stood with about four hundred other people in a line outside the Lesbian and Gay Community Services Center, waiting to hear Larry Kramer speak. I was exuberant, bouncing on my toes with anticipation. My companions were less thrilled. Neither knew the backstory or the objectives of Larry's speech, but had I told them, it wouldn't have raised their interests higher than a mild indifference. Gregory's political concerns didn't expand beyond his affair with Congressman Galbreath, and Erik didn't voice any views stronger than garden-variety gripes about how elected officials, regardless of party, were corrupt. I'd convinced the two of them to join me by promising to pay for our dinners and drinks later that night.

"I got me a taste for crab cakes. Let's go to Schaffer's," suggested Gregory, just to be a pain in the ass.

"Nope," I said.

"Why not? I hear good things about the food and the service."

This had become a game I was growing weary of playing. Gregory kept trying to make me squirm by hinting at and slowly revealing to Erik an embarrassing or scandalous episode from my life. The best way to spoil my roommate's fun was to tell on myself straightaway.

"Erik, we can't go to Schaffer's because I used to fuck around with a straight bartender there, who lived in my old apartment building, and it ended when I told his girlfriend that her man sucked my cock."

Erik blinked. "Okay. I think Schaffer's is overpriced anyway. I'd rather have some Chinese food at Mao's."

"Then that's what we'll do," I said.

I smirked at Gregory. I'd won that round—as far as he knew. What Gregory couldn't see was that I was increasingly distressed by Erik's lack of jealousy. Stupid, I realize. We weren't monogamous. We weren't boyfriends. I just wanted him to be slightly possessive of me. Ask for details of my sexcapades. Show some curiosity about what my tricks looked like. Care a bit more.

The doors opened, and we made our way into the auditorium.

As we got situated in a middle row, I looked around and spotted Peter, Eduardo, and every other participant from my training. We exchanged conspiratorial nods and winks. It felt important; the moment felt historic, and I was a part of it.

Since my training, Peter had told me that Larry had held five more in his apartment. I tried to determine who in the audience were undercover ACT UP members and who were the ones dragged along to fill the room. Posture was the tell. If you were in ACT UP, you kept leaning forward, you were rocking side to side, you couldn't stay still. If you were a civilian, you slouched into your chair.

The auditorium lights dimmed above the audience, and Larry walked onstage to wild applause, which I thought was excessive. We didn't want to signal that the fix was in. The event kicked off with no other fanfare. Someone from the center gave a dry introduction of Larry, and Larry took his place behind the podium and adjusted the microphone. I held my breath.

"Indulge me, please," Larry began. "Could the lights in the auditorium be turned up?" The lights went to full bright. "Could everyone on the right side of the room—my right—please stand up?"

Gregory and I and everyone on our half of the room immediately did as asked. I had to grab Gregory by the arm and yank at him to get him to comply, but he got on his feet.

Looking at us with mournful eyes, Larry directed a heavy sigh into the microphone. Then he said, "You could all be dead in five years at the rate we're going."

He turned to the other side of the auditorium. "Now you stand." Once they had, Larry said, "At the rate we're going, you could all be dead in ten years, and there'll be no one from this community left to mourn you."

In a masterstroke of political theater, Larry did not tell the audience to please take their seats. He left us standing. He kept the whole crowd on its feet because it would make it easier to energize the room.

"You're as good as dead, I tell you," he said, raising his volume and building toward a shout. "You're as good. As. Dead! The question is will you shuffle off to your graves without fighting for your lives!?"

"No!" screamed the crowd in hundreds of voices, in overlapping waves, and with collective might.

The torrent of "No!" continued as Larry matched it in intensity. "Will you die silently while your government twiddles its thumbs?! Will you wait patiently until you're six feet under while the FDA drags its feet?! Will you spend the rest of your short life wasting your precious time at toothless meetings of the GMHC?"

Pandemonium. I'd never heard a crowd that size make so much noise. Larry was tapping into an unspoken anger. An anger at a government that hated fags, at bureaucrats who valued procedure over people in need, and at the groveling political tactics of appeasement embodied by the GMHC.

Larry painted the stark reality of our community's political posture. "We are so desperate for help! We've approached the government on our knees! Begging them to fund research! Pleading with them to release treatment drugs sooner! We lick their boots! Hoping they will take pity on us! And treat us like human beings! And what do we have to show for it! Twenty-five thousand dead! And you'll be joining them! In the cemetery! If you don't get off your knees! And fight!"

He went on for another twenty minutes, explaining the terrible trends. Infection rates rising. The death toll rising. The cost of care rising. A pandemic threatened to wipe us off the Earth, and our government sat in denial of the threat at hand. We had to quit begging and start demanding.

I turned to my left and saw that Erik was caught up in the frenzy. I took his hand and he squeezed mine. Gregory watched the scene unfold with bewilderment, but he knew not to be a contrarian in this crowd. When he saw me looking at him, he pumped his fists in the air and acted as if he was as energized as the rest of us.

Larry ended his speech by asking, "Do we want to start a new organization devoted to political action?" The crowd roared its affirmation. Two days later, three hundred people, including me, met to officially form ACT UP. History bought the myth. I treasure the truth.

NO SENSE CRYING OVER BLOOD MONEY

Several days after my training in Larry Kramer's bedroom, I reported back to Rustin because I believed I could prove to him that ACT UP was going to be a force for good. It didn't feel like snitching. I didn't think I was committing a quid for a quo. We were in the break room at Mt. Morris, each of us clad in nothing more than our towels, and I filled him in on my ACT UP event at Larry's apartment, stressing that the first wave of members would be taught tactics of nonviolence resistance by Dorothy Cotton.

That got Rustin's attention. "They arranged for Dorothy to school you?"

"Yes, she even led us through a practice run. They had two guys really give us the business. Slaps, kicks, and tossed us around. They cuffed us, poured hot water on our heads—"

"And Dorothy condoned this?"

I tried to allay his concerns. "No one got hurt, and you could stop it whenever you wanted. That was the point. The quitters aren't in the group. It was me and about a dozen other people who got through it that night."

Rustin furrowed his brow. "How many times did they hold these trainings?"

"Six," I said. "Again, no one got hurt."

"Still, that kind of trial-by-fire training has been frowned upon since the mid-'70s, and Dorothy knows that."

"Why's it frowned upon? It worked for the Civil Rights Movement."

Rustin got up to pour himself a cup of coffee despite it being 10:00 p.m. "Sure, we did hundreds and hundreds of trainings like that back in the day, and nobody was better at leading them than Dorothy. But you can't risk it now. If something does go wrong, if someone does get hurt, the liability, the negative publicity—it could bankrupt and discredit an organization."

"But nothing like that happened!" I insisted more strenuously than I'd intended. "This wasn't the nightmare scenario!"

"You've made that clear," Rustin assured me as he came back to the slanted folding table. "And I can tell you're worried you've said too much. You haven't, Trey."

"I'd just hate for Dorothy to get in trouble."

He threw his head back and guffawed. "Have mercy, no one alive or dead could reprimand Dorothy. She suffers no fools. Let me tell you, we were having a meeting during the bus boycott, and this might have been the first or second time I had met Dorothy. She sat in the meeting as an equal. She was no secretary, mind you. And Dr. King told her to go make him a cup of coffee. She said ever so politely, 'That's not what I'm here for.' He said, 'But I'm not accustomed to making my own coffee.'" Rustin howled laughing at the memory. "Dorothy said, 'You're a reverend and a doctor. I trust you'll have the brains to figure it out.'"

I laughed and asked, "What did Dr. King say to that?"

"Martin cracked up like the rest of us. Then he went into the kitchen and made a pot of Folgers for all of us. It tasted horrible, but it was the effort that counted."

Relaxed and happy to stop discussing ACT UP, I got Rustin to tell me more stories about the heady days of working with Martin Luther King Jr. An hour flew by. Rustin spoke of the past with no regrets. His admiration for King was all encompassing and, I thought, more forgiving than it ought to have been. I'd been aware that Old Rustin was pushed out of King's inner circle and the movement because of his homosexuality, but Rustin, at last, shared the details of his ousting with me.

"J. Edgar Hoover began to circulate all kinds of stories about Martin," he explained.[62] "One of which was that Martin was a friend of mine and insinuating that there was a homosexual relationship going on between us. This rumor, which I thought was preposterous on its face, managed to scare a number of people around Martin. Those people set up a committee to discover what they should do to counter the rumor, and that committee asked me to leave in 1962, less than a year before the March on Washington."

At first, I was confused by the timeline. "But you organized the march, right?"

"Yes, Mr. Randolph and I were the lead organizers, and I was allowed to continue my work. The committee just had me distance myself from Martin and asked me to stay behind the scenes when it came to the march."

Then I grew incredulous. "You were too gay to stand next to Dr. King, but not too gay to pull together one of the greatest political events ever?"

"You must understand, even the people asking me to step aside felt awful about the position they were putting me in. The times were different. I hold no ill will against the committee or Martin."

Finally, I was angry. "You should. They did you wrong, and it was

---

62. J. Edgar Hoover (1895–1972) was the first and longest-serving director of the Federal Bureau of Investigation (FBI). As FBI director, Hoover abused his power to spy on political figures and used what he uncovered as blackmail material. He also circulated unfounded rumors to damage people he deemed "subversive." While the rumor was never substantiated, Hoover was widely suspected of being a homosexual. He lived with his mother into his forties; he never married; and for more than thirty years, he worked alongside, usually ate lunch with, frequented nightclubs and racetracks with, vacationed with, and bequeathed his estate to fellow bachelor and associate director of the FBI Clyde Tolson (1900–1975).

fucked up. And you can blame the committee, but Dr. King didn't tell them to go to hell, making him a homophobe or gutless—take your pick."

"Cool it with the language and this ugly talk."

"What did Jimmy say when he found out?" I demanded.

Rustin squinted, and it took him a second to catch on that I was referring to James Baldwin by his nickname, as if I were the one who had shared more than thirty years of friendship with the famed writer.

I didn't relent. "Tell me he called bullshit."

"Sorry to disappoint you," Rustin said with edge in his voice, "but Mr. Baldwin and I never discussed the matter."

"What? How is that possible? You were two of the biggest homos in the movement, and one of you got shoved aside for being a homo, and the two of you didn't talk about it."

"There was nothing to say. Or rather, the two of us complaining about a political reality beyond our control was of no interest to us, believe me."

"Alright." I raised my hands in surrender before firing another shot. "It's just shocking is all. Jimmy acts like he wouldn't take shit from no one, but I guess he saw what happened to you and decided then and there that he didn't want the same treatment. Now I get why he won't stick his neck out for Gay Liberation."

"Damn us all then, is it?" he yelled. "Jimmy, Martin, me, our entire generation isn't up to snuff because we didn't burn the country to the ground! No, sir, all we ever achieved was securing rights you take for granted!"

The thunder in his voice left me speechless.

Rustin took a long beat to consider his next words carefully. "It is difficult for the young to understand the strictures of the past. You want your elders to have fought every slight and grievous offense that came our way. But remember, at all times—even yours, even now—there are unjust laws and customs we abide. If you don't believe me, tell people you're gay and try to get a job as a schoolteacher. Take the man you love to city hall and try to marry him.

"We have to be calculating about when to bend and when to rebel. I considered myself lucky to have spent eight years working closely with Martin. In the back of my mind, I knew that my sexuality would eventually be used against me. I knew the ending would be abrupt, and I knew that my departure would cost me less if I conducted myself in an agreeable manner. You see, while I loved Martin, I loved the movement more, and if I'd have made a stink about a loss of status, I would have lost my chance to shape the march. I can live with my choices. I'd bet the same goes for Jimmy and all the homos in the movement you don't know about. There was a great many more than two of us.

"And as for Martin, in my book, he's not the villain. Hoover is the dirty bastard who set these rumors into motion. Once the evil was let loose, Martin could only decide how to address it given the political realities of the day. Martin made the call I would have made had I been him."

None of Rustin's positions tamped down my indignation on his behalf. I wanted to scream at him about justice and equality like Larry might have, but that would have been fruitless. Instead, I shut out all the political argument raging in my head, and I distilled my feelings into a single point of what I found objectionable and heartbreaking about the whole matter.

"You talk about the movement as if you, Martin, and the committee members were all chess pieces on a board," I said. "But you were people, and you were friends. Martin should have been a better friend to you."

My words hit home. Rustin's eyes brimmed with tears. He nodded and rubbed his eyes. "The movement demands many sacrifices," he said.

Our conversation retreated to a safe harbor, and we discussed how we were scoring in the bathhouse that night. Rustin had received a blow job in the dark room. I had gotten fucked in the steam room. I told him that I was going to do one more lap through the maze of hallways and then call it a night.

"Hold on a second," Rustin said. "I think there's a job opening you'd be right for. You do still need a job?"

"Yes, like a hot meal."

"It's not the greatest pay, but I've noticed that you frequent museums, and you've been very helpful telling me what you did about ACT UP . . ."

And there it was: the quo I hadn't even expected. I gave Rustin information, and he found a job opening for me. I wondered if he would have mentioned this employment opportunity if I hadn't told him about Dorothy and the trainings. But I didn't have the balls to ask him that. I was too poor to be a smart-ass and too afraid that he'd answer me honestly.

———

The following week, I was earning $4.50 an hour working at the information desk at MoMA from opening until closing Fridays, Saturdays, and Sundays. The part-time gig was perfect for me. I earned just enough money to cover my half of the rent, and even before I was hired, I could have walked the floors of the museum blindfolded and never lost my way. I was familiar with the permanent collection and the current exhibits. Best of all, my enthusiasm for art was genuine and infectious.

From the moment I arrived for my interview, everyone working at the museum was courteous and effusive toward me. Of course, the fix was in, and the job was mine. But it was more than that. My prodigious vocabulary, my unrestrained exuberance, and my tailored dress shirts and slacks weren't merely tolerated; they made me a star among the staff.

While I'd love to attribute my instant success at MoMA to my winsome personality, I suspected I owed a debt of gratitude to another gay man who'd paved the way for me. In the autumn of 1951, poet and art critic Frank O'Hara clocked in for his first day of work on what was then called the "front desk" at MoMA.[63] By 1960, he was the museum's assistant curator of painting and sculpture exhibitions. O'Hara was not a wallflower, and I believe his openly homosexual sensibilities shaped the ethos of the museum in a way that more than twenty years after his death made MoMA a welcoming environment to a colorful fairy like me. Such is the importance of groundbreakers. Thanks, Frank.

My supervisor at the information desk was Elizabeth "Libby" Robinson. Pushing seventy and widowed, Libby came from old money and kicked back her salary to the museum as a small part of her annual donation. She had no children and took the job overseeing the information desk to give herself purpose and to meet new people. Libby doted on me like I was her favorite grandchild.

At the end of my first week, Libby treated me to lunch in the museum's café. She listened and took notes as I pitched my grand idea for MoMA to make more money and enhance the gallery experience for visitors: at each exhibit, visitors should have the option to rent a Sony Walkman loaded with a cassette tape that had prerecorded music that would speak to the era and/or the tone of the art on display. I warned against the inclination to score every exhibit with classical music. We were a museum of modern art. We shouldn't be afraid to incorporate modern music. I volunteered to be on the music selection committee.

When I was done with my proposal, Libby closed her notebook and said, "What you've put forward is divine. I'm for anything that pulls the public in. Look at what Diana Vreeland does for the Cos-

---

63. Frank O'Hara (1926–1966) was an influential figure in the New York art world through his position at the Museum of Modern Art (MoMA), his generally positive critiques of the contemporary scene, and his friendships with leading artists like Jackson Pollock (1912–1956), Willem de Kooning (1904–1997), and Larry Rivers (1923–2002). O'Hara's most notable collection of poetry, *Lunch Poems* (published 1964), was written at his desk and during his lunch breaks at MoMA. O'Hara died after being struck by a jeep late one night as he walked along a beach road on Fire Island.

tume Institute at the Met.[64] We should be harnessing the zeitgeist to our advantage."

I drummed the table triumphantly. "Exactly, Libby. Exactly. So you think the higher-ups will run with my idea?"

She flashed a tight-lipped smile, took my hand, and said, "Probably not. There are quite a few more fuddy-duddies in this museum than there are daring visionaries like us. I will push for it. You must remember that it can take years—even decades, I'm afraid—to move an institution this large."

"Decades?"

"Don't fret. You're young. You have decades to spare." She signaled the waiter for the check. "Which is why I do hope you stick with the museum and come back to us after your gap year."

I was worldly enough to know better than to disabuse her of that lie. I did, however, want to know if this "gap year" notion was how Libby explained to herself why I was nineteen years old and not enrolled in college, or if someone had misled her.

"Oh, Mr. Rustin told you about my gap year, did he?"

"No, I didn't speak with him," she said. "It was your mother. She and I got on like a house on fire."

I tried with all my might to maintain the smile on my face even though bile soaked my tongue. My mother. She was inventing polished answers to appease high society; I called this her *Lady Fiona* mode. Once she locked into that persona, she was status conscious and crafty enough to be a member of an Elizabethan court.

I should have guessed that my mother would craft a story to explain where her eldest son had gone. The truth would be too embarrassing: *That ungrateful sodomite decided to forgo college and moved to New York City, where he'd rather starve to death than touch a dime of*

---

64. After an unceremonious end to her eight-year reign as editor in chief of *Vogue* magazine, Diana Vreeland (1903–1989) became a special consultant to the Costume Institute at the Metropolitan Museum of Art (the Met) in 1973. Vreeland curated exhibits that went beyond catering to academics and proved to be blockbuster attractions for the general public.

the hard-earned money that we put into a trust fund for him. He doesn't call, he doesn't write, and we expect the authorities to notify us any night with the news that he's been killed. Yeah, Lady Fiona simply couldn't say that at League of Women Voters socials or at strategy meetings for the National Rainbow Coalition.

"Gap year"—that was a clever spin. It sounded sophisticated and vaguely educational. Never mind that I'd been on my own for two years, my mother had an explanation that would withstand casual scrutiny. And landing a job at MoMA was a boon that played into her hands. Hoosiers would be quite impressed by that, and Lady Fiona wouldn't have to acknowledge how I'd rejected her, my father, and their lifestyle. She wouldn't have to give me that satisfaction.

Furthermore, Lady Fiona was not going to allow me to bring her standing as a Black mother back into question. She had endured every variation of misery when Martin was abducted and (presumably) killed, and one of the more perverse torments turned out to be a whispered debate about her culpability as the victim's mother.

Oh, the people must have their say about everyone's business. So while strangers pitied her with condolence cards and congregations prayed over her in churches, plenty of adults speculated about whether my brother would still be alive if my mother had kept a tighter leash on her children. Parents of my friends suggested that my mother had been too career-driven, too disenchanted with the thankless work of motherhood, and too caught up in Jesse Jackson's orbit to do right by her own children. My mother was the target of a bullshit misogynistic double standard. Yet she craved the approval of those who stood in judgment of her, and how would it look if she lost contact with her other son?

For the record, I didn't hate my mother. I just didn't know how to be myself around her without disappointing her and sparking a nasty argument between us. We were designed to be at odds: she was always clad in artifice, and I longed to strip naked.

Despite my efforts to appear delighted, the mix of anger, disgust, and sadness I felt for Fiona must have shined through.

"Oh dear," said Libby, "she hadn't told you that we talked."

The waiter arrived with the check, and before he could set it on the table, Libby offered up her credit card.

"No, she hadn't mentioned it," I said.

"And all too late, I can see why. She wanted to avoid the appearance of being an interfering mother," Libby surmised. "Listen, Trey, you mustn't be cross with her. In fact, I implore you not to mention this at all to your mother. I've talked out of turn. Forgive me, and let this be our secret."

Her guilt was my advantage. "I will on one condition. Tell me what she said about me."

Relieved, Libby happily obliged. "Alrighty. She said you're a maverick. You've always been an independent thinker and set your own course. You're very well-spoken. Let's see, she mentioned your great memory. You've got a brain like a card catalog. It's all up there, organized, and retrievable at your fingertips."

The review was so positive I was tempted to question Libby about whether she was certain she had spoken with my mother. Instead, I asked, "What are my drawbacks? Mom always evaluates people and options based on their advantages and drawbacks."

"Well," Libby stalled as she searched for euphemisms to soften my mother's critique, "she suggested that you could be obstinate . . . and sometimes you can get carried away by your passionate feelings and do things that come back to hurt you."

I translated Libby's words to figure out what my mother must have divulged. "She told you that I moved here on my own and I support myself—hand to mouth."

"She said you insisted on it over her objections." Libby winked at me. "That's when I knew you and I would get along. You're not the first person to walk away from a fortune to find out what you're made of."

The waiter returned with the receipt, and Libby tipped him and signed it.

"So talking to her helped convince you to hire me?"

"Yes, it was one of the factors, along with Mr. Rustin's letter of recommendation to my boss. And, of course, your interview. You see, you've got a lot going for you, Trey."

———

That night in Erik's apartment, I explained to him how and why I owed my job at the museum to Rustin and my mother, and I concluded, "I have to resign from MoMA."

Erik didn't respond right away. He bobbed his head from left to right as he tore off a piece of injera and used it to scoop up some yellow peas. I thought he'd speak before putting the food in his mouth, but he kept me waiting as he ate the bite. Ethiopian cuisine was his favorite.

Finally, he spoke in that languid way of his whenever his dancing life had left him nearly depleted. "You work at the info desk, you don't resign. You just quit."

"Semantics aside, you do think I should quit?"

"Do you have another job lined up?"

"No."

"Then you absolutely don't quit."

Wearing nothing but a pair of silk boxers, Erik was reclined on his couch with his ankles iced and elevated on pillows. I was sitting on the floor at his side, and our take-out order was around me in Styrofoam containers. As I ate, I lifted the dishes Erik was hungry for when he pointed at them.

I'd presented the fasolia, and he reached for it, almost getting it before I pulled the container away and said, "Have you been listening to me? Rustin called in a favor to get me in the door because I'm his double agent in ACT UP, and my mother, who I haven't spoken to in two years, is making up lies about me to save face. The job is tainted now."

Erik winced as he shifted his body to sit up. He patted the cushion he'd been lying back on and told me, "Put your ass here, and I'll lay my head on your lap."

This was a major act of gallantry. Usually, Erik didn't share the couch, and it was the only furniture he had in the sparse living room / kitchen of his one-bedroom apartment. When we were at his place, which was 90 percent of the time, we primarily stayed in his bedroom, where his eleven-inch television sat on plastic crates. I would have enjoyed cuddling up to each other eating pizza in bed while we watched old movies, but Erik had a strict rule against getting crumbs in his sheets. Suggestions that he buy a modest table and a couple of chairs for his kitchen were denied without a moment's consideration. He needed to keep the living room / kitchen free of clutter so he could practice his ballet jumps and combination steps.

Hand to God, I could strangle him sometimes but not when he looked sexy and attentive with his head in my lap. Looking up at me with his soft brown eyes, he placed my left hand on his bare, tight stomach. I was all his.

"Trey, you never want to think too hard about why you got a job," he advised, "because it will only drive you crazy. I've gotten lead roles not because I was the best at dancing the solos but because I was the only one the lead ballerina trusted not to drop her during the lifts."

"That still speaks to your talent and strength."

"How about the roles I've played because the choreographer got off on correcting my body during rehearsals? Or the times I was cast because they wanted someone dark, but not too dark? I once got called into a fitting with three other dancers that obviously would have killed onstage and leaped circles around me, but the artistic director picked me because the costumes for the revival fit me like a glove, and he didn't want to pay to have the costumes altered."

"That would bother me," I said. "I'm not sure I'd be able to dance under those circumstances. My principles would—"

"You work at the info desk," Erik repeated. "It's not a big deal, and it's really none of your business why they hired you."

"None of my business? How can it be none of my business?"

"Their reasons are their reasons. Your responsibility is to do your job. And that's it."

"You're not getting it," I insisted. "If I stay at MoMA, I'm accepting a payoff from Rustin, and I'm giving credence to this fantasy my mother's invented about me being on a gap year."

"You're giving me a headache talking in circles." Erik kicked off the ice packs and sat up. "No one takes their principles to work with them. It's a gig, it's a show. You do it, you go home. Leave it at that."

"I don't know how to turn my brain off like that."

For the first time in our undefined relationship, Erik raised his voice, "Your brain could use some rest!"

I squared off for a shouting match, and Erik walked off into his bedroom. I was too stunned to yell after him. I'd never seen anyone silently decline to engage in an approaching argument. The nerve! Erik closed his bedroom door behind him, and I stood alone in the living room / kitchen with our take-out food at my feet. I considered barging into his room and cursing him out, but I figured it would only make him feel superior. I'd be deemed the immature kid that he had to cut loose for growing too needy and quarrelsome. Erik prized being cool. Okay, I could do that. I could play his game. I sat on the couch, quietly finished eating my portion of dinner, and let myself out.

On the long walk back to my apartment, I thought hard about Erik's points and determined that he did have the correct instincts but settled on the wrong conclusions. He was right that it is impossible to know all the motives of the people that hire me for a job, and I could go mad speculating as to their intentions. Erik was also spot-on when he asserted that a candidate was almost always chosen for dubious reasons that have nothing to do with merit. That's the way of the world. Erik's failure was accepting this without any further thought as to what he owed for receiving opportunities that bloomed from twisted roots. He danced and went home.

More was required. More than crying over the nepotism, cronyism, and other bogus reasons that determine who benefits and who doesn't. More than resigning in a snit. I'd landed a job at MoMA, which would connect me to a world of cultured and influential people. How I got the job was grubby and left me feeling unclean. The way to rectify my misgivings—to balance the score—was to wring what I could from this gig to serve the greater good. The solution was subversive action, not tears. Through me, MoMA was going to support the Gay Rights Movement.

Lesson #15

SOMETIMES IT'S NOT ABOUT YOU

I heard the telephone ringing, but it was around nine in the morning on a Thursday, and I had roamed Mt. Morris until dawn, so I turned over in my twin bed and put my pillow over my head. Gregory, who hadn't been called in for a temp assignment, ran out of the shower dripping wet to answer the phone.

"Slow down, lady," he said. "Who? . . . Got it . . . Yeah, I'll tell him. Bye."

I felt Gregory's hand on my back, shaking me gently, and I knew I was about to be told something awful because the soft touch was not my roommate's style. If he had to wake me, he usually did it with a shout or a fiery slap to the ass.

"Hey, lil man, wake up."

I turned to face him. He was naked and crouching next to my bed, and he eyed me like I was a skittish animal that needed to be handled with care.

"Just tell me," I said.

Gregory sighed. "That was Angie. Barney died this mornin'."

I just cried. No cursing, no wailing. My vision went blurry as heavy tears ran down my face, and I wondered for a split second if Gregory thought I was crazy or foolish. Here I was crying over a man that I had known for about two months. A man who had already accepted his imminent AIDS-related death before I met him in Angie's apartment.

Gregory began massaging my neck. "Barney was the Broadway guy, right? Worked with Lena Horne and all of them?"

I nodded, genuinely impressed that he had been listening and remembered who Barney was.

As if he could read my thoughts, Gregory added, "You talk about him more than anyone else." Then he lifted my blanket and climbed into my bed. I shifted to my side to give him room, and he wrapped his arms around me, pulling our bodies together. I was in red long johns, and he was nude, still quite wet, but warm from the shower. I continued to cry as he softly kissed my face and lips. I felt his erection pressed against my thigh.

Here, at last, was my big chance to go all the way with Gregory. After countless sex dreams and jerk-off sessions featuring his body, he was mine for the taking, as he offered to me what he sold to others. This was not a casual or meaningless gesture. He was holding me tight and grinding against me because this is how he showed love. Tender and available, free of charge.

I got hard, too. I considered wiping my face and reciprocating his kisses. Finally, I would discover if he lived up to his legend, and I suspected I would be more skilled and adventurous than he imagined. Win-win. We would cross from brothers to lovers to back again. God, I was willing; I wanted to fuck and be fucked by him. But my tears wouldn't stop, my mouth wouldn't open, and my arms clung to Gregory's torso, and he soon realized that I needed him, on that morning, to be my brother. We lay together for an hour before I sat up, thanked him, got dressed, and left.

———

By the time I walked to Angie's apartment, my eyes had run dry and my head was throbbing. I looked so distraught that Angie insisted on talking to me in the hallway outside her front door. She was afraid that if she let me in and the men in her care saw me, it would upset them.

Angie was not gentle like Gregory had been. "What's gotten into you?" she began. "You saw him two days ago. He was in agony."

True indeed. Barney had coughed his throat raw, and it hurt so much to swallow that he'd taken to drooling into a cup. Whenever he lifted his head off his pillow, he suffered nauseating vertigo, which made showering or going to the toilet impossible. We sponge bathed him and changed his adult diapers in the primary bedroom as he lay flat on the mattress wearing nothing but the diaper and a cheap, terry cloth robe.

"He shouldn't have died like this," I said. "Where were all the people he talked about?"

"Barney kept them away. He didn't want them to see what we saw—to remember him that way. He came here to hide out and die."

"He's the first grown-up I've ever met who I wish had been part of my family."

Angie pouted for effect. "You saying you don't want an Aunt Angie?"

"You know what I mean. Barney was Black and gay. Imagine if I'd had him in my life as a kid, watching out for me, showing me the ropes."

"Are you sad about his death or your childhood?"

"Fuck, Angie, I came over here because I thought maybe you'd be sad about Barney, too. I forgot no one gets to you. They come, they die, you move on."

She raised her hand to slap me, and determined not to dodge it or look away, I braced for the impact. Angie caught herself. She lowered her hand and her head.

Staring down at the worn green carpet in the hallway, Angie said, "I can't afford to indulge my grief. I've got other guys—there are always other guys—that need looking after. I can't be there for them if I'm hung up on someone else. But if it's so goddamn important for you to hear what's on my heart, I'll tell you this once. I loved Barney, too. He was special."

"Thank you. I'll get out of your hair now," I said as I stepped toward the stairs.

"One more thing, Trey." Angie was serene as she explained, "He wanted the pain to stop. This morning, Barney said to me, 'I'm ready to die.' He said it over and over. His death was a release from all that needless agony."

———

The address on the letter for Neil Constable brought me to a sandstone apartment building in Morningside Heights. I pushed the button next to his name on the buzzer.

Over the intercom, Neil asked, "Who is it?"

"Hello, my name is Trey Singleton. Barney sent me to give you a letter after he died."

Immediately, the front door clicked and unlocked. I entered the building, afraid that I'd somehow ruin my solemn mission. It felt like I should say more than, "Here you go," hand over the letter, and leave. But I wasn't sure what words suited this occasion. As I approached Neil's door, I decided to follow his lead.

Neil let me into his condo, where the living room walls were painted fuchsia, a bust of Marlene Dietrich sat on a grand piano, and the sofa was lined in gray fox fur.[65] Neil, at fifty, maintained a trim figure and wore his chestnut hair in a mess of curls on top and shaved tight on the sides. Dressed in a black T-shirt and black jeans, he told me that he had learned that Barney passed away that morning; a mutual friend of his and Barney's called to break the news.

---

65. Marlene Dietrich (1901–1992), who was one of the first and brightest of film stars to transition seamlessly from the silent film age into talkies, cut an enduring and tantalizing figure with her incandescent brand of androgyny in movies like 1930's *Morocco*. Dietrich, a bisexual, managed her public image scrupulously. Much about her love life wasn't known until after her death.

"I pretended I already knew Barney was dead," explained Neil. "That way, I didn't have to give a big performance, you know? People tell you a thing like your ex-lover is dead, and they expect you to fall to pieces."

After he hung up, Neil said the phone just kept ringing. A barrage of good friends, forgotten drinking buddies, one-night stands, and sympathetic ex-lovers lit up his telephone line until Neil couldn't take it and left the phone off the hook. The busy signal sang to him for a few minutes. Then there was silence. Neil said that he hadn't cried yet, which surprised him as much as my arrival. He insisted I stay awhile.

"Of course Barney wrote a letter on his deathbed," Neil said after taking my coat and ushering me to the sofa. "He always had a flair for the dramatic." He sized me up. "Have you read the letter?"

"No, sir. What he wrote to you is your business. I wouldn't snoop."

"Please, honey, call me *Neil* or *darling* or *sugar,* but not *sir.*" He went to the wet bar next to the fireplace and began to fix himself a cocktail. "I can't believe he's gone. I'd heard he was sick. I considered going to see him, but there were conflicting reports as to where he'd gone during his final months. Besides, he hated being caught off guard. He *arranged* surprises, you see. He was never *to be* surprised. A quintessential Aries." He took a sip of his Moscow mule and then looked over his shoulder at me. "Would you like a cocktail, honey?"

To be polite company, I said, "A gin and tonic, please."

Neil raised his glass in appreciation. "Right on. Thank you for not making me go through the motions of twisting your arm. Few people can admit they'd like a drink nowadays. They have to be talked into it. It's terribly boring."

"Barney told me about a lot of the parties you two used to throw. Did you really drink white wine out of Joni Sledge's shoe?"[66]

---

66. Joni Sledge (1956–2017), along with three of her sisters, was a founding member of the vocal group Sister Sledge, who recorded the 1979 R&B hit "We Are Family," which was embraced as a gay anthem.

Neil scoffed. "Is that what he told you? No, honey, it wasn't white wine. I drank champagne out of one of her high heels. Joni's feet were very clean, and I was pretty sauced by that point." Neil brought me my cocktail. "What else did he say about me? Am I the court jester in all his tales?"

"No, not at all. He told me about your stage shows. He said you were the best drag—" I caught myself. "—female impersonator in New York."

"How dear of him." Neil clinked his glass against mine, and we both drank long sips. "Did he mention why he felt my talents were limited to the city? Was there someone he felt was better elsewhere in the country or on the planet?"

He asked the questions with such a dry deadpan, I was taken aback.

Having shocked me as he intended, he laughed. "I'm only kidding, honey. Charles Pierce has a standing engagement in Vegas, and as long as he's onstage, I'll never be the fairest one in all the land."[67]

"Charles Pierce—I haven't heard of him. What makes him such a great drag queen?"

Fuck, I'd said the forbidden words. Barney had warned me. Neil clutched his glass in his hands, got up, crossed the room, and leaned against his grand piano like a femme fatale in a film noir.

"Do you know what drag queens are? Frustrated cabaret acts." Neil sat down on the piano bench and began playing "Falling in Love Again." "These are men who can't sing," he insisted, "so they lip sync. They can't achieve a resemblance to a real star, so they give themselves silly names and act like buffoons. Don't get me started

---

67. Charles Pierce (1926–1999) was widely considered the preeminent female impersonator of his era and skewered movie stars such as Bette Davis, Joan Crawford, Carol Channing, and Mae West with his comedic takes on their personas. This had not been Pierce's career goal when he moved to Los Angeles. He'd wanted to be a screen actor but couldn't get substantial work due to homophobic attitudes against men who read as gay. Pierce's club act developed as a way to make ends meet.

on that freak show of theirs—Wigstock.[68] There's no professionalism to what they do. Anything goes.

"Female impersonators, on the other hand, have rigorous standards. We have to look, move, and sound exactly like the stars we're portraying. You can judge our work against the real thing. I had eight silver screen dames in my repertoire, but Marlene was the jewel in my crown. Tell me you've seen her movies or listened to one of her records."

"Yes," I said, "a boy I fooled around with in high school was a big fan of hers and played me *Dietrich in London,* or *Dietrich in Rio,* or Dietrich someplace."

"The location is unimportant. What matters is you know her voice. Listen to mine." Neil's eyelids dropped to half-mast, his bottom lip dipped a fraction to the left, he gazed out onto an imaginary audience, and sang in a German-accented contralto, "Men cluster to me. Like moth 'round a *vlame.* And if their *vings* burn. I know I'm not to blame. *Valling* in love again. Never *vanted* to. What am I to do? Can't help it."

His rendition was camp but couldn't be dismissed as only mimicry and affectations. Neil infused the lyrics with soulfulness. He felt every word he sang, and he made me feel it, too.

"That was awesome," I said. "I'd believe you're the best in the country."

Neil reached for his drink. "Thank you, honey."

"I'd love to see you onstage, dressed like her and everything."

"Oh, I gave it up a year and a half ago." He polished off his drink and got up to make himself another one. "I'm a freelance makeup artist now."

"Why'd you quit?"

"The scene is fading. There used to be a dozen venues I could play in and around Manhattan. Now the only way to make any real

---

68. Wigstock was an outdoor drag queen festival held in Manhattan annually from 1984 to 2001, then again from 2003 to 2005, and sporadically since 2018.

money is to go on the road, accept smaller booking fees, pay for my own hotel accommodations."

"That's a shame," I said. "You are great."

His hands started to tremble, causing the ice cubes to clink against the glass, and he stared out the window. "I have a gift for a dying art. It happens. I'm proud I got to stop on *my* terms. I didn't chase the scene until it died in my arms."

I thought this was the moment. The ice in his glass continued to rattle. Neil's face became a mask of pain, and his breathing grew erratic. The dam was going to break. He was going to cry for sure.

"Did Barney die alone?" he asked.

"No, my friend Angie was with him. She and I looked after him the last couple of months. He lasted a lot longer than most I've seen. In the end, Angie held his hand, and Barney told her that he was ready to let go."

Just when I expected a flood of tears, Neil steadied his hands, turned his head high in defiance, and went to retrieve a leather-bound photo album from a bookshelf. "There's this picture of Barney and me that you should see, and it's a miracle because it's the only time we ever both looked handsome in the same photo at the same time. We were out on Rehoboth Beach, celebrating the Fourth. Have you been to Rehoboth?"

"No, I'm not even sure where that is," I admitted.

"Delaware," Neil answered as he joined me on the couch and opened the large photo album across his right leg and my left leg. "There's nothing happening out there except this gay area of the beach. Far less expensive and trashy than Fire Island." He bowed his head and sighed. "I'm not keeping you, am I? The last thing I want to be is a bore."

"Not at all. Barney told so many stories about the two of you. I've been curious about what you guys were like together." For a second, I was going to leave it at that, but Neil was being so open with me, I felt I should reciprocate. "Fifteen years together. I've never met two men who stuck it out that long."

"It was all luck. There is no secret formula. Just be lucky. Everything between us was so easy. We hardly argued. Loved the same movies and plays." He flipped through the pages to find the Rehoboth photo. "We were young, and we didn't have a lot of money, but you didn't need a lot of money to have fun in those days. Every night, there seemed to be a party, and he and I were everyone's favorite guests. Rooms would cheer when we entered. 'Barney and Neil are here!' Honey, I loved being us."

"If you don't mind me asking, what happened?"

He found the photo. "Here we are. Look at those Adonises."

They did look radiant embracing on the beach. Both shirtless. Barney in yellow swim trunks, and Neil in a blue speedo. There was an ease and intimacy to their posture. Arms intertwined and bare torsos pressed together, Barney and Neil appeared content. An interracial gay couple in the early 1970s, and they'd found each other, and together they were all they needed.

"Perfect. The two of you look perfect," I said before sitting back and finishing my drink.

"Yes, we were for a while. This was well before the years of paranoia and death."

"What do you mean?"

I didn't say I wanted another drink, but Neil took my empty glass from my hand and got up to make me a second gin and tonic.

"We had this marvelous circle of friends. We all worked in theater—mostly off-off Broadway and occasionally on the Great White Way. We'd meet up to help each other with our shows, and we partied until dawn after the curtain came down. Guys fell in and out of bed with each other back then, and it was no big deal. You'd sleep with a friend just to try it out—for the experience of it. No hard feelings."

Neil handed me my drink. I took one sip and realized I could drink no more of it. He'd given me a glass full of gin and forgotten to cut it with tonic.

"It was 1974 when Cyril caught pneumonia," he continued, "then double pneumonia, then died. He was thirty-three. We thought it was a bizarre fluke. The next year, Scottie got these lesions, lost weight. The doctors couldn't figure it out. He went home to his parents in Memphis because his folks insisted. What did New York doctors know anyway? We stopped hearing from him. Barney was the one who phoned Scottie's parents' house, and they told him that the Lord had called Scottie home. In '76, we lost Jamal and Ryan."

I couldn't accept what I was hearing without confirmation. "To AIDS?"

"Yes, honey. You don't think the deaths started when *The New York Times* decided to write about it?[69] AIDS was killing us long before we gave it a name.[70] Our friends—usually the Black ones, in the beginning—started dying, and no one could give us any answers. No one seemed to care. I was shocked by that. Barney wasn't. Anyway, honey, the fear, the accusations—it got ugly. Unforgivable things were said. Some of us suspected it could be passed through sex. Others were convinced kissing could do it. We didn't trust each other. We blamed each other."

"Is this when Barney got it?"

"I don't know. Maybe. We were practically celibate by 1980. We broke up in '82. He got tested in '85, and he was positive. I got tested, too, and I'm negative. It's never made sense to me. Who gets it? Who doesn't? Who dies in months? Who lives for years?"

"I'm sorry," I said.

---

69. The first *New York Times* story about HIV/AIDS was published on July 3, 1981. The headline of the article speaks to how much public understanding of the disease has evolved: RARE CANCER SEEN IN 41 HOMOSEXUALS.

70. The earliest detected case of HIV/AIDS in the United States is believed to have befallen an African American patient in St. Louis, Missouri, named Robert Rayford (1953–1969). Rayford, who was suspected of being an underage gay sex worker and/or molestation victim, sought medical treatment in 1968 for genital warts, sores, and swelling. He claimed he first noticed those symptoms in 1966. After he died of pneumonia, an autopsy revealed that his lesions were Kaposi's sarcoma. In 1987, Rayford's tissue samples were tested, and the antibodies against all nine detectable HIV proteins were found in his blood.

Neil downed half his drink in three big gulps. "One year, twenty-six of us rented seven houses all next to each other on the south end of Rehoboth. Now there are five of us left." He paused.

I stayed for two more hours. Neil drank three more Moscow mules. He showed me other pictures and shared hilarious stories about his beautiful, gifted deceased friends. I would have stayed longer, but Neil's boyfriend, Victor Flores, burst into the condo. Middle-aged and heavyset, Victor was sweaty and panting. He'd only learned within the hour that Barney was dead, and when he called the condo to check on Neil, he'd gotten a busy signal. Fearing that Neil had harmed himself, Victor ran several blocks from his office in the admissions department at Columbia University to the condo he shared with Neil.

To calm himself down, Victor went to get himself a beer out of the refrigerator. While Victor was in the kitchen, I noticed that Neil had hidden Barney's letter between the pages of the leather-bound photo album.

"I should be going," I said.

Victor shook my hand and thanked me. Neil hugged me good-bye. Out in the hall, I felt light-headed. The result of alcohol on an empty stomach. I took a second to gather myself. Then, even though I knew it was invasive, I stood outside Neil and Victor's door listening for a minute. I heard muffled chatter until suddenly I could make out the sound of Neil crying. I was glad he wasn't alone.

THERE'S NO PREPARING FOR EVERY CIRCLE OF HELL

The night before the first ACT UP protest, I didn't feel anxious or afraid like Peter had warned I might. But I suppose I had some sort of longing because I did something I hadn't done in months: I told Gregory to hand me the telephone when he whispered that my sister was on the line.

Jackie sounded surprised and thrilled to hear my voice, but she wasted no time on catch-me-up pleasantries. Instead, she asked playfully, "Do you know what you're gonna get me for my birthday?"

I joked, "Same thing I got you last year," which was nothing.

Jackie laughed her head off, then said, "Make sure to put it in a big box with a bow on top."

With her fifteenth birthday less than a month away, Jackie was mildly sarcastic and sweetly self-centered, eagerly rambling on about her life without prying into mine. For most of our conversation, I just listened and followed her in my mind's eye as she roamed through Ashmount, the mansion that I had fled and that she still lived in with our parents.

Our father, who was among the first to have a car phone installed in his Cadillac, had bought a cordless phone for the mansion. So I could hear the stairs creak in the pitch and order that told me that Jackie was going down from the second floor to the first. When she entered the living room with its high ceilings, I knew exactly where she was because of the way her voice echoed.

After a while, I lay on my bed and closed my eyes, and as Jackie talked about her high school friends, crushes, and rivals as if her world were a soap opera that I'd been following, I began to feel like I was sitting in the old green armchair that I missed, and Jackie was curled up on the gray couch. I was home, and it was ordinary and uninspiring. Just another night in Indiana.

And I'll admit, for once, the deafening lack of excitement was welcome. The doomsday scenarios that every protester had been trained to anticipate stopped beating their drums. The nagging doubts about my ability to be brave when attacked quit blasting their horns. I breathed easy. Tomorrow was kept at bay by the sound of Jackie's voice.

Fortunately, on and on she went, and I didn't interrupt her to mention my fears or problems. In fact, I spoke less than a hundred words during the entire call. Two hours passed before Jackie had to run, and I was startled to see that it was almost midnight on my end of the line.

"Love you," she said.

"Love you, too," I replied.

After I hung up, I wrapped myself in my bedsheets and pretended I was in my childhood bedroom until I fell asleep.

I had set three different alarms to wake me up early the next morning, Tuesday, March 24, 1987. After a bowl of hot oatmeal and a cold shower, I put on a jockstrap and inserted an athletic cup over my cock to protect it from knees, kicks, and batons. I wore military-green corduroy pants, thick wool socks, and a pair of ratty, comfortable sneakers. My T-shirt bore the slogan GAY IS GOOD,[71] and the black, crushed-velvet women's jacket that I'd bought at a

---

71. "Gay Is Good" is a political slogan coined by gay rights activist Frank E. Kameny (1925–2011). The slogan was modeled after the consciousness-raising message "Black Is Beautiful."

thrift store had a button fastened to the lapel that read: HELP THE POLICE—BEAT YOURSELF UP.[72]

Gregory rolled out of his bed to see me off at the front door. "How soon after you stop traffic will the government surrender?" he asked.

"Reagan should be waving the white flag by noon."

"For real, though, lil man, don't be gettin' cute with the cops. You ain't gonna make it through life if you get any uglier."

"Ahh," I said sweetly, "fuck you, too."

Gregory grabbed me by the hand. "Please . . . stay in the background."

"I'll be careful, I promise."

Half an hour later, Peter and Eduardo met me outside the back doors of MoMA. They were fifteen minutes late. I acted peeved but had built their tardiness into our schedule. I banged on the big metal door to the beat of "Shave and a Haircut."

"Holy shit, this is just like an art heist!" cheered Peter entirely too loudly.

"Shut up," I snapped.

The back door opened, and a bald, portly man named Leland McCaffrey barked in his gruff voice, "Get in, quick!"

Peter, Eduardo, and I hurried into the unadorned corridors of the museum that were primarily used by deliverymen, maintenance crews, and trade workers for the in-shop services. A wad of two dozen keys jingled against Leland's hip as he led us down a musty hallway that dead-ended at a large workroom. This was the signage department, where sixty-eight-year-old Leland was the last word on quality control for exit signs, floor plan maps, executive nameplates, celebratory banners, art piece wall summaries, and exhibition posters.

Leland was a MoMA lifer, having worked his way up to the top

---

72. "Help the Police—Beat Yourself Up" and "Support the Police—Beat Yourself Up" are satirical slogans used to ridicule the prevalence of police violence toward marginalized communities. While their origins are unclear, the phrases began appearing noticeably on buttons and signs in the early 1970s.

of signage over the course of a forty-two-year career in the department. I'd met him when I was sent from the information desk to find out if we could have a sign discouraging flash photography in the museum, a growing crisis due to Polaroid-crazed tourists from the Midwest and California. Leland was brusque, but professional. He didn't treat me like a kid, and he completed our order in less than a day. I dropped by the next evening after my shift and thanked him with a bottle of Jack Daniel's because I'd noticed a number of shot glasses on the shelf behind his desk.

"Unnecessary and much appreciated," he said. "Take a load off, and we'll test the goods." He poured two shots and slid one across his desk to me. "You are old enough to drink? Wait! Don't answer that."

We knocked back more than one shot, and I got Leland talking about his tenure at the museum. Turned out, he didn't give a flying fuck about art. Frank O'Hara used to call him a philistine. What kept Leland loyal to MoMA was that they looked past his 1943 arrest in a fairy raid at a gay bar called Carrico; in addition to being thrown in jail, Leland's name and those of the other homosexuals booked that night were published in several of the New York City newspapers.

"'Deviant Behavior' was the header," Leland said. "Any of my pals will tell you, I've never been deviant a day in my life. I didn't expose myself to anyone. I didn't dance with other men. No matter, I was a deviant in print."

With his homosexuality confirmed (and my persuasion being self-evident), we delved into what Leland's life was like pre–Stonewall Riots.

"More than anything, you wanted to stay under the radar," he explained. "If you were found out, they could ruin you."

Leland considered himself lucky to be hired on at MoMA despite the mark against him, and the humiliating ordeal left him determined to avoid receiving a second strike. He would attend all-male house parties, but not gay bars. He had friends in the Mattachine

Society, but he would not join it. He supported the goal of the Sip-In, but wasn't one of the agitators at Julius'.[73] When the Stonewall Riots broke out, he remained locked away in his bachelor's apartment in Hell's Kitchen.

I dared to ask, "Do you wish you'd done more?"

His gravelly voice was almost a whisper. "From time to time, I do."

March 24 was Leland's chance to redeem himself. He took Peter, Eduardo, and me into a back room. On a wooden table, there were three stacks of twenty-four-by-thirty-six-inch, hard-stock posters. One poster said: DON'T PUT A PRICE ON LIFE; the second one said: AID$NOW; and the third had a black-and-white headshot of President Reagan stamped with the word AIDSGATE. Leland had made twenty of each poster.

"I'd give you more," he explained, "but I can only write off so many discards in a month without raising eyebrows."

"These are beautiful," said Eduardo.

Leland puffed up with pride. "Thanks. I did my best."

"And we are grateful," added Peter.

I patted Leland on the back. "We're going to put these to good use."

Peter, Eduardo, and I concealed the posters in three cardboard boxes, smuggled them out of MoMA, and caught a cab to Trinity Church on Wall Street. On the ride over, Peter rolled up Eduardo's sleeve and wrote on his forearm with a black marker.

---

73. The Sip-In, which was orchestrated by the Mattachine Society and the American Civil Liberties Union (ACLU) in 1966, was a successful effort to abolish a discriminatory New York State Liquor Authority policy. The policy forbade serving drinks to known homosexuals in public bars. This ban on serving alcohol to homosexuals was often the pretext for police raids on gay bars. To challenge the policy, three men disclosed that they were gay to a bartender at Julius', then ordered a drink. When denied service, the ACLU filed a discrimination claim that ultimately was upheld by the New York City Commission on Human Rights, effectively ending the "no-service" policy targeted at homosexuals in bars.

Then Peter turned to me. "Take off your smoking jacket and show me some skin."

"Why?"

"I'm gonna write the number of the law firm that's handling our bail in the very likely event we get hauled off by the cops."

I took one arm out of my crushed-velvet jacket and presented it to Peter.

"This is your one phone call," he said as he scribbled the telephone digits onto me.

It was 7:00 a.m. when the cabbie dropped us off, and more than one hundred ACT UP members were already gathered outside Trinity Church. The energy in the air was electric. Many of our fellow protesters carried SILENCE=DEATH or homemade signs that railed against corporate greed. Nonetheless, there was a frenzy when Peter ripped open our three boxes, and Eduardo and I started passing out Leland's posters. I had never felt more alive.

The first disruptive demonstration of ACT UP was about to commence, and we had a surefire plan to attract the police and the media. We were going to bottleneck the morning rush hour traffic in lower Manhattan by laying our bodies down on the road at the busy intersection of Broadway and Wall Street. We'd chosen that spot to send a message to the New York Stock Exchange and its legion of financial profiteers who prioritized revenue streams over the lives of people battling HIV/AIDS. We also took specific aim at the Food and Drug Administration (FDA), a rat's nest of bureaucrats that could take up to nine years to approve a promising new drug, and the rapacious pharmaceutical company Burroughs Wellcome, who manufactured the only approved AIDS drug available at the time, AZT, and charged $10,000 for a year's worth of the medicine.[74]

By 7:30 a.m., there were more than 250 of us gathered outside the church, and honestly, it wasn't clear who the hell was in charge. I'd

---

74. Accounting for inflation, $10,000 in 1987 is equivalent to $23,916.90 in 2021.

seen Larry Kramer, Vito Russo, E. D. Galecki, and Dylan Stalder in the mix, but none of them, I suspected, wanted to be accused of attempting a power grab. So there our group was—teeming with explosive energy and righteous indignation, and no leader, no direction.

At last, Theodora Divine, a Black, trans woman who was also the best waitress at the Have Mercy Fish Shack, climbed on top of an overturned garbage can and shouted, "If we doin' this, let's do it now! Hit the street, bitches!"

The crowd roared and stormed the intersection waving our posters and signs overhead. It was bedlam. Cars swerved and zoomed to avoid getting trapped in the flood of bodies. Once we secured the center of the intersection, a furious chorus of car horns blared around us. The noise was deafening and sustained. Some drivers tried to intimidate us by revving their engines and edging forward. Dumb move. We pounded dents into their cars' hoods. Smart drivers realized they'd have to find another route to their destinations and began making U-turns. Within five minutes, we occupied the whole intersection, and in the distance, police sirens squealed.

I sat on the street next to Peter and Eduardo and had to scream for them to hear me, "So far, so good!"

"We're just getting started!" yelled Peter. "It ain't a party until the boys in blue get here!"

Alarmed, Eduardo pointed to the northeast corner of the intersection. "What is that? Who is that?"

I turned and saw Helena and a group of young white men pulling a long rope to hoist a mannequin dressed in a cheap suit into the air beneath a streetlamp. The sight triggered a visceral reaction in me. I broke out into a cold sweat, and my face felt tingly. Was I really seeing what I was seeing? At a glance, the mannequin looked like a real person, and only when the effigy twirled and faced me could I read the name on a piece of cardboard affixed to its chest: Frank Young, a reference lost on me. What I did know is that the image of a pack of angry white guys hanging a body to the delight of a white woman was not the message we wanted captured and broadcast across the country.

I got up and ran over to confront Helena. We had to yell over the commotion, but admittedly, my opening words could have been more diplomatic. "What the fuck is going on here? You all look like a lynch mob!"

Helena didn't back down. "Frank Young deserves a hanging!"

"Who's Frank Young?"

"The incompetent FDA commissioner!"

"People aren't going to get that!" I screamed as several police cars formed a barricade around our demonstration.

"What?" Helena shouted.

"This makes us look crazy and violent!"

"Huh?"

"Take it down!"

"We're about to burn it now!"

A fire. And not the ordinary contained garbage can fire. No, this would be a swinging mannequin in flames over the heads of dozens of people in a congested area where it was too noisy to issue warnings or instructions.

"Absolutely not!" I screamed. "Don't burn it!"

She heard that and put her hands on her hips. "Who says? You?"

The drawbacks of an army without a hierarchy came into sharp focus. People couldn't be ordered to do anything; they had to be persuaded. There was no chance Helena was going to accept me as the final word on the matter. Reflexively, I almost lied and told her the command came from Larry, but I remembered how hostile she'd been to him after our training session. Then I recalled who she did respect.

"Vito! He's worried a fire will cause a panic! The fire will be the story! Not our message!"

Helena glanced around, hoping she'd spot Vito. When she didn't, she sighed. "He's probably right!"

The effigy remained hanging, which I didn't love, but it wasn't ablaze, which I would have hated more. The politics of activism in a nutshell.

I rejoined Peter and Eduardo, sitting on the street. We chanted, "Release the drugs!" or "We're angry, we want action!" off and on for half an hour. The crowd swelled around us. News helicopters began circling us in the sky, adding to the racket. It felt like the ground was rumbling beneath me. A police van pulled up to the perimeter, and when I noticed that a few cops huddled together were smiling, my blood ran cold.

I put my mouth close to Peter's ear. "The cops are about to hit us! They're going to clear us out of here!"

Peter put his lips against my ear. "Don't let Dorothy down!"

I wondered if he was referring to Dorothy Cotton or Dorothy Gale.[75] Before I could ask, cops in teams of two shoved their way through the crowd of protesters. I saw Dylan, among others, knocked to the pavement. People screamed; some pushed back against the cops. I counted ten police officers heading toward us from the south side of the intersection. I imagine there were at least that many cops closing in from the other directions.

The crowd began to collapse in on itself. People weren't watching their steps. Fear was setting in. Peter, Eduardo, and I tried to get up on our feet, but it was too late. Bodies were falling back, tripping and crashing in on us. Peter balled up onto his shins and knees and covered the back of his head with his hands. Eduardo wiggled and wormed, bodysurfing the crowd away from us. I was less Zen in my approach. I bucked and jumped and grabbed ahold of anyone higher than I was and pulled on them for leverage up. I got to my feet.

The cops weren't actually trying to clear the entire crowd. Two officers would select one protester and drag that individual away to be arrested. It seemed random, but it revealed its racist slant. Easily

---

75. Dorothy Gale is the full name of the main character in *The Wizard of Oz* (released in 1939), portrayed indelibly by Judy Garland (1922–1969). Due to the movie and Garland's large gay fan base, a coded way of discussing or disclosing a person's homosexuality is to refer to them as "a friend of Dorothy's."

90 percent of the ACT UP demonstrators were white. I saw the cops grab a Korean man. I saw them grab Theodora. Two white cops zeroed in on me.

As soon as one of them yanked me by the arm, I went limp. The second cop tackled me, and we rammed into a wall of people before tumbling to the street. He let his full weight come down on me. I couldn't breathe. I felt him driving his knee into my crotch. He was disappointed to discover I was wearing a cup.

The cop on top of me yelled in my ear, "How'd you get your nigga dick in such a small cup?"

I managed to shout, "Your daddy did it for me!"

He ripped the button off my jacket and jabbed me repeatedly in the ribs. His partner pulled him off me, and the two of them hooked me under my shoulders and carried me away. At the police van, my hands were cuffed behind my back, then I was tossed inside the van face-first. My head smacked against the metal floor, and I was semi-conscious as they loaded up the van. Seventeen ACT UP protesters were arrested during our first demonstration, and fourteen of them were people of color.

———

I didn't get to dial the telephone number that Peter wrote onto my forearm. I'd completely passed out by the time the police van reached the precinct, and I was separated from the other detained protesters. There was a knot on my forehead the size of a golf ball.

I woke up on the floor of a dank solitary-confinement cell. My vision was blurry, and my head was throbbing. There was one chair in the cell, and a middle-aged Black man in a gray suit was sitting in it.

"Good, you're back with us," he said. "We can talk now, and we must hurry. There isn't much time left to save you."

In the small cell, the man's voice echoed, aggravating my headache. I crawled over to a wall and rested against it as I sat on my butt.

I attempted to study the face of this Black man offering me his help. It was difficult to get a fix on him since I saw at least three overlapping outlines of him, but what I could piece together was that his comforting words didn't match his demeanor.

"Save me from what?" I asked.

He leaned forward and put a hand on my knee. "Your affiliations."

I jerked my knee away from him. "Who are you? Are you my lawyer?"

"I'm not your lawyer, but—"

"I want my lawyer now, please."

"But!"

The volume of his echo sent a searing shock wave through my skull from temple to temple. I fell to my side and groaned softly.

"But," he continued, "I can be your advocate. Unlike my colleagues, who would let the inmates at Rikers go to town on your Black, nelly ass, I'm sympathetic. I've got a cousin who's queer. He can't help it either."

"You're a *fed*," I said with naked disdain.

"Yes, Mr. Earl Singleton the third, I work for the bureau."

All at once, the game at hand was clear, and I knew exactly why I had been separated from the other arrested activists. I was someone this FBI agent thought he could bully, trick, or bribe. I was his weak mark. Never had I been more insulted in my life.

"Wrong move, sending a Black agent to try and flip me," I said. "Nooooo, what you need is a faggot fed. Does the FBI have one of those? An Agent Mary who can at least suck my dick before asking me to betray my brothers and sisters."

"Whoa!" he yelled, using his volume again as a weapon. "Forget your so-called friends out there. You need to think about yourself, Earl. Think about how this path you're on will hurt your real family. I've looked into you. Your parents are respectable, civic-minded people. What you're doing would break their hearts."

I laughed in the agent's face. "I thought you assholes tapped phones. Didn't you see there are no calls between me and my parents? I'm not going to be your informant to please my mommy and daddy."

The agent shifted gears without the slightest hesitation. "Okay, then let's talk incentives. Maybe you're tired of living in a small apartment with a male prostitute for a roommate. I can find you a place of your own—rent-free."

My suspicions that I was under surveillance were confirmed, and I felt vindicated, then violated. How long had the government been examining my life without my consent? I wondered if this nameless Black agent had tailed me by himself. Was tracking me his day job?

"Pathetic." I lean against the wall as I dared to stand up. "There's nothing you can do to me, nothing you can give me to make me your spy."

As soon as those righteous words came out of my mouth, I remembered my deal with Rustin. I had agreed before I even joined ACT UP to be his inside man, passing along information about the group. Obviously, there was a world of moral difference between the FBI and Bayard Rustin, but I felt compromised. I couldn't speak truthfully in absolutes.

My conflicted feelings must have registered because the agent grinned like he had spotted an opening. He wagged his finger at me and insisted, "There's something you want. You just thought of it."

"No, I didn't. I wasn't—"

"How many of the people you got arrested with can you name? How well do you know them?"

"That doesn't matter," I said.

"You owe them nothing—or think of it this way, you owe yourself more. You owe yourself first."

"You're boring me. I want my fucking lawyer."

"You don't get a lawyer," he said, "because this isn't an interrogation. I'm here to offer you a chance to get something out of this besides the knot on your forehead."

"I've got nothing more to say to you."

There was knocking on the cell door.

The agent spoke to whoever was on the other side of it. "Alright, I'm wrapping it up." Then he came to stand right in front of me. He rested the palm of his hand on the wall to the left of my head. "I don't want to say this too loud," he whispered. "I'm not supposed to mention it. But come to the federal building. We're on Foley Square. Give them your name at the front desk, and they'll find me. And I'll let you read a file that will blow your mind. It'll explain why your brother was kidnapped and why his body still hasn't been found."

I gasped but couldn't exhale. The agent left, the cell door closed behind him, and I remained frozen with my lungs holding in the air and the shock. Martin. Poor Martin. He was dead, long dead. No changing that, so the details in an FBI case file were ultimately immaterial. The details could offer no salvation . . . but some answers, some closure—maybe. Oh fuck, my head was throbbing worse than ever, and as I stood breathless in that cell, I realized the agent had found my soft underbelly.

Lesson #17

LEAVE THE FALLEN BEHIND

I was released five hours later than the other sixteen ACT UP protesters, and when I walked out of the precinct, I was greeted by the applause and whistles of at least fifty of my fellow activists, including Peter, Eduardo, Theodora, Larry, and Vito. The knot on my forehead was regarded as a badge of honor. A tear in the right shoulder of my crushed-velvet jacket revealed a red silk lining, and just about everyone who hugged and kissed me also advised me to never have the rip mended. I still felt a bit unsteady on my feet, but it didn't matter because I was so lovingly mobbed, there was no room for me to fall down.

After waving goodbye to the crowd, I climbed into a cab with Peter, who kissed Eduardo and promised to meet up with him later. My lower ribs started to ache when the cab pulled into traffic. I closed my eyes to rest.

"Hey, golden boy," said Peter, "I agreed to pay for this ride out of my own pocket because I expect you to spill. What happened in there?"

I kept my eyes closed as I explained, "Believe it or not, but I was put in solitary confinement, where a Black FBI agent tried to make me his government informant. I swear, I told him to fuck off."

"I believe you," he said to my relief. "Probably won't be the last time they come at you. They can be persistent and go to extremes.

The law doesn't apply to law enforcement. When we were protesting Nixon and the war, I knew plenty of people who got snatched up without warrants or any due process. And those people would disappear for days. It was mostly the FBI, sometimes the CIA. Looking for proof of foreign influence, they called it." Peter chuckled. "I'd bet my balls the feds have got files on all our leaders and members. Phones tapped, people followed. That's been the extent to this point. But I suspect it'll get more hardball. ACT UP is an escalation."

I looked Peter in the eyes. "I'm telling you this so you'll know I told you everything. The agent said he'd let me read the file on my brother's death. I could really learn what happened to Martin."

"Oh," Peter groaned. "That's low, even for a fed. You realize he's full of shit, right? They're eavesdroppers, not crime solvers."

My throat tightened as I fought back the sudden urge to cry. Peter was right, of course, but damn, how I wished there was a stack of pages that would explain the end of Martin's story. I didn't recognize just how badly I longed for those answers until they were teased in front of me.

"They've got nothing in that bag for you," Peter assured me.

I nodded.

"Listen, you just keep your nose clean and bask in the limelight," he suggested. "Off of what happened today, you'll be the belle of the ball in Chelsea for weeks."

When we reached my apartment building, Peter walked me to my unit. Gregory opened the door when he heard me rattling with the keys.

"Don't be mad," I said.

Gregory took one look at the welt on my head and glared at Peter. "How come nobody ain't fuck up your face?"

Peter raised his hands in surrender. "I didn't hurt him."

"No, I get it," Gregory seethed. "You pulled him into the streets, but you come out clean, and he got his head cracked. And now you've come to drop him off before you go on your merry white way."

Peter objected, "Hey, I'm an ally to the cause—"

"Leave before I yell some thangs that'll have brothers runnin' out to beat your ass."

"Call me later, Trey," said Peter, scurrying off.

"Thanks, Peter."

Gregory pulled me inside our apartment and slammed the door. "Whatcha thankin' him for?"

"He's not to blame for how the cops behaved."

"He's to blame for thinkin' cops were gonna play fair," said Gregory, "and you to blame for not stayin' in the background like you promised."

"I tried."

"Not hardly, by the looks of it."

"I'm not a wallflower," I explained. "The cops zeroed in on me. People always zero in on me."

Gregory opened the fridge to get me some ice for my welt, but our ice trays were empty. He filled them with water and put them back in the freezer. I started to get undressed. I wanted a long, hot shower.

Gregory informed me, "The government didn't surrender, and you all was a blip on the news. You got that egg on your head for nothin'. You see that, don't you?"

"Maybe," I said, "or maybe not. It's too early to tell."

———

Although I assumed Peter was joking, it turned out he was correct about the rise in my celebrity status among politically minded gays. Whether I was at the museum, in the subway, or out drinking with Gregory, queers of all ages approached me with smiles and open arms. They knew my name ("Trey, it's an honor to meet you.") and were eager for me to confirm the folklore growing around that first ACT UP demonstration ("Is it true you sang 'You Know How to Love Me' as the cops led you away?")[76] Some of the men who recognized me wanted to have sex with me. I obliged more than a few of them.

Beyond the social scene, my newfound cachet earned me a spot on the unofficial—but absolutely necessary—advisory committee for ACT UP. Publicly, the no-hierarchy principle was inviolable. Realistically, ten to fourteen people, depending on availability, met at each other's apartments or, when I hosted meetings, in an available conference room at MoMA to discuss ACT UP's next steps.

Despite Gregory's doubts, we had reason to believe that we could make a positive difference for those living with HIV/AIDS. Our first demonstration became a leading national news story, and while we were denounced by the likes of the right-wing grand wizard of bigotry, Senator Jesse Helms, in the weeks following our protest, Burroughs Wellcome lowered the annual cost of an AZT prescription from $10,000 down to $8,000, and the FDA cut its nine-year approval process by two years.[77] This was irrefutable progress. More needed to be done, but in one strike, ACT UP had advanced our agenda better than years of polite quaint lobbying by our sister organizations in the struggle.

The challenge was to arrange a second ACT UP demonstration that was even more provocative and politically potent than what we'd done on Wall Street. By mid-April, the unofficial advisory committee hit upon a brilliant scheme: ACT UP would *piggyback* on—no, wait, *infiltrate*—no, no, no, *respectfully participate* in the Second National

---

76. "You Know How to Love Me," released in 1979, was an R&B/disco ballad originally sung by Phyllis Hyman (1949–1995). While the song was a modest hit, peaking at number six on the disco charts, "You Know How to Love Me" was a perennial on the playlists at homosexual dance clubs, skating rinks, and lounges, and became a minor gay anthem.

77. Senator Jesse A. Helms (1921–2008), a Republican representing the state of North Carolina, minced no words when expressing his homophobia. He called homosexual people "weak, morally sick wretches," and in his opposition to federal funding for AIDS research and treatment, he maintained, "There is not one single case of AIDS in this country that cannot be traced in origin to sodomy." As to stemming the AIDS epidemic, Helms predicted an ominous solution: "Somewhere along the line we're going to have to quarantine people with AIDS."

March on Washington for Lesbian and Gay Rights, scheduled for October 11, 1987.

The potential for dramatic disruptions in D.C. was spectacular. We could barricade ourselves inside the office of Secretary of Health and Human Services Otis Bowen. We could storm the floors of the U.S. House of Representatives and Senate, bringing Congress to a standstill. No stunt was deemed out of bounds as long as it remained nonviolent. At our third committee meeting, someone—I wish I remember who it was—proposed that we get the ashes of gay men who had died of AIDS and toss those ashes over the gates at the White House.[78] We were looking to cause good trouble.

Therein lay the problem. Planning for the Second National March had been under way since July of 1986. In addition to a march, the event was a coordinated push to lobby politicians in the traditional, thirty-minute-meeting-by-appointment-only mold. Organizers were aiming to attract five hundred thousand people to the rally. The goal was to present the queer community in a positive and sympathetic light. It seemed foolish to expect the organizers of the Second National March to let ACT UP into the tent given the obvious risks we carried with us: as an organization, ACT UP was less than two months old; we had no designated leaders; our members openly expressed their outrage and anger; our approach was confrontational; we welcomed getting arrested; and we had no mechanism for controlling or disciplining members should they go rogue.

Larry attended the meeting where the unofficial advisory committee decided to send an ACT UP emissary to approach the co-coordinators of the Second National March, Steve Ault and Joyce Hunter, about the possibility of our inclusion. Dylan was nominating himself for the role.

Larry cut him off and said, "Send Trey. They'll adore him to pieces."

---

78. On October 11, 1992, ACT UP activists marched to the White House as part of a controversial protest called the Ashes Action, which culminated with activists tossing the ashes of at least eighteen loved ones who had died of AIDS onto the White House lawn.

I had received no heads-up from Larry that he was going to champion me for the assignment. And I wasn't sure I wanted to do it. Between working at MoMA, volunteering at Angie's, and my new ACT UP obligations, I was feeling overextended as it was.

"Be serious," said Dylan. "Trey doesn't have the gravitas to represent this group. No offense, Trey."

Okay, fuck that. How dare anyone dismiss me out of hand. I had been paying attention at our meetings and reading the briefs on the Second National March's logistics and goals. Suddenly, I did want the assignment.

"We don't need gravitas. We can't bully our way into an invitation," argued Larry. "Look at Trey. He's wilier than you think, and he's got something you and I lack, Dylan. Trey is naturally likable."

I blushed, and the other committee members, except for Dylan, laughed.

"This is no trivial asset," Larry continued. "The fear is that ACT UP is a pack of angry hooligans. Who better to put forward than the adorable young man—I hope I'm not embarrassing you too much, Trey—that kept his cool while the police manhandled him on Wall Street?"

The debate as to my merits and shortcomings lasted for fifteen minutes. It was fascinating to watch a group of older white adults discuss me as if I weren't in the room. Finally, Larry asked me to weigh in on the issue.

"I can do it," I said. "I noticed on page seventeen of the Second National March manifesto that they're desperate to bring more Blacks and Latinos into the fold. They won't turn ACT UP down if I'm doing the asking."

Larry actually smiled. "See, he gets it."

The matter was put to a vote, and the decision was nearly unanimous (Dylan voted against me): I was the ACT UP liaison to the Second National March.

———

The rest of April, the whole of May, and the first half of June were nonstop marathons of commitments for me. Convincing Steve Ault and Joyce Hunter to allow ACT UP to participate in the march was a tough hurdle to clear, but I eventually managed to do so by agreeing to the stipulation that someone from our fledgling group would help with the monumental task of organizing a large march on Washington. I became that somebody.

My main role was helping to secure sizable hotel room blocks in the D.C. area to accommodate all the out-of-town marchers. I made the long-distance phone calls, an expense I couldn't afford, from whatever conference rooms were unoccupied before and after my shifts and during my lunch breaks at MoMA.

Nailing down room blocks turned out to be a giant pain in the ass. Hotel managers weren't exactly tripping over themselves to open their doors to thousands of gay guests, a sizable number of whom were HIV positive or living with AIDS. I learned to be vague. I described the Second National March as a grassroots campaign to improve the lives of American workers. I mentioned that César Chávez was one of the keynote speakers, and that helped because by 1987, he'd transitioned from radical troublemaker to mainstream do-gooder in the public consciousness.[79]

A wiser man would have gotten more sleep than I did during this whirlwind of work and activism. Instead, I frequented Mt. Morris, where I now could count on one or two steady fuck-buddies to be there whenever I turned up around 11:00 p.m. Occasionally, I'd run into Rustin, keeping him abreast of how ACT UP was playing nice with other gay organizations and picking his brain to guide the planning of the latest march on Washington.

---

79. César Chávez (1927–1993), a Latinx civil rights advocate and labor leader, rose to prominence in 1965 as a key organizer of the protracted Delano grape strike. During that five-year labor dispute, Chávez was monitored by the FBI and branded a communist subversive, an accusation that lingered for decades. Yet, toward the end of his life, he was hailed as a "folk saint." A year after his death, Chávez was posthumously awarded the Presidential Medal of Freedom.

When I wasn't out past midnight at the bathhouse, I was likely palling around with Gregory, who snorted enough recreational coke to dance at the Saint until it closed and then go talk his head off until dawn as we split cheesy fries at Claudia's Diner. He had a knack for cajoling me into being his sidekick, although by the summer, Gregory was spending several nights a week in Long Island with closet-case Congressman Leslie Galbreath.

Gregory's absence turned into Erik's gain. Lonely and horny for his touch, I showed up unannounced at the ballet dancer's apartment door. He let me in. We didn't talk about the night he'd insulted me and I'd walked out. We didn't ask each other how we had been doing the past three months since we'd last seen each other. Erik led me to his bedroom, where we stripped naked and fucked like wild animals. Then we fell asleep, and when I woke up, he had already left for rehearsal. There was not even the pretense of romance between us. We weren't in love with each other. That was damn clear. So what drew me back? Honestly, Erik didn't demand much of me, and we consistently had the best sex I'd ever experienced, and that was an informed opinion.

Above all—and it pains me to admit this now—I simply didn't believe, at nineteen, that I could do better than the arrangement Erik and I had. I wasn't even convinced that "better" was possible. For all the different people and lifestyles I had seen in the city, I had yet to witness a healthy, monogamous, lasting relationship between two gay men. So be it, I figured. I had no interest in pursuing a fairy tale when I could hook up regularly with a ballet Adonis who didn't care if I fucked around on the side. I considered my hard-nosed assessment of gay male romance to be a sign of my maturity.

I mention my legitimate commitments and my foolish extracurricular activities because they contributed to why I blamed myself for what happened to Angie. I put in fewer hours volunteering with her, and when I was there, I wasn't as observant as I should have been. She was burning out, and I let her down.

Death increased its turnover rate among the men in Angie's care.

In the spring of '87, it was not unusual for me to arrive on a Tuesday, be introduced to a new admission on her couch, only to return on Saturday and be informed that the man had died. I guess I grew numb to it. I had other demands to occupy my mind.

Not Angie. She'd made running that makeshift hospice her sole mission. No days off, no escape. She seemed so impervious with her gruff bravado that Peter, the other part-time volunteers, and I assumed she would always hold up under the strain. I can see now that our faith in Angie was rooted in selfishness. We told ourselves she was superhuman because if we admitted that she wasn't, we would have to do more to help her. What lousy men we were.

Then came the day—Sunday, June 28, 1987—that I couldn't ignore Angie's distress and the danger it held. I'd been in her apartment for two hours, tending to fifteen men while Angie devoted her attention to Dale Tharpe in the primary bedroom.

Dale was a twenty-nine-year-old elementary school math teacher from Kansas City. He'd created a couple of fun games that were incredibly effective at teaching fractions to kids, and the notoriety got him recruited to join the faculty at Cathedral Preparatory School and Seminary, a prestigious Roman Catholic school on the Lower East Side. Dale, who was the only Black teacher at the school, was beloved by students and staff until sarcoma appeared on his hands. He confessed to the school principal that he was HIV positive, and the holy priests, compassionate nuns, and enlightened educators of Cathedral terminated Dale's employment, stripping him of an income and health insurance.

When he arrived at Angie's apartment, Dale was deteriorating fast. Angie and I figured he'd live another week at most. When time allowed, I would sit next to Dale and fill in the numbers on this puzzle game he introduced me to. The rules baffled me at first because it was so unfamiliar. The game was called sudoku, and years later, damn near everyone was playing it.

By June 24, Dale had been with Angie for nine weeks. He'd been in the primary bedroom, which was customarily reserved for those expected to die within forty-eight hours, for nearly two weeks. Despite being in a state of constant pain, Dale kept eating, and he was often lucid. His body just would not die. Angie lamented, "If that sweet boy were a bird, I'd find a goddamn rock and put him out of his misery." I chalked up those remarks to being part of Angie's vivid, rough language. It was just how she talked.

Angie fretted over Dale to an extreme I'd never seen before. It was as if they were the only two people in the apartment. I think that's why she didn't hear me or react when I entered the bedroom.

"Angie, I served lunch. Did you—" I froze.

Angie was using a hypodermic needle to inject a colorless drug into Dale's arm. Dale was unconscious. Angie appeared to be in a sleep-deprived trance.

I waited until she withdrew the needle from his vein before speaking. "Angie, what have you done?"

She looked up at me and stared for a few moments as if she were determining whether I was real or a figment of her exhaustion. Once she accepted that I was indeed present, she screamed, "You should knock before you enter a room! Or did you not learn anything in Indiana!"

"Never mind that. What did you give Dale?"

"I won't stand for you fucking spying on me."

I walked toward her slowly. My voice was calm and firm. "I'm not going to turn you in, okay? This stays between you and me, but I need to know what the hell I just saw."

"It's for the pain," she pleaded. "I gave him something for the pain."

"We have pills for that. What was in the needle?"

Angie set the needle down on the bedside table. "Morphine."

"Where'd you get it?"

"A friend of a friend nicked it for me."

"Did you give Dale enough to kill him?"

She nodded. "Won't be much longer now."

"Come here."

She hesitated. Angie, for once, was afraid of me. I opened my arms, inviting her to hug me. She rushed me, wrapping her arms around me tightly.

"You understand, don't you? Dale told me he was ready to die."

I held Angie close to me because I didn't want her to see the terror on my face. I remembered her telling me that Barney had confided in her that he, too, was ready to die. She made similar claims about dozens of men in our care.

"Have you done this before with the morphine?"

Angie pulled away from me. "You are on my side, right, Trey?"

"Yes, yes, absolutely. Dale suffered too much. His death is a mercy."

Strictly speaking, I meant every word I said; my loyalty to Angie was fierce, Dale was in excruciating pain, and motivated by compassion (and fatigue), Angie overdosed him. Still, I knew it wasn't Angie's place to take his life. This couldn't happen again.

"Look at Dale at peace," she said.

His breaths were shallow, and the gaps between inhales and exhales grew longer. He did not look peaceful to me. He appeared ravaged—a husk of a young man, bent and wizened. He should have died weeks before, and I'll never understand why his body hadn't given out on its own. Why couldn't he let go?

"Poor bastard," I said.

"Poor bastard," Angie echoed. "I couldn't stand to watch him go on another day. Is that so wrong?"

The burning question inside me was, *How many men had Angie euthanized?* I considered grabbing her by the shoulders and demanding she tell me everything, but she had started to weep and soon crumpled to the floor. I looked over at Dale and realized that he had stopped breathing. I needed to call Dr. Stolberg, who served as our "attending physician" so that he could arrange for the coroner to issue the death certificate and for a funeral home to oversee the cremation. I needed to dispose of the morphine and the needle. I needed to get Angie in a condition to think rationally. In light of the immediate challenges, my curiosity could wait. There would be time to talk it all through later.

First things first—I led Angie to a quiet cot in the darkest corner of the living room, tucked her in, and heard her snoring before I left. Then I tended to Dale. I checked for his pulse, and there was none. I wiped the drool from his mouth and combed his matted little Afro. I called Dr. Stolberg, and before he arrived, I threw the needle and the small vial of morphine into the apartment building's trash chute. I checked in with the other men in our care, assisting a few to the restroom and fetching ice water for some others. Dr. Stolberg showed up with transporters from the funeral home, and I kissed Dale on the forehead before they took him away.

Once they were gone, I realized it was time to get dinner started for the men. Based on what I spotted in the pantry and refrigerator, I whipped up a large batch of chicken salad with mashed potatoes and macaroni and cheese as sides. I ran the hospice by myself all night until Angie woke up late the next morning.

"I'm surprised you didn't call Peter for backup," she said, pouring herself a cup of coffee in the kitchen. She still looked like hell, but her vigor was restored.

"That might have created more problems than it solved."

Angie nodded. "Peter can be nosy."

"And you were a fright to behold."

"I was tired, so shoot me!"

"You were more than tired," I said. "You were overwhelmed. This has become too much."

"Oh, I see. Should I kick everyone out now, or is checkout time at eleven?"

"Don't cop an attitude with me," I warned. "Not after the position you put me in yesterday. Things have got to change."

Angie scoffed. "I take orders from you now?"

"Look at it this way. I did you a huge favor, and you're going to pay me back by getting on the phone, calling the other women running home hospices, and sending a dozen of these guys to them. You've got to lighten your load."

I was prepared for a screaming match, but Angie didn't argue. She didn't tell me I was right or hug me either. Instead, she picked up the telephone mounted to the wall and made the calls I told her to make. By that afternoon, Angie had seven men remaining in her care.

Before I left, I asked, "Was Dale the first one you've helped die like that?"

"Yes," she said, "first, only, and last." She raised her right hand like she was swearing an oath.

———

By August, not only was I confident that the worst was behind us, I had largely put the circumstances surrounding Dale's death out of my mind. Angie wouldn't admit it, but cutting her workload did wonders for her. She got more sleep, she ate better, and she seemed happier. Angie and I also had an agreement that she would never care for more than eight men at once, and if she ever felt the burden was too heavy to carry, she'd call me.

On the morning of Friday, August 21, Angie called me, alright. I was on duty at the info desk at MoMA when Libby pulled me aside and told me that a distraught woman dialed the museum's main line demanding to speak with me. Libby insisted that I take the call in her office so I could have some privacy. "Brace yourself," she suggested.

I ran to Libby's little office. Angie was on line three. After I took a seat and cracked my knuckles, I felt ready. I'd already seen Angie on her worst day. Whatever was upsetting her could be addressed.

I picked up the receiver and pushed the line. "Hello, Angie."

No reply. Just labored breathing.

"Angie, it's Trey. What's the matter?"

"You're gonna have to come take over for me," she said. She sounded choked up as if she'd cried hard and stopped moments ago. "You're gonna have to get to my place before the police do."

My heart sank, but I tried to suppress my alarm. "Tell me exactly why the police are coming. What happened?"

"Bruno's brother is angry he died. That stupid, rich, yuppie asshole thinks he could have bought Bruno a cure for AIDS at some experimental hospital in Switzerland."

I should have guessed the trouble had something to do with Bruno Devonte. Five other home hospices turned him away because so many of the other dying men in their care refused to spend their last days on Earth in the same apartment with Bruno. Apparently, the once-attractive thirty-four-year-old had fucked his way through a sizable swath of the gays in the New York City tristate area while violently denying that he was homosexual.

There were countless stories of Bruno shoving and threatening to beat the shit out of gay men who crossed paths with him and dared to say hello while he was with his Catholic, Italian family or at work. The most notorious incident that I heard of involved a gay sommelier, who was accompanying his mother while she shopped at Gimbels, when he recognized one of the salesmen from a night of barebacking at the Continental Baths.[80] The sommelier subtly proposed sucking Bruno off in the department store's men's restroom. Seemingly receptive, Bruno gave him the nod, and the two men entered the restroom, where Bruno took off his dress shoe and used the heel to strike and break the sommelier's nose.

The altercation was reported to the store, but Bruno claimed that he had merely reacted as any hot-blooded straight man would have after the sommelier had groped him by the urinals. It was a version of

---

80. The Continental Baths (1968–1975), at one point the most well-known gay bathhouse in the United States, distinguished itself from other homosexual sex venues by presenting live performances from talented entertainers on the rise, including the bawdy songstress Bette Midler, the experimental comedian Andy Kaufman, and the influential DJs Frankie Knuckles and Larry Levan.

the gay panic defense, and Gimbels allowed Bruno to keep his job on the sales floor.[81] The sommelier went to the police, who refused to even write up a report on the assault because it was a "he said, *she* said" situation. The kicker, of course, being that the sommelier's career was ruined; his nose healed, but his sense of smell was forever warped.

Angie was the one who took pity on Bruno. She was aware of his rep, but the four Black men in her care had never heard of Bruno, and Angie was committed to an unshakable principle: everyone deserved to die with dignity. Bruno, who lost his job when Gimbels went out of business, was destitute and blind. He was a broken man, and in his hour of need, he didn't turn to his brother or any of his blood relatives. Instead, he sought refuge in the community he had abused. Did he deserve to be accepted into the fold? Honestly, I wouldn't have had the compassion to open the door to Bruno, but Angie did. I loved that about her.

"When did Bruno die?" I asked

"This morning, and his brother banged at my door a couple of hours later. He had a million questions and hated everything I told him."

"Like what? What did you tell him?"

"That no one comes to me hoping for miracles. Bruno decided on his own to quit taking his meds. He didn't have any more fight left in him. That sent his brother through the roof. He called me a dyke lunatic."

"Did you punch him in the face? Is that why the cops are coming?"

"No, but Bruno's brother threatened to sue me."

"Let him try. Like you said, Bruno chose to move in with you. He knew the score."

---

81. The *gay panic defense* is invoked in courts of law to justify the assault or murder of a homosexual(s). The crux of the defense is that the perpetrator, who does not deny committing the violent act(s), was temporarily insane or suffered diminished capacity due to a same-sex sexual advance from the victim. The gay panic defense is controversial; sixteen states and Washington, D.C., have explicitly banned the gay panic defense, which is to say, it remains a legitimate legal strategy in thirty-four states, as well as in federal court, in the United States of America.

"He's not only going to sue," she said, then choked up.

"Angie?"

"There'll be an autopsy."

My words ran ahead of my thoughts. "So what? He died of AIDS. There's no mystery—"

The penny dropped. Angie had done it again. She'd eased Bruno into death with morphine, and the unprescribed morphine would turn up in the autopsy.

"You promised," I said.

"I won't blame you if you hang up."

I didn't hang up. I told Angie to stay put and not to do anything rash. I promised I'd find a way to get her out of this mess. She thanked me because she believed me.

Claiming that my family was in crisis, I left MoMA and went looking for Peter. I figured the two of us could organize a defense for Angie. Get her a brilliant lawyer, maybe from the ACLU. We could frame this as a gay rights issue. Let's spin Bruno's death as a sympathetic case of assisted suicide, and publicize Angie's dedication as a caretaker to men dying of AIDS. Peter was a night copy editor at the *New York Post*, and surely there was a reporter on staff who would run with that angle. When Angie was inevitably arrested, the Gay Men's Health Crisis should post her bail. ACT UP could lead demonstrations and marches to galvanize the gay community to support this lesbian who had given so much to so many. I pictured Angie's face on buttons under the words FREE ANGIE.[82]

---

82. The FREE ANGIE button that Trey described is patterned on the FREE ANGELA buttons that circulated after the political activist Professor Angela Davis was apprehended by the FBI on October 13, 1970. In a case fueled by questionable political motivations, Davis, an avowed member of the Communist Party, was charged with the aggravated kidnapping and first-degree murder of a judge—even though she wasn't a participant in and had no foreknowledge of the botched kidnapping. During her incarceration and trial, "Free Angela" was a rallying cry for young African American and progressive activists. Davis was acquitted by an all-white jury on June 4, 1972. In 1998, Davis publicly acknowledged that she is a lesbian.

When I got to Peter's apartment in Tribeca, Eduardo answered the buzzer and told me that Peter was working a dayshift at the *Post*. I rushed over to the newspaper's Midtown office, and by the time I arrived, I'd mapped out a twenty-five-point plan to save Angie. I was wild-eyed and amped up.

I spotted Peter on the other side of the newsroom bullpen and shouted, "Peter! Peter! We've got to talk! It's an emergency!"

He glanced up from the article he was proofing and waved me over to his desk. I could tell from Peter's smirk that he assumed whatever I'd come to discuss was going to be amusing to him. I felt awful realizing that I was going to deliver news that would wring the joy out of his eyes.

Conscious of being in a room full of reporters, I whispered the story of Angie's use of unprescribed morphine, Bruno's death, his angry brother, the threat of a lawsuit, and an imminent autopsy. As he listened, Peter clenched his jaw tightly, a vein in his neck surfaced and throbbed under his skin, and sweat dotted his forehead. He opened a desk drawer and retrieved a pack of cigarettes.

Peter stood up and walked to the elevators. I followed him, and we rode together in silence to the top floor, then took a half flight of stairs out onto the roof. There were three or four other people taking smoke breaks and gazing out at Manhattan's thicket of skyscrapers. Peter and I found a private corner. I'd never known him to go this long without speaking.

I got the ball rolling. "There are several ways we can get Angie out of this. You and I should decide which of the possible approaches we like best. Otherwise, when we bring in additional support, we'll get bogged down by everyone else's opinions. You and I have to hammer out this plan and keep everyone else on task."

Peter lit a cigarette and savored the first drag. "Angie fucked herself, and we've got to cut her loose."

I balked. "Are you joking? Because this is a hell of a time to joke, even for you."

"I'm totally serious. She's radioactive."

I was astounded by Peter's immediate betrayal of a friend and fellow activist that he'd known for nearly two decades. He wasn't going to fight for her. He wasn't even going to consider fighting for her. I backed away from Peter out of fear that if I got any angrier, I might snap and push him off the ledge of the building.

"What's the matter with you?" I shouted. "The first day I met both of you, you're the one who talked me into sneaking Walton's dead body out of Angie's apartment so he wouldn't get cremated."

"Lower your fucking voice," Peter demanded. "That was different. That didn't threaten to burn the whole house down. Don't you see what happens if Angie gets arrested and stands trial? They'll crucify her. She'll be the mean, butch villain those inbred conservatives have prayed for. That alone would be very bad for our tribe. But the dagger in the heart will come when they investigate how she ran her hospice. The money will lead back to me and GMHC."

"Why's that a problem? She runs a GMHC program to care for—"

"It's off the books," he confessed. He tried to soothe himself with a long drag off his cigarette. "I funnel the cash to Angie and more than a dozen other women doing exactly what she's doing. No one else at GMHC knows, or at least no one else officially knows. Hell, I've been at this for three years. I don't even remember anymore how much tacit permission I bothered to get when I started."

"I see. You're afraid you'll go to prison, too."

"Fuck you. I've spent more time behind bars than you, Mr. ACT UP superstar." Peter flicked the ash off the end of his cigarette in my direction. "It's not about what happens to Angie, Dr. Stolberg, or me. It's how the government will use what Angie and I have done to destroy GMHC. They'll also shut down every other home hospice we've got going. I mean, none of this shit is regulated."

My mind was spinning to keep up with the extent of the damage Peter was predicting. I hated to agree with him, but I could see the scenario he envisioned. Still, I couldn't help fixating on the pieces I didn't understand.

"Why would Dr. Stolberg get in trouble?" I asked.

"Huh?"

"You said it's not about what happens to you, Angie, or the doc."

Peter exhaled smoke to the heavens. "Who do you think supplies the morphine?"

"Got it. Then you've always known Angie was mercy killing guys."

"They all do it. Not to everyone, but to the ones this disease refuses to quit torturing. The straights won't understand, but the women running these places have learned when to intervene." Peter looked out over the city. "We can't afford to let all our good work go down the tubes."

"Fuck." I sighed. "Then what do you want Angie to do? Off herself?"

"No, no, no," he said. "She needs to plead guilty. Quietly. No resistance. No trial."

"And we let her hang for this?"

Peter stamped out his cigarette. "She got caught. She's gotta take the hit."

"I don't really see Angie going down quietly."

"That's why I've got to talk to her. You've got to talk to her. We've got to move her in the right direction."

———

I believed that I had one more card to play before I agreed to side with Peter, and I convinced him to give me a day to see if I could solve our problem without sacrificing Angie. Bruno had been dead for no more than a few hours, and the chronic bureaucratic delays of crime-ridden Manhattan, for once, worked to our advantage. The morgues were full of obvious homicide victims riddled with stab wounds and bullet holes; it would be at least twenty-four hours before an autopsy was performed on Bruno.

I used the white pages phone book to look up the address for

Rustin, B., and it turned out that Old Rustin had an apartment in Chelsea. I'd walked by his building dozens of times with Erik. I wondered if Rustin had ever spotted me and didn't say hello because it seemed like a breach of protocol. I get why he might have felt that way. I wouldn't ordinarily have dared to contact Rustin at home, but these were extenuating circumstances.

Rustin did greet me at the building's front door with some apprehension before ushering me quickly into his apartment. "This place is filled with gossips," he explained. "A young man calling on me while my partner is out of town is exactly the sort of thing that will send their tongues wagging."

"In that case, I'll cut to the chase," I said. "Angie McBroom is likely to be charged with murder for—"

"Stop. You're being far too specific, and I'm a tad too old to be caught up in a criminal conspiracy. So please, let us talk in hypotheticals."

Rustin invited me to have a seat on the worn leather couch in his living room. From what I could see of the apartment, it was crammed with open books, scattered documents, yellowing newspapers, and abandoned coffee mugs. In contrast to his surroundings, Rustin was dressed impeccably: polished dress shoes; creased, royal-blue dress pants; a starched and ironed white French-cuff dress shirt with round gold cuff links; a black necktie; and a gray-and-blue plaid sports coat. It was striking to see him so crisp and stylish. Then it hit me that I'd never seen him in clothes before— just Mt. Morris's extra-large towels.

Rustin sat in a mahogany rocking chair and prompted me by saying, "Alright, Trey, let's suppose you had a friend who may have broken the law . . ."

Peppering my sentences with *what if, for instance,* and *picture this,* I presented the facts of Angie's case, its likely ramifications, and my ideas for mobilizing a winning defense. Rustin listened with his hands folded in his lap and his eyes locked on me. After fifteen minutes, I concluded, and he leaned back and began rocking in his chair.

Neither of us said a word for a couple of minutes. I sat perched on the edge of the couch, too anxious to relax.

Finally, Rustin spoke. "It is a bitter irony that those who devote the most to a righteous effort are often denied the opportunity to enjoy the rewards. Neither Moses nor Martin lived to see the promised land. Even today, take Nelson Mandela, who is confined to a cell and will most certainly die there before there is an end to apartheid in South Africa.[83]

"You see, despite the loftiest of goals, political struggles are themselves unjust. Leaders are assassinated or imprisoned. Allies are slain or disgraced. The movement can't stop to mourn them," he said. "The movement must carry on. It is a collective concern, not an individual one."

I'd heard enough of that philosophy, and I was sick of talking in hypotheticals. "Peter already tried to sell me that bullshit," I said. "You want Angie to give herself up. To put the movement ahead of herself, the way you tell yourself you did when they decided you were too gay to stand next to Martin. I'm not—"

"Damn it!" Rustin boomed, startling me. "Trey, I don't care what becomes of Angie. I'm invested in what becomes of you. Your passion, smarts, and guts could make you one of the great leaders of your generation. But you've got to learn to live with the losses."

"They could throw the book at Angie. She could spend the rest of her life behind bars."

"At least you'd have a place to visit her. Tell me where I go to see Andy Goodman!" Rustin hopped to his feet and turned away from

---

83. Events turned out more positive than predicted: After being denied freedom for twenty-seven years as a political prisoner, Nelson R. Mandela (1918–2013) was released in 1990. He took part in the painstaking national negotiations that led to the end of apartheid in South Africa in 1994. That same year, Mandela was elected president of South Africa.

me. "I shouldn't have said that. It was unfair of me. You've probably never even heard of Andrew Goodman."[84]

"No, but I gather he's dead."

Rustin nodded. "Such a beautiful young man." Then he returned to his chair. "My point is if you don't learn how to keep walking past the fallen, then you will be driven crazy, and the movement will leave you behind, too. That's just the way it is, son. Now, you can let Angie be an inspiration that fuels your work for the rest of your life, but you can't remove the morphine from the needle or put breath back into the lungs of the man she killed. You can't spare Angie from her fate. Make peace with the loss."

I didn't argue back. A realization washed over me as Rustin continued to lecture me on the inevitability of being separated, through death or political calculations, from allies. He preached the gospel of emotional resilience. He commanded me to keep my eye on the sparrow, not the lost lamb. I nodded, shook his hand when he was through, and thanked him for counseling me.

I pretended to be converted and left without making more of a fuss because it hit me that Rustin was speaking to me about another time—he was speaking to me *from* another time. This brilliant man had shared with me what he knew of national politics, grassroots protest movements, coalition building, and social revolutions. What worked, I would keep. What no longer fit the present world, I would abandon.

I never rebuked Rustin—or Peter, for that matter. Both had given me all they could offer as mentors. I loved them despite my bitter disappointment at their advice to sacrifice Angie. To keep the peace, I continued to maintain a relationship, but the two men soon came to realize they had lost their sway over me. I sat like an obedient student at their feet, but I trusted my own judgment over theirs.

---

84. Andrew Goodman (1943–1964) was one of three activists who was volunteering to register African American voters in Mississippi when he was shot, killed, and buried in an unmarked grave by members of the Ku Klux Klan. The two young men murdered alongside Goodman were James Chaney (1943–1964) and Michael Schwerner (1939–1964).

Lesson #18

BURY YOUR OLD SELF

It was late afternoon by the time I got back to my unit in the Harlem River Houses. I hadn't eaten since breakfast. I'd been revved up and running around since Angie called, and the weather was unseasonably warm. So I thought, for a second, that I was hallucinating when I saw my mother leaning against the hallway wall outside my apartment door.

She was wearing a dark purple wrap dress and tan wedge sandals. A white purse dangled from her right shoulder. Her hair was straightened, parted on the left, and reached her collarbone. Very chic. My mother saw me approaching and gave me that small, closed-mouth smile of hers. A smile that conveyed no affection and, in fact, revealed nothing of the emotions behind it. She seemed shorter than I remembered, which made me question if it truly was her. The smell of her perfume, Charlie by Revlon, assured me that she was real.

Why was she here all alone and without warning? Someone had died, I thought. Perhaps my father. No, if she were a widow, she would have dressed the part. Instead, my mother looked radiant. This was by design, as was her surprise visit. Her strategy in dealing with me had always been to knock me off balance, and my only defense was to do the same to her.

"Hello, Lady Fiona," I said with a bow.

"Why, that takes me back," she said. "Me, Lady Fiona. You, the

Duke of Earl. You made me stop calling you that when you were nine or ten."

I'd forgotten how mesmerizing her speech pattern could be. Words shot out of my mother's mouth at a rapid-fire pace. The decades of political campaign work had honed her ability to deliver complex ideas in the blink of an eye. Yet despite the lightning speed at which she thought and talked, her diction remained perfect. *Ums* and *ahs* didn't pollute her sentences. Lastly, my mother said everything with a sly wit—her observations could double as insults; her questions could serve as accusations; her asides typically camouflaged her convictions; and her criticisms were the Trojan horses concealing her love.

Inside my apartment, my mother began her inspection of how I'd arranged my kitchen cabinets and refrigerator as if we'd had an appointment for her to come over and do this. I acted as if it didn't annoy me.

"Were you just passing through the neighborhood and decided to drop in?" I asked.

"Your father owes me ten dollars. He was certain I'd find you living in squalor." She started to rearrange the spices on a shelf. "But I told him that if you came across a cockroach or a rat, you'd burn the building down before you'd sleep another night there."

"I'm glad you won," I said. "Did you and Dad have me followed by a private investigator?"

She threw away a cracked bottle of turmeric. "Only for the first year or so."

"Do you think the way you parent is normal?"

"Of course not. God didn't give me normal children."

I hated it when she bested me verbally. "It's good to see you're still quick. Can we play catch-up another day? I'm in the middle of an emergency."

She put her hands up in defense. "There's no need for you to fly off the handle at me."

"Fly off the handle? I didn't yell or curse."

"Your tone is giving me attitude, and you're kicking me out less than a minute after I got here."

"You can't just show up after two years, Fiona, and expect me to drop everything! I've got a life—"

"Do you hear that? Sounds to me like you're yelling."

"Yes, I'm yelling! You win again."

Force of habit almost made me storm off to my room, but I stood my ground. This was my apartment. I brushed by my mother, grabbed an apple from the fruit bowl, and bit into it.

"The sink is right there," she said. "How much effort would it take to wash that apple?"

As I chewed, I asked, "Did you get on an airplane and catch a taxi to Harlem to have *this* conversation?"

"No, I did not."

"Okay, then. Let's have it. Why'd you finally turn up at my door?"

My mother moved on from the spices to rummaging through a drawer that was an unruly mix of plastic utensils, unused chopsticks, small condiment packages, and measuring spoons. "Trey, baby, I didn't come to fight, but I take issue with your phrasing."

"Please, by all means, write my words for me." I took another bite out of the apple.

"That's not what I'm doing. The simple fact is your phrasing, 'finally turned up,' implies that I should have come sooner."

She flashed me that tight-lipped smile again. It was remarkable how the gesture dampened my anger. Instead of firing back at her, I found myself distracted by how gorgeous she remained. Dark skin. Amber eyes. Long curled eyelashes. Thick lips shaped in a cupid's bow. The bone structure of a queen. And a beauty mark on her left cheek. Had she been taller, my mother could have been a high fashion model. That I had inherited some of her feminine facial features was not lost on me. My admiration of her looks was tinged with narcissism.

Her attractiveness notwithstanding, I was determined to hold my mother to account. "I think it safe to say that most parents wouldn't have waited as long as you and Dad to check on their child who moved to a new city."

"Forgive me, I didn't realize I was meant to chase after you," she said. "Not after the way you demanded that we give you freedom as if we enslaved you. Not after the way you told us you were too good for our money and you didn't need us interfering in your affairs."

"I wanted space. I didn't expect you and Dad to pretend I never existed."

"How do you find anything in this drawer?"

"For fuck's sake, leave the drawer alone, and let's have a real conversation for once. Start by telling me why you iced me out."

My mother smacked the kitchen counter with her hand. "Because I didn't want to give you another chance to humiliate me! The way you talked to your father and me. You have no idea how much it hurts to watch a child that you've poured your heart into treat you like you're a monster. I assumed that if I reached out to you or if you saw me on the street, you'd walk on by me."

"I see, in your version, you're Juanita Moore, and I'm the ungrateful daughter who can pass."[85]

"Your father was right. I shouldn't have come." She shut the drawer. "You're only interested in belittling me."

She grabbed her purse off the kitchen table and headed for the door. She was going to walk out and not look back. If I let her go, this might very well be our last conversation.

I said the unsayable. "You're the one who makes me feel small. You blame me for Martin's death."

---

85. Juanita Moore (1914–2014) was an African American actress who received an Academy Award nomination for Best Supporting Actress for her role in 1959's *Imitation of Life*. In that film, Moore's character has a daughter who is hell-bent on using her light complexion to pass for white. In a pivotal scene, the daughter breaks off her relationship with her mother with the instructions, "And if by accident we should ever pass on the street, please don't recognize me." The mother offers her unconditional love while promising to respect her daughter's decision.

My mother stopped in her tracks. "Well, you weren't blameless, were you, Earl?"

Her words instantly gutted me. I dropped the apple onto the linoleum floor and hunched over the kitchen sink. I felt like I was going to vomit. I squeezed my eyes shut as hard as I could and took deep breaths in and out.

"You lied to the police, you lied to us." My mother's voice grew louder as she came nearer. "The cops spent days looking in the wrong location. You muddied the waters." She was right beside me. "I was furious at you. I was even terrified that in my grief, I'd hurt you." She spoke directly into my ear. "But I forgave you years ago—just as I forgave myself."

I turned the faucet on and washed my mouth out with cold water. My mother picked the apple up off the floor, placed it on the counter, and backed away from me. After I dried my lips with my shirtsleeve, I stood up straight, looked at my mother, and realized that her hands were trembling. Her eyes refused to meet mine.

"Are you alright?" she asked softly.

"Are you?" I hugged myself tightly. "You been waiting a long time to get that off your chest—to tell me off."

"Oh, is that what I did?" Her gaze met mine. "Your life will improve tenfold the day you learn to listen."

In no mood to be lectured, I bristled at her tone. It would take years, in fact, for me to understand what she meant and to recognize what she was offering. I grabbed the apple and took another bite because I hoped it would make her look away. And it did.

"I got arrested at a protest in March, and the FBI questioned me."

I had her attention again.

"They wanted me to be an informant for them."

My mother smirked. "They got the wrong boy for that."

"Yeah, I told the agent to go fuck himself, and he dangled a carrot in front of me. He said he'd let me read the file that explains what happened to Martin."

My mother sighed and said, "The feds will say any crazy old thing to play you."

"I know they've got nothing new to tell me," I assured her. "But you do."

"Earl, whatever notion is in your head, drop it."

"There has to be more to the story than what I did. Mom, who do you think killed him? What do you suppose they did with his—"

My mother spoke as if she had one breath left to plead her case. "I came here with wonderful news. Your father spoke with the president of Georgetown University. They'll accept you as a freshman next month. You'll even receive credits for your volunteer work with ACT OUT and your job at MoMA.[86] You've proven your point, Earl. Two years on your own. Very impressive. Now let's get you back on track."

That was her wish: for me to shut up about Martin and enroll at Georgetown. I'd be a son she could be proud of, and we'd be a family to envy despite the faint specter of a distant tragedy. She was so desperate for me to play my role in her version of reality.

It was heartbreaking to witness how grief, denial, and a blinding faith in the appeal of social status had warped my mother's judgment. She somehow clung to the hope that I'd drop the topic at hand in exchange for a spot at a prestigious university, in addition to the other perks she and my father would undoubtedly lavish on me: a new wardrobe; a generous spending allowance; a coveted internship at one of the Smithsonian Museums.

Poor Lady Fiona. She'd arrived in New York City too late. If only she'd knocked on my door with her temptations after my bike accident resulted in a broken collarbone and a fractured left arm, or after I'd gotten attacked at Mt. Morris, or even when Gregory and I first faced eviction from Fred Trump's ghetto tower, I very well might

---

86. ACT UP was in its early years repeatedly referred to mistakenly as ACT OUT, and many gays thought ACT OUT was the better name since it was a play on the word *out*, and *coming out* is often the first political act in a queer person's life.

have packed my bag and gone with her. But I was someone else now. I was a brazen, unapologetic, cutthroat New Yorker.

I refused to back down. "Tell me everything right now, goddamn it, because I deserve to know as much as you do about my brother's murder."

My mother covered her face with her hands, but she didn't cry. She gritted her teeth and let out a guttural shriek. It was unnerving, and I feared for a moment that she was going to attack me.

Instead, she lowered her hands and said, "The boys that chased you—they did it. They dumped Martin's body in the creek, and the cops just couldn't drag it up." She shrugged. "There was a known child molester who lived near the creek. He did it and dug a shallow grave somewhere in the woods."

My voice caught in my throat and broke as I said, "Mom . . ."

She continued, "A couple of months after Martin disappeared, a junkie attacked a couple of kids down by that wretched creek. The junkie did it. A drifter did it. No one did it, and as he waded across the creek, Martin fell into the deep end of the water and drowned. At least, that's what I think. I think all those things and a thousand more. Satisfied?"

"No," I pleaded, "there has to be more. A lead, a direction."

"Nothing. We have nothing to tell us what happened to my darling boy after you lost sight of him." My mother shook her head. "You've known as much as I have the whole time. So do yourself a favor and pick a story—any story—that you can accept and move on."

"Is that what you did?"

"It's what your father did. I still blame countless boogeymen."

"And I'm one of them."

"Not anymore, not for years." She looked up and locked eyes with me. "I don't believe I've been too hard on you. You abandoned your brother. You failed him. You didn't shoulder more blame than you deserved."

Fiona and I didn't console each other and hug as we waited on the sidewalk for a town car to arrive and take her to JFK airport. I felt wrung dry, but my mother wanted to discuss my future.

"You intend to stay the course?" she asked. "Live as you do."

I repeated her words in my head: *Live as you do.* What a tidy understatement. A pleasantry meant to encapsulate my sexuality, my museum work, my political activism, my commitment to residing in the city, my disinterest in returning to Indianapolis, and my distance from my family.

"Yes," I said. "I can't see myself anywhere else."

"And you won't be needing financial support from me or your father?"

I got defensive. "I haven't asked for a dime since I left."

"I know, and I commend you." She searched the oncoming traffic. "Going forward, do you see yourself maintaining total independence?"

"Of course."

"In that case, I think you ought to sign over your trust fund to Kareem." My mother saw her town car approaching and raised her left hand into the air.

I rolled my eyes. She'd questioned me to prime my answer in the direction she wanted, but she needn't have bothered. "Fine. Do whatever you want with the money."

"It's not that simple. As you've been told multiple times over the years, the trust is irrevocable. We can't just give it away. You have to sign it away."

"Okay, I will. But tell me, why is this on your mind right now. Because we argued?"

"No," she insisted. "This is the conversation I flew out here to have with you."

I was confused. "What about the Georgetown offer?"

"Your father set up Georgetown. I swore I'd float the idea past you. I knew you'd refuse—just like I knew you'd relinquish the trust fund. I'll have the paperwork messengered to you."

"How'd you get so all-knowing?"

"After the big lie, I made it my business to learn how to read you." Her town car pulled up in front of us. "You're very much like your father when he was young."

I winced. "Leave before you say anything else cruel to me."

"Boy, you could do worse," said my mother as she climbed into the back seat and closed the door.

After Fiona departed, I went back to my apartment and lay on my twin bed for a couple of hours. I felt numb, and my mind presented me with ideas and scenarios like I was a neutral spectator. At first, I thought through all the possibilities about Martin's death that my mother had suggested and a dozen more of my own making. With each one, I imagined how my life would have been different if I'd believed that version of my brother's death when I was eleven. There would have still been plenty of guilt and sorrow to consume me, but maybe I wouldn't have considered myself worthless, damned, and unredeemable. So much needless pain.

Then my thoughts drifted to a place I rarely allowed them to go: I imagined who Martin would be if he were among the living. He'd be seventeen, in his senior year of high school with his sights set on an Ivy League college, a goal he'd achieve in stride. Martin was a better student than I was and more naturally competitive, which in a child is an early sign of later ambition. I pictured his appearance, aging him from a nine-year-old boy into a young man. He'd be taller than I am. He'd have continued to favor our father with a square jaw, wide nose, and broad shoulders. He'd have been handsome. So much needless pain.

There remained a field of thought I didn't have the nerve to cross: Would Martin have liked me? We loved each other as brothers, but we weren't the closest pair in our neighborhood. I remember how the Walker brothers and the Holmes boys who lived up the street moved as one, thought as one, and fought the world as one. Martin and I didn't have that kind of bond. Sibling rivalry could have ruined us. And he might have disapproved of my gay lifestyle. No, I couldn't bear to examine the matter closer. So much needless pain.

To shake off the weight of Martin on my soul, I forced myself out of bed and went over to Angie's apartment. She was dicing celery in preparation for cooking a vegetable soup for the men in her care. I took my place next to her at the kitchen counter, opened a bag of thawing peas and carrots, and rinsed them clean in a strainer. No longer distraught, Angie had settled into a gallows humor about her impending doom.

"That sweetheart Peter called me," she said with sarcastic cheer. "He felt the need to forbid me from telling him anything about the past forty-eight hours. I put his mind at ease. He's no longer someone I'd burden with my troubles."

As upset as I was at Peter, I didn't have it in me to get worked up bad-mouthing him. I said only, "I'm pissed at him, too."

"He informed me that he can no longer bring me any cash. That I'll have to shut down. I mean, no shit. Why bother telling me that? I'm gonna be serving life in Bedford Hills before too long."

"You don't know that for sure," I insisted. "I think I can get Helena Costas to represent you."

"No kidding?"

"Yeah, we've been hanging out in the same circles."

"I like her. She's got balls."

"You'd have to listen to her. Do what she advises. Is that possible?"

"Yes, Scout's honor. I want to get out of this." She nudged me. "I'm starting to doubt that a woman's prison is going to be the dyke fantasy I've always imagined."

"These are the kind of things you can't say to strangers or reporters."

She laughed and draped an arm over my shoulder. "You're not a stranger."

I helped Angie serve dinner to the last four men she'd ever nurse and shelter. As a treat, she opened two bottles of white wine, allowing each man a glass. Angie drank considerably more. I wondered if we couldn't still put the pieces back together. If only we could raise Bruno from the dead. If only we could remove the morphine from the needle . . .

A risky idea occurred to me, and I bolted from the table, yelling, "I'll call you and explain later!"

———

I caught a cab to Penn Station. From there, I navigated the sprawling Long Island Rail Road, arriving in the sleepy, bayside town of Patchogue an hour later. My adrenaline rush hadn't waned since I'd imagined the benefit of blackmailing Congressman Leslie Galbreath. I'd envisioned myself rushing past his secretary and barricading myself in his office, where I'd remind him of who I was and what I'd seen. He'd reassure his secretary that everything was fine. Then he'd do my bidding.

However, the longer I rode the train, the more implausible it seemed that I'd be able to ambush the congressman in his office. For starters, I was seeing fewer and fewer Black people the farther east the train headed. By the time I reached the Babylon stop, I was the last nonwhite person continuing on. Even more disconcerting is that the dozens of white passengers seemed familiar with each other. They talked like friends, and they eyed me before whispering conspiratorially. This damn sure wasn't Manhattan, and I was not going to have the luxury of being inconspicuous.

I walked to Representative Galbreath's district office. It was a two-story brick building that could have been the headquarters to a regional insurance company. The sun had set, so the lights were on in the occupied offices. I walked around the building with my head down and saw the congressman through the window of a corner office on the upper floor. I almost leaped with joy. I'd figured the odds of finding him here were good since Congress was in the middle of its August recess, but I'd also prepared myself for the possibility that I had come a long way for nothing. At the very least, I would get my shot tonight.

When I strolled past the front of the building for a second time, a white security guard stepped outside, making no bones about watching me. I paid him no mind and kept on down the sidewalk for another half a block until I ducked into a tiny bar.

I ordered a rum and Coke. The bartender asked to see my ID. I was speechless. No one had made such a request in over a year. I didn't even bother carrying a fake ID with me. Eager to avoid any fuss, I changed my order to a Coca-Cola without ice.

Once I finished my drink and paid for it, I returned to the parking lot of the district congressional office and waited. My heart was pounding. I wished I had gotten that rum into my system. If I got caught "loitering" out here, I would be arrested instantly.

Over the next forty-five minutes, staffers left one and two at a time. I hid behind a fence separating the parking lot from an abandoned building. Finally, Congressman Galbreath walked out with a female aide. Under the light of a lone streetlamp, she chatted his ear off to the point that he was clearly annoyed, jingling his keys like an agitated rattlesnake. At last, the aide got into her car, and the congressman remained in place to wave goodbye to her as she pulled off. Now was my chance. He was alone.

I took a deep breath and was about to step from behind the fence when the congressman stage-whispered, "Gregory? It's okay. Merv, the security guard, said he saw you. You can always just come up to my office. Hell, Merv is sweet on you, too."

I stepped out into the light. "I'm not Gregory. I'm his roommate."

Not listening to a word I'd said and reacting to the color of my skin, Galbreath pulled out his wallet and cast his eyes to the ground. "Whoever you are, go on and take the money. I haven't seen your face. There's no need to get rough."

"No, this isn't a stickup. Look at me. Do you remember me?"

He tentatively gave me the once-over. "Yeah, I believe we've met."

"I saw my roommate pounding your ass on Election Night, Congressman."

"Gregory said he talked to you. This wasn't going to be a problem."

"It wasn't. Except I need you to pull a political string for me."

"Or what?" Galbreath put his wallet back in his pocket. "You tell your story, and I tell mine. From what I've heard from Gregory, you're a slutty faggot who'll say anything to get what you want. And Gregory will deny sleeping with me, so I'm not—"

"I have pictures of the two of you," I lied.

"How?"

Fuck! I'd expected him to fold with less resistance. I had only one guess to bolster my bluff. I wasn't aware of the congressman's sexual habits beyond our brief first encounter, but I had an encyclopedic knowledge of Gregory's rent boy playbook. My roommate was a creature of habit.

"You two meet at the Warwick Hotel. I've followed you. You guys have gotten careless, and I snapped the kind of pictures they love to splash across the cover of the *Post*."

Galbreath snickered and shook his head. I feared he'd seen through my bullshit, but his contempt was for himself. He conceded with a friendly tip. "If I were you, I'd take the money, kid. Freshman congressmen aren't exactly powerful."

"You can handle this one. You were a big shot prosecutor for the district attorney."

"What is it? You violate probation?"

"There's going to be an autopsy on a gay man named Bruno Devonte," I said. "He died of AIDS, but I'm afraid they'll find morphine in his system and draw the wrong conclusion."

The congressman was baffled. "And where do I figure into this?"

"Call the coroner. Make sure he leaves the word *morphine* out of his report."

"And this is happening in Suffolk?"

"No, Manhattan."

"Who do you think I am?" Galbreath asked. "Tampering with a murder investigation outside of my district could ruin me if it goes sideways."

I put his options in perspective. "Which will be harder for you to explain? Why you tampered with an autopsy or why you spread your ass for a Black boy?"

Galbreath covered his mouth with his right hand and ruminated on the political realities of 1987. "Bruno Debonee."

"Devonte," I corrected.

"I do this, how do I know you won't be back next month asking me to get one of your buddies off death row?"

"I'll burn the negatives in front of you."

"Alright, then." He headed back toward his office, then turned around. "Gregory in on this?"

"No," I said. "I think he really likes you."

"Then he's more fucked than I am."

———

Later that night, I got back to my apartment and called Helena. She agreed to represent Angie. Around midnight, Gregory and I smoked a joint, which only made me more paranoid that the phone would ring, and the congressman would tell Gregory what I'd done. Or maybe the police would kick in our apartment door and arrest me on trumped-up charges crafted by Galbreath. At 2:00 a.m., Gregory went to bed. I didn't sleep a wink.

The next morning, I was a zombie at work, listlessly giving museum visitors directions to exhibits and the restrooms. I wasn't sure when or how I'd find out if the congressman had met my demands. As the day wore on, I began to worry that I'd gotten far out of my depth. I'd given Angie a hope that might prove false. I'd betrayed Gregory. I'd intimidated a congressman into breaking the law. And if my gambit failed, I had no way to cover my ass. I'd have ruined lives with nothing to show for it.

Libby pulled me aside after lunch. "Trey, you're clearly out of sorts."

"I'll pull myself together," I said.

"Would it help to talk?"

"Alright. I made some big decisions yesterday for my family—people who are like family to me." I rubbed my sore eyes. "Decisions that will shape the rest of their lives. What if I've got it wrong? I'm trying to be a hero. What if I'm the villain?"

She cupped my jaw in her hand. "Oh, honey, villains never stop to consider that they've done anything wrong."

I took solace in Libby's wisdom. Two hours later, I was returning from an errand that took me down to the signage department, and as I approached the information desk, I saw Angie describing my height and build to one of my coworkers. She appeared stern, but that was her natural disposition. She'd come with news.

I stopped walking and yelled, "Angie!"

She turned to me. The corners of her mouth were downturned, and the bags under her eyes were puffy. She held still for a few moments. Then she let loose a piercing, joyful squeal and ran at me full steam. Everyone in the museum's entrance hall watched as she wrapped me in a bear hug, swept me off my feet, and twirled me around in a circle. When she placed me back on the floor, Angie planted a kiss on my lips. MoMA visitors and staff members applauded and cheered our celebration. If they'd only known the half of it.

I needed to hear her say it. "You're in the clear?"

"Helena called. The coroner ruled that Bruno died of AIDS-related complications. Case closed."

My happiness was total. Nothing else mattered, and nothing could diminish how good I felt. I clocked out early, went to the nearest bar with Angie, and we each drank a martini to mark our victory. We didn't say much to each other. Smiles and laughter bridged the meaningful silences.

Angie paid the bar tab and splurged to give me cab money back to my apartment. I got the usual bear hug and kiss as I said goodbye. I raised my hand to flag down a cab, and Angie yanked me backward to hold me once more.

"You're a goddamn angel," she said. "Don't ever let anyone tell you different."

The cabbie dropped me off in front of my apartment building, and I was ready to crash and sleep for a solid twelve hours. The stress had caught up to me. I wasn't even going to bother taking off my work clothes before I crawled into my twin bed.

As soon as I entered my unit, I realized there would be hell to pay. The floor was redecorated with most of my albums, which had been broken into hundreds of vinyl shards. A lot of my dress shirts, which had lost their buttons and were torn at the shoulders, were strewn around the living room and kitchen. And standing in the middle of the mess was Gregory with a pair of large, sharp dressmaker scissors in his right hand.

He walked toward me slowly and said, "I oughta kill you—you loudmouthed, no-good bitch boy."

There was no use in trying to run or to play dumb. "It was always going to end between you and that pathetic hypocrite. At least this way something good came out of it."

He pointed the scissors at my throat. "You had no right to fuck up my business."

"You'll find plenty of other down-low white men willing to pay to play with your cock."

"He was more than that," Gregory snarled.

I'd have laughed if he hadn't looked so sincere. He actually believed what he'd said. Amazing—Gregory had caught feelings for a mark. Even more tragic, he was under the illusion that the mark cared for him, too.

I attempted to shed light on his absurdity with a gentle question. "So then he forgave you?"

"You forced his hand."

"So then he cut you out?"

"We're losin' this apartment. I got to the end of the month. Your ass is out tonight."

I nodded. "I get it."

My cool acceptance of his terms enraged Gregory. "What the fuck, lil man! You ain't even gonna say you sorry? You don't care that you fucked us? You don't care that you fucked me?"

It might have been smarter to lie, but I was too tired to speak anything besides the truth. "Sorry would mean I'd do it differently, and I wouldn't. I had my reasons. I wish things could be different, but they can't. That's the way it goes. You know how it is."

He squinted at me like he was trying to remember who I was. "This city would've sent your sweet punk ass packin' if not for me."

"Thank you," I said, "and I mean it."

Gregory scoffed. "I'm gonna need the negatives you took of us."

"There are none. I bluffed him."

He stepped back and lowered the scissors. "You bluffed him?"

"Yeah, he started asking what kind of proof I had, and I made up the part about following you two and taking pictures. I mean, shit, you ever seen me with a camera? I don't have the—"

Gregory lunged at me. He opened the scissor blades and drove them at the soft flesh of my stomach. I fell back against the door and caught the blades with my left hand. He squeezed the scissor handle, cutting into my palm. I screamed and headbutted him with all my strength. Gregory dropped to the floor with a thud. I kicked him twice to keep him grounded. Then I grabbed a mangled navy-blue dress shirt of mine off the couch and wrapped my bleeding hand with it.

"You ain't shit!" he cried.

"Attack me again," I said, "and I'll kill you."

I left the apartment with nothing but the clothes on my back, my state ID, my MoMA staff badge, and the money in my wallet. I got some looks in the subway with a bloodstained shirt tied around my wounded hand, but no one was too alarmed. No one asked me if I needed medical attention.

As I jostled in my seat and kept pressure on my sliced hand, I did wonder how much Gregory was hurting. I wasn't just his best friend—I was his only true friend. And I had betrayed him. Guilty as charged. However, I desperately wanted him to see that it wasn't an easy decision. I took no joy in it. But I did what I had to do. Angie was free, and Gregory would land on his feet. He always did. That was one of his talents. In a sense, I was banking on his survival, and I held on to the hope that when Gregory came out the other side of this (maybe in a couple of months, maybe in a couple of years), we would not remain enemies.

I got to Angie's place, and she cleaned, stitched up, and dressed my palm. I swallowed three aspirins for the pain. Then Angie let me sleep in the primary bedroom since none of the men in her care were expected to die within the next couple of days. It was odd at first. I couldn't help thinking of the numerous men who had passed away on this mattress and under these sheets. Their storied lives ended in this very spot. Yet here I was, and in the morning, I would open my eyes and go on with my life.

ACKNOWLEDGMENTS

All I had to do was write. The rest fell into place because of other people. My husband, Jonathan, convinced me to send a query letter to Jim McCarthy, who signed on to be my literary agent, and Jim knew the manuscript belonged in the hands of Nadxieli Nieto, who agreed to be my editor. As with any creative project I take on, T. J. Brady, Ted Neill, and Alex Goldsmith talked me out of quitting whenever I got too discouraged. My kids, JoJo and Max, grounded me whenever I got too grandiose. I am forever in the debt of this brilliant tribe. I love them all, especially the first one and the last two mentioned.

The novel is inspired by the LGBTQ+ and Civil Rights movements in the United States. I am a lifelong student and benefactor of these twin histories. The movements to end discrimination based on race and sexuality are responsible for shaping my worldview and for making many of the freedoms I enjoy possible, and anyone who contributed to the advancement of liberty is a hero to me.

If you are interested in learning more about the people and the events that informed the world of this book, I suggest you read or listen to the following: *We Are Everywhere: Protest, Power, and Pride in the History of Queer Liberation* by Matthew Riemer and Leighton Brown ◆ *Let the Record Show: A Political History of ACT UP New York, 1987–1993* by Sarah Schulman ◆ *Not Straight, Not White: Black*

Gay Men from the March on Washington to the AIDS Crisis by Kevin Mumford ♦ *Funeral Diva* by Pamela Sneed ♦ *A Queer History of the United States* by Michael Bronski ♦ *Making Gay History: The Half-Century Fight for Lesbian and Gay Equal Rights* by Eric Marcus (also listen to the companion podcast, *Making Gay History*) ♦ *Dying to Be Normal: Gay Martyrs and the Transformation of American Sexual Politics* by Brett Krutzsch ♦ *History Is Gay,* a podcast by Leigh & Gretchen.

ABOUT THE AUTHOR

Rasheed Newson is a writer and producer of *Bel-Air*, *The Chi*, and *Narcos*. He currently resides in Pasadena, California, with his husband and two children. *My Government Means to Kill Me* is his debut novel.